HONOUR

Printed in Australia

Cover and internal design by Shawline Publishing Group Pty Ltd

First printing: June 2024

Shawline Publishing Group Pty Ltd

www.shawlinepublishing.com.au

Paperback ISBN 978-1-9231-0192-0

eBook ISBN 978-1-9231-7102-2

Hardback ISBN 978-1-9231-7114-5

Distributed by Shawline Distribution and Lightning Source Global

Shawline Publishing Group acknowledges the traditional owners of the land and pays respects to Elders, past, present and future.

 A catalogue record for this work is available from the National Library of Australia

HONOUR

WILL SPOKES

Also by Will Spokes
Lusine's Blessing
Death on the Ferry Hygeia

DEDICATION

This book is dedicated to the hardy, uncomplaining men and women early settlers who built the country we now take benefit from and the men and women who went unhesitatingly into battle with Nazi Germany and the fanatical Japanese who threatened invasion of Australia.

My father was one of these people who served in New Guinea at Port Moresby and a horrid place on the northern coast called Buna Gona. Dad was a navy man, a telegrapher sweating over his telegraph key while bombs rained down on Port Moresby. He also saw service aboard some of Australia's fleet of small ships, the corvette class.

He was aboard HMAS Stawell intercepting the Japanese as they island-hopped down the Dutch East Indies archipelago, relating stories to me sprinkled with exotic place names like Java, Salamanca and the Celebes. They sometimes intercepted vicious pirates who had operated in those waters for hundreds of years and even still do today.

The HMAS Castlemaine, another corvette upon which Dad served, is now a floating museum in Williamstown on Port Phillip Bay and I have visited it and stood in Dad's tiny 'office' where he was stationed directly below the bridge.

I tried to imagine him sitting there, thousands of miles from home, perhaps writing one of the many letters he sent home to his new wife whom he would not see for some time.

Sadly, Dad and I did not always see eye to eye as often happens between fathers and sons, but I still honour him and his generation for protecting us from an evil and determined invader, often at great personal cost.

Lest We Forget.

NOTE FOR THE READER

Better travelled people than I might question the descriptions of landscape, cattle stations and farming throughout sections of this story. Military historians might also question the detail of events of the war in New Guinea. I am not from the bush; I'm a city boy, but I have experienced life in the bush in a limited way. Nor am I a military historian and in taking these liberties – historical, geographical and topographical – it has been totally intentional on my part. The same may be said of the technicalities of flying, although I have had more experience with aircraft than farming implements. These things have been altered to suit the narrative and its characters and without which the tale might be quite dull. I beg the indulgence of the reader and trust that you enjoy this work of fiction.

Will Spokes

FOREWORD

'Greater love hath no man than this, that a man lay down his life for his friends. John 15:13

Courage

To confront pain, difficulty or danger.

Valour

Courage or bravery especially in battle.

Heroism

Someone who displays great courage and valour is referred to as a hero, their actions are considered to be acts of heroism.

Honour

The quality of knowing and doing what is morally right.

Credit to Macquarie Dictionary for the above definitions.

CHAPTER ONE

Fully matured, the Eastern Taipan, one of the world's deadliest venomous reptiles, had been hunting along the dry creek bed and was making her way back to her home among a tangle of tree roots, where the creek bank had collapsed. Perfectly adapted to her harsh environment, the snake was still hungry, having only taken a tiny sandy inland mouse. Despite that expenditure of venom, she still carried enough to kill a dozen grown men and hoped to use it to secure more prey.

She had been exploring her territory, seeking game in the drought-affected country. The lack of water had driven much of her usual target species away. The landscape had changed and she needed to relearn its subtleties and dangers. She was moving quickly, but cautiously, through the leaf and bark trash, mulga grass and dead shrubs. Her 3-metre-long slender body moved silently; her large head highlighted by a pale face and snout, still seeking left and right optimistically for the heat flare that would indicate prey.

She suddenly became aware of a series of strange vibrations ahead of her and was instantly on high alert. She was driven to keep moving, in fear of being caught by the rising sun exposing her to the ever-present wedge tailed eagle. She moved over and around a fallen tree and stopped in her tracks. Lying across her path was a huge creature of a type she had never encountered. Her curiosity drew her forward, her long, bluish tongue flickering in and out, sampling the air, trying to identify the creature's risk potential.

She was now only several feet from it, well within her striking range, when it suddenly stirred and rose up. She immediately went into self-defence mode. The deadly pose was unmistakeable, rearing up, her head now two feet from the ground, her body drawn up like a coiled spring, ready to strike whatever that threat was.

Known as *Dandarabilla* to the indigenous people, they knew the chance of surviving a bite from this viper was exactly nil.

Harold Eldon Cuthbertson had slept well after a tiring day exploring his territory; a huge parcel of land in south western Queensland, recently purchased by him near Longreach and named Courtland Downs. He too needed to learn its limits, its dangers and subtleties.

This was no country for soft white men accustomed to the green plenty of the land they had migrated from. A harsh climate, plague levels of the ubiquitous maddening flies, infrequent rainfall leading into long crushing droughts and blinding dust storms, broken only by destructive floods. Stock succumbing to thirst, hunger and disease. Cattle losses to local tribes were frequent and annoying, leading to friction between the races and legal intervention should any settler be unwise enough to seek retribution.

Harold Cuthbertson was no soft European. He had been brought up to believe you had to earn what you got and fight to keep it. But within these precepts, there was an instinctive wisdom that allowed him to separate losses from vengeance. He intuitively understood the natives' attitude to possessions. Cattle wandering about on their land were fair game. In fact, they were wonderful game that just stood about waiting to be speared. Very little tracking and chasing involved and the reward was enough meat to sustain the mob for a week or more.

They resisted the white man coming into their camp with their guns, whips and clubs. To the natives, it seemed odd they should hold these animals so precious and yet strangely let them roam free in the bush.

Harold could see the futility in this conflict and sought to befriend and educate the tribesmen hunters to white men's ways while learning all he could about the Aboriginal culture and beliefs. In doing so, he found ways to grow trust between the two and offer some valuable assistance to the natives.

Over time they nurtured a reciprocity where Harold was trusted with vital information about water sources for which he traded beef or cloth. An axe was held in awe by the primitive people whose dependence fell upon stone instruments. They had carried them forward for millennia, however, the sharpened steel of a modern axe could not be bested for butchery of kangaroos or cutting firewood supplies. Not to mention putting fear into their enemies. These tools enabled the people to survive over millennia.

Harold had been mapping out surviving water holes and assessing the parched country's capacity for bearing stock. He was being guided by an elder of the local Bulawai tribe who had been invaluable in locating springs and water holes. Harold had a great deal of respect for the man and his bush skills, using his tribal name Jirrah, instead of some anglicised version for his own convenience. They had camped together by the creek bed where the soft sand provided a comfortable base for their bedrolls.

Sitting up, he yawned, stretched and looked up at the stars still filling the pre-dawn sky. They were so bright and the air so clear, he swore he could reach out and touch them. His legs were sore and stiff after a day in the saddle and he needed to get up and stretch them, working the blood back into his lower limbs. Harold never complained about the legacy of pain from hard work. He considered it a small price to pay for what his God had granted him in this new land.

He noticed Jirrah was already out gathering wood for the dying fire. He would brew a pot of tea and they would breakfast on salted beef and the remains of a damper left from the previous night before the two set off again.

Some primitive sixth sense, a tingling sensation on the back of his neck, alerted him to a danger he was yet to see. A slight noise, a kind of sibilant whispering behind his left shoulder drew his attention. Turning slowly, he was terrified to see the large snake rearing up in a strike pose three feet from where he now sat.

Warily, he scanned the camp site for a weapon or a way to escape the inevitable painful death, but his shotgun was out of reach. His feet were tangled in the blanket that had covered him as he slept and any attempt to dive away would be far too slow.

Harold was frozen in fear, while almost resigned to his fate, when Jirrah shouted and with all the skill of an experienced hunter, hurled a length of wood like a boomerang in a flat, whirling flight that caught the snake one foot below its deadly jaws and carried her away down the dry embankment, her spine broken by the blow.

Jirrah was on it in an instant, his pure white teeth flashing in a huge grin as he stood proudly holding the now dead Taipan for Harold's inspection; its nervous system still threshing. He would make a meal of it later and offer to share it with his fussy white man friend.

Harold remained frozen to the spot and, for the first time in what seemed like an age, he released a huge sigh of relief. Turning to his still grinning and laughing guide, he realised how close he had come to an agonising death but for Jirrah's intervention. He would always owe his life to his new friend, to whom it was just another little slice of life in the bush.

Harold never forgot the experience and was forever grateful to his wonderful guide who became a great and very wise friend, helping him understand the limits and dangers of the land they shared.

The vast grazing property just outside Longreach in Queensland, *Courtland Downs*, was settled by Harold Eldon Cuthbertson in 1876, just a few years before one of Australia's earliest recorded nationwide droughts. It would not be the last drought old Harold would experience, but he was smart enough to learn from it and prepared well for the next one. This circumstance of climate may have been why he was able to purchase such a large parcel of land. This highly developed foresight of his, enabled Harold to maintain stock numbers above the average of similar properties around the country and secured his future wealth and the security of his legacy for generations of his descendants.

The property was bordered by the Thomson River and consisted originally of 30,000 hectares carrying several hundred sheep for wool and meat. The Thomson River, as with all the rivers in the Lake Eyre Basin, never reached the sea, and instead, either evaporated or, in an exceptional flood, emptied into Lake Eyre many miles south west. Floods were relatively common because of the summer monsoon rains. Due to the flat nature of the country the river could then become many kilometres wide, causing major difficulties for Harold and his neighbours. For much of the time, however, the river did not flow, and became a line of billabongs.

Relying on the sparse native grasses for cattle feed, Harold had few concerns about water as his property sat above the Great Artesian Basin, an aquifer system, from which he and many other settlers drew an unlimited supply of cool, fresh water for their cattle and their own use.

Cattle was another matter. With the arrival of cattle ticks into North Queensland in 1896, it became apparent that maintaining

British bred herds in the harsh tropical environment was virtually impossible. Consequently, graziers, like Harold, began experimenting with crossbreeding to overcome the perennial problems of drought, cattle ticks, heat, eye cancer and many other problems that reduced production and profitability.

Courtland Downs was well watered, but still suffered in the frequent droughts which killed off the grasses Harold had to rely on to feed his stock. Still, he managed to farm the sheep and some beef cattle in fluctuating numbers according to conditions. Future generations of Cuthbertson's would run cross breed cattle reasonably successfully but that was a long way in the future of Courtland Downs.

Harold married Henrietta Constance Croft, who became a very important contributor to the success of the endeavour. Without her support, life out there would have been intolerable. At the end of the day, when Harold returned to the homestead he had built to replace the old shack he had constructed in the early days, he would find that Hettie, as he called her, had added some homely touches to the newer building and put a decent meal on the table, instead of the fly struck boiled mutton and potatoes that had been his fare as a bachelor.

These were the very early days in the Cuthbertson dynasty but things would improve with a whole lot of hard labour and good luck. The hard labour began with the design and construction of the new homestead.

The construction of the new accommodation began with the arrival of a load of massive logs, ordered by Harold to serve as the stumps, raising the floor above the potential flood levels and providing an airway to cool the main building during the summer months. The logs were sawn in half and set into the ground, protected against white ants, each with a metal cap to keep rats and mice at bay. The end result was a secure comfortable farmhouse that became known as a "Queenslander", large, spacious and airy with a huge useful area beneath it for a workshop and storage.

After a period of time, Hettie was able to run a scruffy bunch of chickens and ducks that gave them some meat and eggs when the native dogs and hawks left them alone. Kangaroo meat graced the pot now and then, along with a bit of chewy emu from time to time. Fresh vegetables were a problem for a while, until Hettie was able to establish a garden, but then it had to be guarded very closely because there were plenty of hungry mouths that would devour a crop in a night.

Hettie was far more than a housekeeper-wife. She became a very competent horsewoman, keeping pace with Harold and even some of the crack stockmen. Her lightweight frame, stretched out along the neck of 500 kilos of half broken stock horse at full gallop, in pursuit of a stray, was something that made the breath catch in Harold's throat.

Hettie could take the eye out of any dingo, that threatened their precious stock, at 100 yards with her handy well-kept Winchester 30.30 rifle. Despite these masculine talents, Hettie never became coarse and scolded any bad language; she read the Bible and the classics and built up an impressive collection of poetry. She also had a deft touch with a paint brush and palette, producing some beautiful portraits of family members and some stunning landscapes, which often included their loved indigenous stockmen recruited from the local Ininga mob, and especially their beautiful doe-eyed children. Hettie was, in all things, a true product of her English heritage and education.

The soil of western Queensland around Longreach existed in one of two states: cloying mud that could trap and drown stock when on the odd occasion it chose to rain; or more consistently, as choking dust when it didn't. The predominant soil type was known as a *vertosols* which cracks open when dry. A large belt of grey and brown vertosols ran from the New South Wales border to Charters Towers. Harold's station sat right across this belt.

All the essentials of life that could not be produced on the land, like flour and salt, dry goods such as cloth and building materials, would be hauled in by bullock wagons. These heavy plodding wagons hauled along by a team of up to 18 oxen, generally driven by a tough character who skilfully plied a long whip, cracking it just above the heads of the slothful beasts, peppering the air with a nonstop salvo of ear blistering obscenities. They were the heavy transport of their day hauling massive loads of produce out and essentials in.

Harold and Hettie, as cattle producers, said the good thing about cattle was they walked themselves to market and, until Harold had built up their sheep numbers and had a reasonable clip, there was no wool going out in the first few years anyway. So he rarely had outgoing cargo for the bullocky. But almost like a kid at Christmas, he always anticipated the arrival of the next team that might be carrying fencing wire, milled timber, feed for the poultry, seed for Hettie's garden or other provisions that would improve theircomfort levels.

Harold had employed a manager-foreman, Bartholomew (Barney) Jones. Barney was built like the proverbial brick outhouse and possessed a power to weight ratio that would almost rival a bull ant. Harold had witnessed Barney effortlessly dragging a yearling heifer from a bog and then heave the exhausted creature onto his shoulders and place it on to the wagon. They put on a number of local blacks who worked for supplies and a small allowance and who thought Barney was some sort of yowie. Harold found it hard to argue, as he wasn't too sure about Barney himself. Thus the large man became the butt of a few jokes among the indigenous cattlemen who began to warn their children that the yowie man would come for them if they misbehaved.

He was a huge man by comparison with the average male, towering over Harold at six foot, three inches. His large head was a mass of curly hair that covered the back of his neck. His face was almost obscured behind a wild bushy beard. The first time Harold saw him with his shirt off, cooling down in a billabong, he was amazed at the thick hair that covered his entire body. Poor old Barney couldn't understand why the children screamed and ran for the bush when he visited their camp. The men would be rocking back on their heels, chuckling and exchanging knowing looks.

Harold learned early that if he paid the blacks a cash wage, they wouldn't know how to handle it, so he paid them with supplies like flour, salt, tobacco and some second-hand clothing and boots. This way, he gave them fair value for their input and was able to keep a reasonably consistent workforce, enabling him to plan a day or twos work in advance.

But after a while, he managed to sort out a decent bunch of hands and, under the guidanceof Barney, the workers started to make some significant gains. The truth was the blacks were slightly terrified of the big man and jumped every time he barked out an order.

Harold, on the other hand, was good to the native workers and respected them and their strange ways. He endeavoured to understand their culture which he found fascinating. He began to understand how their wanderings were not just random but related to the seasonal appearance of game and fruits in the bush. They were the product of centuries of experience and wisdom and they had much to teach him.

He was an educated man and, like many of his kind, he was interested in the sciences. The branch of science of special interest to him was anthropology and here he was in a living laboratory. At every opportunity, he would sit with the locals and interview them, attempting to learn their language, superstitions and customs, taking copious notes and making accurate sketches of the men and on visits to their camp, he was permitted to sketch the women and children. They demonstrated some of their arts to him and he was delighted when they brought him some of their native bark paintings as a gift. They taught him how to track and find water and food in the bush. Skills that proved invaluable in the way he treated the land. They would drink tea, smoke their pipes and share genuine affection for each other.

Hettie would sometimes have to break up these talk fests by shooing the natives away with a gift of damper or cold roast meat. There were two prominent tribes in the south west of Queensland, the Ininga and Kuungkari, from which the stockmen came. There didn't appear to be any friction between them and Harold and Hettie treated them equally.

Clearly, being a pastoral property, meat for the house would come from their stock. A beast would be cut from the herd and led into the house paddock and allowed to settle down before slaughter. It was eerie the way the animals seem to sense their fate, trembling and snorting with fear. Harold, or Barney, would try to spare them unnecessary trauma and dispatch them with the minimum of fuss. Traditionally, an animal would be slaughtered and hung under the water tank stand, hauled up by a pulley system constructed for the purpose to bleed out. The beast would then be eviscerated with the lights and offal being put aside.

The hide would be taken off and put aside for later tanning, to provide material for repairing harnesses and footwear etc. Then the carcase would be broken down and prepared for storage in the cool room. There was little room for waste.

During the summer, the meat could spoil on the same day, so preserving it quickly was important. If it was to be eaten within a few days it would be par-boiled or par-roasted as soon as possible and then the cooking was completed just before consumption. For longer periods of time, meat would be pickled by stacking it in layers in barrels, separated by salt, saltpetre (potassium nitrate) and brown sugar and then soaked in brine. Harold often made sure to provide a gift of meat to one of his stockmen who had performed particularly well.

Harold had access to plenty of chopped wood and had constructed a smokehouse. Choice cuts of beef and pork were treated in it, which involved hanging the product above a fire of mulga wood. When smoked like this, the meat would last for weeks or months at a time and would have a beautiful smoky flavour as a bonus. Bacon produced this way from a small parcel of hogs was sensational. Most of these skills exercised by Harold were transplanted from the old country where it was, admittedly, a cooler climate but still presented the same problems with preserving and storing produce.

After time, his descendants would take this further, producing many varieties of smoked meats, including sausages, that were turned out in the "surgery" as they jokingly called the butchery.

Fruits, when they could get supplies of them, could be dried by covering them with cheesecloth in direct sunlight, on the roof of the homestead. Once shrivelled and hard, they were hung in the cool store until needed. When consumed, the fruit was stewed in water and sugar, however it wasn't very palatable, being tough and lacking flavour.

It took time for Hettie's orchards to start bearing good crops and when they did, she would preserve the stone fruits or convert them to wonderful jams from recipes she had brought out to Australia with her. These would be put up in the cool store and enjoyed in the winter months. A much preferred result to the old, dried fruits.

The native hands were good with the animals and had a hand in locating aquifers and digging the wells that would keep up a supply of precious water forever and a day. Cattle troughs were continuously fed by the wells at strategic spots, such that stock would not need to walk miles to quench their thirst

This was real pioneering work vital to the viability of the station and Harold knew it would be to the benefit of those that came after him. He was building an empire, an opportunity that was denied him in his homeland, where all the farmland was held in an iron grip by the privileged classes. The best he would have been able to hope for was to take a lease on someone else's land and be forever in their debt.

Australia represented a chance for men of Harold's ilk to forge a future for themselves and their descendants, free from the ancient mores and restrictions of Europe. Not only did his labours profit Harold, but would eventually be passed down to their eldest surviving son Hugh, and thence to William Luther (Big Bill) and his younger brother George Clement (Books), by which time it was a secure debt free and profitable agricultural concern; droughts, floods and bushfires allowing.

Life on these remote cattle stations was extreme. The pastoralists and families had to endure punishing heat and dust that made its way into every nook and cranny, frustrating the housewife's vain attempts to fight it.

Flies!

The Australian outback had cornered the market on flies. These irritating, little, black bush flies would crawl into eyes, ears and nose of man and beast alike. Without some sort of net protection over the face, they were capable of literally driving a person insane. It's claimed that flies have influenced the Aussie accent by forcing people to talk with a closed mouth to keep the pests out and introduced the great Aussie salute, the constant waving to move the flies on.

It would be a few years yet before civilising facilities such as a post office and the railway arrived at the town of Longreach. In fact, it would be 1892 for the rail. In the meantime, supplies would continue to arrive by bullock dray. An early settler had to be made of sterner stuff to imagine a life out there and have the stamina to see it through. Old Harold was such a man.

As mentioned, the homestead was built by hand with materials brought in for the purpose by bullock dray. Old Harold Cuthbertson had money behind him and a comfortable timber structure was designed and built by a party of labourers and tradesmen led by himself and Barney over a period of a couple of months. Deep verandahs with fly screens provided a sanctuary around the core of the house and kept the heat at bay by opening or closing the shuttered sections that were placed where they could capture the cooling evening breezes. They also provided a safe environment for the children, when they came along later, to play out of the weather and away from snakes.

Old Harold, as he was always referred to by his descendants, brought his young English bride, Henrietta Constance, to this home on the hot and dusty Queensland plains where it was expected that the delicate English flower would wilt and die. But she would have none of that and from day one, showed the mettle of a seasoned pioneer, swinging an axe, pumping and carrying water and even after time, wielding a castration knife like an expert.

No one sat idle in those days, least of all Grandma Ettie, as she became known. There were sheep to shear and drench, meals to cook for the shearers and station hands, laundry and the dusting. The never ending dusting. Harold looked on proudly as his little flower became a self-sufficient tough-as-old-boots settler's wife.

Not that she lost her femininity, as when they went to town for supplies or to partake in some social activity in later years, she would spruce up and become the unmistakable ladylike Henrietta Constance Cuthbertson once again; even sporting a little powder and perfume. Her work hardened hands were covered by delicate, cotton gloves.

These were hard days, but days of accomplishment; small wins were great triumphs. The first wind-powered well, the completion of functioning stockyards, the first sale of steers where, for a magic moment, income beat outgoings, if only for a moment or two.

When it came time to bring the cattle in, Harold was presented with a uniquely Australian cattleman's problem. Find the blasted cattle. On 30,000 hectares there were a thousand places they could be and risk and reason would not find them. They would always be in the last place they looked. Once they got the mob together, moving them wasn't too bad; just head the strays in and keep an eye open for any small mobs in pockets of bush as they went.

The sound of a large mob of cattle was unmistakeable and would often draw the small clusters out of their hidey-holes.

Once back at the stockyards, a count would be taken and any sick or lame beasts would be culled out. A mob would be put together for the sale yards and, after giving the beasts time to rest and take on water, they would head off under the encouragement of the stockmen who made up the droving team.

Horses, dogs, cattle and men, in a moving cloud of dust just over walking pace and generally making more noise than a circus. Whips cracking, dogs barking, men shouting and the support wagon providing a musical background of rattling pots and pans, accompanied by the creaks and squeals of harnesses and snorting of horses.

The cattle would feed from the crown land on the roadside when cattlemen owners were forced to take their herds on the road in time of severe drought and feed was scarce. In time this came to be known as "the long paddock".

CHAPTER TWO

1881

Harold had known Henrietta when they were children growing up together in England. She was a second cousin on his mother's side. It was a given that the two bright, young things, who had an undeniable affection for each other, would one day be betrothed. This sort of arrangement was very common in those days with sometimes first cousins marrying. He was six years older than her and smitten by the pretty, cheerful, young girl who was a more than competent horsewoman and who, despite her obvious feminism, Harold could see an underlying steely resolve. She was no shy retiring wall flower and joyfully engaged in the rough and tumble of the boys' games, often getting the better of one or two of them.

Before he left for the great southland, they were betrothed and with the promise that as soon as it was possible to provide an acceptable lifestyle for her, he would send for her to join him. They corresponded regularly; Henrietta always responded in a delicate cursive on beautiful, scented writing paper embossed with the family crest. Henrietta wrote with a quill pen and Indian black ink. Harold preserved every letter and would sit by the fire reading them over and over as he smoked his pipe and dreamed of the day she would join him. He would respond to every letter, confirming his love for her and informing her of the day-to-day activities on the station. He hoped she would join him soon and he prayed for her safe arrival and for that day to come quickly.

After much hard work and a determined effort to provide a civilised homestead for her, Harold felt the conditions were such that the time was right to send for his bride. That wonderful time had finally arrived and Harold's letter advised Henrietta that should she still so desire, he could offer her a comfortable home, suitable to her expectation and standing.

An exciting return letter arrived early in February 1881, informing Harold that Henrietta was delighted to accept his invitation and she had secured a berth aboard a suitable ship and gave him the approximate arrival date.

Henrietta boarded the ship, *Scottish Knight*, arriving in Townsville 15th June 1881, having departed from Plymouth 3rd March 1881. A journey of 104 days. As a first class passenger, she shared her time at the captain's table with like fellow passengers who were all good company and made the time pass pleasantly. Henrietta's ship docked in Townsville harbour under the looming Castle Hill.

The journey was long, but not without its pleasures. Before sailing down the west coast of the African continent, they had restocked with fresh fruit and water at Tenerife after a gruelling crossing of the Bay of Biscay. There were few other ships encountered on the journey with only the occasional sighting of a cloud of sail on the horizon, which made Henrietta feel sometimes as though they were the only people on the planet.

They enjoyed fairer weather and relatively smooth seas on the way to Cape Town, South Africa, once more replenishing supplies for the long haul across the Indian Ocean to the Dutch East Indies. It was here they put into Batavia where the captain hoped to take on a cargo of spices that would fetch a high price in their final destination.

Henrietta was stunned by the colour of the crowded exciting port, seething with traders, travellers, livestock, dozens of chattering children, beggars seeking alms and one or two cunning pick-pockets and thieves.

The waters of the harbour were populated by a fantastic variety of water craft. The famous Chinese junks, three masted clipper ships, flat bottomed punts and barges, all loaded down with cargo of one sort or another. Sacks of rice, crates containing delicate china ware and the big money crop of the day, tea.

The tea was packed in large square crates and piled high dockside waiting to be trans- shipped to the bowels of the anxiously waiting clippers who would reap a rich reward for being first home to the eager markets of England. Prices of the time were the equivalent of gold, pound for pound, and security of the cargo was a high priority.

The air was redolent with the aroma of a rich variety of cloyingly fragrant spices thecaptain was seeking. It was a vibrant, exotic moving feast for the eyes and olfactory senses.

High pitched insistent voices of vendors, calling out the virtues of their wares in strange languages, mingled with weird music from fascinating instruments she had never encountered before, let alone heard.

Her senses were assaulted by the overwhelming sight of weird and exotic fruits and colourful vegetables, the heady scent of dozens of different spices, the squawking and chattering of strange animals and birds in bamboo cages, all competing for her attention. Bananas, pineapples, dates, olives, nuts and many fruits neither she, nor her escort, could name. There were stalls buried deep under bales of wonderful garishly coloured silks and fabrics, while carvings in jade, ebony and ivory were displayed in abundance. Brilliant jewellery in gold, silver and jade, decorated with precious gems and pearls and mother ofpearl, were displayed proudly by their vendors.

Henrietta looked on fascinated, as the many street vendors cooked a tantalising variety of food right there on the street. Huge pots containing daunting stews, coloured by chillis, spices and any number of odd vegetables. Massive tubs of rice were steamed over wood fires that added the aroma of wood smoke to the ambient air.

Smoked meats were displayed and the carcasses of goats, sheep and cattle were butchered by gore-covered workers, sweating over their tasks, who made no attempt to keep the sweat and ever-present flies away from their product. A huge range of seafood stalls were competing, side by side, along the waterfront offeringevery type of fish in the ocean. Some still live in tubs such as huge live crabs with their pincers firmly tied and a myriad of crustaceans in a bewildering array.

She returned to the ship with the third mate, who been her escort on the insistence of the captain, her head spinning and pulse racing. A virginal girl from the counties witnessing sights and sounds she had never dreamed of. Eventually, the captain secured the produce he wanted, preparations were made and orders were given to get his ship underway.

The penultimate leg of their journey required some accurate navigation, threading a cautious route through the complex archipelagos and the myriad islands and atolls that made up the Dutch East Indies, and a watchful eye as there were many native pirates attacking shipping around the islands. The captain was no fool and had sailed these waters before learning to avoid the bloodthirsty raiders, but he was also pragmatic and so as not to alarm the passengers, had subtly briefed and armed the crew in preparation for any threats they may encounter. Anti-boarding nets and weapons had been placed where they were readily accessible and the crew were instructed to play dumb if the passengers asked any questions about them.

The run down from Cape York to Townsville was a less stressful exercise uneventful and unremarkable except for the wonderful weather and the azure sea and skies. The little ship rolled along at a business-like clip, all canvas aloft 'with a bone in her teeth' as the sailors described the brilliant white foaming bow wave. Again a watchful eye was needed on their navigation as there were many uncharted reefs to catch the unwary.

Finally, the brave little ship made Townsville. After a pleasant and restorative stay in a local hotel, Henrietta stepped aboard a coastal trader on 20th June which took her south to Rockhampton. She was experiencing her first taste of Queensland weather as the little trader left Townsville behind. It was a beautiful clear day with mild temperatures. These pleasant conditions stayed with them all the way to Rockhampton to which they were gently driven by a warm breeze and a pleasant following sea.

Henrietta had maintained the dress standards of the day on the ocean voyage and she was still dressed in that style aboard the trader. The 1880s was a decade of severely tight and restrictive corsetry that was worn (or endured) under dresses with long boned bodices, tight sleeves and high necks. It gave Henrietta a very modest, and even prudish, look. Dresses could weigh 15-20 pounds, hardly a suitable garb for tropical Queensland.

Sailing down the coast inside the Great Barrier Reef on a glorious June day like this, the traveller could easily be convinced they were in paradise. The sea was a glorious sapphire blue, reflecting the azure sky above as the small ship moved to a gentle ocean swell, highlighted by the stark fluorescent white of the occasional breaking wave.

They were escorted part of the way by a huge school of dolphins that seemed to delight in their company, diving, broaching and rolling on their backs, looking directly into Henrietta's delighted eyes, with their broad grinning mouths, uplifting the spirits of everyone on board including the most hard-bitten deckhands.

Seabirds of all descriptions wheeled about in the sky above them, including the majestic albatross of legend. Swarms of gannets were in a feeding frenzy, plummeting into the sea in pursuit of the schools of baitfish below the waves, screaming and screeching greedily.

The sea delivered a fresh breakfast to the passengers aboard the trader on the first morning at sea. Overnight, schools of terrified flying fish, perhaps being pursued by the dolphins or other ocean predators while flying low over the wave tops to escape, impacted the sails falling to the deck to be eagerly gathered up by the crew. Cleaned and then fried in butter, they made for a delicious breakfast treat. Without any further events to remark on, the trader finally sailed into the Fitzroy River. Henrietta's extended sea journey was finally over.

✳ ✳ ✳

A telegram had reached Longreach from Townsville and was duly delivered to Harold. It advised him that Henrietta would be arriving in Rockhampton by coastal sailing ship approximately four days later. Harold was beside himself and made preparations for her arrival. He had previously arranged for a lady from Longreach to come and help him improvethe homestead to a reasonably acceptable standard. He rushed about pulling out chests stuffed with carefully preserved Manchester, bath towels and all the frippery a woman would expect. Curtains on some windows, floor rugs and the careful placement of some long-stored vases and other ornaments were put about to soften the rather harsh and masculine bush interior. Finally, he stood back, hands on hips, gazing about critically and decided he had done all he could do. Further improvements would be made in time.

The railway west from Rockhampton was commenced in 1867 but didn't extend to Longreach until 1892. In the meantime, it provided a more comfortable and swifter form of transport than the Cobb and Co coaches, although Henrietta still had to take a coach to complete the journey.

Passage aboard a Cobb and Co stage coach was arranged by telegraph and Henrietta would have to endure a dusty journey inland to Longreach where her betrothed waited impatiently for her arrival. Harold was very familiar with the road from Longreach to Rockhampton, having travelled it more than once when delivering his wool clip to the port. In the early days, it was little more than a track that was likely to spring a few surprises by way of attacks from natives or holdups by bushrangers. Like most of the inland settlers, he was impatient for the rail to make it to Longreach, delivering swift and secure transport for their produce to the port of Rockhampton. Until then, he dealt with an agent who purchased his clip and made all transport arrangements, meaning he hadn't been down the road (which would become the Capricorn Highway) for a couple of years, but all the same, he was aware that it was a rugged trip for a gentle flower of England to be travelling.

While she waited for her coach, Henrietta had time to explore the burgeoning township of Rockhampton and it gave her an opportunity to shop in one or two women's fashion stores. The shopkeepers admired her clothing, which it could be said was the very latest from London. Several asked permission to take measurements and sketches to allow them to repeat the fashions. At the same time, Henrietta was able to obtain advice on the appropriate dress for where she was going. The result was another suitcase full of outfits more suited to the wife of a pastoralist.

The coach, bearing Henrietta's arrival at Longreach, was heralded by thundering hoof beats and jangling harness, throwing up a huge cloud of dust in its wake. The coach driver had thankfully toned down the curses he used to urge his team of horses along as they entered the town's perimeter. Henrietta had never imagined such colourful language and hoped she wouldn't have to endure the experience again. She had delivered a sharp rebuke to the driver that left him in no doubt that the lady was very serious and if he wanted to keep his job he would need to adjust his vocabulary.

Now that the great day had dawned, Harold was dressed smartly in a tweed suit and high-topped riding boots, polished to a high gloss. The whole outfit capped off with a handsome bowler hat. His open-necked shirt was enhanced by a brightly coloured silk neckerchief knotted about his neck with the free ends reaching down to the top of his waistcoat that was adorned by a gold pocket watch and chain. The whole outfit projected the image of a man of substance, the very impression he wished to convey to his bride to be and anyone he met along the way.

He stood straight-backed with his chest out and proud as she stepped delicately down from the coach that had pulled up in a cloud of dust, jangling-jingling harness and snorting four-in-hand of horses responding reluctantly to the driver's impatient commands.

She had managed to preserve her elegant gown from the dirt and dust of the journey and wore a fetching little bonnet, which assisted in keeping her hair tidy and the punishing sun from her yet to be acclimatised English complexion. Over her left arm, she carried a beautifully embroidered silk purse and in her right hand a parasol. Henrietta was a stunning spectacle to the onlookers lounging about the coach depot and the sight of her took Harold's breath clean away.

With effort, he regained control of his breathing and politely tipped his hat, offering to take her hand as she stepped down from the coach, while greeting her politely.

They exchanged pleasantries about her travel, the ocean voyage and the weather. Harold enquired after her health and she reciprocated. Finally taking Harold's arm, they strolled casually to the hotel where he had reserved a room for her temporary stay. On arrival, her bags were fetched by Harold's leading hand and brought along behind them. The landlady organised assistant to bring them to her room. Henrietta indicated which of the bags were to go into storage and pointed out the bag that contained her personal accoutrements.

This was a great occasion and one that begged to be celebrated with well-chilled vintage champagne that had been organised by Harold. Crystal champagne flutes clinked together as they looked into each other's eyes for the first time in what seemed like a life time. There was a light smattering of applause from the onlookers and the bar manager, all of whom knew Harold and what this moment meant to him.

Harold and Henrietta brought up a raucous, good-natured cheer as they exchanged an embarrassed kiss and sipped the delightful French wine and stood back to admire each other. Henrietta was desperate to clean up and change and she asked Harold to excuse her while she freshened up.

Harold left her there to refresh and rest while he took advantage of the time and went about the township chasing up various items and orders and settling his account at the dry goods store. Being a gentleman, of course, he left her to find her way up to her room under the care of the landlady, not wishing to give fuel to the local gossips who were already buzzing like swarming bees.

* * *

A number of Queensland towns have their streets named to a theme. In Longreach, the streets are named after species of birds, with the streets running east-west named after water birds and those running north-south after land birds. The main business street is called Eagle Street. Other streets would later honour Hudson Fysh, an Australian aviation pioneer, and Sir James Walker, a farmer and long-serving mayor of the former Longreach Shire Council.

When Harold returned, it was late in the day and he sent a message up to her room, inviting her down to join him. He waited patiently at the bottom of the stairs for her appearance and spent the time chatting to one or two acquaintances. Finally, a faint rustling came to his ears from the top of the stairs and there she stood, as breathtaking to his eyes as she was earlier. He gazed up at her as she made her way down the stairs and wondered again at his incredibly good fortune in winning the hand of this lovely, young woman.

She was very demure and shy, blushing fetchingly, but Harold knew there was a hidden resilience behind those deep, blue eyes that would see her take on the life they had discussed in a hundred letters. He felt his heart skip and lift in rhythm as he walked her to the hotel foyer. After her rest and change of clothes, Henrietta had emerged refreshed and looking lovely, by which time Harold had organised several pillars of the local community to join him and his intended for dinner in the hotel dining room. Henrietta was thus introduced to local society.

She spent her first week in Longreach as a resident at the hotel until their wedding day. Harold proudly took her for his bride in St Andrews Church, before a congregation of fellow settlers, traders and members of his church which was beautifully decorated with flowers, ribbons and lace.

Harold's best man was his overjoyed manager, Barney Jones, and his bank manager, Percy Barker, a great friend, was delighted to give the bride away. The organist followed the wedding party back to the hotel to provide some cheerful favourites as a musical backdrop to the reception on the hotel's almost in tune, upright piano.

They celebrated back at the hotel dining room with a pretty decent spread that impressed the young bride, as well as the guests. Roast beef was the centre piece with a small mountain of roast potatoes, carrots and green beans. Rich, brown gravy was dispensed from a large, silver gravy boat. Wine was not grown locally, but quality wine was shipped from the Hunter Valley in New South Wales and the hotel was well stocked with reds, whites and champagne and many corks were pulled to lubricate dusty throats. Apple pie and custard was served as a dessert with a rich, iced fruit cake, baked for the occasion by the town baker, which was presented as the wedding cake. Several bottles of delightful port helped seal a wonderful reception. Several speeches were encouraged during the meal, brevity and wit being highly prized.

Finally, with a rousing chorus of, "For They Are Jolly Good Fellows", the shy couple took themselves upstairs to a room dubbed the "honeymoon suite" for the occasion. Their landlady had been busy laying out her best Manchester, all scented with jasmine and lavender. The room glowed with the creamy, yellow light from a large, but delicate, candelabra enhancing the usual kerosene lanterns.

The next morning, a glowing Harold and Hettie set off for Courtland Downs and life together as settler pastoralists and the founding of the Cuthbertson dynasty. The combined genes of these two, resilient, intelligent and honourable people would pass down to, and be strengthened by, succeeding generations. The fundamental teachings of their church would also be the guiding light that would bring them universal respect and admiration from all who knew them. Honour was their byword and they would live lives honourable by any measure.

Courtland Downs was not quite what Hettie had expected. The original homestead, which was little more than a shack, had sat on its stumps in a flat, dusty paddock surrounded by stockyards and little else. It had begun its existence as a rough hut to keep out the wind, dust and heat and the cold in winter. But in truth, the only thing the walls of the old shack kept out was the tax man. Harold would often wake to find an animal of some description staring at him with wondering eyes, an experience that could seriously jolt the nerves.

There was a stand of eucalypts at the rear and the bush encroached towards it on the western side, which kept the worst of the summer winds away. It had been good enough for a bachelor squatter but hardly fit for a lady, no matter how hardy.

Harold's replacement homestead was a huge step up from the old shack, which now had other uses. Eventually, a recognisable homestead emerged from the dust to sit proudly in its stead. It would form the core of the household over the ensuing decades and would be subject to the needs of each subsequent generation, advances in technology and building techniques.

This was still the 1800s and Harold's best efforts had produced a homestead that provided a comparable level of comfort that could be found anywhere in the developing nation at that time. But there were some things the city dwellers had never experienced and would probably baulk at. Inside, the building was hot, airless and dusty. Henrietta was going to have to get used to the dust. You couldn't beat it, and if you tried, you were on the losing side.

Harold had tried to make this a home, bless him. Their bedroom was neat and tastefully decorated with a large, wrought iron bed covered by a floral bedspread and lace covered pillowslips. Henrietta had a mahogany dressing table, with a large mirror, that was lit by kerosene lamps fixed on either side. Before retiring at night, she sat on a polished, wooden stool with an embroidered seat cushion that allowed her to brush her hair in comfort.

The big surprise though was a bathroom; complete with an indoor water closet that was Harold's *piece de resistance*. He had seen the setup in a newspaper article about English inventor, Thomas Crapper, while he waited to see his solicitor in Longreach. The article found its way into Harold's pocket before he left. Being the inventive type himself, he spent some time drawing up his own design, and with Barney's help, Harold had produced a working model. Fitting it and making it work effectively, was something else again, as it obviously required water.

That came from the purpose built tank stand, separate to the one that supplied the homestead. Each of them drew their water from an underground spring. The kitchen was another matter. It was modelled on the kitchens Harold could recall from his youth in England, where he would find a warm haven in which to read his books and perhaps persuade cook, with his puppy dog looks, for a treat to satisfy a young lad's appetite.

It was far more functional, liberally supplied with pots, pans and roasting trays. The central feature was a huge, wood-fired stove that was constantly lit and even now had a big pot of water boiling away and a blackened teapot sitting to one side. There were plenty of storage cupboards, but adjoining one side of the preparation area, was a large pantry fully stocked with everything needed to feed a small army.

The homestead had a separate store where bulk items were held, and protected against the elements and rodents, under lock and key.

Harold had included the usual features of Victorian housing design, which meant there was a comfortable sitting room, warmed by a cavernous fireplace that was fuelled by massive logs, creating warming fires that were never extinguished during winter.

The original hut he had built years before, would probably fit within the walls of the generous sitting room. The homestead boasted a central hallway aligned in such a way as to take advantage of cooler breezes in the summer, but could shut out the cold winter winds that came in off the plains. Whilst the temperature never descended to the freezing levels they had experienced back in Mother England, it frequently decreased to single figures and, fuelled by a cruel wind, would soon have man and beast looking for cover. Heat was the main threat, often soaring into the 40 degrees Celsius plus range in the mid-western Queensland summer.

The building was still unfinished and lacked touches like skirting boards and stained and polished woodwork, but it was warm in winter and cool in summer and did effectively keep out, not only the tax man, but the wind, rain, reptiles, cattle and some dust. Harold, as a final civilising touch, surrounded the house with fencing to keep the stock out of the house and kitchen gardens. Across the front, he even managed to install a decorative fence of fancy patterned wire that was quite common in the city those days. Admission was gained through a swinging gate that matched the fencing and had a little roofed shelter builtover it.

Henrietta showed the character that Harold admired and didn't utter a word of complaint and simply got on with her duties as a settler's wife. She, very diplomatically, uttered wonder and gratitude for Harold's efforts, showering flattering praise on the delights that he revealed to her. She knew she wasn't coming to a baronial manor surrounded by lush gardens and the rich green pastures that she was more familiar with. The differences could not be starker, but she appreciated the enormous difficulties Harold had overcome in pursuit of ensuring her comfort. She looked at her husband, the tough settler, with a renewed admiration and her love.

Hettie set about adapting to the conditions and began to put her own stamp on things. Small feminine touches started to appear about the place. Antimacassars adorned the armchairs, doilies on the dining table, crystal decorations and fine china that came out of the huge trunk that was shipped from England to follow her. There were several crates still to come, packed with all sorts of household goods her family imagined she would require. It would take weeks, if not months, to see the bottom of those crates, if ever.

Hettie was no slouch in the kitchen. The homestead filled with delicious aromas generated by the bread and cakes she would prepare and the wonderful roast meats and even pies. Her new friends in town showed her how to bake a scone, which she quickly mastered, and just as quickly became a staple item on the table when guests arrived.

Hettie would dash off a batch of cakes or a three course roast dinner on a Sunday afternoon when they returned from church services. She prepared lunches for the hands or packed saddle bags for a cattle drive. She would travel out to the drafting camp, where the men were busy branding and castrating the yearlings, and set up a fire and provide meat and veg lunches with damper cooked in the ashes of the fire. She had become a complete settler's wife within no time at all. Harold could not believe the talent, the energy and enthusiasm of his bride and not only that, she was stunningly beautiful, especially when covered in dust and sweat.

CHAPTER THREE

1885

The homestead would not be complete until the voices of children rang out in its rooms and echoed down its long hallway, and as was the Victorian custom, they wished to start on a large family as soon as possible.

Within a couple of sad years, Hettie had given birth to a still born child they sadly christened Morna (*Gaelic: Dearly loved*) and interred her tiny body in a shady spot reserved for the family plot. Twin boys were the next born babies, presenting in good health. After which, Hettie gave birth to a very healthy and vocal girl, Hannah Constance.

Hugh and Julius, the twins, were good lads, both burly and adventurous and were the embodiment of Australian youth; rough-riding, hardworking young men, even in their early teens, who survived everything the bush and Harold could throw at them. But there were some things in outback Queensland that denied the strongest wills and most powerful physiques. While mustering strays in a far-flung corner of the station, Julius had an unfortunate encounter with a deadly taipan that delivered a quick and painful death from its loathsome fangs.

Hugh was devastated to lose his twin brother and lifelong companion. He felt as if he had lost his right arm, and for months he would turn his head expecting Julian to be there to share some event or comment on a beast in the herd. Once or twice when hard at it, he would suddenly stop and point at a rare sight, calling for Julian to look and see, before realising his brother was no longer there. Harold and Hettie tried hard to help him through the depression brought on by his loss, which they obviously shared. However, the demands of their lifestyle made no room for too much mourning and the responsibilities of the stock and the station's animals had to be met.

This was an unfortunate part of life in the outback and too long spent in mourning could see the seeds of neglect begin to take root. Julius was laid to rest alongside his tiny sister; prayers were said and the work went on.

Fortunately, there were many good times to balance the sad and tragic times. The Cuthbertson's created a reputation for hospitality and generosity. Harold had imported a piano for his musically-starved and talented wife. He surprised her with it on her birthday, having had it hidden in the barn after it was delivered along with the mail on a bullock wagon.

Keeping the instrument hidden until the right moment was no mean feat. The clumsy men, led by Barney, who probably could have lifted the darn thing by himself, despite every effort, they could not avoid jolting the instrument, causing loud clanging non-musical clamour from the precious piano. In the calmness of the dusk, they thought the awful row would be heard for miles and it wasn't until it was finally secreted quietly under a canvas sheet and further disguised by a layer of hay, that they were assured their secret was safe. But the tremendous effort was worth the joy it gave Hettie, and Hugh told everyone he thought his dear mother would wear the ivory off the keys inside of a week.

Both the children seemed to have an ear for music as well and before long Hannah became almost as proficient as her mother on the instrument and had a delightful singing voice. Hugh had picked up an interest in guitar from one of the hands and soon he was strumming away tunefully on his own guitar alongside his mother or sister. This music would fill the house when there were guests to be entertained or when time and opportunity allowed. Harold would join in the singing with his pleasant baritone. Favourite songs of the period included: 'Swing Low Sweet Chariot'; 'Put on Your Old Grey Bonnet'; 'In the Shade of The Old Apple Tree'; 'Wait Till the Sun Shines', 'Nellie and Silver Threads among the Gold'.

Hettie had a great love for the classics and her very favourite, Beethoven's *Moonlight Sonata* could be heard often as the station settled after dinner. She had requested sheet music from her parents back home: Mozart's *Turkish March*; Beethoven and Mendelssohn, which arrived on a regular basis. Each new piece gave her and Hannah a fresh challenge. The tradition of music in the Cuthbertson dynasty was assured.

While the Cuthbertson Empire was emerging from the dust of outback Queensland, a dark shadow was thrown across Europe and the world with the outbreak of the Great War, the war to end all wars.

1914-1918

Across the other side of the world, the war to end all wars had raged on and the infant nation of Australia gave up its finest youth to fight, struggle and die in the mud of the battlefields of foreign lands. Hugh avoided military service due to the fact he was a primary producer and the product of his labour was sorely needed for the war effort. Like all the brash young men of his age, he was itching to go on the big adventure and had no idea of what horrors lay over the horizon. Besides, Harold was slowing down these days and was more dependent on him around the property than ever.

Newspapers arrived at the station a few days out of date and Harold took his time reading them by the fire, while puffing on his favourite pipe. Shrouded in clouds of tobacco smoke, he would read passages of interest to Hettie while she knitted or darned. Hugh would have his feet up in another club chair and, on occasions, slurping a home brew or a cup of tea. They would discuss the war news and scan the list of casualties, sadly and too often, finding the names of young men who were the sons of Longreach. These names would also be called out at Sunday services to a solemn congregation. The war dragged on and on with all its horrors but the work on the station never ceased and it seemed like they were living on separate planets.

Following the example of her mother, Hannah would either be at the piano or practising her art work. Whilst Hettie preferred landscapes and portraiture, Hannah adored the bird life the station supported and had built up an impressive portfolio of delightful sketches of them.

Her favourites were the tiny little wrens, all the way up to the emus. The black station hands collected feathers and sometimes dead specimens for her and showed her nesting sites where she could sketch the chicks and observe how the parents cared for them. The waterholes and the river provided a home for many gorgeous species. There were at least half a dozen varieties of kingfisher, numerous ducks and geese. In the grasslands, there werequail and brush turkey along the tree lines. Watching overhead for the main chance were kites, hawks and eagles.

The noisiest of the lot were the budgerigars and parrots whenever they arrived in great swirling masses for water or departed at dawn for their favourite feeding grounds. It was always a spectacular sight to see them rising as one from their roosting place into the sky, like a cloud of dark smoke and then, as if obeying some singular mind, head off to their feeding ground, still in a tight flock. Any stray birds were in danger of providing a meal for the ever present birds of prey. Such was the variety and vivid colour of the birdlife, there was barely enough paint supplies in her paint box to do them all justice.

Hannah attended an art class in Longreach where she learned some of the finer points of her skill. In time, her work was forwarded to a gallery in Brisbane, which was administered by a relative of her art teacher. She was flattered to receive many plaudits from more than one art critic or bird lover and serious ornithologist, who wished to hire her as a guide and have an opportunity to explore the countryside with her.

Sadness descended on Courtland Downs when Harold contracted Spanish Influenza and passed away very quickly in a shivering fever. It was 1919 and the deadly virus, brought home by the returning soldiers, delivered swift death to thirty million people around the globe. Henrietta was devastated. Her life partner was gone; the man who everyone thought would live forever. A "tough as nails" old settler who had laughed at all sorts of perils over the years and now, suddenly, he was no more at the age of 65.

Hettie was inconsolable and never really overcame her loss. The piano lay forgotten in the sitting room and the homestead was dimmed with dark curtains over the windows and nothing could bring back her smile. Within six months, she had sickened and died. Henrietta, the stoic settler's wife joined her husband in the family plot, which was becoming quite populous now. She was only 55 years old.

Hettie's interment was conducted in a touching service conducted by the family's minister, Reverend Thomas Mc Cloud, and attended by many of the community's leading dignitaries. As original settlers who had the courage to come into this harsh land to establish a prospering cattle station and produce a family that continued to bring prosperity and honour to the district, their passing was a notable event.

With the passing of the old folks, Courtland Downs now passed into the hands of Hugh. At the age of 27, he was now responsible for the management of 30,000 hectares of land, 5,300 head of cross-bred Brahman cattle, 1,550 sheep, 15 pigs and mixed poultry and God alone knew how many dogs.

He was also responsible for his beautiful young sister, Hannah. At the age of 21, Hannah had blossomed into a very attractive woman who was currently being wooed by the son of a neighbour. Alfred John Woodward would ride over on his parents' buggy on weekends to take her to town or on a picnic. There were also the usual dances and sporting events that kept the young ones entertained. Alfred became known as AJ by all and sundry who found his first name a bit dull; but AJ was far from dull. Much to Hugh's delight, AJ was a very handy sportsman, playing rugby and opening the batting for his cricket team. He was also like all his generation, a good horseman and a crack shot with a rifle.

Hannah and AJ were married in a simple ceremony and went on to have several healthy children. AJ inherited his family's station and became a well-known and respected pastoralist who consistently produced top quality cattle that brought top prices at the Rockhampton cattle market.

It was in 1925 and as the master of Courtland Downs, it was high time Hugh brought a wife to the station, which was not all that easy in the wide brown land. The only opportunities to meet and socialise with members of the opposite gender was by attendingthe rounds of dances, sporting events and church socials. But Hugh had that covered already.

Hugh had spotted Frances Lilly McLeod in the congregation at church, when he was still a youth. He had noticed her peeping at him from under her bonnet and cheekily winked his eye. She had blushed furiously as she hurriedly turned away. Eventually, Hugh had an opportunity to speak with her and she found him to be a courteous and amusing companion. Over the following years, their fondness for each other developed as they grew and matured. As young adults, they spent more time together and were a constant at socials and parties.

Love blossomed from there and flourished between them, leading to a joyful marriage in St Andrews, their family church. Frances' wedding gown and veil were made locally by a school friend, who would become a very successful fashion designer. Her best friend from school Margaret, and Hugh's sister Hannah, were her bridesmaids and her little sister, Joanne, was flower girl. Frances' father, Jock McLeod, proudly walked his beautiful daughter down the aisle.

Hugh's best man was his old rugby team mate from school, Gordon Andrews, always called Gordo, another pastoralist from a similar family property further north of Longreach. The boys looked incredibly handsome, but incredibly uncomfortable, in formal suits and ties, topped off with stylish Homburg hats with bright hat bands.

Hugh brought his new bride, Frances Lilly, back to Courtland Downs immediately after the ceremony and a small reception in the church hall. No time for a honeymoon, there was work to be done and a wool clip to get in. Frances, as a daughter of the soil, understood and pitched in where she could.

Frances came from a farming family and was well schooled in her responsibilities. Her late mother-in-law, Hettie, had worked wonders in laying out the kitchen gardens all fenced and well-tended. She had instructed Harold in building henhouses and a piggery but over the years they had deteriorated a little. There was no time to waste; the seasons wouldn't wait for anyone.

Frances had Hugh build an efficient cool store that benefited from the shade of several large gums within easy reach of her kitchen, which she also had him remodel to her liking. She then set about laying out an agenda that would hopefully take them somewhere towards self-sufficiency.

The local soil was unforgiving so Frances had raised beds constructed and built up the soil with manure from the stables, thick with straw and compost from the household waste. Garden cuttings all joined to make a viable growing medium and before too long her gardens were a joy to behold.

Hettie, before her, had planted out a substantial orchard of apples, pears, oranges and lemon trees which were now mature and delivering a constant supply of fresh fruits. There were also flourishing flower gardens full of roses. The apples were baked in superb rhubarb and apple pies. Pears were preserved and put down in the cool store which contained other necessities and kept the oversupply of all these items fresh.

Frances' garden was managed systematically year round, to produce the fresh green vegetables and staple items in their seasons: tomatoes; carrots; cabbage; spinach; crisp, fresh peas and all the cottage garden herbs. The house gardens were home to flocks of chickens and ducks which, when released from their pens, kept her kitchen supplied with fresh eggs and poultry and managed to keep the number of pests down. Frances even managed to grow strawberries which were savoured with the ice-cream made in her kitchen when ice was available.

But if this sounds like a home gardener's dream come true, it was far from it. Frances waged a constant war against an army of rodents, insects and animals that believed all this fare was laid on for them. By the back door opening out to her gardens, Frances kept her armoury. She had a light weight .410 shot-gun, a 22 rifle and Hettie's old Henry Rifle, plus an array of bells and whistles that she brought into play before reaching for the more lethal defences. She depended on noise to frighten away the wildlife and would be very reluctant to take the life of any animal if she could avoid it.

Guns and bird nets could repel the larger predators, but more subtle techniques were required to keep insects at bay. Frances rotated her crops religiously and had found information about companion crops with insect repelling properties. Of course, healthy plants offered the strongest resistance to disease and insect invasion, so her gardens were well tended and fertilised. Frances may have been one of Australia's first organic farmers.

The brothers, William Luther and George Clement Cuthbertson, were born in that order, two years apart. William in 1918 and George followed on in 1920. As they matured, they seemed, to family and friends, to grow in different directions, remarking on their physical differences and approach to life. William was a strongly built boisterous lad who couldn't wait to get on a horse or a tractor. He developed into a big, athletic youth who gleefully excelled at sports and was captain of his schools rugby team. From about the age of eight he was always referred to as Big Bill.

Bill was a very popular young man for whom nothing seemed impossible. He was always onhand to help his friends and neighbours alike and would be the life of any party. In fact, no party really got underway until Big Bill arrived. Bill, despite his size, was an excellent dancer and every girl would be delighted to have him as a partner on the dance floor. He was a very courteous and considerate partner and all the mothers would be pleased if he was to be their daughter's escort. He liked to slake his thirst with a cold beer now and again, but unlike many of his mates was never known to drink to excess.

George was diametrically opposed to his older brother in every way and could usually be found with his head in a book. His room was almost wall to wall with reading material of all kinds. He was a brilliant student, excelling in his studies, winning scholarships and prizes. It wasn't long before he was dubbed "Books" by his brother and station hands. Like Bill, he enjoyed a beer at day's end if one was offered and like his big brother he was almost a teetotaller in practice.

Swimming parties were held at a beautiful billabong, forming part of the Thomson River when it flowed and could be relied on when the rains failed. Picnic baskets and folding chairs were delivered by horse and cart and the children and their friends would splash about until they were called back to eat. Hugh would have his guitar and they would be serenaded as they ate. Tired and sunburnt, they would load up on the wagon and make their way home again singing cheerfully, with the children nodding sleepily in the back.

The boys had a little sister, Elsie Henrietta, who was much loved and she played happily with her pretty little dollies and little toy stove and sewing machine. She was such a contrast to the rough and tumble happening outside, as to be a miracle to the lads, when they came in from their chores all covered in sweat and dust. Here was Elsie, sweet little thing singing nursery rhymes and chattering away in her own childish language. She would rush to meet her big brothers as they appeared on the door step. She was younger by eight years than Books.

Another daughter, Edwina, was lost to influenza that had lingered in the area and she was now lying along with other deceased family members at the back of the property shaded by a big old peppercorn tree. Designated as the family plot, she joined Grandpa Harold and his wife Henrietta and her uncle Julian. The plot was always kept neat and tidy, with headstones of Carrara marble inscribed in gold lettering. It was shaded by glorious bougainvillea in a variety of colours, which leant a cheerfulness to the site and all was well cared for.

Frances would often bring her darning out into the fresh air and light of the generous verandah, choosing to sit in one of the overstuffed armchairs in the cool shade away from the heat of the kitchen, which always had a wood fire burning day and night throughout the seasons. Hugh would often join her with his pipe and guitar. There was a bookshelf loaded with quality reading materials and a huge old trunk full of toys and girl's items that Elsie would drag out and spread all over the floor. When the boys came in from their duties they would wash up and join their parents discussing events of the day. Elsie would pester them to play with her and the whole scene was one of joyful domesticity.

The work was demanding in this climate, seven days a week building stockyards, fences and shearing sheds and other buildings for all sorts of storage, such as a stable and tack shed, machinery and other farming equipment. When all the building was done, the endless maintenance of machinery began and to that there were dams to be dug, wood to be cut and gathered for the home fires and a hundred other jobs to make life a little more tolerable. Then there was the mustering and branding of the cattle or castrating the bulls, shearing and lambing season. The work never ended, it only varied. Every chore was conducted with a maximum of energy, noise and dust, as if they were racing some demanding schedule.

Cattle bawled in fright or pain, or both; dogs yapped like crazy; the men yelled and yahooed at the herd, whips cracked, horses neighed and snorted and pounded the dusty ground with their hooves; the whole scenario disappearing in a dense shroud of fine dust. The horses needed care as well and all stations were equipped with a smithy where shoes could be forged and fitted. Parts for broken equipment would also be forged here by a skilled artisan. The number of parts that made up a harness for a dray was almost as complex as a modern motor vehicle and was the realm of expert horsemen.

Generally, one of the family men could handle the relatively simple task of shoeing a horse but more specialised work required a trained hand. Distance was the tyrannical master that dictated any veterinary emergencies were administered by the men of the station. If it couldn't be cured by their often crude doctoring, then it was brought to a merciful end with a bullet.

And the dust and flies were unrelenting. Drought struck often and if the grazier was slow to move his herd onto better ground, all that was left for him was to stand and watch his cattle going mad with thirst and dying in agony. It was that or put a bullet in them. The eight year drought of 1895-1903 was serious, and if not for the wisdom of old Harold, it may well have meant the end of them. They were just recovering from that awful event when another came along in 1911 and lingered for five years.

On other properties that had been overstocked, despite the advice freely handed out by Harold and now Hugh, trenches would be dug and the poor starving beasts herded up to them to be dispatched with a bullet to the head. Sheep were tougher, as their demands were less, but eventually, in a long drought they would fall to the same fate. The grazier, having literally worked 24/7, almost to the point of collapse to grow his herd and his wealth, would see it all blow away like the dust that was now choking him. The country was also subject to floods and bush fires, so there was always something to concern the landholder and keep him guessing.

These were the trials and tribulations that forged the steadfast Cuthbertson character.

CHAPTER FOUR

1940

Before Bill's departure, the family gathered for a farewell get together at Courtland Downs. Bill had requested a roast lamb dinner, his favourite. The table was piled high with a huge plate of superbly roasted potatoes, supported by all the usual vegetables grown in his mother's house garden outside her kitchen window. The centre piece was, of course, the mouth-watering lamb, flavoured aromatically with rosemary and basking in gloriously rich gravy. His father, Hugh, entertained as usual on guitar and Bill joined in on the family piano. Lydia and Elsie providing backup vocals.

It was a lovely night, but in the morning it would be time for him to leave. His parents were not content to say farewell from Courtland Downs so they planned to follow their son and his bride into Longreach to send off the young warrior at the railway station.

His mother, Francis, was tearful as he made a short, impassioned speech after dinner about his love for them all, imploring Hugh and Frances to take care of Lydia and themselves. He had discussed plans he and Hugh had in play for the property and Hugh reminded him, not for the first time, that Bill was exempt from military duty being a farmer, but Bill was having none of that. He believed he had a debt of gratitude to his country and he was determined to repay it. Hugh knew better than to argue. Books followed up with a speech in support of his elder brother that would have brought the house down as a vaudeville act, relating previously unrevealed tales of the brothers' adventures growing up. He finished with a short prayer of thanks for all they were blessed with and the early safe return of Big Bill.

After dinner, Lydia walked Bill out onto the verandah and they sat together on the old dusty couch looking out across the countryside they both loved so much.

The night was mild, almost balmy, and redolent with the mixed aromas of cattle dust and eucalypts. The sky was exceptionally clear and ten thousand stars glittered above them. It was hard to believe the world was at war again.

In the morning, Hugh and Francis followed Bill and Lydia into Longreach to farewell their son and wisely allowed them to spend the last few precious minutes in private.

Bill had his muscular left arm around Lydia's shoulder as she snuggled her head into his chest. She sat upright, turned and looked him squarely in the eyes then quietly told him she was with child and as it was September, he would be a father by June. Big Bill hugged and kissed her with delight and swore he would be home for the birth. There was a lot of water to go under that proverbial bridge and, unfortunately, he did miss the actual birth due to military duties but did make it home on leave eventually to meet his new son and heir, Robert Hugh Cuthbertson, and attend his christening in St Andrews.

Australia, with the other British dominions, had adopted the Empire Air Training Scheme (EATS) to provide trained aircrews to fight with the RAF. Australian recruits received elementary training at air bases around Australia and many of them were then sent overseas for advanced training.

Big Bill, with his previous flying experience, was able to waltz through every stage of the training course and was soon on his way to the UK. Like a lot of Aussie lads, he baulked at the stuffy disciplinary mores of the British but managed to put it aside to concentrate on the job at hand. There he joined a RAAF Beaufighter Squadron, (Dominion Squadron) flying missions over France and into the fiords of Norway. He also flew missions as a night fighter at which he excelled, scoring several quick victories, eventually achieving recognition as an ace with his fifth victory in the air. The massive firepower of his Beaufighter simply blew the enemy apart. The Battle of Britain was a very tough introduction to war for the Aussie pilots but a huge victory for the Allies and a demoralising defeat for the fat pompous Air Marshal Goering who had promised his Fuhrer to destroy the British air power, allowing the Germans a trouble-free crossing of the channel and invasion of the island nation.

Big Bill won admiration for his courage and aggression when attacking enemy shipping, or conducting night fighter missions, which he relished. He became an integral part of his Beaufighter, so much so that he could swear he felt pain if it was ever hit.

The common attitude to the Nazi enemy in those days was revulsion and very little pity was wasted on them. When Bill claimed his first confirmed kill, he celebrated with his squadron mates. And after every subsequent victory he felt the same surge of adrenaline and personal sense of satisfaction. Bill continued to win admirers as well as air battles.

There were many losses on the allies' side and quite a few of Bill's comrades flew out from their base and never returned. The empty chair in the squadron mess became the symbol of fallen comrades for the pilots in the conflict but these courageous young men continued to take to the air day after day.

Even though the Battle of Britain was won and Hitler denied his victory over the British Isles, there was still a lot of fighting to do. Bill's squadron was engaged in raids into France and Norway attacking ground targets and shipping. U-boats were an especially prized but rare target and Bill longed to get one under the nose of his aircraft and let his rockets and guns put paid to the nemesis of the North Sea fleets.

Although the chance never crossed the gun sights of his powerful fighter, he made up for it in other ways, fearlessly attacking heavily defended German targets wherever they were assigned. Targets were assigned by HQ as a result of intelligence information supplied by resistance fighters, reconnaissance flights or observation by other services.

Bill managed to catch up with his brother Books in London during a few days leave and they had a great reunion. Books remained very tight-lipped about his work and never mentioned Bletchley Park, except to confirm his work was top secret and they hoped to shorten the war with it. Bill entertained Books with tall tales and true of his air war against the Nazis bringing approving comment from his younger brother who knew the facts and admired his brother's courage.

They were both concerned for the family back home of course, and the situation with the Japanese in the Pacific and exchanged the little information they had received in letters from home.

Unsurprisingly, the brothers drank too much and stayed too long before they exchanged a brief bear hug and wished each other well, swearing to survive the war and be reunited back home at Courtland Downs, before breaking off and returning to their billets.

With the terrible pressures of war in the air and so many losses, young men became oldbefore their time. New recruits could only hope to survive long enough to gain the experience and survival skills that would give them a fighting chance.

Big Bill came into the war armed with a comparatively high number of flying hours which was a great advantage. Many of the new recruits were still learning to fly, as well as trying to master the art of war in the air. It wasn't long before Bill's flying skills and leadership won him promotion to Squadron Leader. When he became an ace, he was awarded the Distinguished Flying Cross for destroying six enemy aircraft in night fighter operations and for exemplary leadership and initiative that inspired his comrades who were in awe of his courage, determination and unfailing cheerful personality. Bills rear gunner/ navigator Flight Sergeant Bluey Mansfield was awarded the Aircrew Europe Star.

Because of Bill's experience in the harsh Australian outback, he had taught himself the self-reliance adapting quickly to the exigencies of a night fighter pilot.

The development of radar was accelerated and it was becoming more sophisticated and deadly accurate, which proved to be an invaluable weapon in the squadron's arsenal. Bill and his flight would be vectored by the radar to an incoming enemy group with great accuracy, until they could see the flame from the exhaust of the Nazi aircraft, allowing them to approach stealthily, swooping in to take up an attackingposition from below, firing a deadly burst of machine gun fire and rockets into the belly of the hated enemy before the Nazi pilots knew they were there.

At the other end of the world and much closer to home, things were looking very grim, as the "yellow tide" of the Japanese advance in the Pacific was called. Again, no sentiment was lost on the cursed Japs because of their unprecedented cruelty.

A horrible example of what the Japanese Imperial Army was capable of occurred during the second Sino-Japanese War. The Nanking Massacre was an episode of mass murder and rape committed by Japanese troops against the citizenry over a period of six weeks, starting on 13 December 1937, the day he Japanese captured Nanking, the capital of the Republic of China. During this period, Japanese soldiers murdered Chinese civilians and unarmed combatants who numbered, at best guess, somewhere between 40,000 to over 300,000 and perpetrated widespread rape and looting.

Alarm bells began to ring throughout the Commonwealth as the axis powers of Germany-Italy-Japan claimed victories across the globe. Every man and woman in Australia would be called on to help halt the barbaric flood that seemed to be making its invincible way to the south.

With the swift and savage advance of the Japanese in the Pacific, Flight Lieutenant William Luther Cuthbertson DFC was seconded back to Australia to join No 30 squadron RAAF at Richmond Air Base.

After a joyful reunion with his adoring wife and his newborn son proudly christened Robert Hugh, Bill had a few days leave to enjoy with Lydia. The time seemed to race by and they filled every moment until it became time for him to leave and report back to Richmond airbase. He rejoined his squadron as they transferred to Townsville, keeping him a little closer to home and able to get away from time to time to for a visit to Courtland Downs in a borrowed vehicle.

The road trip was almost 800 kilometres and took the best part of nine hours when he couldn't beg an unauthorised ride with a sympathetic DC 47 pilot, a flight distance of 530 kilometres, taking about two hours. He would be picked up at Longreach by Hugh to be driven home. Getting back to Townsville was another matter, but he managed it often enough to make the loss of sleep worthwhile. The squadron, in the meantime, was engaged in escorting anti-shipping patrols which kept them pretty busy. These trips home were soon curtailed as the squadron was on the move. Once again Big Bill took his wife in his arms and said his emotional farewell.

Bill was still as patriotic as they came, but he cursed his squadron, the air force, the war and, in particular, a special curse on the bloody Nips that were now depriving him of his family and home. He was looking forward to bringing the enemy a little pain. He needn't wait too long as his squadron received orders to set a course for New Guinea.

Bill's aircraft was the Bristol Beaufighter, a very reliable and durable plane. The Beaufighter was developed during World War Two by the Bristol Aeroplane Company in the UK. Originally conceived as a heavy fighter, it found its niche as a night fighter during the Battle of Britain. As a larger aircraft it was able to carry heavy armaments as well as radar without the loss of performance. In later roles, it operated as a torpedo bomber in maritime action and, armed with rockets, it performed magnificently as a ground attack aircraft.

The RAAF Beaufighter was heavily deployed in the Battle of the Bismarck Sea in an anti-shipping role. The RAAF eventually had seven squadrons of Beaufighters. The aircraft had a crew of two and was powered by twin 14 cylinder radial engines pushing out 1600 horsepower each, giving it a top speed of 320 mph and a ceiling of 19,000 feet.

A total of four forward firing 20mm Hispano cannons were mounted in the lower fuselage area. The cannons were supplemented by six .303 Browning machine guns in the wings. The Beau's fighter armament was among the heaviest of its time. Beaufighters were developed as fighter torpedo bombers using their firepower to take out anti-aircraft fire and hit the enemy's escort vessels and small ships. The recoil of its guns could reduce the plane's speed by 25 knots.

The pilot sat in a fighter cockpit with big windows providing excellent vision. The navigator-radar operator or bomb aimer sat to the rear under a perspex bubble. Both crew had their own hatch in the floor. The pilot's hatch was behind his seat which, on entry, collapsed so he could climb over it to take his seat. In an emergency, the pilot could operate a lever that released the hatch. He would then grasp two overhead steel handholds, swing his legs over the hatch and drop through. The navigator's hatch was directly in front of him and unobstructed. The pilot could exit by flipping his cockpit open to starboard and stepping out onto the port wing and likewise, the navigator had a similar arrangement.

It was widely rumoured the Japanese had labelled the Beaufighter, "Whispering Death" supposedly because the attacking aircraft was often not heard or seen until it was too late. This was the fighting machine that took Big Bill into Port Moresby in 1942 where he and his squadron conducted low level ground attacks in support of military actions against the Japanese infantry and shipping.

The flight from Townsville was uneventful apart from, in their pre-flight briefing the Met Officer advised them to expect heavy weather on approach to Moresby. They took to the air in the pre-dawn darkness showing no navigation lights, each one looking for the blue formation light of his neighbour. They climbed to their nominated cruising height and formed up in a loose formation that appeared to lack the precision a civilian might expect but had proved its efficiency in Britain's air war.

Although they were flying into poor weather and a hot war zone, Big Bill still had time to enjoy the magnificent cloud formations that were revealed with the dawn from the large, uncluttered windshield of his aircraft. Flying still made his heart soar and the glistening lapis lazuli blue of the Coral Sea below contrasted against the blinding white towering, cumulonimbus clouds and, in a moment of impiety, shared the thought with his navigator that they were like the ancient Greek Gods. The Japanese would soon find they were more like airborne hellions.

Bill brought his squadron into the Port Moresby Airfield (Jackson Field, named in honour of Squadron Leader John Francis Jackson, D.F.C. 75 Squadron RAAF aged 34. He was killed in action on 28 April 1942).

The pre-war Port Moresby airfield had been taken over and expanded by American forces. Revetments were constructed to protect parked aircraft and defences. RAAF fighter Squadrons 75 and 76 Kittyhawks and P40s, were operating out of this field before Big Bill's arrival. Their role was to conduct ground actions and target enemy shipping. The P40s had suffered considerable losses to date.

When elements of 30 Squadron were assigned to Milne Bay airfield, they found a different set of conditions. These pilots were using the unfamiliar Marston matting, the brilliant, perforated steel matting used all over the Pacific to rapidly construct airfields on very disagreeable swampy ground. The runways were narrow strips and called for precision when landing, which was not made any easier in the brief and frequent rains squalls.

The strips were slightly unnerving as the matting could move up and down as much as a foot. Earthen revetments were banks of earth in a large U shape, providing a relatively safe parking space and had been established to provide protection for the planes from the frequent enemy attacks.

Squadron Leader William C Cuthbertson DFC was at war again and duly reported to his commander Group Captain Brian "Blackjack" Walker DSO.

The Japanese were now using landing barges out of Buna and Rabaul to island hop and larger troop ships were reported in the Coral Sea in their advance in the Pacific. They became an important target for the Beaus who hunted them relentlessly in and around the Entrecasteau Islands, East Britain up to Rabaul and Buna on the north coast of New Guinea. They continued their support of naval activities with their attacks on Japanese shipping.

One 30 Squadron patrol led by Bill caught a convoy of Japanese troop ships. The fleet consisted of a mix of auxiliary craft, two small 650 ton Nozaki class and one larger Iroko classof 9,570 tons. The small fleet was sailing on a southerly heading and on the first pass by the Beaus, the two smaller vessels were found to be packed with troops.

The Beaus went on the attack immediately and, without mercy, raked the decks with lethal machine gun and cannon fire to subdue the anti-aircraft defences and then followed up with deadly rocket attack. It was possible to feel sympathy for the soldiers on the exposed decks, until one remembered what their mission was, to invade New Guinea and ultimately Australia.

Bill circled and attacked several times, inflicting terrible damage to the ships, one of which pulled out of formation, turning to port aimlessly with a huge column of black smoke streaming from it. The upper decks and bridge, a shattered mess of twisted scorched metal. No 30 Squadron was supported by US B25s of the 8th Bombardment Squadron out of Jackson field, dropping bombs and launching torpedoes. It was a crushing blow to the Japanese, sending the badly savaged fleet staggering back towards Rabaul.

Bill's reputation for aggression came to the fore, bringing his plane down to mast height, blasting the enemy shipping with the full force of his terrifying guns. His aircraft sustained several hits from the Japanese defence. Shrapnel and machine gun fire tore through his port wing and tail plane. Bill was completely unaware of it until he landed after the mission and his ground crew pointed it out. They were immediately set to work, making repairs so Bill could get back into the air and harass the Japanese before they could reach sanctuary. Bill and his crewman, Flight Sergeant Bluey Mansfield, retired to the mess for a well-deserved hot meal and a cup of tea before getting a couple of hours' kip.

It was exhausting and stressful duty and the pilots and crews took every opportunity to grab some rest when they could. Soldiers and airmen in combat quickly learned not to pass up a chance to rest because there was no telling when the next opportunity would come along. The Squadron felt they were making a difference in their support of the hard-pressed ground troops and never complained.

Whatever the mission assigned to him, Bill always pressed home his attack with great courage and ferocity, personally affronted by these barbarian invaders who would threaten his country and his family and beliefs. Bluey was in awe of his leader and, more than once, said he would hate to be the enemy in Bill's sights. He had never once heard him complain or waver in his duty. Bluey Mansfield would fly into hell with the big Queenslander and never doubted that the mission would be completed and more importantly get them both home in one piece.

The Japanese tactic of island hopping in small landing barges, managed to move large numbers of troops and equipment out of their stronghold port of Rabaul in New Britain and made a prime target for the Beaufighters of 30 Squadron.

The Daihatsu barge was 65 feet long and displaced about 15 tons. They were capable of carrying 170-190 fully equipped troops or 25 tons of supplies or a truck. Two small tanks were landed at Milne Bay from one of these barges. They were an effective form of transport for the role and a juicy target for Allied aircraft and stood little chance once the Beaus' sights fell on them.

The Beaufighter would lay down terrifying firepower from their cannons and machine guns. Anything in front of an angry Beau stood little chance of survival. Combined with their stealth, they were rightly feared by the Japanese and worthy of their nickname "Whispering Death".

In May of 1942, American naval forces, commanded by Rear Admiral Frank J. Fletcher, intercepted the Japanese fleet in the Coral Sea, which had embarked on an invasion of Port Moresby, New Guinea.

Air combat units from both sides proved to be wasteful, missing their target opportunities but when they found them, they were able to prove the incredible value of air cover at sea.

The Americans struck first, sinking the light carrier "Shoho". When the main forces came to trading air strikes, the Americans lost the carrier Lexington and suffered damage to Yorktown. Lacking air cover, the Japanese withdrew, delivering a tactical victory to the allies.

This four-day intensive engagement was marked as the first air-sea battle in history, with the Japanese seeking to control the Coral Sea on their way to invade Port Moresby. Although both sides suffered damages to their carriers, the battle left the Japanese without enough planes to cover the ground attack of Port Moresby, resulting in a strategic allied victory.

This air battle created great excitement among the air and ground crews of Big Bill's No 30 Squadron, remaining a major talking point. If there were still any doubters, they would finally be convinced of the importance of air superiority, having seen Hitler's plans for the invasion of England thwarted in the Battle of Britain and now Tojo's plans for domination in the Pacific had suffered a similar major setback, brought about by air power.

Now this is not the end. It is not even the beginning of the end. But it is perhaps the end of the beginning – Winston Churchill at the end of the Battle of Britain.

Perhaps this could be equally applied to this important event.

The struggle for control of New Guinea began with the Japanese taking Rabaul on the northern tip of New Britain, an important strategic base, providing a considerable natural anchorage and was ideal for the construction of an airfield. Over the next year, the Japanese built up the area into a major air and naval base. The allies were unable to prevent the Japanese landing at Buna on the north coast of New Guinea, but their next move to take Milne Bay was not to prove as easy or successful.

The ultimate prize was the colonial capital, Port Moresby, on the south coast. Capturing this strategic port would deny the allies their principal forward base and serve as the springboard for the subsequent planned Japanese assault on the Australian mainland.

The Japanese had poor intelligence of the allied numbers in the area and believed it was lightly defended. However, early in June, American army engineers and Australian infantry and an anti-aircraft battalion had landed and work was begun on an airfield.

Kittyhawk's from 76 RAAF Squadron, under the command of their legendary Squadron Leader, Keith "Bluey" Truscott, landed on the strip in July and 75 Squadron followed three days later. Some of the planes found conditions a bit challenging with water over the runway causing them to skid off and become bogged. They were to be joined later by a small contingent of the Beaufighters of No 30 Squadron in September.

By mid-August some 8,500 Australians and 1,300 Americans were on site. The Japanese arrived on August 25th and the battle began. The Nips believing there weren't many allies, landed a force equivalent to a battalion, maybe two or three companies of between 80-250 troops.

Allied aircraft destroyed the Japanese landing barges when they attempted to land on the coast behind the Australian positions. Despite this they were able to quickly push inland and begin to advance on the airfield.

Heavy fighting ensued, with much of it taking place at night in horrendous conditions of heavy tropical rain and mud. The mud proved effective in preventing the Japanese from fully utilising the two light tanks they had landed, which when overcome by the thick, cloying stuff were abandoned. But the Australian artillery, unfortunately suffered the same fate and proved useless in trying to destroy them.

The Japanese advance encountered the Australian Militia Brigade that formed the first line of defence. Under the command of Brigadier John Field, the brigade consisted of three battalions from Queensland. The militia fell back but the Australians brought forward veteran Second AIF units the Japanese had not expected. Allied air superiority again proved the deciding factor providing close ground support and bombing the enemy's supply lines, finding themselves suffering heavy casualties, outnumbered and without supplies. The fighting came to an end on 7 September 1942. Troops of 55th Battalion were then transferred back to Port Moresby to take up the fightwith the enemy on the infamous Kokoda Track.

Meanwhile, the Australian population held their collective breath and tried to carry on as news of this critical battle was reported. People continued with in their day to day lives in the face of this burgeoning threat.

Author's Note

By 31 January 1942, all British Empire forces had withdrawn from the Malay Peninsula onto Singapore Island. On 8 February, the Japanese landed in the north-west of the island and, within six days, they were on the outskirts of Singapore city, which was also at this time under constant air attack.

Hard fighting continued, but on 15 February, Lieutenant General Arthur Percival, the British commander in Singapore, called for a ceasefire and made the difficult decision to surrender. This included all European civilians, who were interned.

CHAPTER FIVE

1807

Lawrence Garret Parnham was the product of an Australian blue blood family that had settled in the Parramatta region of New South Wales on a 500 acre parcel of land granted to his great, great-grandfather Jonas Oliver Parnham in 1805, which he grandiosely named Chatsworth Park.

It was a premium grazing property which Lawrence's ancestors developed into one of

Australia's finest wool producing sheep stations. Ignoring the trend of other farmers, Jonas purchased a solid breeding stock of pure merinos from John MacArthur and continued to preserve the pure breed with their fine wool, instead of cross breeding. It was hard work that took time to achieve, but eventually, it paid off in a very big way.

Macarthur had been cross breeding two varieties of sheep, hoping to produce fine wool in NSW. Two ships were sent from Sydney to the Dutch Cape colony by Governor Hunter in 1796 to obtain supplies for his own colony. Both commanders were friends of Macarthur who asked them to take up any good quality sheep they might find.

People say that luck's a fortune and so it proved to be in this case as, by chance, the King of Spain had presented some of the very finest merino sheep to the Dutch Government. Originating from the Spanish royal flocks of El Escorial, they were closely guarded and highly prized.

The sheep were put into the care of a Scottish gentleman who died shortly thereafter and the flock became the subject of a long running dispute between the man's widow and the government who ordered them sold to end the matter. A number were purchased by the two captains and were ultimately delivered to Macarthur. The magnificent merino sheep that included three rams in the flock, were bought by several landowners.

It was from the resultant pure bred flock that the foundation of the Parnham fortune was established when a fine selection of breeding animals was purchased from Macarthur's flock in 1807 and set to graze on the lush pasture that was Chatsworth Park. Macarthur, if not a mentor of Jonas, was a powerful influence over the young settler. Governor Phillip had brought vine cuttings to the colony in 1788 and in 1794, Macarthur obtained cuttings from which he produced port and actually sent samples back to England. In time Jonas' sons would develop viticulture in NSW.

Jonas added a fine vineyard after seeing the success of John Macarthur's. From this time on, by modelling his agricultural and grazing enterprises along the same lines as his wealthy and successful neighbour, the Parnham family fortune never took a backward step.

With wool reaching record prices in Europe, especially during the Napoleonic Wars from 1803 to 1815, there was a large influx of merinos into Australia.

By the end of the 1850s, sheep numbers across Australia had reached 16 million, or around 39 sheep per head of population. In the late 1890s, lower wool prices and the infamous Federation drought devastated the industry. Sheep numbers dropped by half and industrial action by shearers seeking better wages and conditions, also took its toll. The unions, formed by the shearers, became the Australian Workers Union in 1894 and eventually helped give rise to the Australian Labour Party. This put a shiver up the spine of the average squatter, the Parnhams included. They continued to look for other crops and perhaps industries into which they could diversify.

Jonas had married well of course, and Almira Genevieve Hartwell became his wife in a simple ceremony when she arrived in Sydney Town, three years after Jonas had established Chatsworth Park. However, she insisted on staying in the township until he could provide the standard of housing she was accustomed to.

This gave impetus to the labours of Jonas, which he passed down the line to the hired help. Eventually, he had completed the basis of the homestead that would expand over the coming decades and was of sufficient quality to satisfy his aristocratic wife.

A simple cottage-style building constructed from handmade bricks and stone, quarried locally, surrounded on three sides by a broad verandah, an architectural style instantly recognisable to most Australians. An equally basic floor plan gave him a large bedroom with its own fireplace on one end and a comfortable sitting room with a second fireplace on the other, separated by a spacious area in the middle that was both kitchen and dining. It may not have been an English manor house that Almira had been raised in, but by the standards of the day it was a little bit above the average.

As the years went by, the simple cottage grew into a far more substantial homestead as the Parnhams' wealth and security increased. By the time Jonas' grandson, Jefferson, had matured, it boasted three more bedrooms, a formal dining room, a guest wing, an expanded sitting room, a small but adequate ballroom, a business office and an extensive wine cellar, plus a huge pantry with cool room.

Lawrence, the great, great grandson of Jonas, had his character formed as a farm hand just like his ancestors before him, by mucking in around the farm. No job was considered below him and he would join the hired help, shovelling manure from the stables or crutching sheep to prevent fly strike. Lawrence worked long and hard and he was not spared from any of it.

The busiest time of year was shearing time when the huge flock of prize merino ewes and rams were yarded in preparation. The rich pasture could support heavy stock rates, but the Parnham's were neither greedy nor stupid. Quality was the catchword at Chatsworth Park and that meant careful husbandry of stock and pasture.

Lawrence loved the bustle and excitement of shearing time when the rough, hardworking, hard swearing and drinking shearers occupied the billet that was their sleeping quarters while they worked to remove the prize fleece. His father, Alexander, was a stickler for discipline during this time, as there was a great deal at stake. Any shearer found drunk, or displaying anti-social tendencies, was dismissed on the spot and the contractor who employed him would feel the wrath of Alexander.

Despite this, Lawrence enjoyed the camaraderie of the shearers and joined them around their fire, singing and swapping yarns. They teased the young squatter good naturedly, knowing they would be answering to him one day as heir to Chatsworth Park. These tough nomads recognised his place in the scheme of things, but such was the nature of their own tough upbringing, their courage and strength was frequently tested by violence. It was part of their rite of passage that they saw and accepted as part of becoming a man.

It was not unsurprising then, that one of their number would present a challenge to the young Lawrence when he had gained the physique of a man. Lawrence had always appeared as a strong lad who had never shirked hard work and was always cheerful and respectful. However, when, without any provocation on his part, a hard bitten young shearer pushed him against a wall so violently that the back of his skull smacked hard against the stone work, emitting a sharp cracking sound. Instead of defending himself and standing his ground to knock the lout down, he fled to the safety of the main house and sought the comfort of his father.

Alexander was less than impressed by his son's weakness and, in anger and embarrassment, cuffed him soundly across the head and sent him back out to take up the ruffian's challenge with his ears ringing from another unexpected blow.

Lawrence was more intimidated by his father than the young shearer, who he found laughing by the fire at the humiliation of the "would-be master" of Chatsworth Park earlier. Seeing the look of determined aggression on Lawrence's face, the shearer was swiftly on his feet and ready for combat. In the blink of an eye, the two came together in a violent clash that lasted less than thirty seconds with Lawrence delivering a powerful left hook to his opponent's short ribs, taking the wind out of him and causing him to bend forward in agony, only to be pole-axed by a follow up round house left to his jaw. Without further ado, Lawrence stepped over his prone antagonist's unmoving body and walked straight back to report his success to his father.

The onlooking shearers were stunned. One minute, Lawrence had run off apparently too terrified to fight and then returned and shaped up like a seasoned prize fighter taking out his adversary, in what would have been a knockout in the first round of an organised boxing match. The contradiction was inexplicable and would be repeated much later a long way from Chatsworth Park, in much harsher circumstances, with devastating results.

Lawrence was a gun at school sports and showed no sign of timidity on the playing field. He wore the number two proudly for the first fifteen and took on the fiercest tacklers, backing up with a great turn of speed to score a bag of tries. He was a strongly built young man, thanks to the hard work about the farm, who also enjoyed swimming in the inter-school championships and brought honour to his team. He came fully equipped with a barrel chested, powerful physique, and with a huge reserve of stamina, he was unstoppable. Academically, he consistently achieved results in the upper five percent of his year. Alexander was unapologetic in his praise for his son, at a time when one was wise to practice humility. He saw a great future for the lad and would move heaven and earth to see that he had every advantage to make his mark on the world.

The Parnhams were a very proud and, some said, arrogant family. Their perceived arrogance was born of personal success and the confidence that it brings. Even in those times, Australians loved to cut down the tall poppies and the Parnham's stood tall in their community.

In establishing the family, Julian Wesley Parnham succeeded his ageing father Jonas, as head of the family and manager of his estates. On a trip back "home", as many Australians called England in those days, Julian met and courted his wife. He was aged 22 and she was 19 and had seen several of her friends already walk down the aisle. Too young by current standards to be called a spinster, but the sands of time were running through the hour glass at an astonishing rate and the object of Julian's desires had, with great diplomacy, shut down several suitors. All her friends had been at least betrothed by the age of 18 and it was with great relief that her father welcomed Julian's request for her hand and was jubilant when his precious child accepted his proposal.

She was a genuine English Rose, fair skinned blonde haired and with astonishing deep blue eyes that put Julian in mind of the oceans he had crossed to arrive on those shores.

Victoria Elvira Westchester was the second daughter of a minor titled aristocrat who, unlike many of his peers, treated Julian with respect rather than the usual sneers directed at him as a colonial, or worse, a convict settler from the colonies. These disturbing insults were thrown at him when he first arrived on English soil, but Julian was made from better stuff and quickly learned it was a waste of time trying to rebuff this nonsense. He noted it was generally the "chinless wonders", the under achieving or overindulged brats that were attempting to overcome their sense of self-loathing by putting other people down.

After gaining permission from Victoria's father, Julian organised a picnic in the beautiful English summer countryside. They took a horse and buggy out across her father's grazing land to a very beautiful grassy bank of a small local stream. In the shade of an ancient oak tree, and at a suitable time, Julian fell to one knee, produced a sparkling diamond and ruby ring and proposed marriage. His supplication was accepted with great excitement by his young fiancée. Julian and Victoria were married in autumn in the Westchester family chapel, that was decorated with garlands of flowers from the estates gardens, before family and friends. Victoria's sister Emily acted as bridesmaid and her young brother Christopher was best man to Julian. It was a beautiful occasion blessed by the warmth of a late summer. A sumptuous wedding supper followed in the great hall of Rothley Manor, the family's ancestral home.

The celebratory repast consisted of all the ingredients of a generous English feast. Roasted meats of beef, lamb and pork all smothered in a variety of rich, dark brown gravies to suit. If this was not enough, then Julian could tuck into three different roasted game birds: pheasant; partridge and delicate little quail. Lashings of vegetables and many carafes of wine, produced on the estate, and huge jugs of the rather flat, warm beer the English are fond of. It was a feast worthy of his second daughter and, after some long overly sentimental speeches and one hilarious rather bawdy one from a cousin, the feast moved from the dining hall to the ballroom and the rest of the evening was spent in nonstop exhaustive dancing. Julian and Victoria discreetly left the celebrations and retired to their bridal room where their union was consecrated.

After a decent interval, which allowed them to visit and be visited by a host of uncles, aunts and cousins all keen to impress the happy couple with splendid meals and entertainment, they were anxious to be on their way. Before they said their final farewells, they made a special effort to spend some time with Victoria's grandparents, who were unlikely to ever see their beautiful granddaughter again after she sailed away.

As Victoria's papa and grandmother saw them off at the door, the old gentleman pressed a small parcel into her hand, muttering that it was a little of her inheritance that might come in handy. Victoria later found that it was a surprisingly generous 500 pounds which would indeed be handy.

After respect had been paid to what seemed like hundreds of relatives, Julian and his bride departed for the colony of New South Wales and his home aboard the barque *City of London*, a tidy little vessel of 395 tons on 16 March, arriving after a reasonably comfortable voyage, in Sydney Town on 12 July 1838. There were eleven fellow passengers in first class whose company they enjoyed on the journey, including Mr Robert Dickson, a surveyor from whom Julian learnt quite a bit of useful information. They formed a friendship that would endure after their arrival. Julian and Victoria also befriended another good natured fellow, Dr Neil Campbell, a skilled surgeon who would set up his practice with Julian's advice and support in the burgeoning settlement of Sydney Town.

Travel by sail to the colony of New South Wales was a matter of pot luck where the weather was concerned. Many a sailing vessel ran into problems depending on their timing and point of departure. The Bay of Biscay, with a coastline shared by France in the north and Spain in the south, was a trap for the unwary. Any captain getting too deep into the bay on a leeward sea would have great trouble trying to tack out against the westerly pushing them in deeper and deeper against the coast.

The vicious sea that would be the undoing of any unsound vessels, plus the square-rigger's poor performance sailing to windward, make it a sea respected by sailors and one better left well to port heading south.

Sailing down the east coast of Africa, a stop was often made at the Canary Islands' largest land mass, Tenerife, for replenishment of supplies before "running their easting down" to Cape Town, as the old-time sailors termed it.

Cape Town has a history as a victualling port for sailing ships headed for the Far East. Ships sailing for New South Wales on Australia's east coast rounded the Cape and headed east with the prevailing winds blowing unimpeded, east to west, almost like a conveyer belt. Ships heading into the Pacific and beyond, would follow the east coast of South America south, before chancing their luck and sailing skills with the storms and wild seas of Terra del Fuego, the feared Cape Horn with its contrary head winds, huge seas and powerful tides. A large part of the early shipping traffic were whalers out of New England and New Bedford Massachusetts in America.

After leaving Cape Town and the prominent landmark of Table Mountain behind, ships would generally dip further south to merge with the unimpeded winds of the Roaring Forties between latitude 40 and 50 to take them across the Southern Ocean to reach the southern coast of Australia. Some would continue on, leaving Tasmania on their portside rather than risk running the gauntlet of the infamous Bass Strait, which claimed the lives and ships of many traders, explorers and migrant ships. The southern coast of Victoria was dotted with sad little burial plots of the dead recovered from the cold, green seas after their ships struck reefs or were driven ashore by savage Bass Strait storms.

Up to this point the *City of London* had experienced better conditions than most, although coming out of Cape Town, the passengers and crew were astounded by the gigantic following seas, with some gargantuan swells, towering over ninety feet dwarfing the fragile craft. They came from behind them in a regular metronomic rhythm, the little ship lifted from the stern rising up to the crest where the wind is at its strongest threatening to tear the rigging away then feeling as though their vessel was sliding down the face of the monster like a nightmare toboggan ride. It takes a very talented helmsman to keep the ship from surging forward into a broadside attitude known as broaching down the face of these monsters. It's a weird and frightening sleigh ride that can end with the ship driven below the waves or being 'pitch-poled' that is, turned end over end.

Passengers were confined below and the ship was rigged fore and aft with safety lines for the protection of the crew who were still required to attend the ships rigging. The ships motion was a repetitive surge forward with the rushing sound of the sea against the hull parting about them, then a strange lull as they settled down the back of the wave. The ship felt as though they had almost stopped and were actually going backwards.

One of the perils in these massive swells was a dismasting which happened when the sailing vessel was lifted to the crest of the wave from the sheltered trough, where the ship gained temporary shelter in the lee of the following swell. Then suddenly, the vessel would be exposed to the full force of the screaming winds of the Roaring Forties that would fill the exposed sails with a loud crack, putting tremendous pressure on the upper rigging.

The upper reaches of the masts on sailing ships from stem to stern are known as the Topmast, Topgallant (T'gallant) and the Royal mast.

One way to combat this effect was to carry only top sails, hopefully keeping them clear of the crests and into the wind stream, maintaining consistent pressure on the canvas and lessening the impact of the sudden change in pressure.

At the suggestion from a passenger that they should seek calmer waters, the captain turned away, muttering into his copious beard about landsmen being 'nowt but talking cargo.' He was a gruff, serious man as he needed to be in his chosen profession due to the absolute responsibility for his ship, passengers, cargo and crew. The ship's master, however, had a wealth of humorous adventures to relate, like any good sailor, which diverted their attention away from such perils, keeping them all in good spirits as they took their supper in the ship's saloon.

The food was tolerable enough without being anything like sumptuous. The trick at times was to consume the meal before it hit the deck as the ship plunged and rolled on the ocean swells. The saloon table was edged with a timber guardrail standing an inch above its surface, known as a fiddle. This should in most cases, save a passenger's plate flying off the table onto the deck, but occasionally it proved to be a little inadequate in these waters and one or two fine meals finished as decoration on the saloon deck.

In time, they finally pointed the ship's bows north as they rounded the south-eastern coast of Van Diemen's Land on their way to Sydney Harbour some 600 miles north.

On a clear, warm day on a calm sea, a sincere religious service was conducted by the captain on the main deck with the passengers and crew giving their grateful thanks to God for seeing them safely through the tumultuous seas to this the final leg of their arduous voyage. The spirits of the passengers and crew rose in correlation with the passage of the tough, little barque into the prevailing southerly current, which slowed them imperceptibly as though the seas wanted to keep them in its fold for as long as possible. But not to be denied, the *City of London* eventually made it to Sydney Heads, the two kilometre wide entry to Sydney Harbour on 12 July 1838.

After farewelling their fellow travellers with promises to keep in touch, Julian received a hearty slap on the back and best wishes for their future.

It was 1838 and Port Jackson was a few years away from being declared the city of Sydney. The population of the colony was a mere

3000 in 1800 and would reach 39,000 by 1850. It was still a colony in the early stages of its evolution, nevertheless, was a bustling port. The first edition of the Sydney Herald was published in 1831 and David Jones opened its doors in 1838. In the next few years, transportation of prisoners would be halted and Sydney

Julian arranged for accommodation in the settlement, before taking to the road that would lead them to their home at Chatsworth Park, approximately twenty kilometres away. He felt they should rest and refresh before taking the journey by horse and buggy. The rail line would not reach Parramatta until 1855.

Julian had spent considerable time describing the property to Virginia, so she was under no ilusions as to what to expect. He had in fact played it down somewhat, hoping it might surprise her with its comforts. Even he was delighted to see the landscape green and lush from the early winter rains and the paddocks dotted with sheep grazing contentedly in the home fields.

His father, Jonas, and mother, Almira, were alerted by a messenger sent ahead thoughtfully by Julian and they waited anxiously to greet them. It was winter in the southern hemisphere; a light drizzle of rain was falling and there was quite a chill in the air, so the young couple were grateful for the roaring log fire that was blazing in the sitting room and the glass of restorative brandy on offer.

After the initial excitement of reunion and introduction, the family sat down to a magnificent roast lamb dinner with all the trimmings of fresh vegetables. It was the most enjoyable meal put before them since they had left London and made all the more enjoyable by the company.

Jonas allowed his son a brief settling in period for everyone to get to know each other and, in particular, for Victoria to find her place in the household. An early settler like Jonas knew full well the price of complacency, finding work for Julian in the fields. Almira was busy showing Victoria the way around her kitchen and explaining her regular routine in managing the household. There was much to do and still only 24 hours in a day. She would be expected to feed and water the poultry, tend the vegetable gardens and eventually, the fruit orchard, which was reaching maturity now. She would need to supervise the ticket of leave staff they had employed to assist with the domestic chores.

Julian was soon working hard alongside his father in the fields, supervising the day labourers they employed and assisting in the construction and maintenance of the property. Building the flock in number and quality was the top c priority for them. One chap, a convict, whose sentence had expired, had earned sufficient credit with Jonas and Julian to be assigned the status of station foreman. This was a common circumstance in the colony where people convicted of petty crimes were transported for a set period. This was not so much a fight against crime, but a thinly disguised solution to the overcrowding of its cities, as rural dwellers moved in to take advantage of better conditions and opportunity. A false hope, as all they found was poverty and starvation, leading the desperate to commit the theft of food or small items to stave off death.

Victoria spent many hours with her mother-in-law, Almira, discovering the ins and outs of her new home. Almira still ruled the household and the servants answered to her, but it was important for Victoria to be recognised for her status as mistress in waiting. The stations accounts and records were managed by a gentleman servant who, under the careful supervision of Jonas, kept the all-important breeding records.

Almira and Virginia were assisted by an assigned convict (ticket of leave) servant, Polly, who performed most of the cleaning and laundry duties. She had a teenage daughter, Clarissa, a delightfully cheerful young woman, with her who proved to be a willing helper.

Julian had shipped in a piano on a ship that arrived not long after they did and Virginia would entertain the household, accompanying her singing and encouraging the others to learn the lyrics of the current popular songs and join in. But where she really shone was playing her favourite classical pieces from Chopin and Mozart.

Julian would come in from the paddocks and, as he approached the homestead, he would be greeted by Beethoven's Moonlight Sonata or one of Mozart's compositions, the beautiful notes ringing out from the sitting room into the night air.

Julian was delighted by the adventurous nature of his wife, who had cheerfully accepted the harsher life of a settler, compared to the more sophisticated and comfortable life she could have enjoyed had she wed locally and stayed in England. She totally embraced their lifestyle and quickly earned the genuine admiration and love of her in-laws.

All early settlers had to be self-sufficient and there was of course an extensive kitchen garden and poultry yard. Jonas kept English honey bees whose nectar was a treat spread generously on the fresh bread baked in the large wood-fired cooking range in the spacious kitchen. The ladies spent much of their time there cooking, preserving and sewing and darning, enjoying the warmth of the stove against the winter winds.

The men, meanwhile, worked at building the flock, shearing, fence building and improving the pastures. There was always something to occupy their days and when the ewes began to drop their lambs, it was almost a 24 hour a day job. The precious lambs had to be brought into the sheds and protected against the marauding native dogs, which were a bigger problem than the Aboriginal locals who seemed to have no idea of ownership and would wander in and spear a prize ewe or ram if they were not dissuaded.

Jonas took a less than benevolent attitude to the blacks although, while he was firm in his determination to keep them away from his flock, he was disgusted by some of his contemporaries who would just shoot them on sight. In their defence, many of the settlers were victims of native attacks, suffering death or terrible wounds inflicted by their vicious spears. It always paid to keep a firearm handy, regardless of the attitude of the individual. There were rumours also of some settlers giving them the "gift" of poison-laced flour although this remained unproven.

Jonas was shocked to hear of the murder of 28 Aboriginal men, women and children, who had been camped peacefully on the banks of the Myall Creek in northern New South Wales, by 10 Europeans and one African in 1838. After two trials, seven of the 11 colonists involved in the killings, were found guilty of murder and hanged. The presiding prosecutor, John Plunkett, ironically, was an opponent of capital punishment. He became attorney general and served in that role until 1856, presiding over many significant law reforms.

Two cultures in conflict like this were not unheard of and the dominant race would always prevail. But so would the law of the land. Jonas took the view that it was a huge country and there should be room for all. In the meantime, an attitude of tolerance to the natives was the preferred option for Jonas, so long as they left his prize rams alone. If they should make the mistake of taking one from his flock, Jonas was not above finding the nearest camp and bringing down his wrath upon them without such niceties as proof beyond doubt. This was an aspect of the life of a squatter that was best kept from the fairer sex.

The attitude of Jonas to the native population was not dissimilar to his attitude to "other wildlife" as he put it. In other words, he recognised their right to exist but only tolerated them up to the point where they became a nuisance.

Not long after these messy events, there were some significant changes in the colony with the ending of transportation in 1842. The Governor of New South Wales, George Gipps, also prohibited the assignment of convicts for domestic service in the towns when he took up his appointment in 1838. They could only be assigned to work in remote areas and Chatsworth Park qualified in that regard, which meant that Polly and Clarissa were legal. Although Jonas had enough experience not to have employed any old "lags" that may have presented a risk to the household.

The son of Jonas was to meet and conduct matters of law with the prosecutor of the infamous case of the slaughter of the Myall Creek natives, Mr John Plunkett. Plunkett came to the colony from Ireland in 1832 to take up the post of solicitor general. The colony was formed by three distinct groups. Convicts, some of whom were incorrigible, but many were decent enough; emancipated convicts who had served their time and were largely determined to make something of their lives, and of course, the squattocracy.

The squatters generally thought themselves superior to the other two groups, but somehow the disparate classes managed to build the early settlement into a thriving colony.

It would be fair to say that most new arrivals in the township were not that interested in the indigenous population and took little notice of them, preferring to build a life in the burgeoning settlement of Sydney Town. Where the two races came together out in the hinterlands, there was inevitably aggression from both sides. There has been much made of the arrival of the white settlers as invaders. This was little different and probably not as tyrannical as it sounds, considering the experience the indigenous people of many lands who had been usurped by marauding invaders over thousands of years.

Sir Henry Parkes arrived in the colony from his home near Coventry with his wife, Clarinda, in 1838 and became a very vocal advocate for the abolition of transportation, which led to the commencement of his political career. The speeches and the passion of Parkes were intoxicating to the young Julian Parnham and before long, he had become involved in the politics of the day, promoting his *laissez faire* style of economics and social attitudes. His interest and compassion for the Aborigines resulted from his shock and abhorrence of the Myall Creek affair, which sparked an interest in the indigenous people and their culture.

Author's Note

The truth is this is the way of the world. The settler's homeland of England, after all, has been subjected to ruthless invasions from many foreign races for thousands of years. The list of these aggressors is long and bloody. Romans, Saxons, Angles, Jutes, Vikings and Normans, just to name a few. And in recent living memory, Adolf Hitler's army of thugs in Europe and the Japanese Emperor's barbaric army attempting to invade Australia. It's not hard to imagine how the Nipponese army would have treated the indigenous race had they been successful in defeating the allies and taking the Australian continent in the light of their behaviour when invading the Chinese city of Nanking.

The recently conceived Welcome to Country ceremony, which has become compulsory at every public gathering now, in those days it could well be a spear through the chest of the white man or the native from the next tribe. Aborigines spent a lot of time stealing each other's women and children and killing each other long before the white man came.

So it's quite surprising that the comparatively benign occupation of the Great Southland could cause so much continuing grief. If we are honest, and can disregard ideological and political motivations of the various antagonists, the arrival of the white man has brought many benefits to the descendants of the previous indigenous occupiers of the land. Just as the subsequent arrival of people from over 170 different lands and cultures since has been a cultural blessing in building a united, prosperous nation.

* * *

The years passed without great personal trauma, despite the turn of events in the colony. The Parnham's flock increased, as did their wealth and standing in the community. Victoria gave birth in 1841, to a son christened Jefferson Gideon. The little chap was soon joined by a sister, Mary Frances, the following year. Both children were the delight of their grandparents and the pride of their mother and father.

When the children were old enough, Victoria began to school them in reading and writing. The old bookkeeper, Burton, was delighted to add arithmetic to their curriculum and so by the time Jefferson was 10 years old, he was thoroughly schooled and was enrolled as a boarder at Kings School, Parramatta beginning a family alignment with that academic and social establishment of New South Wales.

Mary continued her education at home with her mother, which concentrated more on domestic matters, including cooking, sewing and artistic pursuits. Management of the household, including the gardens and poultry, were part of the training she received from her mother and Polly. It would be many years before female students were thought worthy of exclusive schools of their own.

Jefferson Gideon proved to be one of the first and most successful graduates of the Kings School and later graduated in Law at Sydney University. With the Parnham name and reputation, he joined a leading Sydney law firm and passed the New South Wales bar entrance.

Jefferson soon established a reputation as an aggressive and clever advocate with a high success rate sought after by most of Sydney's elite. He had married young to Charlotte, the daughter of a Scottish wool merchant. Charlotte fell pregnant and after a difficult labour produced a son, Alexander, in 1875. Sadly, Charlotte was unable to bear any further children.

Talent like Jefferson's was bound to attract attention in certain quarters and before too long, a group of power brokers began to court him as a conservative candidate in the next election. By means of cajolery, and many late-night dinners, they were able to sway him to their purpose.

And so it came to pass that in 1880 the Legislative Assembly was dissolved, and writs were issued by the Governor, Lord Augustus Loftus, to proceed with an election. Jefferson was duly elected to the

Legislative Council of New South Wales and at the age of 39 proudly took his place in the House on 15 December 1880.

There was no recognisable party structure at this election, instead the government was determined, by a loose shifting factional system, which was a perfect arena for Jefferson, to expand the influence of the Parnham's.

Favours granted, favours received, were an everyday part of the fledgling government and a favour granted to the right person was an infallible investment for future support.

Jefferson's sister Mary, unsurprisingly, married into another legal family. The offspring of Julian and Victoria were beginning to give the Parnham's' and their extended family, a powerful influence in the business of law in Sydney.

Jefferson's heir, Alexander Morris Parnham, followed his illustrious father's path through the King's School and the law. He also became an advocate and represented the electorate of West Sydney as a Member of Parliament. Alexander married Winifred Jane Stevenson, the daughter of a greatly respected magistrate. It was one of Sydney's first society weddings, attended by all the leaders of the legal community and all the grazing blue bloods from the Parnham circle.

The reception was a glittering affair in a magnificent reception room and announced to the world that this was a wealthy and influential family who would set the standards of the community for decades to come.

On the surface, the Parnham's were the pillars of the community, providing support for many charitable causes and, through one or two commercial enterprises, they provided employment and training opportunities for many men and quite a few women as well; although the females were more likely employed in simple clerical roles or domestic duties as was the norm at that time. Young men were taken in from families that were experiencing difficulties and, in some instances, a ward of the court. All of these grateful workers became loyal supporters of their benefactor and could be counted on to round up voters on polling day and get them to the booths to cast a vote in favour of Alexander.

Factory workers, farm workers and domestic staff eventually equalled a substantial voting bloc. Compulsory voting was not invoked in New South Wales until 1928 which meant Alexander had a considerable march on his opponents.

Should a sharper pair of eyes take a closer look at some of the commercial activities of Alexander Morris Parnham MP KC, they might find cause to question some of his enterprises. Perhaps a shadow of doubt, or perhaps more properly, the morality or otherwise in how a parcel of land fell into the holdings of Chatsworth Agricultural. And that significant share of a city development, was it an astute investment or blind luck or something else? What if an enquirer were to follow the paper trail relating to a particular parcel of shares in a very prosperous mining company? Was that a shrewd reading of the market or, heaven forbid, reward for his support for a particular piece of legislation?

No one would dare accuse such an important and powerful member of the legal community of any nefarious dealings for fear of public ridicule and a possible law suit. And so the Parnham empire continued to grow wealthier and more powerful, unimpeded by the constraints of an over active sense of morality.

As old Alex often said to himself, 'What the eye don't see, the heart don't grieve over.' But a wily politician such as old Alex always had a plan B in the event of some misfire.

Next in line to the Parnham family name was Lawrence, a handsome and intelligent young man, soon joined by twin sisters Laura and Lilly; two incredibly beautiful little girls who charmed everyone they came in contact with. As they grew, so did their charms. Both had amazing musical talents and would sing, dance and play piano and violin to the delight of anyone fortunate enough to witness the impromptu concerts they would perform in the sitting room at Chatsworth Park. Music would always form a significant part of the Parnham culture.

The girls adored their big brother, Lawrence, who doted on them, and when he went off to Kings Boarding School in Sydney, they were devastated. Their early education was conducted at home by their mother, Winifred, until they were old enough to attend a local school at the end of year six, at which time they were enrolled in MLC Burwood, their mother's alma mater.

During term they resided at the family apartment in the city from where they commuted to school each day. Term holidays and Christmas breaks, the girls gleefully headed for home at Chatsworth Park where they would be reunited with their dear mother and Lawrence, their horses, dogs, cats, kittens, chickens and all the things a farm can deliver, including the broad fields and the surrounding bushlands to energetic young children.

Lawrence was an excellent scholar and a favourite with the majority of his teachers and fellow students. He seldom got into trouble of even the mildest kind. He was a very competent batsman in the school's first eleven cricket team and held the important role of third man in. In other words, he was the first replacement after one of the openers was dismissed. His quick hand-eye co-ordination made him a valuable slips fieldsman as well.

As a good all round sportsman he was very quick over the ground and won medals in athletics for his school.

His tutor and the school chaplain had a conversation about him one day in the staff room when he was in fifth form. There was nothing they could put a finger on, but they both felt uneasiness about Lawrence, as though he had a hidden secret, but when they raised it with their colleagues, they were scoffed at. Most felt he could do no wrong. He was a hardworking, honourable student. And yet one or two boys had shown some reluctance to be paired with him in activities, which wasn't unusual at an age where alliances and lifelong friendships could be forged or broken over the smallest thing.

Given that Lawrence was a boarder there was ample opportunity for mischief of all kinds. Sometimes the best indicator of a boy's character was to gauge the reaction of the lads around him.

Lawrence took a differing route from his illustrious father. On passing at the top of his year at King's School, he had no problem being accepted into Law at Sydney University and seemed to breeze through his studies, graduating with Honours. After which, he sought permission from his father to join the AIF. After some protracted, and a little heated, debate in an attempt to preserve the family tradition in law, Alexander might be expected to deny his blessing. Instead, he gave way to his proud son's desire and wished him well in his chosen career.

Given his father's blessing, he enlisted with the Second Australian Imperial Force. He then applied with his commanding officer's permission and was accepted to train as an officer at the Royal Military College, Duntroon. His colleagues were from some of the country's finest families, blessed with an education in the very best private schools. Lawrence developed a close friendship with another cadet with a similar background to himself.

Arthur Kingston's family farmed cattle further west than Chatsworth Park. In fact, a long way west where the average cattle station was measured in square miles rather than acres. Lawrence had matured physically into a tall, athletic, young man with an aquiline nose, framed by bright, clear, blue eyes above a square jaw. All in all, he was a handsome specimen who caught the eye of more than one young lady. Standing six foot three inches tall in his stockinged feet, and weighing a solid 180 pounds, he was an automatic selection when speed and power were called for on the football ground.

Lawrence took to the discipline and military studies as he had in university and there were no adverse reports to speak of. He and Arthur spent a lot of time together spurring each other on in every field of endeavour. They competed with the results of their studies, the physical training, obstacle course, cross- country running and sharpshooting. Every activity, either academic or sporting, was seen as an opportunity to challenge each other. As officer cadets they would spend a further year at Duntroon before being commissioned.

Arthur happened to have a very fetching younger sister who came to visit him, requiring Arthur to introduce her to his new best friend. It was an instant hit. Lawrence struck up a relationship with Frances Esther, which very soon blossomed into passionate love and took the usual path. Lawrences proposal for marriage was accepted.

Alexander was both elated and apprehensive when Lawrence decided he wanted a military career, however his chest swelled with pride at his passing out parade. The pomp and ceremony and the marshal music had a stirring effect on all the parents and participants and made for one of the most important and memorable days of their lives.

Frances stood proudly alongside her future in-laws, looking like a film star. Many of the graduates had a problem maintaining discipline as they passed by her. The occasion was decently celebrated at the Hyatt Hotel, Canberra.

Lawrence was commissioned to his old 55th Battalion as a lieutenant commanding a platoon of around thirty soldiers. By this time, he had established a reputation as a popular leader. He was firm in his handling of his command, his men knowing if they crossed the line, the "Boss", as he was called, would come down hard.

Before Lawrence was given his commission, he and Frances were married in a brief service attended by the bride and groom's parents, with Arthur acting as Lawrence's best man and the twins, Laura and Lilly, acting as bridesmaids to Frances. They exited the church to an honour guard of fellow officers with their ceremonial sabres forming the traditional arch. Although spartan by comparison with Lawrence's parents' nuptials, it was still a joyous occasion, celebrated with the reception held in a private room called The Bevery in The Hotel Australia.

While Lawrence was still in New South Wales, he was still able to get home on leave to spend time with his gorgeous wife Frances and the rest of his family. Frances had taken up residence in the extended wing of the old homestead, a beautiful, airy self-contained wing with its own private bathroom, sitting room and verandah. Winifred saw to it that, as the future lady of the house, she became familiar with all the household routines and restraints. This was almost a tradition now, where the women joined company in the vast station kitchen where, not just victuals were discussed and prepared, but the family businesses and especially politics, which was at the heart of this dynasty. All of which was grist for the conversational mill.

Lawrence's battalion was transported to Newcastle, New South Wales and set up defences along the coast in the Raymond Terrace-Stockton Beach area, around twenty kilometres north of Newcastle.

The following year, as the outlook across Asia deteriorated with the fall of Singapore, the battalion prepared for a move. In May of 1942, they were transported to Port Moresby. Initially, they were used as a labour force and had little opportunity to train. In July, the battalion was split into A, C, D and E companies.

Lawrence was 24 years old and, as a man at war, his strength of character, leadership skills and courage would soon be put to the test in deadly conflict with a ruthless enemy. After a brief conversation with his battalion chaplain about his future in the army as an officer, one annoying thing kept popping up in his mind, from Proverbs 16:18:

Pride goeth before destruction and a haughty spirit before a fall.

CHAPTER SIX

May 1942

Lawrence's war began with a shovel instead of a gun, alongside his men undertaking the construction of the Port Moresby defences. The work was punishing in the tropical heat, but it was nothing that the men were not used to. It was a well proven fact that a soldier spends more time digging holes and waiting in them for something to happen than actually firing his gun.

While American engineers built the airstrips and wharves, the Australians worked on roads and accommodation. The small force of sappers was reinforced by infantry and Papuan labourers. The massed forces around the Port Moresby area consisted of various units of US, Australian and British forces.

The harbour was a busy scene with merchant shipping and warships of all types calling in on various missions from time to time, but always with an air of urgency. No ship's captain wanted to linger any longer than necessary with Japanese bombers regularly attacking. This was the prize the Nipponese army wanted desperately, giving them a launching pad or springboard from which to attack mainland Australia.

Port Moresby was attacked regularly by Japanese Mitsubishi Betty Bombers, supported by Zero Fighters and was defended by army anti-aircraft batteries and machine gun units. In March, RAAF Kittyhawks of 75 Squadron arrived. Later that month, the Australians were joined by American A24s and, for a short period, six P39 Airacobras. Further aircraft arrived over the following months and included the Australian Beaufighters of 30 Squadron, one of which was flown by Squadron Leader William Luther Cuthbertson DFC.

The American A24s had arrived in Australia in very poor condition being heavily worn from their training duties in the US. After some amazing ingenuity displayed by the Australian engineers, some of the aircraft were brought up to airworthy standard.

The 3rd Bombardment Group and 8th Bombardment Squadron were assigned to the defence of New Guinea but sadly losses mounted swiftly. In July 1942, from a flight of seven A24s, only one returned.

The 55th battalion learned very quickly about jungle warfare. The Japanese were advancing very aggressively down the Kokoda track and were being met by units of the 55th among other Australian battalions. One of these units was led by Lieutenant Lawrence Parnham.

The fighting was close, fierce and lethal. Jungle warfare is like no other; the soldier is the hunter and the hunted simultaneously, and he learns quickly or he dies in the same amount of time. The Japanese were fanatical and merciless fighters, driven by the code of Bushido, 'the way or the morale of the warrior.' An unforgiving culture that treated its defeated enemy with no respect or mercy.

The over-riding belief was that surrender brought great shame on one's ancestors and the Emperor. Better to die. Enemy troops that surrendered to the Japanese were therefore treated as shameful creatures to be abused or simply dispatched by sword, bayonet or bullet.

A section from F Company was sent to Milne Bay under the command of Lieutenant Lawrence Garret Parnham, to reinforce the Australian Militia Brigade who were expecting some action from the Japanese forces landing on the northern shore of Milne Bay. The Japanese had received faulty navigational advice from a local and landed some six miles from where they wanted to be. The terrain here was swampy and the light tanks they had brought with them soon found themselves in trouble, sinking into the soft sticky mud becoming useless. Which was just as well for the defenders, as their anti-tank guns suffered the same fate and the sticky bombs,* developed to destroy tanks, proved ineffective in the wet and humid conditions. An improvised explosive attack weapon that depended on a 'sticky' surface material to adhere to the target.

The invaders suffered serious setbacks when part of their invasion force lost their landing craft to allied air attacks undertaken by the Beaufighters and P40s of the Americans, as they attempted to land on the coast behind the Australians.

The Japanese quickly pushed inland and began to advance on the airfields. Heavy fighting ensued as they encountered the Australian Militia Force that formed the first line of defence and who were steadily pushed back. However, the Australians brought forward the veteran 2nd Australian Imperial Force units, which caught the Japanese by surprise and sent them packing back into the jungle with their tails between their legs. They were learning the Aussies were no pushovers.

Again, allied air superiority helped tip the balance in the defenders' favour providing close support to the troops in combat, as well as targeting logistics. The Australian troops directed the ground attacking Beaufighters to strafe the Japanese positions with lethal results. The worst place in the world to be was in front of an angry Beaufighter.

Aussie Beaufighters and US P38s caught a Japanese supply fleet of eight ships in the Bismarck Strait, plus their escorts, and totally destroyed them with bombs, rockets and cannon fire. It was a huge blow to the Japanese and a confirmation yet again of the value of these frighteningly effective aircraft.

Jungle warfare at night was a special form of hell and high tension. Impenetrable darkness, strange sounds, clicking, buzzing, whirring, rustling and unaccountable crackling of dry twigs and leaves. The musty smell of rotting vegetation lingering in the still night air, sometimes sour, sometimes tempered with the perfume of jungle orchids or other exotic blooms. At times, you would swear you can hear the enemy breathing and you dared not breathe loudly yourself in case he could hear you.

The jungle was seldom silent, as a rich cacophony of bird calls echoed through the undergrowth. New Guinea was home to hundreds of bird species that Lawrence could swear were all calling at once providing a cover for their ambush.

The Japanese were masters at night fighting, creeping stealthily up to their enemies' positions with great patience, which made it a nervous watch for the Australian sentries. The inexperienced allied troops soon learned to deal with this threat after paying a heavy price. Trip wires and other booby traps and forward pickets provided some measure of security, but it was the cool battle hardened veterans who turned the Japanese strengths against them.

Parnham, who had led his patrol into an ambush position, lay patiently in wait on the floor of the fetid jungle for the decisive moment to strike at an enemy that was almost within arm's length. Night falls dramatically in the jungle, the heat of the day unrelenting. Sweat ran down Parnham's nose dripping onto his forearm that supported him. Rivulets ran down his face from under his slouch hat stinging his eyes. He dared not reach for his water bottle despite a desperate thirst. The airless, heavy humidity was fuelled by frequent tropical downpours that provided only temporary relief.

He was certain some creature had invaded his shirt via the back of his neck. He hoped it was not a centipede, or some other spiteful pest; bad enough that he was defenceless against the insatiable mosquitoes drawing blood many times over the last few hours and would continue feasting unabated until he could move again without fear of detection. He wouldn't have long to wait now. The humidity was draining and his mouth dust dry. Dehydration, fatigue, nerves or the combination, had his tongue sticking to the roof of his mouth but he dared not move a hand towards his canteen.

His right hand was around the handgrip of his Thompson sub machine gun and in his left he held a Mills bomb. Ranged around him in the brush, heavily camouflaged were other members of his platoon similarly armed and alert waiting for his order.

Little more than twenty feet away, a unit of Japanese soldiers were sitting around in a combat ready formation, weapons across their knees, eating cold rice and dried fish. They chattered away in hushed tones, completely unaware of Lawrence and his men who were about to add some spice to their meal they hadn't planned on.

The one with the keenest hearing, had he been listening instead of talking, may have heard the tiny metallic sound of the pin being removed from the grenade in Lawrence's hand. He may have picked up the rustle of Lawrence's clothing as he drew his arm back to throw the explosive into their midst, but he sure as hell didn't miss the thud as the unexploded item landed at a point, three feet from his crossed legs.

Then, anybody within several hundred metres would have heard the unmistakeable dull whump of an exploding grenade that lifted the enemy's body into the air, spraying several others with lethal shrapnel, sending them to their ancestors. Immediately, the rest of Lawrence's squad were up in firing positions pouring bullets into the stunned survivors of the blast.

The heavy hammering of the Bren gun, and the sharper reports of the Enfield rifles, supported now by the harsh staccato of Lawrence's Tommy gun, smashed the jungle silence, sending birds and small animals flying in panic, adding their screeches to the sounds of the well-executed ambush. The whole action had taken less than a minute after several hours of patient stalking. Nine Japanese would play no further part in the invasion of Milne Bay and one very frightened one ran helter skelter through the dense underbrush faster than any native boar would manage. Terror may have given him wings, but it deprived him of rational thought as a short burst from a strategically placed digger, armed with an Owen gun, stopped him in his tracks and curtailed his war.

The Australians approached the fallen Japanese carefully, in the event that one or two might be playing possum. Any sign of life was quickly despatched by rifle fire to the head.

Lawrence gathered his men in close like a football coach, checking that no one had been wounded. Several of the Japanese had got off a few rounds, which mainly went into the tree tops before being gunned down. He complimented them on a job well done and issued orders to quickly search the bodies for any intelligence, then directed them away from the area before Japanese reinforcements arrived. The platoon moved swiftly and on high alert, with the release of the adrenaline flooding their systems.

After a quick hard slog over some rugged terrain away from the scene of the ambush, he finally felt it was safe for them to take a smoko. They all drank greedily from their flasks before pulling out their smokes. Lawrence's hand shook noticeably as he held a cupped match to his hand-rolled smoke. No one was foolish enough to share a lighted match around, (however unlikely) being familiar with the World War One stories of the third man who lit up, copping it from a sniper.

They sat and chatted quietly, just as their victims had only minutes earlier, until Lawrence was satisfied they had rested sufficiently and needed to move swiftly back to where the rest of their company were manning the defensive lines around the airfield. As a reconnaissance mission, Lawrence's men had done a fine job and now it was important to relay the information they had on enemy positions, back to their base.

CHAPTER SEVEN

Milne Bay is a V-shaped rift that cuts 30 kilometres into the far eastern tip of the island of New Guinea. This location allows domination of the sea lanes leading towards Port Moresby and Northern Queensland. The bay has palm-fringed beaches backed by cloud-shrouded mountains, but the initial impression of a tropical paradise was soon dispelled for the men who arrived there to fight.

Allied ground forces at Milne Bay reached a total of around 7,500 Australian Army, (both regular and militia infantry forces, plus some artillery), and 1,400 American airfield construction engineers, all under the command of Australian Major General Cyril Clowes. For the young Lieutenant Lawrence Parnham, the conditions at Milne Bay were a shock. Mud, voracious insects, rain and humidity would have been bad enough, but they were expected to fight a war in this swamp. The marshy ground caused a number of different problems, one of which was establishing any sort of foundation for the building of runways and securing artillery pieces accurately. Plus it was tiresome dragging artillery and one's feet out of the clinging mud.

The Japanese had been surprised by the strength and determination of the Australian troops they found themselves up against, but were undaunted and would continue to push for the capture of the airfield at Milne Bay, which would provide the springboard for their ultimate goal of Port Moresby. Following his successful mission and back in the privacy of his tented accommodation, waves of nausea wash over Lawrence. He was shaking and sweating as he wrestled with another bout of malaria. The mosquito repellent supplied by the army was ineffective and his mosquito net was still in the hold of the ship when he last thought about it.

The army took haphazard precautions when it came to the malarial threat. Quinine was in short supply. They had been prescribed ten grains per day but adequate supplies had yet to catch up. This was serious. If allowed to continue, the disease was capable of incapacitating the entire allied force in Papua.

Lawrence's thoughts were far from the malaria problem as he reached into the bottom of his kit bag for the bottle of brandy secreted there. He laid back and took a deep draught from the bottle hoping to suppress the horrors of a previous mission.

The one he had just led, the carefully laid ambush, had been an unqualified success and he had managed to strike a real blow against the enemy without one of his men sustaining more than a few scratches inflicted by the bush.

The tension was eased momentarily, finally allowing him to fall into a deep, exhausted sleep. Before too long, he began to stir restlessly, lathered in perspiration. And the dreams came. Not the dreams of a man at peace far from conflict, more like the hallucinations of a fevered brain. Images recalled from earlier conflict and terrifying hallucinations brought on by stress and guilt, leaving an indelible imprint that would stay with him, floating at the back of his conscious mind when he awoke.

Images of men torn apart by machine gun fire or exploding mortar rounds; men screaming, their hands frantically trying to prevent their intestines from spilling on the ground; a man dragging himself to God only knows where, with both legs a mass of ground flesh and bone behind him. One man kneeling on one leg looking back up the hill toward the enemy, composed as if for a photograph, except that the top of his skull had been sliced cleanly off, leaving it open like a ghastly anatomical specimen. Some weird force of physics and corporeal magic kept the man's body there in perfect balance.

Then he sees the enemy. Short, thick body on somewhat bandy legs; a grim determined individual with a samurai sword on one hip and a pistol holster on the other. The pistol is in his hand as he strides toward Lawrence. He halts half a metre from him and presses the Nambu pistol barrel firmly against the centre of his forehead and pulls back the cocking knob. His finger tightens on the trigger and Lawrence knows this is the end. In his dream he screams, the shock of it wakes him; he swings his feet out of his bunk that's saturated in his malarial sweat, his head spinning. His hand is shaking alarmingly as he reaches for the brandy bottle once more, knowing he may never rid himself of the horrors he has endured in reality that have become his nightmares.

As part of the 55th Brigade at Milne Bay Lawrence's platoon had been one of the first to have contact with the Japanese that landed on the northern shore of the bay. The Japanese main force of over 1,000 men and two Type 95 Ha-Go tanks had landed away from their intended target due to faulty navigation. They quickly sent out patrols to secure the area and were intercepted by Lawrence and his men.

The previous 'walkabout', as the men had begun to call their patrols, resulted in a short, sharp fire fight with the Aussies having the worst of it. The Japanese had been spoiling for a fight after enduring attacks from Kittyhawks without being able to fire a shot in retaliation. This fight was not going to end happily for the diggers.

Surrounded and with heavy casualties that included his sergeant, Lawrence gave the order to surrender. The Japanese ran over the top of them, smashing men to the ground with rifle butts and laying into them with their boots. Lawrence protested loudly to their stocky little leader with the dimensions of a tree stump, and received a rifle butt in the stomach for his trouble. Clearly this was not going to be good.

The Australians were all rounded up and a quick survey carried out in the most brutal fashion. Stumpy marched along the line of soldiers and, with not the slightest hesitation, shot the wounded in the head with his semi-automatic Nambu pistol. Now there were only nine men, including Lawrence, left alive. These shocked survivors were forced to their feet and made to march behind Stumpy and three of his men with another group of Japanese bringing up the rear. Others had fanned out like the experienced fighters they were, providing cover from point and dropping back behind to the rear.

They marched like this for several kilometres; the Aussies being encouraged with kicks, punches and rifle butts, as they staggered forward through the knee-deep mud.

Their captors urged them on until they came to the encampment of the main contingent. Again, Lawrence was separated from his men who had their arms held behind their backs with a stout length of bamboo around which their elbows were secured with rough twine.

They were now all kneeling in a line with several soldiers standing over them. Lawrence was given special treatment, tied to a bench and his torso beaten repeatedly with a bamboo pole until he passed out. He was revived with cold water and beaten again, all the time being screamed at and spat upon and cursed. He was cut free and dragged upright to face his men.

A Japanese officer approached the men and, without a word, went along the line beheading the first five of them. He stopped as the senior officer and another soldier, speaking clear **English, cam**e to Lawrence and began hectoring him to detail the allied troop dispositions and weaponry. Lawrence shook his head and told him to get stuffed. He kept this up as long as the Japanese officer kept at him, slapping his face, brutally, swearing and cursing him.

When he ran out of patience, the beheadings began again. Lawrence could feel his courage running out like water from a holed bucket into the sand on which he kneeled.

They forced him to watch, as one after the other the last of his men went quietly and bravely to their deaths, without one of them begging for his life. Lawrence threw up. The translator said to Lawrence that his men were very brave, but he would need to have much more courage, because if he failed to give them what they wanted, he was going to experience the agony of being burnt alive. Off to one side, a large pile of dry coconut fronds and dry material from the forest were being piled up in readiness for Lawrence's live cremation.

To give him a taste of the agony he was in for, a red hot ember was forced against his back. Lawrence screamed and simultaneously the Japanese put a torch to the pyre. Lawrence's innards had turned to stone, his courage totally gone, his mind frozen in utter terror. He seemed to slide into some sort of catalepsy, his mind whirling, bright flashing luminescence at the back of his eyes. He was unable to control his bowels, or his thoughts. He is kicked and punched again and again, until he spits large amounts of blood and some teeth onto the ground. They worked on his kidneys with sharp punches, the pain blinding.

He slipped into a symptomatic zombie like state; seeing but not feeling; uncomprehending but still cognitive; strangely, oddly floating through the agony, almost as a detached observer. The next passage of time was lost to him as though his brain had expunged it as it occurred; all memory of it instantly erased. His ears were screaming with the white noise induced by the slaps and echo of detached voices. He saw a pencil and a sheet of paper. There was a hand; was it his? The hand was writing, drawing lines and squiggles. Blackness overcomes him again and mercifully he collapses. The black curtain rose again and he was talking, talking. He had no conscious awareness of what was being said, only that mercifully the pain and violence had stopped. Cool water had been splashed on his face and neck, providing a brief relief but he still felt close to death. In fact he couldn't be sure he was still alive.

He woke again with the translator talking to him quietly, revealing that he had been a prisoner for three days. He was still alive, due to his co-operation, which had been of great assistance in their campaign and he would soon be joining his comrades in an honourable death.

Lawrence could not believe what he is hearing. Had he collaborated with the enemy? This could not be real; it went against everything he believed in. He was not a coward, dammit! What had happened?

The senior Japanese officer had appeared again, jabbering at Lawrence with a smile that would curdle milk. He wanted to have another little chat, just to confirm one or two little points. Lawrence had gained strength and courage again and was determined to give him nothing; even if it meant burning to death, he would get nothing. He told them to get stuffed once again and spat phlegm and blood at the little yellow bastard's polished boots.

He never saw the punch coming, but felt it; the impact ringing in his head as he keeled over backward into the sand. He was dragged up and punched down again. The Japanese seemed to be letting out all sorts of suppressed rage on him. He didn't believe he would survive this brutality, but it was a better way to go than burning alive. His world went black again.

He had no idea of how long he had been unconscious or even if it was the same day, but someone had poured water on his face again, talking soothingly to him with an Aussie accent! What the hell?

It seemed another Australian contingent had caught the Japanese napping and, in a wonderfully successful attack, totally annihilated them, save for the stunned interpreter who was sitting there with the thousand yard stare on his oriental dial, wondering how he would explain this to his emperor.

Around them, Aussies of the 2nd Division were cleaning up the Japanese bodies, dumping them into a communal pit. The Australian dead were being buried, with due dignity, into individually marked graves, their ID tags carefully collected.

Lawrence passed out again and when he recovered this time, it was dawn and the troops were getting ready to move out. He had survived remarkably well considering the punishment meted out to him.

His abdomen gave him the most grief. Perhaps he had some broken ribs, but apart from a little blood in his urine, he didn't appear to have suffered any internal injuries. He was severely dehydrated and nauseous, his head was reeling from the concussion, a product of the sustained beating. After attempting a hot cup of tea that felt like he was drinking lava, he managed to drink a cooler version to wash down some pain killers out of someone's field kit. Now urged on by his fellow officer, he was as ready to go as he could be.

Then suddenly, the horror of what he witnessed and experienced over the previous days, hit him like a sledge hammer and he fell to his knees, retching and crying like a child, deep heartbreaking sobs from way down in his chest. His fellow officer Lieutenant Andy Kerrison puts a sympathetic arm about his shoulder and raises him up muttering encouraging words in his ear and urging him to hang on until they're back to base and relative safety. Kerrison is a tall, rangy Aussie, raised on a cattle station in Western Queensland. He was deeply tanned and fit, his sinewy arms as strong as a blacksmith's. Armed with an Owen Gun slung from his shoulder, his command consisted of entirely capable looking soldiers who, like Lawrence Parnham, had learnt the hard lessons of war very quickly.

During the night, and while Lawrence was comatose, Lieutenant Kerrison had been conducting an interrogation of the translator. What he learned was shocking.

The Japanese officer accused Lawrence of being a traitor and a coward. Under torture and interrogation, Lawrence had broken down and given his enemy what they wanted; a complete description of the displacement of the defences around the airfield at Milne Bay and details of the work he had supervised at Port Moresby, including the airfield defensive trenches and revetments for aircraft, the roadway systems and underground administration facilities. The information had been despatched by runner to the Japanese main force, in all likelihood, was behind an attack on the airfield by the Japanese that was fortunately repulsed. The interpreter told Kerrison that a satchel, containing the original information and the dead captain's report, was in the shelter used by the Japanese officer. He would find it hidden toward the back under a length of canvas, having been quickly secreted there when the Australian rescuers attacked.

It was now imperative to get a warning to the defenders to prepare for any further attacks at Milne Bay and, more worryingly, on Port Moresby. Lieutenant Kerrison selected Johnno Reeves and Curly Carlisle, two very fit soldiers, who had proved their value on more than one occasion.

As the lads took off, Kerrison uttered a prayer for their success. The rest of the Aussie defenders would need to know their displacements had been compromised.

Now with the satchel recovered from its hiding place, Lieutenant Kerrison led the unit back toward their base, bringing with them the ghastly story of the total annihilation of Lieutenant Parnham's unit and the captive Japanese prisoner accusing Parnham of treachery and cowardice.

Kerrison believed their support would be vital in defence of the all-important airfield and double timed his troop in the direction of the airstrip. He had two men at point and two sweepers coming up behind. The sun was not fully above the tops of the palms but the heat was already building quickly and the humidity was like a steam bath.

Lawrence was transported in a sling below two lengths of bamboo, carried by two soldiers. It was hard work and awkward but far more efficient than trying to get the badly beaten man to walk. The troop rotated the arduous duty between them. As a result, they made good time over the muddy ground and tough undergrowth. Wary eyes on the jungle around them, trying not to follow an obvious route that could lead them into ambush or booby traps.

One of the men let out a yelp, as though he had been scalded with hot water, dancing around like a madman swatting at his clothing, swearing and cursing. Kerrison jogged swiftly up to see what was wrong. The unfortunate man had run headlong into a nest of green tree ants that constructed a hive-like structure from cut leaves suspended in the undergrowth. They were almost impossible to see and had a way of making their displeasure known to whomever or whatever disturbed them and the unfortunate digger had brushed his hat heavily against their nest. The digger dropped his weapon and stripped his shirt off, waving his arms and hat wildly with his Lieutenant feverishly brushing the very angry insects away.

As if they didn't have enough problems, nature was now pitching in to delay them. They both suffered multiple stings like hot needles and swear and curse, but they have to get moving. There's no time for sympathy.

Lawrence's transporters took the opportunity to relieve themselves of their burden and carefully lowered their patient to the ground where he lay oblivious to this charade. The ants were finally overcome and the troop continued their cautious progress.

Resuming their journey, the platoon had spread out down the rough track. Lawrence had a field medic on one side keeping a wary medical eye on him. Through the haze of pain, Lawrence noticed an NCO hovering closely by his side. Was he a guard? Was he under suspicion of something? The translator was right beside the NCO who carried his revolver in his right hand. Was he under guard in a similar way? It was all too hard for him to fully comprehend under the influence of a heavy concussion.

Lieutenant Kerrison had called a halt to rest his men. Lawrence was administered more pain killers with a tepid cup of tea and asked for assistance to stand. Ironically, his greatest discomfort was from a straining bladder. His legs were threatening to collapse and he felt like he might pass out at any time, but he managed to clear his manhood with hands shaking and wracked with nausea. The pain from **the body blows inflicted on him with the bamboo rod was excruciating and each time he coughed, stabbing pain shot through his chest and he tasted blood in his sputum. As he urinated, his flow coloured with blood as well. His nose had stopped bleeding, but he was sure** it was broken.

Suddenly, the realisation hit him like a hammer blow; that all of the unfortunate comrades under his command were dead. Every one! All of them were volunteers, brave young lads from the 55th Battalion recruited and trained in New South Wales to fight this vile enemy and protect their homeland gallantly. Not to be slaughtered like livestock. His overall memory of events was very patchy, but he did have the image of the beheadings etched into his brain.

Suddenly, there was a burst of activity from the front. It was the two men on point, running back, looking panicked and heading straight for Kerrison. The news they carried was not good. Johnno Reeves and

Bluey Carlisle had been found dead on the track ahead of them. They appeared to have been surprised and bayonetted swiftly and silently.

Kerrison acted quickly and snapped out a series of orders, getting his men into defensive positions in anticipation of an attack. Lawrence and the Japanese prisoner were left behind in a secure spot with an alert young digger watching over them both. Lawrence couldn't be certain, was it his nerves, his head injury or poor judgement that was causing him to be paranoid? He was simply a mess of nerves.

For his part, Kerrison was still not convinced that a fellow Australian officer would do what the translator said he did. But he would take no chances either. The Japanese captain's report on the matter was, of course, written in Japanese and was incomprehensible to him. But that was not his responsibility. His duty was to get Parnham and the translator back to where a higher authority would extract the truth and act accordingly.

The interpreter was a vital first hand witness, even as an enemy combatant. The allies had their own interpreters but this man's evidence would be examined and cross examined intensely. Perhaps he was playing games to put the Aussies off guard. If so, he was a very cool customer.

Besides, Kerrison had had scant time in which to try and make sense of it, so decided to err on the side of caution. He knew Parham's reputation as a graduate of Duntroon, a member of a semi-aristocratic grazing family and that his father was a federal minister destined to lead the Country Party in coalition with the Menzies opposition to the Fadden Labor Party. So it was best to tread carefully and let the matter be handled by his superiors. Plus, he had very little personal one on one experience with which to judge the man. A soldier comes to realise that discipline and orders are his best friends; when followed they take away the need for individual thought and action.

The men waited nervously, fingering their weapons, listening intently for any give away sounds. The bird life provided a great first warning, fluttering noisily into the air if disturbed and sometimes their cheerful song would cease as they assessed a perceived danger. In any event, it paid the jungle fighter to heed the birds. They didn't have long to wait; half a dozen colourful parrots took panicked flight, followed immediately by the rattle of small arms fire that burst out on the right flank and was rapidly followed by several thumping grenade explosions. The Aussies responded, but too late for one or two who had already fallen. The platoon had two Bren guns which opened up with their rapid fire 303 ammunition, slashing the jungle foliage, punching back hard against the Japanese attackers.

Now the defensive gunfire had peaked in answer to the Japanese' initial fusillade that had levelled off as they took casualties. The antagonists were separated by a matter of several metres and almost hand to hand with neither attackers nor defenders gaining the ascendency. The Japanese suddenly fell back for a brief pause during which they reformed to shape up for another run at the Australians.

The Australians heard their officers screaming 'banzai' at their soldiers leading them in some kind of mantra like a football coach building team morale. The Sons of Nippon had decided on a bayonet charge and the diggers were more than happy to take them on. They burst from cover, screaming like fanatics. Convinced by years of propaganda of their invulnerability and their desire for an honourable death in battle. Hand grenades were hurled among the charging Japanese who barely broke stride, as if they were eager for death, and they met it with withering fire from the Aussies who were more than happy to help them on their way.

Despite their own casualties that were mounting, the Australians were giving the Nips a hiding. They were falling in unsustainable numbers, their officer screaming abuse with threats like a maniac, driving them on with kicks and punches. If he kept up he wouldn't have any troops left.

Kerrison put a burst into the fanatic's chest and settled the matter for him. The rest of the attackers were now without direction, turned and fled back into the jungle from where they had, with a steady stream of angry Australian gunfire seeing them off.

Kerrison called a cease fire and to stand down. They all relaxed a little and started to take toll of the dead and wounded. The wounded Japanese were dispatched without fuss and left where they lay. It was not out of anger or retribution; it was hard core pragmatism. They did not have the resources to take prisoners, especially wounded ones.

The Australian dead were left in shallow marked graves and their ID tags recovered. Kerrison turned to check on Lawrence and found him wide-eyed in shock; the Japanese interpreter was laying behind him, unmoving. He was dead. How he came to be dead was not apparent.

The cause, however, was obvious; a perfectly placed bullet hole in the middle of his forehead was undeniable and raised a question mark in Kerrison's mind, but unfortunately there was no time to investigate further. But this was a blow, as the interpreter would have been a valuable prisoner to interrogate. He would have also acted as a witness to back up the claim of treason against Lieutenant Parnham that he believed was included in the captured documents.

Kerrison's NCO had rounded up the troops and set them in defensive combat positions and they moved out once again. They found the bodies of their comrades, Johnno and Bluey, and give them a decent burial in shallow graves. Kerrison thought digging graves had become far to frequent for his liking.

After saying a quick prayer over their fallen comrades, they set off once more finally reaching their headquarters at Milne Bay and were met by bad news. The Japanese had attacked, as expected by Kerrison, who had been unable due to circumstances, to get a warning through to his commanding officer. The result was the Japanese had partly overrun the airfield and inflicted many casualties and damage. Fortunately, the Kittyhawks' were airborne somewhere on a sortie and the Beaufighters were giving Japanese shipping a caning. So only one plane, an A20, that had seen better days, was damaged by a grenade and caught fire.

Just when it looked like it was all over and the Japanese had succeeded, a couple of returning Kittyhawks had come in and given them a spray. The enemy had swarmed across the runway towards the Australian defenders and were cut down by the intense machine gun and cannon fire from the fighter aircraft.

Communications in the area were a bit dodgy, but on this one occasion, air-control had managed to alert the fighter patrol who came back with all haste and made mince-meat of the attackers.

Lieutenant Kerrison reported back to his captain who, understandably, had his hands full and asked his subordinate to prepare his report and they would debrief him later. Lieutenant Kerrison checked on his men then found a spot to prepare his mission report, which was a little more complex than usual with the added accusation by the enemy against a fellow officer.

At that point, Kerrison was the only one who knew the full story of this and he toyed with the idea of ditching the whole thing. Given Parnham's status as a fellow officer and his standing in the community, he wondered would his, that is, Kerrison's head be the one to roll. Further to that he knew his fellow officer had suffered greatly at the hands of the enemy and questioned whether he himself would have been able to withstand the torture and have the courage to choose death before dishonour.

He decided the material, while unreadable in the Japanese commander's satchel, may be vital intelligence and there could be information included that could blow back on him if he failed in his duty to tell the whole story. He began to type on the company's *Royal* typewriter, a rugged portable with most of the keys functioning.

When he had completed it, he reported back to his commander and requested a confidential meeting, even asking for the boss' aide to leave the meeting. He then laid out the story verbally, being as precise as he could be. Captain Fullmore, a career officer, was aghast when he heard Kerrison's story. Kerrison knew he may be called on to give evidence at a later date and was preparing for that by putting down the foundations. He would need to repeat the story more than once and there had better not be any contradictions or deletions. He placed his report on the captain's desk and produced the Japanese officer's satchel. He removed the report, some scribbled hand written notes and what looked like a rough attempt at several maps, but clearly a map of Port Moresby and another of Milne Bay.

The Japanese captain must have been a canny devil, Kerrison decided. These were clearly copies kept by him, while the originals were sent to his command centre. While crudely done, they would certainly give the enemy a pretty clear idea of what they were up against. This was a shocking revelation.

They discussed the matter for a half hour. Kerrison sent for his NCO who was subtly questioned by the captain about his observations of Parnham, being careful not to reveal damaging information that would reflect on their investigation.. The soldier informed his superior that Parnham seemed to be settling very quickly but his injuries would take some time yet to fully heal. His assessment was that Parnham should be fit for duty again in about two weeks. He made no allowance for his mental state.

The NCO was dismissed and Captain Fullmore produced his pipe and lit up. He indicated for Kerrison to follow suit and he did so gratefully. They sat in quiet contemplation for a while, puffing intently on their pipes while they mulled over the situation. After an interval, Fullmore cleared his throat and delivered his decision. He ordered Kerrison to take the Japanese papers and a copy of his report back to Battalion HQ in Moresby. There he was to make his statement and present the evidence to the Senior Intelligence Officer for his decision. In the meantime, Parnham would be considered innocent until proven otherwise and would report for duty after his recovery.

Kerrison was sworn to secrecy on the matter and, given all they knew about Parnham, it would be as well to keep their noses clean as it could be more than their careers were worth.

It was several days before Lieutenant Kerrison was able to hitch a ride in a RAAF transport back to Port Moresby and report as ordered to Battalion HQ. There he was subjected to an intense interrogation by his senior officers at the conclusion of which he felt as though he had committed some misdemeanour himself, so vehement was the ordeal. Eventually, he was sworn to secrecy under the Official Secrets Act and dismissed to re-join his company.

There followed quite a hubbub as the intelligence officers poured over the Japanese written report with the aid of an interpreter and was overlaid on Kerrison's version of events. The reports of the attack on the Milne Bay airfield, when the enemy very nearly overran the defenders, were re-examined in detail for evidence of prior knowledge by the enemy that would indicate some veracity in Lieutenant Kerrison's report on the matter.

They believed there would be enough evidence to warrant further investigation and put through an order to have Parnham report to HQ as soon as possible to be interrogated. A very subtle suggestion came from the intelligence officer, who doubled as a propaganda specialist. Making sure his audience was confined to the two senior officers; his advice was to delay this as long as possible. Instead of interrogating Parnham, send him back out into the field as soon as he was passed fit and the problem may well resolve itself.

His none too subtle tactic was not missed by anyone in the room and while they mostly thought it was a stroke of genius, they were still shocked by the depths of their individual desperation and duplicity. It would not be the first time such a scandal was dealt with by battle hardened senior combat officers inured to civilian morality, protecting their troops and careers against morale depressing stories such as this.

In fact, about this time, a US bomber fully loaded with explosives as well as full fuel tanks, suddenly plunged into a marshalling yard as it attempted to take off. In that crash zone an Australian battalion was boarding trucks to head out for their combat duties. Approximately 240 of Australia's finest young men perished instantly in the massive conflagration that followed.

Tearful observers witnessed a long line of trucks bearing the dead to their resting place in the rapidly expanding cemetery for the war dead. This was the greatest single loss of Australian lives in action in the war to date and the news, if released, would have had a devastating effect on civilian morale. The incident was immediately subjected to an embargo of the highest order and the reports, and all references to it, were locked away, not to be opened for 50 years.

By this time, Milne Bay was considered secure against the Japanese who had pulled back, suffering their first real defeat of the war. Their navy had been met in the Coral Sea and suffered great losses and their land forces were now rebuffed by a determined allied defence.

The units of the 55th AIF, that had been fighting around Milne Bay, were recalled to Port Moresby to bolster the forces defending the Kokoda Track. Lawrence Parnham was with them; however, he was admitted to the field hospital there to receive further treatment for his injuries. After a brief stay of one week, he was discharged back to his unit.

Author's Note

Milne Bay Battle Summary

In all, 171 allied servicemen were killed and 216 wounded. Included in these figures were seven RAAF pilots and three Americans killed and four wounded at the defence of number three strip and in the sinking of the transport ship *Anshun* in the bay. In total the Japanese landed 1943 men at Milne Bay. Of these, 625 died and 311 were evacuated wounded. An additional 21 Japanese aircrew were lost. While the Japanese had occasionally been temporarily repulsed in attacks in Malaya and the Philippines, this was the first time a major Japanese operation had been comprehensively defeated.

CHAPTER EIGHT

Lawrence had been admitted into the field hospital's casualty clearing station to spend a week recovering from the wounds and bruising inflicted on him by his captors. After a period of seven days, the company medical orderly, (under orders,) passed him fit to leave the hospital to resume light duties, even though still badly bruised. In reality, he was still physically and mentally unable to assume a command.

The MO was puzzled by the order. Here was a man, clearly at the end of his endurance, who should be evacuated but he had been ordered to pass him fit for duty. Five days later, the MO received a stern rebuke for failing to pass him fit for combat and was ordered to re-examine him and amend his assessment. Lawrence duly reported to the MO, still light headed and in obvious pain, and was shocked to be told he was now fit for service in the field.

However, Lawrence didn't question his orders, despite feeling less than fully fit. The current military situation required his input and he was determined to do the best he could and lead a platoon back into the field. The situation, militarily, was still very much in the balance and every hand urgently required in such a tense time. He was assigned another platoon to conduct search and destroy in the dense jungle against the Japanese still stubbornly clinging to the hills and ridges between Milne Bay and Gona. The Japanese had refused to accept defeat and moved a small troop along the coast from Gona to test the allies in and around Milne Bay.

His command had decided, as nothing was proven, they had to consider him innocent until proven otherwise. They were very nervous about bringing charges against the son of a prominent federal politician and would prefer to kick the whole thing down the road. As there were no duties worthy of his rank and experience behind the lines, his CO thought privately along the same lines as the intelligence officer. If the bastard was killed in the line of duty, they could tidy the whole mess up neatly.

Miraculous how great minds think alike in times like these. The troop that had been put under Lawrence's command were a mixed bunch of experience. Some ex-2nd AIF Rats of Tobruk, a few new green recruits and one or two wily jungle fighters from the Milne Bay arena who had been in New Guinea from the start.

In warfare, its kill or be killed. Similarly, you ambush and guard against ambush. Death can come from many directions and in many forms. The Japanese Betty bombers were still infrequent visitors and their deadly loads seemed to strike with a careless randomness that made death capricious. The bomber pilot didn't deliberately select an individual to receive his bombs, as a sniper in a tree with a high powered rifle and telescopic sight would do. The victim was collateral to the intended target and, in reality, a bonus to the enemy.

The Zero attack was different; he would look for trouble anywhere and everywhere. If he wasn't challenged by the opposition fighter aircraft, then he had free reign to strafe his enemy on the ground. That was personal and terrifying. The Zero came in fast and low; his machine gun's rapid staccato chatter dispensing death and destruction to everything in its sights.

Man to man combat in the jungle was just that. See the enemy first and kill him before he killed you and that was the tricky part. A Japanese sniper would tie on to the top of a tree, well camouflaged, and wait patiently for his target who wouldn't hear the shot that killed him.

The general run of combat around the Milne Bay area had been close quarters, although the allies had the upper hand now. Reports had come through of a Japanese unit infiltrating from the north, possibly having worked along the coast from Gona.

Lawrence's troop was assigned to sweep the area, engage and eliminate the enemy.

The conditions were still appalling, steep muddy slopes providing a massive challenge to Lawrence Parnham's men. His experience fighting the Japanese further south around Milne Bay, was much the same as this. The mud and jungle were the same, the enemy was the same, fighting up and down the energy sucking hilly terrain was a different world again. This time he couldn't count on the air support he had enjoyed previously.

It was one thing to face the horrors of the Japanese "Banzai" charge but this business promised to be deadly and exhausting at a level he found hard to credit.

Most of the allied soldiers had heard rumours about the Banzai charge which had largely been exaggerated. It was certainly confronting, but it had proved to be a losing tactic.

Screaming, 'Tenno Haika Banzai' which meant, 'long live the Emperor' they would charge, without regard for their own mortality, at their enemy. Lawrence and his men had heard about this Bushido, or Way of the Warrior, inspired willingness to die for the emperor, rather than face defeat in utter shame.

The charge, while terrifying, was generally used when the Japanese, as a smaller force, were losing or lost a battle and was almost always repulsed by sometimes smaller forces that could hold their nerve and lay down effective disciplined fire, which would cut the attackers down like wheat. The Japanese were also committed to suicide if the attack did not succeed and this meant using grenades to kill their enemy by throwing themselves amongst any allied soldiers who failed to gun them down. This human bomb style was a forerunner to the suicide bomber or kamikaze.

Another tactic was to pretend to be dead or wounded and wait for the enemy to come close enough to spring a surprise attack with whatever weapon he had on hand: knife; handgun, or most usually, the grenade. Another common method of taking out the enemy "post mortem" was to booby trap an enemy body by placing a grenade underneath it with the pin removed. When the body was disturbed for any reason, the grenade would explode.

True or not, Lawrence knew it was very effective propaganda, but from what they had seen so far in the Battle of Milne Bay, the enemy may need to be a little more prudent with how he spent his troops.

Lawrence led his new platoon out on patrol again. It was raining hard, effectively drowning any tell-tale jungle sounds but providentially providing cover for the troop. But if it was hard for the patrol, it was equally hard for the enemy they searched for. One advantage these young soldiers had was their upbringing on the farms and in the rural areas of New South Wales. They had all learned to hunt and shoot from an early age and they were mostly armed with the unwieldy Lee Enfield Mark 111 .303 rifle. It was deadly accurate with an effective range over 500 metres. It was the weapon many of the troops who had served in North Africa were used to. It was a great weapon in the wide open desert where the war was fought over long distances as at the siege of Tobruk, but of questionable value in the jungle at very short range. It was no lightweight either, weighing in at just over four kilos, not counting spare clips.

The platoon moved cautiously in single file on each side of the muddy track with Lawrence in the lead carrying his powerful Thompson sub machine gun, weighing over five kilos loaded, plus spare clips and a Webley Revolver .455 on his hip. They all carried fresh water and some rations. The simple act of carrying a water bottle was hard work in these conditions and the men needed to take rest breaks fairly often as a result of lugging their weaponry in the continuous fight against the clinging mud. Many of the men preferred to go shirtless in an attempt to beat the heat. They cursed and swore under their breath, but still they pressed on, keen to give the Japanese a bloodied nose. Those with the .303's were lugging them along with bayonet fixed.

Many of the men preferred to go shirtless in an attempt to beat the heat and humidity. The Bren Light Machine Gun weighed in at over 11 kilograms plus clips etc, but was a much prized weapon by its current owner who preferred the load over smaller, less interesting and lethal weapons. In the tropical heat and humidity these loads were not inconsiderable and took a toll on their endurance. Plus the added effort required to lug the weapons up and down the **steep** terrain while keeping them operational and free from mud.

Tired troops become careless troops. Lawrence would need to be on top of this by calling regular rest stops and ensuring they kept up their hydration. Smoking would be banned once they drew closer to the enemy; the scent of cigarette smoke carried a long way in a war fought at virtual arms- length and would alert the enemy to their presence. Despite the punishing physical trauma Lawrence had received, he was pushing on trying hard not to show any sign of weakness to his men but was every bit as grateful for the rest stops as any of them.

Despite their tiredness, the Australians made good time advancing towards the Japanese positions. Lawrence's platoon was a fairly raw bunch in their combat experience, but they were observing good discipline which meant no bunching up and maintaining razor sharp awareness.

There was no chatter, just the soft suck and slop of the mud that was trying to pull their boots off and an occasional curse as someone stumbled, grounding their weapon that then needed to be cleaned. The jungle on either side was a dense green wall, absolutely impenetrable and threatening.

Lawrence was beginning to feel the effects of his ordeal, pain seeping into his legs where the bruising could still be seen. His heavy breathing was straining his ribs and abdominal muscles. His careful husbandry of his troops with frequent stops was more for his own relief than theirs.

The troop paused where the track was now branching off to the left. Lawrence checked his map, referred to his pocket compass and, satisfied with his navigation, signalled his men to move forward. Cautiously, they formed up once again and followed this much narrower overgrown track. Lawrence called a halt after they had travelled several hundred metres for another rest and refocus. Two men were sent forward on point and they took up positions on either side of the now faint track by pushing themselves against and under the undergrowth until they were almost invisible.

Bird life can be your friend in the jungle. As they go about their business, they announce it to the world with their glorious bird calls. They squabble and brag and sing with *joi de vivre*. They also signal a warning as they loudly renounce any intrusions. It pays to heed the bird calls.

If Lawrence and his men were more attuned to the jungle sounds perhaps they would have had a chance to avoid the next few horrific minutes...perhaps. *If only* they had been a little less weary and a little more wary.

"If only", the saddest word pairing in the English language. Presaged by a sudden disturbance in the birds' song, the attack when it came was overwhelming and sudden. Machine gun fire was from both flanks, backed up by accurate rounds from grenade launchers. Five of Lawrence's men died instantly without firing a shot in reply. The Japanese were heavily camouflaged and highly experienced, targeting their fire accurately for maximum effect. Lawrence called his men to take cover and return fire. With the best will in the world this was nigh on impossible. There was no solid cover and they had little time to bring their weapons to bear. A mortar round landed beside the Bren gunner, killing him and two comrades. One poor lad was disembowelled and lay screaming in agony.

All of Lawrence's training and discipline had evaporated in the terror now filling his chest. Desperately, he fired long bursts into the scrub where he thought the enemy was.

He fired and reloaded and fired once more. One of his men had lobbed a grenade, which raised screams from the enemy which gave him heart, but his men kept falling, cut down by well-aimed fire inflicting horrendous wounds. Bodies were torn apart by exploding grenades and high velocity machine gun rounds.

The thought was racing through his mind that here was a replay of his capture earlier in the campaign and the horrors that he experienced at the hands of the barbaric Japanese. His blood turned to ice water as he tried vainly to shake off his panic. He tried to gather his thoughts as more ordinances exploded around him. He had to do something or they all faced certain death.

His sergeant had won his stripes in North Africa and growing up as the eldest son of a contract shearer spent his youth manhandling uncooperative sheep the size of small cars. Sergeant Edward "Nugget" Gold sprinted forward and snatched up the Bren gun and found it still operative. With a fresh clip, he poured fire into the advancing Japanese, slowing them momentarily and then, supported by Lawrence, the enemy retreated backwards under the concentrated fire of the two men.

The surviving platoon members gathered themselves to fight back under the direction of their sergeant. Disciplined accurate fire met the Japanese who were beginning to feel the sting of an Aussie backlash. Their return fire had taken the enemy by surprise, but it was still not enough to get them out of trouble. The sudden ambush had now become a slogging affair with neither side willing to give ground, knowing it could lead to annihilation.

Even the best athlete can't run forever and the gutsy Aussies were starting to run out of wind and ammunition. The bloody Japanese seemed to be getting stronger and more determined. Suddenly, there was a blast of machine gun fire tearing into the Japanese left flank and three grenades fell among them with devastating effect.

Reinforcements had arrived, led by an enterprising young officer who was coming back from a patrol with his platoon. They had heard the sound of battle and a scout was sent to find out what was happening. He was able to pin point the Japanese positions and reported the Australians had taken heavy casualties but were managing to hold off a determined enemy. Without losing any time, he organised his supporting attack to assist and ultimately relieve the exhausted diggers.

Lawrence's men had regrouped and the Japanese were now taking fire on two flanks, losing ground rapidly. The Australians expanded their lines to surround the enemy and deliver punishing fire, cutting them down until they were forced to turn and beat a retreat.

Lawrence had gained strength and courage and, spurred on by the sight of the Japanese departing, he ran recklessly forward with the intention of chasing them down and opening another flank, but it was not to be because they had a surprise up their sleeves. They were not running away, they were falling back to a more defensible position where their own reinforcements were coming in behind them, with plenty of fresh ammunition and aggression.

Lawrence found himself cut off, separated from his men by an angry bunch of Nips set on avenging their dead comrades. Lawrence kept firing with the one clip left in his weapon, in short bursts. He knew he was in serious trouble and decided that discretion being the better part of valour, it was time for him to leave the field of battle as quickly as his tired legs would take him.

He fired a last burst in the direction of the Japanese, turned and plunged into the dense jungle behind him, and as the foliage closed over him, he was knocked down. A hot, searing pain exploded in his right arm, his weapon falling out of his nerveless hand.

An enemy round had struck his elbow inflicting a ghastly wound. With his right arm now useless, he tried to free his Webley revolver from its holster with his left hand as he fled instinctively further into the bush.

Now he was in full panic mode, crashing through the undergrowth, his face slashed by thorns and jagged branches. He needed to get the hell away from the enemy and forget all pretence of heroics. Running, crashing through the heavy undergrowth, he stumbled and fell over an ancient fallen tree, landing on his injured arm. He screamed involuntarily and rolled on his left side. There he noticed the log was almost completely hollowed out along on his side.

Quickly regaining control, he shimmied into the cavity, praying he wasn't sharing it with a deadly Papuan taipan which would be as merciless as the Japanese that were now hunting him. In the background, he was aware the sounds of battle had become less intense. The pain in his arm was excruciating, now matched perfectly by his rising level of fear. He clutched the revolver in his left hand. A thought floated through the layers of pain that he was a poor revolver shot with his natural right hand, so he would expect to be bloody hopeless with his left.

Somewhere in his background training, he had heard that moss had astringency qualities. There was plenty of moss in his hidey hole, so with nothing to lose, he tore off a few chunks and pressed the stuff into his wound. It was not perfect, but he was hopeful it might stem the blood flow. He was shocked by the ghastly wound which appeared to have blown his elbow joint apart. If he survived this would surely take him out of the front line.

While the jungle seemed to close in around him he still felt vulnerable and exposed. He was determined not to be captured again and resolved to use his last bullet on himself.

A faint rustling sound came to his ears from somewhere back along the way he had fled. The Japanese were surely following the broad swathe of crushed and bent foliage he had smashed down through the scrub in his panic.

You wouldn't need the skills of an Aboriginal tracker to locate him as even Blind Freddy would have him in a minute. He squirmed as far into the log as possible, determined not to die at the hands of these barbarians. He would not allow them to take him alive. If they found him, he would use the revolver on himself and cocked the weapon awkwardly in readiness.

The subtle sounds grew closer and he could swear that he feared his heart beat was so loud it would give away his position if nothing else would. His eyes were focused on the thick blanket of moss he had just applied to his wound, that was adorning the inner walls of the log and, perversely, his mind registered the simple beauty of it as a small self-contained cosmos supporting a rich variety of insect life. He felt himself drifting off as his mind reacted to the shock and the loss of blood. His eyes, now as heavy as lead, closed involuntarily, as he fought to keep them open.

When he managed to force his eyes open, he found himself looking at a bayonet fixed to the standard Ariska rifle of the Japanese Imperial Army, held by a very fired up Japanese NCO shouting his gibberish at his troops urging them on. Charged with the adrenaline of fear, he was suddenly fully alert. The Japanese soldier had quietly come up on the other side of the log and may have peered over, but seeing nothing relaxed and lazily allowed his rifle to rest on the log, the barrel reaching down over Lawrence's eye line.

The Japanese man was short of leg and stocky, which probably saved Lawrence's life. Those stumpy legs wouldn't take him over the top of the log, so he was forced to forge a path around it and, fortunately for Lawrence, he chose to go around the far end away from the hollow.

How long Lawrence lay there he would never know, but he gave the Japanese plenty of time to move well out of hearing before he moved a muscle. He was losing a lot of blood and tore his emergency wound kit from his belt. He used his teeth to tear open the sulphanilamide powder, removed the temporary moss dressing and sprinkled the antiseptic powder liberally over the gaping wound. Then he fumbled out a bandage which he wrapped around the wound. It wasn't his best first aid work but it stemmed the flow of blood again for a while longer. He was thankful to the Yank with whom he had traded the medical kit, which was superior to the AIF issue at that time.

Carefully, he eased out of his shelter and, as quietly as he could, he backtracked to the scene of the fighting where he caught up with the remnants of his platoon and the other unit that had rescued them earlier. Miraculously, he recovered his submachine gun where it had fallen when he plunged into the jungle, managing to manoeuvre the sling over his left shoulder. He found he would be able to use it left-handed and even if it only had a few rounds in the clip, it gave him a confidence the Webley revolver failed to.

When he staggered back to re-join the unit, a medic quickly attended to his wound, applying a better job of bandaging, cleaning and disinfecting it. Then the medic fixed the elbow with an improvised splint, finally immobilising Lawrence's arm in a sling.

This was not achieved without excruciating pain which, despite a shot of morphine, tore through him like electricity. The pain killer was administered by syrette, a flexible, single dose pack developed for soldiers in the field. After inserting the needle under the skin, the tube of morphine was squeezed much like a toothpaste tube. After injection, the used tube was pinned to the receiving soldier's collar to inform other medical staff of the dose administered. This avoided the potential for a lethal overdose.

Lawrence's fellow officer came to him and introduced himself as Harry Goodman and suggested that, in light of Lawrence's wound, perhaps he, Goodman, should assume overall command of both units.

Lawrence had no problem with that as he was barely conscious due to shock and the effects of the pain killer. The Battle of Milne Bay and the war was receding into time and now all he wanted was to get down the mountains and off this blasted track. As far as Lawrence was concerned the war as a whole would now be over if he could make it back totheir base.

CHAPTER NINE

Lieutenant Goodman announced he and his men would go after the Japanese while they had them on the run and off balance. Hopefully, they could drive them back to the coast where they could say hello to the Bristol Beaufighters currently patrolling there.

He had a scout out tracking them as he spoke and would depart soon with the combination of Lawrence's men and his own, leaving Lawrence in the hands of Sergeant Nugget Gold, the medic and the wounded. Somehow, they would need to make their way to safety or stay put and wait for rescue. Lawrence said they'd be alright and not to worry.

Harry Goodman led his troops out on the double in determined pursuit of the enemy.

The medic, always called Doc regardless of formal qualifications, surveyed the survivors of the savage gunfight, and did a quick appraisal. The wounded fell into two groups: those immobilised by their wounds and the walking wounded. With Lawrence's guidance and approval, he helped the walking wounded into positions where they could still effectively use their weapons to defend themselves and the remnants of their units.

The more strategic area they had taken up was a small, lightly wooded patch on the crest of one of the lesser hills they had been patrolling over. The sun was able to peek through the light foliage, drying out the ground they lay on. It was a pleasure to be sitting on grass warmed by the sun, instead of stinking mud, clothing steaming dry by its rays. In front of them, the tough New Guinea grass grew to a foot high and was broken by occasional small shrubs. Any attack coming from the north would have to expose themselves to the Australians' gunfire as they came across the patch. The disabled were placed behind this pathetically lean line of defence in the shade of the trees that fringed the area.

Lawrence took up a spot toward the centre of the broad arc formed by their arrangement, using a living eucalypt trunk as cover. He scrunched up a handful of its leaves and held them to his nose, enjoying the delightfully pungent aroma so redolent with memories of home.

The wounded remnants of the two platoons settled down for the wait, nursing their pain as best they could while keeping a vigilant defensive position as ordered. Lawrence was finding the Tommy gun a bit of a handful and found an Owen gun without an owner that was considerably lighter and more reliable. Besides, he had only limited .45 ammo for the Thomson and there was plenty around to feed the Owen which took a 9mm x 19mm parabellum or .38 calibre.

Night closed in on them rapidly as it tended to do in the tropics, but before he lost the light altogether, the medic went from man to man, checking their bandages, making adjustments and issuing pain killers where he could. There were the usual grumbles but overall the men were in good spirits realising the seriousness of their situation and also their luck to be still alive. The fittest of them were put to work digging out shallow defensive foxholes which would provide bare protection from any possible attack and at least provide some sense of security. Lawrence shared one such shallow trench with Corporal Douglas who acted as his runner, quietly going about reassuring the men with the boss's words of encouragement. Some of the men had dozed off, including Lawrence, and a calm of sorts had descended over the battle weary and wounded men. Sentries had been posted and they were on full alert as the swirling back and forth contest had already proved anything could happen and so it proved once again.

The determined Japanese had circled around and come back at them from another direction. They could not possibly know the Australian force was now divided in two and the half they were attacking was the weaker target. It was also a sure thing they weren't aware the stronger, aggressive half of the Australian force was tracking behind them and it would not take long for them to work out the Japanese tactics and follow up.

Given the ferocity of the diggers' earlier defence, the Japanese approached cautiously and this was the saving grace for the Australians. The first attack was abrupt and frightening. Coming out of the jungle with the setting sun behind them, firing a burst of random gunfire, accompanied by lung bursting screams, they charged towards the Australian positions in a determined attack.

The sentries fire met them, dropping several and was soon joined by the rest of the contingent as they snapped out of their sleep and went on the defensive. A second wave of attackers followed right behind the first group, putting the fear of God into the defenders. Lawrence, who had been in a blissful morphine-induced state of semi- consciousness, was jolted into awareness, adrenaline pumping through his system as he automatically reached out for his Owen gun, while looking about trying to clear his head and attempting to ascertain the situation.

His runner, Corporal Douglas, was at his side pointing out the main attacking group, which looked certain to overrun the defenders on the right flank. Lawrence was suddenly infuriated by these bloody Japs; he had had enough. It may have been the morphine or it may be Lawrence had reached his limit of tolerance or a deadly wrath. Lawrence was charged with a burning rage and the fabled red curtain descended over him. Disregarding his seriously wounded right arm and snatching up the Owen gun he charged at the startled Japanese, who had not seen him in his trench, spraying them with short effective bursts. Several now caught on and directed return fire at him as he continued to run directly across the face of the attacking enemy line, ignoring the risk to his own life. Years of boyhood cricket practice came to the fore and, like an A Grade slips fieldsman, released the Owen Gun on its sling to free up his one good hand which he instinctively thrust out and caught a Japanese grenade, tossing it back underarm to explode in the face of its original owner.

He continued to run at the enemy, firing one handed and ignoring the pain from his wounded arm, seeing nothing but the hated enemy falling to his gunfire. The Japanese were rattled by the sight of this madman. Their attack began to falter as some turned tail and started to flee. Lawrence realised he had been joined by Douglas, who was supporting him with his own submachine gun, giving the enemy further incentive to run.

Lawrence noticed they were getting the upper hand and continued to push forward. Douglas reloaded his weapon for him and he went on the attack again. A Japanese officer and two men were partly hidden by a fallen tree and were creating havoc among the Australians. Without hesitation, Lawrence charged their position, leaping over the log, screaming like a madman completely terrifying the Japanese, who were too slow to bring their guns to bear and fell under the Owen gun's deadly fire. Finally, the remaining Japanese, completely confused and demoralised by this display of raw courage, began to retreat. Lawrence and Douglas had now been reinforced by several other walking wounded and, between them, beat off the enemy for the second time that day, pouring ammunition into their retreating backs. Finally, Lawrence ordered the men back to their positions, instructed them to dig in further and remain alert as the Japanese soldiers were likely to come back under cover of darkness and try to take them by stealth.

Less than half an hour had passed when Lieutenant Harry Goodman and his platoon returned to a much relieved and exhausted bunch to find Lieutenant Lawrence Parnham lying semi-conscious and almost delirious from the pain and further loss of blood from his wound.

After the shooting stopped, the doc noticed his officer had sustained a further wound to his right side. A bullet had passed through his side front to back, avoiding any vital organs, leaving only the entry and exit wounds which he quickly dressed. It was hard to say whether the man was actually aware of it. The men were standing about talking in hushed tones of Lawrence's courageous feat.

Sergeant Nugget Gold issued orders to get a brew going and make sure those that were able to ingest some food got it. It wasn't long before nearly all the men had their spirits lifted by a hot cup of tea and a smoke. Lieutenant Goodman took the sergeant aside and quizzed him about the chatter among the troops and found he was hanging on every word as the battle hardened sergeant regaled him with Parnham's heroics, backed up by the medic.

It appeared the enemy had had enough and made no further attacks on the depleted Australian platoons and, despite their nervousness, most of them took advantage of it and slept like the proverbial logs. In the morning at first light, Harry Goodman assigned tasks, issued orders and immediately after some field rations and a brew, the battered group moved out, heading back towards their Company HQ.

This is where the local tribesmen proved to be a major asset to the Australian forces, taking on the difficult task of manhandling supplies and the improvised stretchers that were used to transport the wounded. Uncomplaining and good humoured, they were highly valued allies, dubbed Fuzzy Wuzzy Angels by the troops due to their dramatic hairstyle.

Australian casualties could possibly have been much higher if it were not for the selfless and tireless duty performed by these marvellous native warriors who hated the Japanese and were unstinting in their devotion to the care and transportation of the wounded. Wounded soldiers were stretchered through the dreadful jungle conditions, crossing strong flowing rivers and surmounting the muddy tracks down steep slopes, broken by fallen trees and boulders; conditions that would try an unburdened strong man. All the while, the courageously loyal Fuzzy Wuzzy Angels carried on without complaint. At the end of their trial, they would gather together, chattering away in their own dialect, big grins, teeth stained pink with betel nut, splitting their dark faces. The betel nut provided the exhausted natives with a much needed burst of energy. They earned the nickname due to their hairstyle which, in later years in the west, would be called an Afro.

Lieutenant Goodman had spent a fair bit of time receiving reports from Sergeant Gold andthe surviving corporals, on the battle that took place the night before. He wanted all the details of the action while he was pursuing the Japanese who had given him the slip and circled around to pull off their attack on Lieutenant Parnham's group.

Each one reported they were astounded by the incredible courage of Lieutenant Parnham in his almost suicidal attack on the Japanese, which undoubtedly turned the tide and saved the day. Goodman was stunned by the reports presented to him. There was no doubt Lieutenant Parnham should be recommended for the highest gallantry medal in recognition of his selfless heroism which, without doubt, prevented a wholesale massacre of every man in his command, which were mainly the disabled and almost defenceless walking wounded, who no doubt, inspired by Lawrence's heroism, had also displayed great courage by ignoring their wounds in defence of their fellows.

At this time, Lawrence was in a bad way and was still sleeping or unconscious, but closely attended by the medic. Goodman decided to make a stand where they were to enable the men to regain some level of endurance before they set off back to base.

*　*　*

The senior command in Port Moresby were still mulling over what to do with the reports of Lawrence's behaviour and the charges of cowardice and treason. The reports were still to be fully analysed and were virtually untouched, a matter that had been gnawing away at their conscience. They were very reluctant to act on the evidence before them and had left it mouldering in a locked filing cabinet at the mercy of the tropical humidity, untouched for weeks while they dithered. Secretly but unspoken, even among the three senior officers, was the prospect that Parnham might meet with his fate somewhere up in the hills surrounding Milne Bay. And as it happened, their darkest wishes almost came true allowing them to then sweep it under the rug.

In their defence, there was still the threat of the enemy pushing down the Kokoda Track where the diggers were now fighting and pushing the Japanese back over the Owen Stanley Ranges. The Japanese s frighteningly came within eyesight of Port Moresby which could explain their averseness to this scandalous and potentially politically charged matter. Furthermore, they needed to consider the demoralising effect it may have on the men under their command.

On examination, the Japanese captain's material proved to be very interesting. He had been carrying what appeared to be a code book and a detailed scale map of Port Moresby with some curious notations on various points. When examined in detail, those points aligned with top secret ammunition and fuel dumps and underground communication bunkers. The question was, how to interpret those notations and how did this information fall into Japanese hands? In a full scale attack on Port Moresby, this intelligence could prove to be a fatal blow to the allied defenders.

The Japanese were pressing hard at the time of this reported incident and were virtually at the gates of Port Moresby, having fought their way across the Owen Stanley Range to be within 30 kilometres of their objective. At night they could clearly see the searchlights probing the night sky above the city, looking for attacking Japanese bombers.

Command HQ had plenty of immediate and urgent problems to deal with and a wrong decision on this matter could potentially ruin, not only the young officer's reputation and career, but given his powerful connections, it might possibly take one or two other careers with it as well.

His unit commander, Lieutenant Colonel Arthur Morris, met with Major Collins and Captain Bennet and the die was cast with the decision to get these documents back to Brisbane for expert cryptographers and Japanese language interpreters to ascertain their full import. This was a top priority, top secret mission and had to be undertaken immediately. Or so they said. Perhaps better to hasten slowly and with luck the situation would resolve itself.

However, the fighting was far from over and Lieutenant Parnham should be kept busy until further notice. Should it not sort itself out, leaving the senior officers with no choice but to act on the reports, then they could always fall back on the old bureaucratic stunt of passing the buck. They had held back as long as they could decently explain, if questioned and decided that it had to be sorted, because as far as they knew, Parnham was still breathing and the chances of a Japanese bullet solving the matter for them, was long passed.

Therefore, the decision was made to handball the problem up the line in classic bureaucratic fashion. Or as their American comrades would say, 'Kick the can down the road.'

The decision was made and the machinery put into gear.

CHAPTER TEN

Group Captain, "Black Jack" Walker, was requested to assign one of his long range Beaufighters and volunteered Squadron Leader, Big Bill Cuthbertson, who was due for a break having flown many tough sorties. This milk run would refresh him and be a reward for the sterling service he had provided in supporting Morris' ground troops. Everyone was in singular agreement with the allocation of the mission to Bill, who had built a reputation for aggressive attacks on the Japanese threatening allied positions.

Squadron Leader Cuthbertson had been leading his flight on a variety of targets. In support of the US attacks on Japanese shipping far out at sea and smaller barges making their way stealthily, island to island, as the Japanese pressed south. They had endured attacks by the deadly Zeros who unwisely took them on. They had used their withering fire power against ground targets, catching unwary Japanese who failed to hear their almost silent approach. Bill had his squadron up and flying every hour that weather and daylight permitted, pushing the younger pilots to the point of exhaustion. Everyone, pilots and ground crew, were aware of the critical situation that would ensue should Japanese forces take Milne Bay and then open the door to Port Moresby. They were determined that would never happen.

Black Jack Walker had Big Bill summoned. Bill was none too pleased to be taken away from his squadron and the action, but wisely kept his complaints to himself. Flight Sergeant Bluey Mansfield, Bill's navigator, was catching up on the sleep he had been deprived of in the previous days and weeks of combat duty, snoring like a lord when Bill tapped him on the leg hanging out of his bunk to tell him they were to report to Moresby and he needed to make ready and shape a course for Jackson Field Port Moresby

Bluey shook the sleep out of his head with a quick wash and got his flying boots on and his other gear together. The two men took the time for a quick breakfast of dried fruit and awful coffee and headed for their aircraft.

Taking off in the pre-dawn light, Bill piloted his aircraft to Jackson Field at Port Moresby, about 380 kilometres away to the west. At their cruise speed it took about an hour. They were on high alert as they approached Port Moresby, as Japanese Zeros were still harassing the defenders. There were plenty of clouds about; impressive great clumps floating over the area; huge, towering white masses that could hide a squadron of Zeros. However, the skies were clear of the enemy and they performed a trouble free landing. The moment he parked his aircraft in the safety of a revetment, Bill and Bluey were whisked away and found themselves in front of their formidable commander.

Black Jack briefed them on their mission and told them tongue- in-cheek that he was giving them a holiday. Compared with what they had most recently been doing, it would be a welcome break and by God, a chance to see family.

Bill was reluctant to leave the field of battle when they were beginning to see a return for their sacrifices but even he admitted to himself that a break would be most welcome. Turning the Japanese army back before they could build on their advances and noting a difference in the volume of their shipping. Their air to ground attacks on Japanese troops and equipment with the Beaufighters' terrifying fire power was devastating to the enemy. The continuous support for the Aussie soldiers, for whom he had great respect, was important but his arguments were in vain. The mission had overriding importance.

But the chance to see his family was all the incentive he needed. The decision was made, the orders delivered and now Black Jack told him, in no uncertain terms, to pull his head in and get on with it. Black Jack handed Bill a sealed blood red packet made from an almost indestructible resin coated canvas folder, heavily decorated with stark printing advising that the contents were TOP SECRET and for the eyes only of an intelligence officer at GHQ.

Bill was instructed that it was of extreme importance and the envelope was not to leave his hands until he reached Brisbane and placed it into the hands of the senior officer named on the front panel of the gaudy packet. The gravity of the mission was beginning to sink in.

Bill and Bluey met with the weather officer to begin plotting their flight plan. They could expect the usual August weather for New Guinea and northern Queensland. Port Moresby, on departure, would have a high of 29 degrees Celsius, low of 23. Light south-west winds, clear visibility with scattered alto cumulus clouds with a base of 5000 feet. They might encounter patches of rain but nothing they weren't used to and shouldn't cause them any grief. On reaching the Australian mainland they should have similar good flying conditions. First light would be at 6.26am.

Bill's navigator, Flight Sergeant Bluey Mansfield, was plotting their course with the assistance of the squadron intelligence officer. It was a pretty simple route heading almost due south of Port Moresby to intersect the Queensland coast, north of Townsville.

He was advised to lay the shortest course across Torres Strait, avoiding the unlikely possibility of any enemy aircraft activity over the Coral Sea, then follow the Cape York coast line south, reporting when abeam of, and inland from, Townsville. At this point they could make the decision to refuel at RAAF Base Townsville, however, the Beaufighter carried enough fuel to fly to Brisbane direct with a big safety margin, which was the major reason to assign the mission to them; that and the Beaufighters high speed and self-defensive capability.

Bill had planned to put a little swerve in his flight path and the less mucking about with unnecessary refuelling stops, the better. Bringing Bluey into his confidence, he asked him if would mind if Bill did a little fly-over Courtland Downs. Bluey had a problem resisting that big wide country boy grin of Bill's, as he assured him with a wink it would only be just down the road a bit and add just a 'few minutes' to their journey. The answer was of course in the affirmative. Everything in outback Australia is just down the road, which could be anything from 100 kilometres to 300 kilometres. Anything less than 100 kilometres was right next door.

The leg to Townsville would take two hours, 30 minutes with a further two hours, 45 minutes ahead of them to Brisbane. The total trip to Archerfield was approximately 1300 miles giving them a fuel reserve of one hour 40 minutes, well within safety requirements for the mission, even taking Bills 'swerve' into consideration.

Bill and Bluey retired to their respective cots to grab a couple of hours sleep before their mission. Bill was woken at 4am by a batman with a strong cup of sweet tea. He took it sitting on the side of his bunk and began to think about the day ahead. He wondered if he dared try to catch up with his dear wife, Lydia, although war time travel was very difficult and Black Jack made it blindingly clear that he expected him back ASAP, because every plane and crew were vitally important at the moment. Group Captain Walker was very reluctant to release one of his precious aircraft and was verballed into the decision.

Bill was up and about, bright-eyed and eager to get going. All he wanted to do was get this bloody mail run over and get back here to re-join his squadron.

He reconfirmed weather conditions once more and then joined with Bluey Mansfield in the canteen where they filled up on something resembling food, washed down with more tea. Bluey filled Bill in on the course he had plotted and they discussed a couple of plan Bs in the event of weather interfering with his existing flight plan.

Bluey headed for air traffic control to lodge his flight plan; something he hadn't been required to do for some time. They were normally briefed and vectored to their targets by command HQ and then their position was determined by the battle as it unfolded.

Bill caught up with the ground crew and conducted his pre-flight checks. The boys saw him coming and offered some half-hearted salutes, not out of disrespect, but in the usual Aussie laid back style. His Beau had been fuelled up and given a thorough pre-flight, but Bill left nothing to chance and wandered about the aircraft, running his eye over the control surfaces and looking for obvious things like damage from stones thrown up from the rough runways or the odd enemy inflicted minor damage that may have been overlooked in the interests of expediency.

Ordinarily, in combat conditions he would trust in his ground crew to have taken care of all these items, but he had time now and was enjoying himself, until he heard one of the ground crew ask a mate in a stage whisper if this bloke was auditioning for an airline job. They had removed the heavy rockets and topped up Bill's 20mm ammo for the cannons and the .303 ammo for the machine guns. An orderly was on the spot again with a packet of sandwiches and a thermos of hot tea for Bill, and the same for Bluey, apparently ordered by a considerate Black Jack as a farewell thought.

Bill walked under the belly of the big plane and reached up to release the access hatch with its built-in spindly ladder, he gave the ground crew a wry grin and thumbs up, as he climbed up inside the fuselage. Once aboard, he had to step over the back of his seat to get snugged down into it. Bluey gained access by way of a similar hatch a couple of metres behind the pilots hatch and took up his usual position as tail gunner/navigator. The two experienced crew attached their safety harnesses, connected their intercoms and set about doing their pre-flight checks, exchanging a few brief comments through their headsets.

Finally, they were ready to go. Bill switched on his intercom and checked with Bluey to see if he was set to go and proceeded with the start-up of both the huge Hercules 14 cylinder radial engines. The Beaufighter was an imposing aircraft standing on the ground but when those mighty engines roared to life, the observer suddenly understood what a powerful weapon of war it was.

The huge radial engines turned over, wheezing and sputtering, bursting into life with a roar and a massive cloud of blue exhaust smoke billowing out of each exhaust system. Bill runs them up a bit with his foot hard on the brake the whole plane vibrating and jigging about with the torque, anxious to go like a thoroughbred racehorse. He locks eyes on the ground controller who indicated that he was clear to go. Releasing the brakes, he taxied his lumbering aircraft out to the duty runway. The big plane lined up on the runway, sitting there with the engines running up while Bill had eyes anticipating the all clear, to be signalled from the tower.

He held on the runway threshold, one hand on the control yoke, with the fingers of his right hand embracing the twin throttle levers. He looked up and saw the control tower signalling clear for take-off. The time was 0640 hours. In the tower, his aircraft squadron number and time of departure were noted. Bill pushed the throttle levers forward and the big Hercules radials roared as the Beaufighter lurched away from the holding point, gathering speed as it hurtled down the runway, reaching its take-off speed swiftly.

Bill pulled back on the yoke and rotated the nose launching his plane into the air, then gently applying a bit of left rudder to compensate for the torque of the big engines, willing the plane to yaw to starboard. He retracted the undercarriage and, as usual, liked to build airspeed at this point. After raising the flaps he lowered the nose just slightly and watched the airspeed indicator climb to a comfortable level. With a shallow turn to starboard, he brought the aircraft to a climbing attitude, giving him 500 feet per minute rate of climb.

Observers on the ground spotted the rising sun glinting briefly off the starboard wing and tailplane. They disappeared behind a low cloud floating in on the south westerly breeze from Torres Strait.

The ground crew continued to watch as Bill climbed away to the south west making for Cape York, but it might as well have been bloody New York for all they knew. All they did was service 'em and launch 'em. Job done, they headed for the canteen and breakfast. Just another plane and just another take off.

The commanders, Lieutenant Colonel Arthur Morris, Major Collins and Captain Bennet watched Big Bill's Beaufighter disappear into the skies on its way south, as it receded to a mere dot into the azure sky. They had managed to stall the inevitable for 17 days since receiving the initial report and they were mightily relieved to see it now winging its way south, hopefully never to involve them again. Over breakfast they lamented the bloody uproar this would cause when it hit the desk in General Headquarters.

Two days later, the senior group were enjoying breakfast when they thought the potentially career wrecking event was finally off their hands. They were thoroughly put off their breakfast by a package of documents which was delivered to HQ from an officer in the field somewhere at Milne Bay detailing an action that had taken place five days ago in the hills north of the allied airfields there. The usual battle report and casualty lists were accompanied by another report, endorsed by a senior sergeant and two corporals, who witnessed the incident recommending Lieutenant Lawrence Garret Parnham be awarded the Victoria Cross.

'For most conspicuous gallantry in defence of his unit. While seriously wounded, Lieutenant Parnham displayed great personal courage. Ignoring the risk to his own life in the face of heavy incoming fire, he charged the enemy lines inflicting such severe casualties on them that he turned a certain annihilation of the soldiers under his command into a rout of the enemy.'

The commanders were dumbstruck. They had just sent off one report with a recommendation to investigate an officer from a prominent Australian political family for treason and cowardice and, almost simultaneously, a fresh report of a separate engagement has arrived, recommending the same officer for the army's highest award for courage under fire. There was strong evidence from eye witnesses to the event, including a written statement from the unit's medical orderly who treated Parnham's ghastly wound.

They looked at each other for answers, and then went back to the report. They took it in turns to stare out the window or sit with their heads in their hands. Fists were thumped into the tabletop and curses muttered. They knew if they signed off on this and sent it back to Canberra, they would look like fools but they had no alternative.

Was Parnham a hero or a coward? Was he a traitor or a patriot? Dear God, what should they do? If only this had arrived before the Beaufighter took off for HQ.

Lieutenant Colonel Arthur Morris made a ruling. They must personally interview the witnesses and participants in the action to confirm Parnham's reported valour or find a loophole that would get the command off the hook in making a decision on the matter.

Orders were issued to gather the relevant personnel together in Port Moresby for a thorough interrogation that would prove the validity, or otherwise, of the report. The central character in this drama was currently no more than a couple of hundred yards from where the anguished commanders were trying to come to terms with his future recovering in the hospital having had an amputation of his right arm

Over the ensuing days, the participants were assembled, after much back and forth, and each in their turn stood before the panel of senior officers to answer questions and give a first-hand account of the events leading up to Parnham's alleged heroics and a detailed description of the critical action that led to their conviction that he was deserving of the nation's highest gallantry award.

It must be said that the panel approached the matter with what may have been a jaundiced view, but they were determined to make a fair and just assessment. Each one put his view forward based on his interpretation of the statements of the witnesses who all presented as professional, well-spoken and experienced combat veterans. The panel had no option but to accept the reports, supported by the verbal evidence of these men.

Sadly, Lieutenant Parnham was the only living survivor from the action in which he was accused of cowardice and treason. His entire platoon was wiped out and the surviving Japanese interpreter, who would have been able to corroborate the written report of his superior, was allegedly killed by fire from his own comrades. The Japanese written report and the hand drawn maps, showing allied displacements, were on their way to Brisbane for analysis and therefore could not be consulted.

There seemed to be no doubt that Lieutenant Parnham had displayed extraordinary courage in defending his soldiers, but what of the Japanese reports of his treachery which have been despatched to Brisbane? What would the translation of that document reveal? In the meantime, they would have to judge Parnham on the evidence they had before them, in assessing his status as a hero. Undoubtedly, the propaganda value of a Victoria Cross winner from the conflict raging on Australia's doorstep would be incalculable; the public morale would be bolstered by a story of epic heroism and self-sacrifice, whereas a very negative revelation of cowardice and treachery would have the reverse devastating effect.

Morris decided to go with the positive and to hell with the consequences. With that, the file was despatched to Brisbane. There being no more time or manpower available to investigate further, Lieutenant Colonel Arthur Morris thanked the men and asked them to return to their units and wished them good fortune for their futures and got on with the business of defending Port Moresby. Thus, Lieutenant Lawrence Garret Parnham became the second of two VC winners from the New Guinea conflict.

Corporal John Alexander French was awarded the VC for his gallantry in an almost identical fashion to Lawrence, showing little regard for his own safety in defence of his men. Sadly, Corporal French's award was made posthumously.

Strangely, the expected response from HQ on Parnham's very serious charges of treason and cowardice had yet to arrive. While the top brass scratched their collective heads and pondered this, the answer they sought came to them in a report of a missing aircraft. It appeared that Squadron Leader Cuthbertson's plane had failed to arrive in Brisbane and a search was being conducted to confirm its whereabouts.

On receipt of this report, the commanders, Lieutenant Colonel Arthur Morris, Major Collins and Captain Bennet avoided eye contact with each other but were no doubt thinking along similar lines. Their thoughts better left unsaid.

CHAPTER ELEVEN

Lawrence spent a week in the Australian General Hospital's Casualty Clearing Station in Port Moresby, where he received treatment for his injuries which included severe dehydration. The wound to his arm was very serious and had become infected. The medics were debating whether his arm below the elbow could be saved. The decision was made for them almost immediately, as an air attack by the Japanese, inflicted several deaths and many more injuries across Port Moresby that required the immediate attention of the surgeons. The bad news for Lawrence was the decision therefore to opt for the time saving option of amputation

The medical teams were now almost overwhelmed and could no longer afford the luxury of debating long term measures. At 3.30 a.m. surgeons amputated Lawrence's arm and effectively terminated his war and active army career as well. He would receive an honourable discharge as a Victoria Cross recipient for his gallantry in his final engagement and the successes he had experienced in his earlier conflicts.

Two days later, Lawrence was aboard the Australian Hospital Ship Manunda and on his way home to Australia. He later came to bless his luck that he wasn't shipped aboard the doomed AHS Centaur, clearly marked by huge red crosses but sunk by a Japanese submarine in May 1943 off the Queensland coast. She went down with the loss of 268 lives from the 332 medical and civilian crew aboard.

AHS Manunda sailed into Sydney Harbour and discharged her relieved passengers into a convoy of ambulances and troop transports, which took them to the appropriate repatriation hospital where they would receive further medical treatment and be reunited with family, depending on the state of their health.

Lawrence was sent to 2/4th Australian General Hospital, Australian Army Redbank. His wife, Frances, had received the dreaded telegram but to her enormous relief, it told her he was wounded and would be repatriated home. She then had to endure a seemingly endless wait to hear news from the army about her husband. When the phone finally rang and she heard Lawrence's strong voice on the other end of the line, she had to bite hard on her knuckles to stop her screaming with sheer, exuberant delight. Tears streamed down her cheeks as she rushed to tell her mother-in-law that her son would soon be home.

The women couldn't contain themselves and completely lost their dignity, shouting and screaming for joy, dancing around the kitchen like mad women. Alexander rushed out of his study, greatly alarmed, thinking the worst of thoughts to find Winifred and Frances spinning each other around and singing at the top of their voices.

Frances made urgent arrangements to get to the Richmond area 30 to 40 kilometres north west of Sydney to meet her man while his parents, Winifred and Alexander, would wait patiently at home for their returning warrior. Neither Frances, nor her in-laws, were aware of the extent of Lawrence's injuries, of course. Only that they were sufficient to have him sent home. However, Frances said he sounded well and cheerful on the phone, so they had high hopes for his full recovery.

The army had generously organised a bus to take wives and loved ones of the newly repatriated to the hospital. It was a hot and uncomfortable journey that seemed to Frances to take an eternity, but eventually it rattled and bumped through the entrance of the army camp that was the 2/4th Australian General Hospital. Lawrence had recovered sufficiently after some convalescence while still in Port Moresby and aboard the AHS Manunda on the trip back to Sydney and was able to move about the ship unaided.

* * *

For a landsman, Lawrence appeared to have good sea legs, unlike many others on board who suffered terribly in the rough seas. The bullet wound in his side had healed well and didn't bother him much, apart from the painful broken rib he incurred. So he was grateful not to be heaving his stomach out with seasickness like the other chaps.

He had recovered sufficiently to be able to look after himself in some matters that had previously been conducted by his predominant right hand, having come to terms with shaving left handed. But one or two things still bothered him, like putting on a necktie, cutting up his food or doing up his shoe laces. He was not the only soldier aboard who had sacrificed a limb in battle so the understanding and assistance of the nursing staff aboard was very welcome.

After disembarking and being transported to 2/4th Australian General Hospital in Redbank, he settled in, waiting for the appearance of Frances. The other patients in his ward were a friendly, cheerful lot who, although seriously wounded in some cases, never- the-less put on brave faces, laughing and joking about anything and everything which included their injuries and how they would carry on with a normal life once they were discharged. Much of the ribald humour centred on their post-discharge sex life and most were keen to find out if their equipment still worked. This had patients and the broader-minded nurses bringing down the house with howls of laughter.

Lawrence told a comrade, if he could shave without opening an artery, he reckoned he could handle anything. That was as far as he was prepared to go with humour, not wishing to tarnish the image of his wife with ribald jokes about their intimacies. At this point, Frances was still unaware of the extent of his injuries, which bothered him somewhat and he was worried about how she would react when she saw him.

Perhaps he should have told her on the phone, instead of confronting her with it. But then he thought she would fret as women tend to do, so he made the decision to tell her only so much. Once she saw him standing straight and tall with no other apparent injuries, he knew it would be okay. Although they had now been married for quite a while, they had spent only a little time together, but he was sure she was endowed with an iron resolve and strength of character that would handle his disability with the love and tenderness she had displayed for him in that time.

He waited nervously for Frances to appear, unsure how she would react to finding her husband, the rugged, powerful outdoors man, previously fit and whole, now minus his right arm. He was now determined that it would make no difference to his outlook on life, after all he was very lucky to be alive at all. He should have died five or six times during his active service, including his reckless charge at the attacking Japanese troops.

Another reason to be thankful was, being spared the extent of injuries some of the poor bastards had, that had made the journey home with him on board the hospital ship Manunda. Some of those poor blokes were coming home with shocking burns, multiple amputations, blinded or insane. No, he was going to be okay. In fact, he thought he could look quite distinguished with a sleeve pinned up. Besides which, he was coming up to 25 years of age, with his whole life ahead of him.

He waited nervously, nonetheless, in the hospital foyer for Frances to arrive. As he waited with a bunch of equally nervous walking wounded for their loved ones to arrive in the bus they were told was on its way, he chatted with the other fellows about nothing.

Finally, here they were, alighting from the dusty old bus painted in drab army brown hues. The passengers were mainly women who stood about in a loose group, a little bewildered with a strange expectant look of concern and happiness as they sought out their man, or someone who would take charge and provide some direction. The old bus rattled off to the parking bay to wait for them after their visit.

It didn't take long for Lawrence to spot Frances among the group of women. She stood out like a rose in an onion patch, as he told her later when they were alone. She, ever the lady, chided him for being unkind to her sisters on the bus. Frances was looking wonderful in the bright spring sunshine crossing the forecourt toward him. She hadn't spotted him yet, so he had a chance to drink in the beauty of his wife and once again thank God for this gorgeous addition to his life. Please, just one more thing God, keep her love for me alive and true.

The group of soldier patients began to separate and join their partners, leaving Lawrence standing alone in the bright sunlight smiling at his wife. Lawrence was a good deal leaner than when he was fully fit prior to embarkation and still deeply tanned. His face was lined with the stress and pain he had endured in the previous few months. Suddenly Frances' eyes locked on him and lit up with instant recognition. With remarkable self-control, she met him halfway across the space between them. As he moved to her, she threw her arms around him and it was only then that she felt rather than saw his empty sleeve.

Involuntarily, she jumped back, her hand to her mouth as she gasped in shock. Tears sprang to her eyes as she took in her husband's loss and pain. She wrapped her arms around him again and kissed him passionately. He crushed her to him with his one remaining arm. She apologised for her initial reaction and he assured her it was natural and of little consequence. What really mattered was that he was here with her now, almost in one piece and he laughed.

He told her of his determination to continue life as normal and how lucky he felt himself to be, compared to the horrific injuries born by the poor devils that sailed out of Port Moresby with him and how he had reconciled himself to his loss and swore that it wouldn't make any difference to who he was and what his ambitions were.

Unlike many of the men Lawrence fought beside, he had only been away from home a relatively short time, but it had seemed like an eternity to Frances and those at home waiting for him. They walked and talked and became reacquainted with the reality of each other. Lawrence drinking in the sweet aroma of her and she aware of his now much slimmer form, the result, no doubt of the stress and pain he had endured. She determined immediately that she would nurse him back to full health when they were finally reunited at Chatsworth Park.

Eventually, Lawrence was passed fit and given leave to return home. His father had sent a vehicle to transport the happy couple into Sydney where he had made arrangements for his son and daughter-in-law to stay at the Australia Hotel, and instructed the staff to ensure they enjoyed a premium dining experience in the hotel's restaurant.

Lawrence had eaten little but army rations and the sight and smell of the simple, but enticing food coming out of the hotel's kitchen had him literally drooling. Despite war time rationing, Sir Alexander's influence guaranteed a quality meal for his home coming war veteran. After they had eaten the delicious food and washed it down with a second bottle of his father's vintage wine, they made their way to their room for the first night together in over a year. The love-making was gentle, warm and considerate, culminating in an extremely passionate re-consummation of their love.

In the morning, after a relaxed breakfast, Frances made arrangements to travel back to Chatsworth Park. Sadly, it involved a train trip and not a chauffeured limousine she felt he deserved, but he made no complaint and was lost in the wonder of his beautiful wife. At the station they were met by Alexander in the reliable old buggy and they set off for home.

Old Alexander was overcome with emotion and shock to see his son's injury, but being the resolute man he was, he tried desperately to stifle his emotions on seeing him for the first time, but failed miserably.

Tears coursed down his cheeks, to his great embarrassment, as he blubbered and stuttered, trying to make a manly job of welcoming him home. Eventually, they all burst into laughter and he thumped Lawrence heartily on the back then pulled up, full of apology, hoping he hadn't caused his son pain. Lawrence put his mind at rest and said that should be the last time he makes any allowance for his disability.

Lawrence and Frances Parnham reignited their life, interrupted by war, back at Chatsworth Park. The estate had been blessed by the assistance of the wonderful Australian Women's Land Army that had assured the continuity of the station's main product; the wool which was used for uniforms, blankets and dozens of different essential items. The land army ladies were paid by the estate and their services replaced the labour of the men who had gone into military service. There had been a severe drought in coastal New South Wales during the war years of 1939-1945, however, Chatsworth Park was fortunate in that they had access to plentiful bore water, and being close to the Parramatta River, they were able to get through without too much stress to their flocks. Cattle numbers had been reduced when the weather forecasts predicted low rainfall and market prices were high.

Importantly, the precious merino flock were sustained and in fact, increased under the stewardship of their new attendants whose exuberant and enthusiastic input provided Winifred and Frances with a lot of cheerful company and some very funny events. The girls were not given the job of shearing the pure bred merinos, as the risk of damage from razor sharp shears was too high in amateur hands, but they pitched in by gathering the clip and after a bit of giggly practice, could throw it out onto the table for the wool to be picked clean of burrs. Lambing time was another source of hilarity and lots of oohs and aahs for one and all as the women played midwife to a flock of birthing ewes.

Alexander spent much of his time away in Canberra attending to affairs of state and establishing Chatsworth Agricultural Co Pty Ltd, through which most of his current and future business revenues would flow. By 1942, with the nation facing the unprecedented war emergency, the Commonwealth government began assuming far greater powers, including the vital power of collecting income tax, formerly collected by the states.

This alone was enough to ensure increased future commonwealth domination of the federal system. During the war years, more than 130 members and future members of the Parliament of New South Wales served in the Australian military forces. Some remained serving members whilst in the military.

Meanwhile, Winifred had been keeping the home fires burning, along with Frances. Lawrence's time away had passed with agonising slowness, but as usual, time on the station was marked by the rhythm of weather and the seasons. This was wartime farming which was a little different due to the demands and expectations of a nation at war.

Lawrence had been home for some time and the farming activities continued on around him. He settled into the study and began taking an interest in the management of the breeding stock and keeping those important records up to date. He was still suffering terribly from war neuroses which, in those days, was called all sorts of things but in essence was Post Traumatic Stress. He endured the agonies of phantom pains where his arm had been, but was weaning himself off pain killers and had rationed himself to very little alcohol, taking a single malt scotch into the study to be enjoyed after dinner.

It was about three months after his arrival home that a telegram came to Chatsworth Park, addressed to Lieutenant L G Parnham, requesting his presence at Battalion Headquarters.

Lawrence telephoned the author of the missive to find out what was going on. As he had been discharged, it was unusual to receive mail addressed to him by his old rank. As he suspected, it was in relation to the gallantry award he had been told he was to receive. This had been advised in a formal letter he was sent sometime after his home-coming.

Lawrence had kept quiet about the matter, not even speaking to Frances about it.

He had a clear memory of most of his time in the field, except for that one passage of time that remained a blank to him. He had come to the realisation that it was his capture and subsequent torture by the Japanese that he could not recall. There was a technical psychological term for this, but he just couldn't recall it. Something to do with shock.

His rescuers had told him the soldiers of his platoon who had survived the original onslaught of the Japanese attack, had been beheaded and he had been handed some extremely rough treatment by the enemy. As he was about to meet his ultimate fate, the Australian patrol tracking a Japanese unit in the area had come along fortuitously and rescued him after a fierce fight.

Medical opinion given by an army psychologist was that the horror of seeing these poor men slaughtered and the torture Lawrence had endured, had caused him to suffer amnesia. Later research will reveal more truths about Lawrence's condition. In a very complex area, about a third of patients with a mild head injury are reported to suffer "islands of memory" during which, the patient is capable of recalling only some events. Unlike a temporary episode of memory loss (transient global amnesia), amnesia can be permanent. This most likely came about by the repeated blows to the head inflicted on him by his torturer.

His dreams were still peppered by odd images he could not explain. The squat Japanese officer pressing his pistol against Lawrence's forehead, the sound of screams and shots and searing pain that would cause him to wake in a lather of perspiration.

But the strangest of the images that swam before his eyes was that of a hand holding a pen or pencil over a map, drawing symbols he did not understand and writing words and numbers he could not comprehend. All of which left him with a very uncomfortable feeling of apprehension and guilt, which he could not explain and the arrival of this summons, however flattering a gallantry award might be, it seemed to fan the flames of his discomfort.

Lawrence decided it was time to bring Frances into the full picture and asked her to join him in the study away from the rest of the household. The couple made themselves comfortable on the chesterfield couch with the sun entering the room over their shoulders, lending an incongruous brightness to the solemnity of Lawrence's revelation. He showed her the formal letter advising him of the intention to present him with the Victoria Cross. He watched for her reaction as she read it, once, then again, shaking her head in wonder. She was astonished he hadn't shared this with her earlier and was a little cross about it, but at the same time, extraordinarily proud of him and told him it was a fit reward for the loss of his right arm.

Then he handed her the telegram that had arrived that afternoon and about which she had been curious ever since. She read it with her vision blurred by tears of emotion. She felt a huge welling up of pride and a little anger at the man before her. He had no explanation for his reticence and brushed it off as a form of modesty and a feeling of unworthiness. He blathered the usual overly modest protestations that he couldn't have done it without the support of his men and anyone else would do what he did, until Frances closed her hand over his mouth and as a tear cascaded down her cheek, she told him he won the award for the very reason that he was prepared to sacrifice his life in order to protect his men.

He then argued that he had gone into an uncontrollable rage and wasn't sane at the time but she wouldn't accept that either. She went to the bookcase and took down the family bible and turned to John 15:13:

Greater love has no one than this; that someone lay down his life for his friends.

He thanked her for reminding him of his faith and revealed an obscure scriptural quote that he said he had written on the inside of his slouch hat. Deuteronomy 31:6:

Be strong and courageous. Do not be afraid or terrified because of them. For the Lord thy God goes with you.

Lawrence had read this before each mission or when he felt his courage ebbing.

Frances called him her knight in shining armour and she would organise their travel, but Lawrence had been told that, as this was a very big deal and the senior command and the army propaganda machine wanted to extract maximum publicity from his presentation, they were sending a car to take Lawrence and Frances into the city for the ceremony where the dignitaries and press awaited.

Frances packed a bag for them both and rang ahead to the Australia Hotel to reserve a room for them. Wartime shortages still applied while the war in the Pacific ground on. However, the Parnham's have a long standing association with the old hotel and she assured that a room would be waiting for them on arrival.

The military vehicle duly arrives and their bag was loaded into the boot while they occupied the rear seat. When they got to the city, Lawrence instructed the driver to take them to the hotel where they unpacked their bag and freshened up while the driver waited for them downstairs. Feeling a good bit more presentable, the couple were whisked away to Lawrence's battalion headquarters where he was met by the batman of two star Major General, Sir Geoffrey Steele, who saluted formally and directed the couple to another chauffeured vehicle. This time a Rolls Royce for heaven's sake! Lawrence asked for an explanation and was stone-walled by the officer who instructed the driver to move off. This was all part of the respect he would be shown during this important event. Lawrence leaned forward and asked the driver what their destination might be. The young soldier told him only that they were headed for Macquarie Street, Sydney. Frances recognised the address immediately and her nervousness turned to excitement. Of course, Government House!

Bennelong Point was surely one of the most spectacular patches of real estate in Australia, overlooking the harbour and its iconic and brutal looking bridge? The driver swung in through the ornate gates where a sentry threw a very snappy salute in their direction and they came to a stop in front of the ornate gothic revival portico of the governor's mansion. A footman stepped forward and opened the vehicle's door indicating that they should follow him.

They walked proudly into the foyer as Lawrence and Frances were met by an orderly who briefed them on the procedures of the ceremony. The valet, for that was what he was, informed Lawrence, in deferential tones, that the governor, on behalf of His Royal Highness, King George VI and in the presence of Major General Sir Geoffrey Steele, family members and fellow officers, would confer upon Lawrence the Victoria Cross.

Lawrence was light-headed and feeling a little intimidated. Frances was proud and excited, feeling flushed and nervous all at once. Reflecting her husband's proud military bearing, she straightened her shoulders, holding herself erect, aided by the pride welling in her chest. They were ushered forward and Frances took a seat beside her in-laws while Lawrence was invited to sit on a gilt chair with plush red padding. Seated behind him in the imposing hall, were several of Lawrence's fellow officers, headed up by Duntroon College Commanding Officer, Brigadier Eric Plant DSO & Bar OBE, his parents, Alexander and Winifred, who were similarly summoned and a number of men Lawrence identified as members of the press, armed with flash cameras and note pads. To one side was a newsreel camera man filming the ceremony that would be up on the silver screen in cinemas across Australia within the week. The next few minutes were a blur as a stirring patriotic speech was made by the major general, who then read the citation for Lawrence's award.

Frances was totally unaware of any of the actions that Lawrence had fought and could hardly believe what she was hearing about the man she loved. She knew he was made of sterner stuff but this was totally surreal.

Finally, Lawrence was called forward and he proudly stepped up, receiving a salute from the general which, of course, he could not return and bent forward in a respectful half bow. On straightening, he removed his cap. The governor came forward and an officer appeared at his side and opened a red velvet-lined jewellery style case which contained the instantly recognisable Bronze Cross with Crown and Lion Superimposed, and the simple motto: "For Valour".

The citation read:

While leading a patrol against the Japanese invaders in the hills to the north of Milne Bay airfields, New Guinea, Lieutenant Lawrence Parnham's patrol was ambushed by a large contingent of the seasoned enemy in a well-planned and executed attack, laying down sustained and intense machine gun and small arms fire.

The suddenness of the attack took the lives of several soldiers under Lieutenant Parnham's command. The ensuing battle was fought courageously under the direction of Lieutenant Parnham, whose discipline and training focused the fire from the Australian troops, forcing the Japanese back. At a critical point, Japanese reinforcement's arrived, gaining the upper hand.

An Australian unit under the leadership of Lieutenant Kerrison returning from another patrol joined into the fray on the Japanese outflanking them, after which the enemy retreated.

Parnham had sustained a serious wound to his right arm and despite this he continued to engage the enemy. Kerrison took his patrol in pursuit of the fleeing Japanese, leaving Parnham in charge of the walking wounded in a more secure position. The enemy had circled back and executed a savage attack on the depleted group and were certain to overrun the Australian contingent.

Lieutenant Parnham, at great risk to his own life, took up a weapon in his left hand, firing until it was out of ammunition. Reloaded by his Corporal, Parnham continued his suicidal attack and was seen catching a thrown enemy grenade, hurling it back into the enemy ranks. Then, with a fully-loaded Owen gun, he charged at the enemy. His fearless attack completely unsettled the enemy who wavered and then retreated in disorder. The troops, inspired by Parnham's selfless actions, rallied to provide additional support where their personal injuries allowed.

Without doubt, the incredible courage displayed by Lieutenant Lawrence Parnham in defence of his men, many of whom were disabled, saved the lives of many.

The whole story was detailed in military prose, highlighted by the intense fight where Lawrence, in defence of his wounded men, performed his heroic deed. The witnesses to the ceremony were speechless with admiration for Lawrence.

The governor pinned the medal with its striking crimson ribbon, to his chest with genuine words of congratulations, thanking him for his courage and service in defence of his country and stepped back as the gathered witnesses applauded reverentially and enthusiastically. Lawrence's head was spinning and he was having trouble staying in control.

Frances came to his side and kissed him modestly on the cheek, providing welcome support. His father and mother politely hung back waiting for the opportunity to join the line of admirers.

The investiture of the Victoria Cross was most often held at Buckingham Palace and presented by the monarch, but the war made that very difficult for a recipient from the southern hemisphere.

Lawrence would receive a letter from the palace congratulating him and this would be in pride of place in his home office. From now on, Lawrence would have to get used to the protocols that came with this extreme honour. If he remained in the service and entered a mess hall, for instance, all ranks would stand and salute a VC holder out of respect for the award. But he would be called on by his local Returned Services Club, schools and organisations on ANZAC Day in April and Remembrance Day in November, where he would be expected to make inspiring speeches to school children and civilians, reinforcing the ANZAC legend and reminding them of the sacrifices the men and women made to preserve their way of life.

The photographers moved in to take more shots, having shot a roll or two during the investiture. They started ordering the couple around.

'Stand here, look there, now look at each other.'

Frances looked adoringly at him. More photos, with proud parents and then with the general and maybe a couple in the grounds. Finally Lawrence called a halt. A steady stream of people have, awkwardly shaken his left hand and he had sat with a senior journalist, permitted to be there for the occasion, who conducted an in-depth interview digging into Lawrence's background. The majority of his questions were bland until he started to ask about family business and some pointed rumours about Alexander's business interests and hinted at a back room deal or two.

Lawrence begged off, declaring ignorance. He'd been at war and what the hell was the relevance of all this? He cut the interview right there and walked away angrily. Lawrence had just received a valuable lesson in not dropping his guard around the press.

His father had sprung into action, calling his press secretary to have the news planted in as many newspapers as possible, including the local Camden Chronicle and, with a small crowd of his father's publicists in tow, they set off to celebrate. Once again the Parnham family headed for their favourite watering hole, the Hotel Australia. Of course, the hero's proud wife stood by her man and both of them were temporarily blinded by flashbulbs popping as he posed on the top of a set of stairs, smiling proudly down at the press.

Alexander crashed into as many photos as possible being the old political hack that he was he was not going to miss any of the limelight reflecting from his heroic son.

This was their favourite watering hole, for good reason, where they made the most of a sumptuous dinner. The hotel's talented chef had performed miracles to prepare the meal for them. Alexander had sent ahead some prime pork and vegetables from the farm, plus fresh butter churned on the estate, wine from the family cellar and cheese produced by their industrious lady cook on the station. Now, all these goodies in the hands of the frustrated chefs who seldom saw such luxury products in these straitened times of rationing, turned out a feast fit for a king.

The politician in Alexander, with his political and native cunning, always made sure the kitchen and waiting staff and hotel management all shared in the spoils, thus they would always be assured of superlative service every time a member of the Parnham dynasty entered the hotel. They would remain premium hotel clients for many years and the glamour and prestige they brought with them ensured their standing with the management.

War time rationing ruled that butter, sugar, meat and a whole host of the products that a wealthy country like Australia took for granted before the war, were strictly controlled and, as usual, the unlawful seized the opportunity to make a fortune stealing those products and selling them on the black market. Alexander would never condone that, but he was not above greasing the wheels with the highly prized produce within his own domain when it counted.

The dining room was packed with federal MPs of all stripes and there was not one who did not wish to shake the hand of a VC recipient and be seen doing so. Many words were spoken, some of them genuine, Lawrence thought cynically, but of course, in reality, every man was looking for some collateral glory that would rub off on their own mundane lives. There was much credibility to be garnered by being personally acquainted with a soldier hero of Lawrence's standing, or taking shelter under the power and influence of his illustrious father Alexander Morris Parnham MP KC.

The evening was outstanding, even by Parnham standards and one or two important alliances were forged over a glass or two of Alexander's vintage shiraz. There was unanimous agreement that if Lawrence wished to stand at the next federal election, then his pre-selection was a foregone conclusion.

Lawrence would be receiving confirmation of his discharge soon and would no longer be a professional soldier and needed to find another outlet for his energies. The farm was not enough for him. He still wanted to serve his country and federal politics seemed to be a natural path for him to follow.

One Sunday afternoon, when Alexander was home for the weekend, Lawrence joined him with their preferred single malt scotch in the room that had become a study they shared. The station's business office was relocated to a separate part of the now sprawling building.

The father and son sat comfortably in two large leather chesterfield chairs drawn up to face the cavernous fireplace. The fire was throwing out the type of bone warming heat that only an open fire can give, its reflected light flickering through the golden liquid in the crystal glasses, tracing dancing patterns across their faces as they sipped the warming liquor.

Alex suggested Lawrence use his war record to build his public profile and stand for office in the forth-coming state elections. Alexander was a minister in the National Party which had formed a coalition with the Menzies United Australia Party which held power in Canberra, becoming the Liberal Party in 1944. He told Lawrence that with his distinguished war service record and his father's support, he stood a good chance to win the seat of Winnago which had once been held by his grandfather Jefferson for three terms.

The old boy was now deceased but his name still held sway as a respected and honoured MP, which would no doubt guarantee great support from the ranks of the party faithful.

Lawrence pointed out, however, with the powerful grip the Labor Party had on New South Wales under the leadership of William McKell, it might be an insurmountable challenge. The incumbent in their neighbourhood appeared rock solid as McKell had gained power by going after the rural seats the ALP had previously ignored. Alexander paid grudging respect for his son's insightfulness and had to agree with his summation.

Lawrence proposed another tactic taking a long term view. He wished to finish his degree with credits in commercial law. He would undertake a post graduate course to complete a Master of Business Administration and present himself as a premium candidate and party member with a couple of years in party service behind him. Alexander agreed it was a reasonable plan and pledged his support. He would appoint a station manager he had been interviewing to keep the family's agricultural fortunes ticking over. In the meantime, their respective wives would perform their part when called on to assist in the image building of their men and always present smiling faces at receptions and official functions.

Alexander was also quietly thinking that it would be tactful to step back a bit from some his business activities, which were beginning to attract unhealthy attention in some quarters. He wouldn't steer his son into those areas; a business manager was far more preferable, so that Alexander remained one or two removes from the business. He would need to find a suitable proxy, a trusted but slightly dull-witted acolyte that would soak up the attention currently being directed at him personally and could be relied upon to take direction from (and the fall for) Alexander and be discreet about it. Absolute loyalty would require his proxy to fall on his sword if necessary.

Lawrence informed his father that Frances was already working on their image, as she was with child and would present him with a grandchild. That would be great for their image for the next federal election. Alexander couldn't believe his luck. This was perfect and his publicist would work this into a dynastic thing.

Should the good Lord bless Lawrence and Frances with a son, Alex cynically thought, such a blessing would be worth a lot of votes. He was surprised that Lawrence seemed to be thinking the same thing in some way. The first thought he had was how the child would aid their election campaign. It's true the fruit does not fall far from the tree. The old politician had to stop and remind himself that he was required to be a grandfather first and congratulated his son on his impending fatherhood.

Lawrence continued preparing himself for his impending life in politics that he felt was **his to claim**. He excelled at Law and, although he found the studies required for his MBA interesting, he was driven to distraction by a boring lecturer and chose to seek out a competent tutor. On his graduation, he was very pleased to find he was in the upper five percentile.

His disability had not proved to be a problem. He took to writing left handed within a short time, and he refused to use it as an excuse for poor performance, even when he was suffering from the phantom pains in a limb that no longer existed.

Frances gave birth to a squalling, boisterous boy who quietened down once he got over the colic that seemed to be with him, from dusk to dawn in particular. **Gordon Alexander had a powerful set of lungs that came in handy later in life.** Lawrence took to sleeping at the other end of the house and when he had a particularly heavy workload, he would sleep in the three bedroom apartment they had since purchased in the city.

Several years later, Frances delivered a sister, Estelle Charlotte, for Gordon and a gorgeous daughter for Lawrence who was immediately infatuated by her little princess charms. **She was** a quiet and reserved little girl who delighted them both with her toddler ways.

And so the caravan of privilege and entitlement moved on. Life at Chatsworth Park continued through the seasons and many high quality clips were taken from the backs of their superb flock. The next generation of Parnham children grew and thrived. There were one or two seasons better than others, but old Jonas had selected his plot very wisely. There was ample water from the many bores on the station that kept the pastures in good shape and provided adequate hydration for the orchard and house gardens. They were never tempted to overstock in the good times, as some of their neighbours did who came to pay for their greed when their grazing land became degraded.

The plans Jonas had made, to spread his interests, paid off as well. Plots of land had been made available by the government and he had been a successful bidder once or twice. When the inevitable droughts came along, the wily old settler was able to rotate his flocks and some crops. Some of his land he put under grain or turned beef cattle out on the acreage and some he held only to sell for capital gain later.

Alexander followed the proven practices of his forbear and invested a large part of those gains into manufacturing businesses, such as wool processing and weaving. This diversity pulled them through all the ups and downs of a burgeoning new world economy.

Lawrence still suffered from recurring nightmares and, like many returned soldiers, he suffered in silence much to the frustration of his attentive wife who recognised that there was some deep seated problem that troubled him. He muttered strange things in his sleep and she could only catch partial phrases amid the groans and stifled screams that made no sense. When she tried to question him about it, he would become angry and break off any conversation, storming off to his office where she would find him later well into a bottle of scotch. She pleaded with him that he would not find the solution to his problems in the bottom of a whiskey bottle where he would drown his career aspirations.

After much self-recrimination and prayer, he seemed to pull himself out of that tailspin and move on. He had the utmost respect for his wife and he was learning to rely on her judgement in many ways. Lawrence swore a silent oath that he would never allow alcohol to rule his life, and although the horrors he had endured came back frequently to haunt him, he never again allowed himself to become intoxicated. He did continue to enjoy a fine wine and an occasional cold beer, but never hard liquor.

The war in the Pacific came to an end as America demonstrated to the Japanese the power of an atom bomb, code named Little Boy, delivered by the American B29 Boeing Superfortress **bomber called Enola Gay,** destroying the heart of Hiroshima and repeating the dose a few days later for the unfortunate Nagasaki. There were three potential targets for the bombs, two of which were withdrawn, one for religious reasons and the second due to weather. Nagasaki was a ship building city and a large military port but was considered unsuitable because of its topographical layout and it had been bombed by conventional weapons five times in the previous twelve months.

The decision to use this abhorrent weapon was hotly debated in Australia, as well as the US afterwards, and the consensus was that many more lives would have been lost in a mainland invasion of Japan than were lost in these dreadful explosions. The battle for Okinawa was an example of what could be expected as tenacious and fanatical Japanese defended their Emperor's homeland.

CHAPTER TWELVE

October 1942

The Royal Australian Navy decided to employ Fairmile ships to provide a fast craft for escort duties, anti-submarine activities and transporting commandos on raids against Japanese held bases. They carried a crew of 10-12 and at 115 feet in length, could get along at a fair clip. Their top speed depended on the power plant fitted, which could be either petrol or diesel that could be 16 or as quick as 29 knots.

One of the first Fairmile's to see action in New Guinea was built by Lars Halvorsen & Sons Pty Ltd at Green Point Naval Shipyard in Sydney. ML 817 was commissioned under the command of Lieutenant Athol Townley who earlier, had played a key role in sinking one of the Japanese midget submarines that had raided Sydney Harbour.

ML 817's last action occurred as Lieutenant Commander Townley took it out of Buna on the north coast, at the end of the Kokoda Track at dawn on September 3, steaming for Morobe, further up the coast. In Morobe Harbour, he placed his craft alongside the RAN corvette HMAS *Shepparton*. No sooner were the lines between the two vessels secured, than 35 enemy aircraft nine Mitsubishi bombers and 26 Zero fighters, swept in from the south- west and pattern-bombed both vessels. ML 817 was severely damaged and, given the lack of facilities, the decision was made to tow her back to Sydney for repairs.

ML 817 was towed across the Coral Sea to Townsville by the tanker *Trinity* in a convoy of ships, and then towed down the east coast to Sydney by the corvette HMAS *Deloraine*. On approach to the Northern Queensland coast, the crew aboard ML 817 noted a single Bristol Beaufighter passing overhead at 0810 hours on a heading of approximately 240 degrees. There were no other aircraft in sight and no enemy aircraft had been reported in the area for several days. The Beaufighter appeared to be flying straight and level and quickly disappeared out of view. The young replacement skipper noted the details in the ship's log.

***

Townsville Air Force Base control tower received a call from a single Bristol Beaufighter at 0825 hours passing inland at a height of 5000 feet and turning 160 degrees enroute to RAAF Station, Archerfield. The commanding officer on duty in the control tower put eyes on the Beaufighter through the control tower's high powered binoculars and reported that the aircraft was at the height reported and seemed to be flying straight and level. Strangely, the aircraft did not immediately turn onto its new heading and continued on, taking it further inland towards Charters Towers until it was out of sight. No response was received from the aircraft to Townsville Control's radio transmission requesting confirmation of its intended course.

Charters Towers airfield, 110 kilometres south west of Townsville, was utilised by various USAF units and the 431st Fighter Group P-38 Lockheed Lightnings were stationed there in the 1940s. Observers there reported a lone twin engine aircraft overhead, at first glance thought to be a Lockheed Hudson, or maybe a US B25.

It was flying straight and level at height and was seen to turn onto a heading of 170 degrees. When it came closer, they were able to identify it as a Beaufighter bearing RAAF squadron markings, LY S bracketing, a blue roundel against the jungle green and brown camouflage.

The pilot failed to respond to radio requests for identity. The Beaufighter continued flying straight and level and disappeared behind some alto cumulus cloud formations to the south. None of this information came to hand until several days after the Beaufighter was posted as missing, by which time the air search had been terminated and the focus was on more immediate matters.

The report hit the in-tray of a desultory clerk who was counting the minutes to lunch and decided, without reference to any superiors, that it was probably already known and immediately buried it under more reports and requests.

No further sightings of Big Bill's gallant Beaufighter were reported and he never arrived at his destination at RAAF Station Archerfield. The following day, the aircraft was reported missing and an air search was undertaken by aircraft from Townsville which included several Beaufighters, Catalinas and Hurricanes of 76 Squadron. The Catalina squadron had just suffered the loss of one of its own. A Catalina with a full crew and two passengers was lost while attempting to land in heavy seas. It was armed with several anti-shipping mines, one of which exploded on the aircraft's impact with the large waves causing massive damage and adding to the loss of life.

Several days were given to the search for the missing Beaufighter and, due to the rather vague last known position, Big Bill's plane was posted as missing presumed lost. His flight plan had indicated a change of course at Townsville to take him to RAAF Station Archerfield. They had to assume he had followed that track and the areas on either side of that was searched thoroughly without a result.

* * *

Lydia Cuthbertson received a telegram at Courtland Downs informing her of the circumstances surrounding her husband's missing aircraft. Family and friends rallied around to support Lydia during the early period of her grief. Hope springs eternal and until it was confirmed otherwise, they held onto the hope that their man was still alive somewhere. Bill was a man hardened by life in the outback and would not depart this earth without a massive struggle. The busy work load involved with the management of the station, plus caring for her energetic and not always well behaved son, left little time for self-pity.

That is not to say that she closed her heart. On the contrary, Lydia prayed for a miracle and mourned every minute of the day and tried hard to be cheerful for her family and her son. She grieved as any war time widow did at the loss of the husband she barely had time to know.

A commemoration service was conducted by their church, St Andrews in Longreach, attended by a huge representation from the local population, joined in their grief by members of the RAAF who had entered service with Bill. As the war had rolled on, telegrams became a sad regular feature of those times arriving at the door of more than one or two other unfortunate families around Longreach. Lydia, sadly, was just another left to grieve on her own, supported by Bill's parents and surviving sister, Elsie, at Courtland Downs.

Pretty soon the demands of station life and motherhood pushed her grief aside until she lay her head down at night and wept silently into her pillow. Sometimes, as toddlers do, little Robert would find his way into bed beside his mother and cuddle into her side, providing some measure of comfort for her as she stroked his little head, nuzzling his hair and inhaling his delightfully sweet baby scent.

Robert seemed to have inherited the very best of the Cuthbertson genes. He very soon became Bobby as it suited his boisterous personality and, still in nappies, he was more than a handful.

In later years, Bobby proved to be a good student, good at his lessons and popular at school. He was not the only child to lose a father or, for that matter, both parents in the war, but all the same, he was aware that something was missing in his life. He lived in a farming community and many of the parents had been exempt from war service as they were considered to be in an essential industry being the supply of foodstuffs to the nation. There were many of his school friends' parents in this category. Bobby came to appreciate that he was in a special group. ANZAC Day became a very sacred day to the family, at which time he heard about the exploits of his courageous father who had lost his life in the service of his country. As a war widow, Lydia was granted special attention on ANZAC Day and proudly wore her husband's service medals over her right breast, the highlight of which was the DFC for gallantry in the air war over Britain and Europe. She was always stirred whenever she heard the words of Winston Churchill in regard to the pilots of that crucial conflict:

Never in the field of human conflict was so much owed by so many to so few.

CHAPTER THIRTEEN

Days seemed to pass into yesterdays before they had time to appreciate them fully; they rolled out with a particular rhythm, dictated by the weather. The Thomson River had delivered flood waters to the station over their history with the land. Harold and Hettie, in their day, had battled a significant flood in 1893 with a subsequent flooding of the Thomson in 1906, 1949 and 1955. The floods and droughts came and went. Time was passing and Hugh and Frances were growing older, but their love for each other and their enthusiasm for life never dimmed. Their many happy years together saw a lot of hard toil, combating drought, floods and all the usual perils of outback Australia, which had worn them down in body, but not in spirit. No, never in spirit. Hugh was still an enthusiastic musician and life of the party. He and Frances allowed Lydia a decent period of mourning, offering hope at first and commiseration and comfort when reality came around.

There was no further communication from the RAAF despite her continuous letters beseeching them for information. Lydia had taken the problem to her local MP and even he was stonewalled by the military with some garbage about security. Big Bill was now presumed dead and, in the absence of his remains, she was without a formal death certificate as yet.

A person may be legally declared dead in absentia or a legal presumption of death declared, despite an absence of identifiable remains. Such a decision is typically made after a person has been missing for an extensive period of time, or after a much shorter period where the circumstances strongly support the belief that the person has died. For example, an airplane crash. And so it would be in the declared death of William Cuthbertson.

Lydia would need the death certificate if she were to receive a war widow's pension and the other benefits provided by the government. Lydia spent a lot of time in a frustrating battle with the pale and resentful bureaucrats who had spent the war shuffling paperwork and whose major physical threat came from a paper cut. Eventually, Hugh blew up, cursing the government's cold-hearted bureaucracy and assuring Lydia that she and Bobby would never go without.

She was a full partner in Courtland Downs and an important contributor to its success and as such, would benefit from its income and capital growth ad infinitum. Added to this of course, was the rather obvious fact Hugh stated firmly, that the station and all its assets were hers to inherit.

VP Day (Victory in the Pacific) is celebrated on 15 August. This date commemorates Japan's acceptance of the allied demand for unconditional surrender on 14 August 1945. For Australians, it meant World War Two was finally over and they celebrated with a nation-wide joyous party. The country's men and women, who had served their country, would soon be coming home to pick up their lives as civilians.

For the relatives of the not so lucky, life would become a hard, lonely road without a much loved partner or a life dedicated to assisting an incapacitated husband or son.

There were many women service personnel among the home comers who, to a greater or lesser degree, suffered the same. The world was about to change in a glorious prosperous way and, while the sacrifices and lessons of World War Two would never be forgotten, life moved on quickly.

The seasons came and went while Bobby grew like a weed, forging his own path through school and the local community. He was a robust little fellow with enough energy to drive a steam train. It went without saying that he had inherited the same spirit of adventure as his father and the talents of his mother. He developed into a gifted amateur musician, filling a spot in the Cuthbertson house band, both on piano and guitar.

Bobby attended his father's school and was an above average student. On the playing field he was not quite so robust as his father, having grown tall and lanky. His mother preferred the term 'loose limbed'. He excelled at athletics, especially the middle distance and mile runs. He loved the pressure and tactics of the mile. His idols were, of course, John Landy and later Herb Elliot and Ron Clarke. He was upset for Landy when Roger Bannister broke four minutes and went into the history books for it. John Landy ran 3.57.9 one month later.

Bobby continued to run and eventually had a fulltime coach sharpening his technique and teaching him tactics. They had fallen into a trusting relationship with his coach, Trevor Dunleavy, selecting the athletic carnivals for Bobby and organising transport and accommodation. All with an eye on the bigger picture, the nationals and what they led to. Bobby followed his father in one important way. He joined the local aero club, took flying lessons and soloed at the age of 16.

Flying became another passion and he quickly gained the endorsements to qualify him, firstly for a private pilot's licence and then he progressed through an instrument rating and several different types of aircraft, including twin engine ratings. At the age of 19, he had a commercial licence and gained many hours as an instructor at the Longreach Flying Club. He had progressed from a pesky kid who gained some flying time washing the planes, to a competent commercial pilot, introducing others to the joys of flying.

He had a yearning at the back of his mind that would only be assuaged by adventure. He wanted to do something monumental. Ever since he was a kid he read about the great Australian aviators like Harry Hawker, Bert Hinkler, Sir Charles Edward Kingsford Smith MC, AFC, and Charles Ulm.

There was one forgotten hero, Smithy's navigator, Gordon Taylor, who during the 1935 Australia-New Zealand air-mail flight, with Smithy and Ulm performed an amazing act of heroism. The starboard engine on the Fokker Trimotor had cut out when they were well into the crossing of the ditch and the portside engine was losing oil pressure.

Smithy calculated they were going to hit the water unless some miracle happened and the decision was made to turn back to Sydney. Taylor took a thermos flask out of the cockpit, balancing on the wing strut, he drained oil from the dead engine, passing it back to Ulm who poured it into a suitcase until there was no further oil available. At this point, Taylor climbed back into the cockpit and went out on the port side and transferred the liquid into that oil-starved motor, having battled the cyclonic wind generated by their forward motion on the starboard side and the backwash of the propeller on the port side. All the time, Smithy was using his almost otherworldly skills to keep them out of the freezing Tasman Sea that was now only 500 feet below them. The choice was simple, Taylor said, stay safe in the cockpit and die, as they inevitably plunged into the sea, or do what he did.

Taylor's actions, with the addition of Smith's flying skills, resulted in the plane making its way back to land safely. Taylor was later awarded the Empire Gallantry Medal which was later exchanged for the George Cross. He was knighted in 1954.

The history surrounding Bobby's local airfield was enough to inspire any lad to want to experience adventure. Longreach had seen the early aviation pioneers coming through on a regular basis and had provided the inspiration for his father, Big Bill, to become a pilot. There was a memorial plaque at the flying club in honour of William Cuthbertson, a graduate of the flying school who lost his life while serving the country.

Bobby would always touch the plaque reverentially for luck and mutter a prayer for the father he never knew, as he passed by.

Bobby persuaded his mother to continue the use of aircraft as commenced by his father. A lot of time had been saved using aircraft in the business of running the huge estate. It was hardly likely, in the circumstances, that Lydia would deny her son's request. After her eventual approval, he supervised the construction of an upgraded airstrip on the original piece of land that favoured the prevailing winds. Most large stations would have a strip that was basically a reasonably flat piece of ground with the grass smashed down. No lights or threshold markings, just a flat strip of dead grass.

Construction was probably a bit grandiose in describing the laying down of the Courtland Downs International Air Terminal, as they jokingly christened it. It had received approval for their private use from the aviation authorities but in no sense as a "major airfield". The slasher was employed to cut down the grass and then it was a process of driving up and down in a variety of farm vehicles until they had a reasonable flat and firm surface. Bobby further persuaded his mother to invest in a restored lovely little Gypsy Moth that was standing in a hangar at Longreach Airfield. To Lydia's astonishment, it turned out to be the very same aircraft that Bill had used to take her on a picnic all those years ago.

When she expressed concern about its condition, Bobby assured her it had been well maintained and loved by her current owner and had airworthy certificates to prove it. Aircraft of all types are subjected to very stringent maintenance programmes which must be completed after a certain number of flying hours. To be registered, an aircraft must present a certificate for the airframe, electronics and engine, all signed by the relevant engineer.

With the formalities completed, the Moth became the property of Courtland Downs Grazing. At home, a hangar was constructed from second hand materials to protect the delicate fabric of the Moth and keep the dust at bay and also provide storage for fuel and oil supplies so that Bobby would have a measure of independence from an official airfield. It was finished off with a crudely written sign, a sheet of galvanized iron with the legend "Courtland Downs International Air Terminal" to perpetuate the long standing joke.

Having established this set up, it was now up to him to prove the value of the investment by locating stray cattle and surveying the boundary fences, noting any breaks and marking them on a map that he would pass to the stockmen. They would then ride directly to the problem area and affect repairs, or recover the stock, saving many hours and stress on rider and mount.

Lydia was a nervous passenger when Bobby suggested he take her on a shopping trip to Longreach in the Moth. Accessing the forward cockpit was a little awkward as the upper wing was directly above it and Lydia felt less than ladylike as she wormed her way into it. It was only a short flight but she thoroughly enjoyed it, despite being sprayed with fine engine oil and having her hair flattened by the leather helmet Bobby insisted she wear. He impressed her with his flying skills and the short jaunt into town became a regular feature they both enjoyed. She told him she had flown with his father on just a few occasions as he was more intent on using the plane in the service of the station maintaining fences and locating stock.

Three days before his 22nd birthday, Bobby decided to take a little jaunt up north, drinking in the sights on the way to Charters Towers to another famous airfield. What could be better than flying a DH 60 Moth over the beautiful hinterland on a glorious September day? The expected temperature was high 20s, wind at height was about 10 to 15 kilometres per hour across his intended track. The distance to Charters

Towers was 430 odd kilometres and the range of his fully fuelled up Moth was 515 kilometres, giving him the mandatory fuel for a further 20 minutes flying time. The Moth's cruising speed of 135KPH gave him a travel time of just over three and a half hours. The forecast was good with the wind from the south east giving him a bit of a shove along. It should be a good flight on one tank with a refuel for the return trip. Bobby had been careful in his planning as it was starting to get to the limits of the Moth's endurance envelope.

Bobby lodged a flight plan with the aid of his chief instructor who talked him through the journey, reminding him of this and that and to be cautious on approach to Charters Towers as it was a busy commercial airfield and Bobby didn't carry a radio. After reviewing the latest weather reports, which augured well for his flight, the instructor wished him well and watched him taxi out to the duty runway. The tower signalled clear for take-off by semaphore and Bobby opened the throttle and rumbled down the runway lifting into the air. Climbing out at a steady 500 feet per minute, Bobby levelled out at 5000 feet and was cruising at 75 knots. The sun was well up in the east and the air smooth. Turbulence would increase later as the sun rose and sent thermals up from the ground to meet his fragile craft. His engine was purring along and things could not be better.

Three hours, 25 minutes after take-off, he was still plugging along into an unpredicted northerly that sprang up an hour earlier, increasing his fuel burn. He had tried to climb above it and descend below it but only succeeded in burning more fuel. He realised he might be in trouble if he didn't make Charters Towers very soon. He had crossed the Cape River which wound away to his right and emptied into the Dalrymple Lake. Just as he noted this navigational waypoint, the de Havilland Gypsy Moth motor spluttered, caught and spluttered again. Then the only sound was the whistling of the wind through the rigging. This was not like the movies; the plane didn't automatically begin to drop like a rock or make that peculiar whining sound the SFX guys used in every plane crash scene.

The Gypsy has reasonably good gliding characteristics giving Bobby a chance to take a good look around for a landing spot. He was still above 4000 feet but his altitude was peeling off quickly and he needed to make a decision. The ground below him was a bit hilly and the Great Dividing Range was in the distance, so he needed a lucky break.

The trick was not to turn too steeply in his search. In general, when a pilot was confronted with a forced landing, he would be wise to try to find his landing spot within a 15 degree arc of his nose. As soon as he adopted a steep turn, he would lose height very quickly.

A steep turn increases the risks of a stall as the wing stops developing lift efficiently. If this happens, the plane will stop flying and gravity will take over.

It was best to look for something under his nose. And right on cue, he saw what he is looking for. Here was a chance, a grass strip on a property just off to starboard. It was like winning the lottery. He just couldn't believe his luck. He began to set the plane up for the landing.

There was not a lot to do actually, except switch off the magnetos and fuel, just in case there was enough of it slopping about in the tank to cause a fire. Like most manoeuvres, landings were subjective. If you can walk away from it, the saying goes, then it was a good one.

Landings involved a number of actions that resulted in a gentle touch down. In a normal landing situation at an airfield, an aircraft joins the circuit area, a square pattern dictated by the prevailing weather. The pilot begins to ease the throttle, slowing the aircraft and lowering the nose. He must always maintain airspeed and keep the nose down slightly. Flaps, if you have 'em, are lowered on the final approach assisting to slow the aircraft and providing extra lift at the slower speed. As the pilot brings his plane in over the runway, he flares out by pulling back on the control column at the appropriate height. Then holding off until he achieves landing speed, the plane will sink gently onto the runway touching down in a three point landing. Simple really.

However, in Bobby's case, he was performing what the old timers called a "dead stick landing". By leaning his head out the left hand side, he could glance at the airspeed indicator and hopefully peg it precisely at 55 KIAS. That is, knots indicated air speed, and then he looked well ahead and occasionally over the bottom wing's leading edge, until he confirmed the right altitude of his plane to bring it down in a well-controlled glide. The little Moth was responding perfectly under Bobby's soft hands, descending gently towards the grass strip in the paddock. Thankfully, there were only a few livestock in the paddock well away from the well maintained strip.

He was rewarded with a satisfying thumping and bumping as the undercarriage met the ground and rumbled along the strip, which he found to be in better shape than his own home runway. It showed signs of regular use. He expelled a huge sigh of relief as he worked the rudder pedals while his plane still has momentum and turned it off to the left, clearing the runway. It was just a little courtesy in case another aircraft needed to come in behind him.

Climbing out of the cockpit, he took a look around at a pretty familiar scene. He was in the house paddock which had a deep pasture of dried grass with a couple of sheep allowed in to keep it down. It was only on his final approach that he caught sight of a substantial homestead obscured by trees on the other side of a small crest. He was grateful none of the sheep were on the strip as he landed, as he would have had no way to go around until they cleared. To his right was a small empty hangar, again in a bit better shape than his own and a fuel storage shed kept separately for fire safety. There is a path leading from this area up to the homestead about 300 yards away and the dogs were barking crazily at this interloper.

Bobby saw a young woman coming through the gateway and heading towards him. As she drew near, he was struck by her wonderful, good looks, straw-coloured hair to her shoulders, a delightful slim figure and tanned skin against deep green eyes. She looked like a cover girl for Town and Country magazine.

As she walked up to him, she blessed him with a gorgeous smile displaying a perfect set of gleaming white teeth and put out her right hand and welcomed him to Beverly Downs. Before he knew it, he is sitting at her kitchen table with a cup of tea and a generous slice of boiled fruit cake, gushing out his life story like a fool.

He was completely in her sway and a good way along to being totally smitten. She had offered him fuel and he used her phone to call both Charters Towers and Longreach airfields to advise them of his plight. But right now he couldn't care less if he was stuck there forever.

Her name was Joanne Wheatley and the property was owned by her parents, Richard and Esther, who were in town taking care of business and expected to return fairly soon. She insisted that since his aircraft was out of action for the moment, he would naturally be welcome to stay for dinner and, of course, she would find him a bed in the shearers' quarters to stay overnight as opposed to sleeping under the wing of the Gypsy Moth. He accepted her kind offer instantly and then hoped he was not being too obvious, but she was totally charming and he began to relax. In fact, he had never felt this comfortable in the company of a woman, and a damned attractive woman at that, in his life.

He was snapped back to reality as the screen door slammed back and Joanne's parents walked in. Her old man didn't look too happy. Her mother followed close behind and appeared close to tears. They saw they had a guest and their demeanour changed immediately, replaced with wide, welcoming smiles. Bobby stood, feeling a little awkward and offered his right hand which was crushed by Wheatley's huge hand.

Joanne leapt up and went to her mother to see what was wrong with them. Her father was angry and upset because dingoes, or stray dogs, had been amongst his herd and savaged a couple of new born calves that he had to put down due to their injuries. He excused himself while he got on the phone, calling the local dog trapper to come and clean them out. He believed they were still in the area and if the professional trapper was quick, he might do them some damage. Bobby, at the age of nearly 22, had garnered enough experience of rural life that such matters were commonplace. He had heard the conversation almost like déjà vu as he'd made that sort of call himself several times.

With the phone call over and arrangements made, he remembered his manners and introductions were properly made. Joanne gave an explanation of Bobby's unexpected visit.

Mr Wheatley suggested it would be a good idea, while the sun was still up, that they give the Moth a good going over to check for damage. It was the responsible thing to do and Bobby should have done it himself if he hadn't been so infatuated with the beautiful Joanne.

The two men set off and on the way Bobby was quizzed about his background and Mr Wheatley, who said his name was Richard and to please call him Dick, was pleased he had another cattleman in his presence. Dick told Bobby that the Wheatley family were heavily engaged in aviation as well. He had an instrument rating in twin engine aircraft and his son, Harvey, was working his way towards a similar level.

After a thorough examination, they gave the plane a clean bill of health, and while they were at it, Dick offered to refuel it and wheeled a drum, fitted with a hand pump and filter, out of the shed.

Bobby climbed aboard, standing in the cockpit and inserted the fuel line into the tank in the middle of the upper wing. The tank held just on 19 gallons and in no time, she was fully fuelled again. The next thing to be checked was the oil level. The Gypsy Moth's inverted engine drank it like water. That taken care of, Bobby swung the prop around a few times to get gas up to the carburettor. Older planes of the Gypsy's era lacked a starter motor and were started by swinging the propeller. Bobby asked Dick if he would be so kind. He obliged cheerfully, being well familiar with the process and after a couple of coughs and splutters, the Moth roared into life. Bobby let it tick over for a while then shut it down for the night.

Back at the house, dinner was nearly ready and Bobby was offered the use of the bathroom in the shearers' quarters to clean up. Over dinner, much family and farming information was discussed and exchanged. Rainfall, cattle prices, wool clips and all the subjects that occupy the mind of the pastoralist, including politics and matters looming in Asia. After an eternity, Dick and Esther, retired to the sitting room to watch the ABC TV news, leaving Bobby and Joanne to chat.

They were strongly attracted to each other and even before he retired for the night, they had made arrangements to get together again for a barn dance that would be held in the townshipin in two weeks' time.

After a restless sleep, Bobby showered and politely knocked before entering the kitchen where breakfast was already on the go. He enjoyed a light breakfast and thanked the Wheatley's for their hospitality. They were impressed by the young man and invited him to call any time at all, but controlled landings were preferred, chuckled Dick.

As another farming family using aircraft extensively in their day to day affairs, Joanne's brother Harvey was away in the family Cessna with a couple of mates attending a cattleman's forum in Townsville. Richard had a Beech Bonanza which was being serviced and was kept permanently at Charters Towers. Dick had extensive business interests up and down the coast and was required to attend board meetings in Brisbane regularly so the Bonanza was his main means of transport.

Joanne walked down to the airstrip with the men. Bobby shyly pecked her on the cheek and thanked her again then said his farewells. Dick swung the prop and the reliable little plane came alive once more. After assessing the wind direction, Bobby waved goodbye and roared off down the runway. Lifting off, he climbed to 100 feet and circled back over the heads of his new friends, waggling the wings. They saw his arm over the side of the cockpit still waving as he headed north toward his original destination.

Charters Towers had been alerted to his ETA and approach by telephone earlier. The control tower noted the impending arrival from the south and if need be they would alert any aircraft in the area to maintain clearance from him.

Bobby overflew the airfield, checking the windsock and confirming the duty runway at 1500 feet and joined the circuit on the dead side, coming down to 1000 feet on the downwind leg and completed his pre-landing checks. Satisfied, he turned on base and began his descent. He was scanning the sky all round him but there was little air traffic. Now, he was on final approach and shaping up nicely on the duty runway.

Following the usual procedures, he flared out and anticipated the thump of the main wheels on the tarmac when suddenly, the Moth yawed hard around to starboard in an unexpected cross wind. The undercarriage hit sideways and tore off; the port wing tip hit the ground hard and snapped off mid wing and the Moth responded by going in a crazy ground loop to port. The broken wing hit and dug in as the momentum carried the fuselage up and over, landing on its back.

Emergency services were already in motion as Bobby hung down unconscious from his harness. The danger now was fire and rescuers had to get him out ASAP.

A fire fighter, clad in protective clothing, supported his weight while a second guy felt for the release on his harness, which let go with a loud click and Bobby was hauled away to safety. He regained some level of consciousness, although very hazy, aware only that he had crashed and appeared to be inside some sort of vehicle, perhaps an ambulance. Then darkness closes in again.

Crash investigators photographed and recorded all the relevant details, witnesses were interviewed and contact details noted. When there was nothing further to be noted, the wreckage was hauled away and stored at the back of a hangar out of the way. Engineers would pore over the aircraft remains, looking for mechanical faults and file their reports. As with all incidents like this, the aviation authorities conducted a thorough investigation into Bobby's accident and tried to determine a cause.

The Wheatley's had been notified of Bobby's spectacular arrival at Charters Towers and were shocked by the news. Joanne, in particular, was very upset to hear of the handsome young man's accident. She had felt a strong attraction to him in the few hours they had spent together.

His emergency landing at Beverly Downs would be brought into question and he would be queried as to how heavy the landing was and if there was any damage incurred that could have had an influence on his crash at Charters Towers. Dick Wheatley was interviewed along these lines and his experience and forthright no-nonsense manner carried the day. The conclusion was that the aircraft had been overpowered by a sudden gust of wind from an unexpected direction at a critical point of its approach. There was no fault put on the pilot's performance leading up to the moment of impact that could conceivably be considered reckless or careless. The control tower would normally have signalled the Gypsy Moth with a flare to warn him off had they been aware of the danger, but the contrary gust came in too quickly for them to act in time.

The verdict was given as an unavoidable accident.

It was too late now, of course, but the problem could have been avoided had Bobby installed the VHF radio sitting in its box in the shed back home. The tower had observed the contrary cross wind and, in all likelihood, would have called him to go around until it settled. Having a radio on board was a cheap and far more reliable and direct system than a primitive flare. Always too much to do and too little time to do it in, well now he would have plenty of time to think about the folly of his attitude. No doubt, his mother would have a bit to say on that subject as well.

He woke in the local hospital and found his mother sitting by his bed and a nurse fussing about with a drip. The news was that the Moth could be a write off but it had been recovered. The wreckage sat forlornly at the back of a hangar waiting for the decision from the insurance company. The aviation authority's investigation would also determine its fate and the fate of Bobby's pilot's licence. The result of the official investigation would go a long way to assisting his insurance claim and also avoid the loss of licence.

On a personal front, Bobby had some spinal bruising but no breaks. His left arm, however, was not so lucky and was encased in plaster. He had a nice pair of black eyes and ten stitches in his cheek that would leave a rather dashing scar.

Bobby had been training seriously with a local athletic club and had competed in many carnivals around the state, rarely being beaten over 1500 metres, which was his pet event and he was being seriously touted as a hopeful for the 1968 Mexico Olympics. His coach was on the phone to the hospital twice a day monitoring his progress and pestering doctors for information. The spinal damage was the greatest concern and he would have to wait until he had undergone further x-rays and consultation with specialists and a fair bit of physiotherapy. It would be a long, tough comeback if he was still serious about running in Mexico.

No one suggested for a moment that his flying should cease or even be curtailed; in fact all the discussion so far had been about a replacement aircraft for Bobby. If it were possible, they would want to restore the Moth which had so much significance to the family history, having been the plane Bobby's late father had learned to fly in.

Eventually at home once again, and after much research, discussion swung around to the idea of one of the new light helicopters that were in use on one or two of the massive million acre Northern Territory stations. In the meantime, they would stick with fixed wing and a search began to find a Cessna 172 with its high wing configuration, making it suitable for the work envisaged for it and its ability to carry several passengers or some light cargo.

Aviation wasn't the only thing developing in the Cuthbertson family, as they prepared to welcome a new member. Joanne Wheatley has become something of a fixture at Courtland Downs after she recovered from the shock of Bobby's prang. She was studying commerce at the University of Queensland and would spend time between studies with her family, or with Bobby, who would fly up to her family property in his new airplane.

And so it would seem that cupid's arrow had struck its target and Bobby had found his life's partner. He couldn't have been happier except for one thing. The damage to his spine in the crash caused him to suffer a lot of pain and discomfort and impeded his ability to run. It would improve in time, his doctors and therapists assured him. But to the immense disappointment of his running coach, he would never compete on the cinder track again.

The two love birds were joined in holy matrimony, presided over by the minister of Wheatley's church, at the homestead in a simple but moving ceremony attended by Bobby's family and select friends. Bobby's best man was a mate from school; a roguish character called Jigger McKenzie who flew in, like most of the guests, in his own plane to the Wheatley's airstrip that took on the resemblance of a major airfield with an unprecedented number of planes parked randomly about.

Jo had defied her father's advice and dropped out of uni and dedicated herself to becoming the partner in Bobby's commercial life, as more responsibility for Courtland Downs fell on his shoulders. Publicly, Bobby wasn't too happy about her leaving her commerce degree behind, but was secretly pleased to have as much time, as the new arrangements allowed, with her at Courtland Downs. It was a bonus.

Her brother Harvey was stepping up at her parents' property as a full partner to Richard, who wanted to slow down and pull back from his farming and business activities to spend more time with Esther, who wanted to see the world by cruise ship.

So, before too long, a new generation began to make its mark on the Australian grazing landscape. Eighteen months into their marriage Joanne announced that she was pregnant. Bobby was over the moon and his mother, who thought she would be an old woman before she saw grandchildren, danced with joy. William Grant Cuthbertson announced his arrival on the property in the usual high pitched squalling way. He was a big, healthy lad of nine pounds five ounces and perfectly formed.

Life in the Cuthbertson household changed for the better with the injection of the energy young William was pumping out. He ruled the roost, as the saying goes, but was never naughty, just a tad demanding and delighted in being chased about the large verandahs dodging between the cane furniture, squealing with excitement.

Hugh was in the twilight of his years now and here he was with a great grandson whom he adored and loved to nurse on his bony old knees. His surviving son, George, who had returned to Australia at this time after many years in the UK, competed with his father for William time.

George had never wed. He was in fact gay and had lived happily in London with a life partner, who sadly passed away from a severe asthma attack. George, who had been working as a public servant, was devastated at his loss. He sold all his goods and chattels and liquidated his UK assets and headed home to Australia. He was the sole beneficiary of his partner's extensive estate, which left him financially independent. He was delighted, on the other hand, to be reunited with his younger sisters and to meet his brother's son for the first time. He was equally delighted to be on hand to welcome William's sister, Elise, into the household, born two and half years after her brother.

George became restless and eventually left Courtland Downs, purchasing an elegant apartment in Sydney, where he started a small business consultancy and ultimately met a new partner. He had had an extraordinary war time career, working as a code breaker at Bletchley Park and had conducted himself honourably as a British public servant. His mind was still as sharp as a tack and his small clientele were appreciative of his intelligent insights.

George was a lover of fine art and classical music and was seldom happier than when he had a book in his right hand and a glass of quality shiraz in his left. Australian cuisine was still in a development phase but if one knew where to look, good cuts of meat and ample supplies of spices and condiments and, of course, fresh seafood was in abundance and easily obtained from the busy Sydney fish market. All that remained was to have the ability to turn these basics into something gourmet. George had enjoyed the cuisine offered in European restaurants and, in particular, the French provincial cooking style.

It was while attending an advanced cooking class that George met his new partner, Phillip, who had been demobbed from Z Special Forces Unit. He had been a member of that legendary force that conducted the famous Operation Jaywick raid on Singapore Harbour against the Japanese shipping. Twenty three of his comrades were killed in action, or by execution after capture, in the ill-fated Operation Rimau, again on Japanese shipping in Singapore Harbour.

Phillip was a quiet man whose waters ran deep. It took George a long time before he could say he knew him well. But they were a well-balanced couple who both possessed a level of intellect that led them to appreciate the finer things in life. Phillip steered away from society gatherings and celebrity seeking people.

George was always an elegant dresser, perfectly groomed and well-spoken . Life on a cattlestation was not for him. He was not overtly gay and, unlike Phillip, he enjoyed the company of the beautiful socialites of Point Piper who were pleased to have George as an attentive and amusing partner at the many social events he was seen at. His handsome, smiling face was seen in the social pages, always with a gorgeous creature on his arm. But when the soiree was over, George would make his way to his apartment to spend the rest of the evening with Phillip among the society he really preferred.

CHAPTER FOURTEEN

Lawrence Parnham's star rose quickly through the ranks of federal politics. The little crimson patch and empty right sleeve gained immediate attention wherever he went and whatever gathering he was invited to attend. The combination of the two eye catching items opening many doors for him and gaining much attention with voting constituents leading to a few extra votes no doubt. He was, as one of his mentors said crudely, a bloke who literally gave his right arm to be in politics, altogether a real vote grabber. There was no doubt about his commitment to his king and country and his skills as an orator grew daily, berating Labor for their tardiness in addressing post war shortages The election hinged on the policies of the Federal Labor Government, especially bank nationalisation.

Prime Minister Chifley intended to bring all the banks under government control, a socialist policy which the coalition argued was not in the country's interest. The coalition promised to end unpopular wartime rationing. The election took place against the background of the 1949 Australian coal strike, the developing Cold War and growing fears of communism.

Lawrence stood as a Country Party candidate for the federal seat of McQuillan and was part of the winning coalition under Robert Menzies. Lawrence was an advocate of opening migration to non-European races, a view supported by Immigration Minister, Harold Holt.

In 1949, as the new Immigration Minister, Holt's decision to allow 800 non-European refugees to stay, and Japanese war brides to be admitted, was the first official step towards a non-discriminatory immigration policy.

Lawrence's performance during the election, and in the first one hundred days in the Lower House, was coming to the attention of the coalition power brokers and he found himself being invited to dinners and club functions and sounded out by the different interest groups struggling for ascendancy.

Sir Alexander Morris Parnham MP KC, having been knighted by King George V, was a powerful influence in the support of his decorated son and made sure all those that mattered were available to meet with him and educate him in the ways of federal politics. The old adage, 'keep your friends close and your enemy's even closer', was conceived in a government or political party somewhere and had particular currency in post war Australian politics. Machiavelli had been a long time pin up boy in Australian politics, seen almost as a user's guide to survival in the treacherous corridors of power and extra copies of *The Prince* were always on order in the parliamentary library. *The Art of War* by Sun Tzu, was another well-thumbed treasure trove of advice on survival in life or warfare.

Lawrence, by now, had developed a valuable network that was made up of legal colleagues, fellow politicians and business people on top of the vast network of acolytes cultivated by the Parnham philanthropy. He also cultivated relationships with some members of the press by leaking a little bit of information here and a rumour or two there. In turn, he was always guaranteed column inches in the major dailies.

It wasn't long before he started to build a file on people of particular interest or influence. This file would be very handy when a particular piece of legislation was being debated. A quiet word about the contents was marvellous lubrication for such sticky moments. This, he thought, was a natural part of politics and not the least bit dishonourable. The earliest lesson learned at the feet of his father was that politics was the art of compromise and he became an expert at obfuscation, convolution and circumlocution. The trick was to slip by a dangerous question while seeming to answer it.

The outgoing Prime Minister, John Curtin, reinforced the philosophy of the White Australia policy, saying, 'this country shall remain forever the home of the descendants of those people who came here in peace, in order to establish in the South Seas an outpost of the British race.'

During World War Two, many non-white refugees entered Australia. Most left voluntarily at the end of the war, but many had married Australians and wanted to stay.

The Immigration Minister of the newly created immigration portfolio sought to deport them, arousing strong protests. However, the major period of government during this time sponsored post-war immigration to provide much-needed population growth and labour, and resulted in a progressive relaxation of the policy as they sought further migrants from different sources.

Lawrence made this cause his own personal crusade and spoke passionately about the benefits the different cultures would bring. His support for increased immigration struck a chord with his constituents on the land who depended on the cheap, hardworking labour and supported him unstintingly at elections.

His ardent speeches in the house almost invariably made the newspapers and his popularity with the public on both sides of politics was undeniable. It certainly had Harold Holt looking over his shoulder at this fire brand from country New South Wales.

Lawrence's second, and no less dedicated cause, was for the welfare of returned service men and women, and the widows of those that did not return to their homeland. He was particularly passionate in his support for those wounded and incapacitated, as one would expect. He created draft legislation submitting them to his party executive and driving his ideas through with an unflinching determination and boundless energy.

Chatsworth Park, meanwhile, continued to prosper. Lawrence was a canny business man and was careful to avoid any conflict of interest matters but it was almost unavoidable that opportunities would be put before him by supporters and favour seekers. By carefully cherry-picking these commercial arrangements and placing them under the control of a shelf company in the name of his wife and his accountant, he skated around the strict interpretation of the law but possibly not the standards of morality that he would often demand of others in the Lower House.

Politics is the art of compromise and principles were often the first casualty. In sport, honour was encapsulated in the phrase, 'In the spirit of the game'. In other words, if the rules of play were stretched, was it in the spirit of the game?

The Parnham family were generous citizens who were unstinting in their philanthropy, beginning with Jefferson Gideon, Alexander's father who in his day endowed a Professorship in Veterinary Science at Sydney University. Sir Alexander continued to build on this reputation for generosity and in a similar manner endowed the law school with a trust fund that would enable a scholarship to be presented to a student coming from humble backgrounds who had shown academic promise.

Over time, one or two of these students on being admitted to the bar, found a position waiting for them in Sir Alexander's spacious and prosperous chambers. Another unspoken qualification for the scholarship was the potential student's political alignment, and in this manner, cunning Sir Alexander built a small coterie of like-minded sharp minds who were astonishingly loyal and would work like the dickens for long hours on his latest crusade.

Sir Alexander's reading of the tea leaves in social development and change had been very acute and he detected an opportunity very early in the cause of the suffragettes. He had canvassed for support for a female to stand for election which came to pass in 1918. This was a big feather in his cap and for the rest of his political career he enjoyed the support of female voters. He rewarded their support by giving his weight in parliament to women's rights across a whole range of important revisions and legislation that would benefit families and, in particular, widows and orphans.

His work led to the expansion of services the Royal Hospital for Women could offer as a principal teaching hospital of the University of NSW in the fields of obstetrics, gynaecology and neonatology. The Royal has a history to this day of innovation in women's health care services, teaching and research.

As a leading Sydney barrister, Alexander had been appointed King's Counsel and taken silk in 1910. This important addition to his profile carried a lot of weight and brought him many prosperous clients who contributed to the growing wealth and influence of the Parnham dynasty in New South Wales. At the age of 55 in 1930, he was rewarded for his contributions to his society and the development of his country and the welfare of its citizens. He was knighted by King George V at a ceremony at Buckingham Palace and became Knight Bachelor Sir Alexander Parnham MP KC.

The Parnham family was now considered, by all who mattered, to be a first family of New South Wales who would bow their heads to none. Wealth, fame, influence and empirical honours established, the Parnham name was part of Sydney society. Sir Alexander and Lady Winifred were among the first on any invitation list, being also on first name terms with everyone of any consequence from the Prime Minister and Governor of New South Wales to the Lord Mayor of Sydney and so on down the social scale.

The crowning jewel of the Parnhams and their greatest pride was their heroic son, Lawrence Garret Parnham VC. An amazingly popular politician in his own right who enjoyed movie star adoration from the working classes, who he staunchly and generously defended. He was particularly supported by migrant groups who appreciated the tremendous work he performed on their behalf and as a result, Lawrence was an honoured guest at many ethnic religious celebrations, plus the weddings and christenings of the children or grandchildren of community leaders he had supported and promoted.

Nothing could throw a shadow over this family whose forebears had been pioneers and who had been major contributors in the development of the nationally important fine wool industry. The Parnham family provided jobs and futures for the descendants of the first settlers upon who they continued to bestow their generosity and paternal guidance wherever it was needed.

In August 1963, Sir Alexander had spent the day inspecting his precious merino flock with his station manager, sat in a buggy with a flimsy canopy and a blanket over his knees. They took a thermos of hot tea and sandwiches but altogether, they offered scant defence against the penetrating cold. The weather was unusually wet and cold and, despite his manager urging him to seek the warmth of the homestead, he insisted on continuing until darkness forced his hand. Later that night he developed a severe fever and passed away at the grand old age of 88 years in his bed days later at Chatsworth Park, surrounded by his loving family. He had contracted a bad chest cold that developed into pneumonia. He hung on grimly for a number of days, but eventually lapsed into a deep sleep from which he never awoke.

A state funeral was provided for the interment of a great citizen and pillar of the community and one of the city's wealthiest men; once again proving that no matter how hard you fight for it, or how many rules you bypass to get it, you still can't take it with you. But to the ordinary Sydney citizens he was a decorated and honourable man.

His many secrets and indiscretions were buried with him and only a fool, who had no further use for his own personal welfare, would dare offer any criticism or direct any suggestion of malfeasance that would put a stain on the reputation of the great statesman.

There were still many people of great stature and power in the community that owed their status and wealth to either supporting or turning a blind eye to some of the questionable deals he had done in his noteworthy career. As one social commentator said cynically, 'No man ever achieved greatness by just helping old ladies across the street or rescuing kittens from trees.'

CHAPTER FIFTEEN

There was little doubt that young William Grant Cuthbertson had inherited a very big dollop of his grandfather's genes. When still crawling about on all fours, his favourite toy was a funny little wooden biplane that Bobby had made for him, to look like the family's historic Gypsy Moth. It was the first thing he would look for at the start of the day and the last thing he put down before sleep.

William was born two years after his mother and father had first met, when Bobby had made his forced landing on the strip of the Wheatley estate. His energies recharged the household to new heights. Starting from daybreak until he fell exhausted into his little bed at night.

He started flying in the passenger seat of Bobby's Cessna as soon as he was big enough to take a seatbelt and cried like it was the end of the world when the short flight ended. Soon, he had become as much of a fixture in the plane as the compass.

Like his predecessors William grew to be an excellent student who enjoyed schooling and sports and was popular with his classmates and teachers. He was brother to his little sister, Elise Joy, and loved and protected her wherever they went, warning her of the danger of bull-ants, waterholes and snakes. They were an inseparable little duo that brought laughter to the family and friends at barbeques and gatherings.

Young Bill had a fruit crate fitted with wheels and wings which was his "plane". Bobby had fitted it with a joy stick and dummied up some instruments on a wood panel. Little Bill loved it and almost had to be dragged out of it at meal times. They caught him one day with one of the dogs hitched up to the front of it, towing him around the yard with Elise in hot pursuit, both of them giggling their heads off.

The children had also inherited the love of music so ingrained in the family genes and watched fascinated as one elder member of the family after the other banged out tunes on the piano or guitar and the two little ones pitched in joyously, adding their little voices to family sing-alongs. So it was no surprise they both learned to play on the ancient piano that was brought to the station by their great, great grandfather, old Harold, for his wife Henrietta, whose portrait hung on the wall above it, looking sternly down on them as if to say, 'we'll have no nonsense here thank you.' The piano held a remarkably good tune considering the extremes of temperature it had been exposed to over the years.

Bill and Elise had harmonious voices unaffected by the temperature or weather extremes and Bill had picked up the guitar as family tradition dictated. Music of the fifties and sixties dominated their preferences from Bill Hayley, Buddy Holly and the Crickets, Elvis Presley and Australia's Col Joye. They lived in the country so country music ruled supreme out there. Slim Dusty, Tex Morton, Buddy Williams and Queenslander Shirley Thoms.

American performers were heard on the radio, the Carter Family and of course JimmieRogers and the singing cowboy Roy Rogers.

Bobby and Joanne entertained often and loved to host parties on special occasions. Music was a dominant feature of these soirees and the music of choice was almost always country and western. Barn dancing was popular with the Heel and Toe Polka, Four around Four and Blaydon Races, and with all of this activity, the old homestead was always lit up and exciting. Many of their guests flew in, landing on the Cuthbertsons' airstrip and camping under the wings of their aircraft for special events such as significant birthdays like old Hugh's 80th. Christenings and funerals were well attended.

Hugh's much loved wife, Frances, great grandmother to Bill and Elise, was laid to rest in the family cemetery in the shade of the gums and peppercorn trees behind the homestead. Out of respect for the pioneering family, Frances was seen off by a large group of mourners who, following tradition, stayed on for a well provisioned wake.

Hugh was deeply affected by the passing of his life's partner, but his indomitable character and love of life and family pushed aside all public display of grief, but when he retired at night and the lights went down, he would always offer a prayer of thanks to his maker for the wonderful times and love he had shared with her. He was most grateful for the children she had born. The ill-fated Julian who had died as a result of stumbling upon a taipan, Big Bill and George and poor little Edwina, his little golden-haired princess who suffered and died from influenza. Hugh remembered them all in his prayers, particularly his son William. A war hero who simply disappeared into the Australian bush without a trace and perhaps his remains may still be laying out there somewhere, his soul lost and waiting to come home.

The outback had its own culture, built around cattle and crops, cooking and craft, church and sport. Conversation invariably came back to one of these subjects and under the heading of sport came rugby and cricket but also rodeo.

Rodeo brought together, not only the rough tough riders, but also the music of the bush and the outback and these events were often combined with a big barn dance and barbeque with the ladies of the Country Women's Association proudly laying out their tempting cakes, scones and all sorts of baked goods. The sale of the food and craft helped to fund local charities and services such as the hospital, uniforms for the junior footballers, netballers or supporting the elderly and infirm in the community. Courtland Downs played host to these events now and again. As usual, the guests would arrive by plane or helicopter, camping under the stars. As flying was a major part of the Cuthbertson clan DNA, was it any wonder that Bill and Elise were both infatuated with it from an early age?

Other girls played with dolls, but Elise was always hanging about with big brother Bill, playing pilots and pestering their dad to go flying. The both of them were among the youngest in their local flying club. As they gained their teens, Bill and Elise went down a familiar road for the Cuthbertsons, loitering in the hangars, talking to pilots and instructors, washing planes in exchange for a ride and generally becoming experts on every type of light aircraft that flew in their part of the world.

They could distinguish one type from another, sight unseen, just by hearing the pitch of its engine as it approached. Their bedrooms were decorated with aircraft photos and models; Elise was more interested in modelling planes than modelling the latest fashions, which was the cause of a little bit of disappointment to Joanne who preferred to see her beautiful daughter pursue more feminine activities. Elise never disappointed, turning heads at the many social events in the area. Even in her early teens, she was a striking beauty who could make a hessian sack look like a cocktail gown.

Both of the young ones were still expected to carry out their duties around the station. There were no passengers on this bus. They were assigned to all the usual chores of **mustering, mucking out stables, mending and fixing, feeding and watering stock and** driving tractors as soon as they could reach the pedals.

As soon as the children reached the minimum age for a pilot's learner permit, they soloed. This was no surprise to their instructor who was pleased to have two students with the skill and enthusiasm they both displayed. Young Elise, being two years behind her brother, was very proud of him but achingly keen to take her own first official solo flight. She was not only younger, but also a good deal shorter and would have to satisfy one other qualification for that step. She had to show that she could actually see out of the cockpit!

When flying with her father, Bobby, she had habitually sat on a cushion to see the view but was far too embarrassed to take her cushion with her to the flying club. However, fresh, healthy, country food and lots of fresh air and exercise soon had her growing like a weed and she proudly took the controls and winged away from the Longreach airfield heading into the sky on her 16th birthday.

A real competition began between the two youngsters. Elise was determined to put her foot forward as a pilot. This was the age of female liberation after all, and she was not going to play second fiddle to her brother, or any other mere male for that matter. She quietly progressed through the various ratings, achieving her full licence and then concentrating to get her night VMC, or her night flying rating and then her instrument rating. She was 17 years old and an experienced pilot who had a plan.

Bill was equally keen to gain ratings and build his hours, but was often distracted by **matters concerning the station which his father insisted he take care of. The propert**y was his to inherit and he had better show a keen interest or go into town and get a job. Bobby didn't mean to be harsh, but it was a harsh country and a tough business and his ancestors had made great sacrifices to develop it and eventually pass it on to their children. The family burial plot now provided the resting place for these resolute and dedicated settlers and it would be an insult to their memory and a disgrace to let the place go to rack and ruin and become another major property falling into the hands of new owners, or worse still, bloody miners and developers.

So preached Bobby to his son and he meant it. His grandparents and Young Bill's great grandparents lay there and one day the widow of his grandfather, and his namesake, would lie there as well. She had said once or twice that if Big Bill's spirit found its way home, he would know where to find her.

So while being the senior and having begun his flying activities earlier, Bill the younger, fell behind his sister's aeronautical advancement. Elise was also using her charms in other directions. Elise had confided in her mother of her 'big plan', which was to be the youngest female pilot to circumnavigate Australia. She was very excited about the prospect and invested a lot of time in researching the possibility. She had quietly accumulated an impressive pile of maps and weather charts and was determined to embark on the great adventure but she didn't want to keep anything from her mother and chose the right moment to broach the subject. Swearing her mother to secrecy, not so much from her dad whom she adored, but her competitive brother, she gave Jo a broad outline of what she hoped to achieve. Her mother listened attentively and, when Elise finished,she asked a couple of pointed questions.

Who would supply the plane? Who would pay for the fuel? Would an insurance company cover the risk? How would she organise the logistical support she would need?

Elise was up to the mark with nearly all of these issues as she had been plotting for some time. The flying club would be the source of most of her support. When she discussed it with the chief pilot and her flying instructor, they had been very excited by the idea and the prospect of exposure it could bring to their club and the district. They immediately set about plotting her track, waypoints and overnight stops, contacting people along the way and making arrangements for fuel and accommodation. Coincidentally, the flying club were in negotiation with the Australian agent for Cessna to update their fleet by the purchase of three new aircraft. They had put forward the idea of the agent's company providing a plane suitably equipped to tackle the journey and hinted a little mischievously perhaps that the Piper representative had got wind of the proposal and had expressed genuine interest.

This, of course, spurred the competitive Cessna agent, who liked the idea, to get on his bike and start pedalling. The bluff had worked and he was already talking to his parent company in the United States for support. Eventually, they agreed to loan Elise a gorgeous little Cessna 152 for her extraordinary adventure which was a great opportunity for the manufacturer to prove the reliability of its aircraft. The minute she laid eyes on it, she named it "Tinker", short for Tinker Bell, the flying fairy in the Peter Pan story.

Rick, the chief pilot, and Jack, Elise's instructor, were also working on a sponsor for her fuel so, all in all, things were already progressing. Jo was mildly shocked by all this information but her chest was swelling with pride for her gorgeous, spirited girl. Elise decided she would not disappoint her supporters and her family, who were unaware of what was in the offing and would soon enough learn of her mammoth undertaking.

While the sponsors were very keen for her success and vowed to give her all the support she would need, she had one more bridge to cross. After seeing how far she had come in her planning and the backup provided by her flying school and the wonderful sponsors, her mother gave her tacit approval, but only on condition that they bring her father in on it as soon as possible.

After a nervous conversation revealing her plans, Bobby had put on a gruff voice and a serious frown pretending for a while to be a little cross that all this background activity had taken place without consulting him. When he saw the crestfallen look on his child's face, his heart melted and he laughed loudly, throwing his arms around her, sweeping her off her feet, announcing how much he loved and was proud of her. Of course he approved and would find some money in the kitty somewhere to help equip her plane or whatever she needed. All she wanted, she said, was her father's love and approval.

The local newspaper had come on as a sponsor and their story was picked up by the mainstream press. Elise found herself giving interviews to a press gallery representing print, radio and television. Pretty soon she became one of the most famous faces in the country being pursued by women's magazines for exclusives.

This could have been distracting but for the fact that they were all waving cheque books. Consequently, Elise's mission was launched in a blaze of publicity with press, television and radio presenting in depth items as they backgrounded 'our latter day Freda Thompson', the first Australian woman to fly solo from England to Australia and the first female instructor in the British Commonwealth.

Before she could take off, there were one or two minor issues to be resolved such as which direction to travel - clockwise or anti-clockwise. She elected to travel anti-clockwise to avoid the monsoons that were due in the north very soon. First and subsequent refuelling points, with the addition of auxiliary tanks, were selected based on Tinker's expected fuel economy and so on. Weather was a further, not quite so minor issue and her instructor was a stickler for such things. She was anxious to get away before she got any older, which meant she would have to deal with whatever weather patterns were current. It could be monsoonal in the north of the nation and winter in the south. Each route would present its own weather problems. She would just have to face it and get through it or around it as best she could.

The Bureau of Meteorology was yet to produce accurate charts of wind and weather that would have been helpful to her, which meant Elise had to rely more on general information and hearsay. Commercial pilots, who flew over a lot of the ground she would cover, provided some information that proved to be very helpful. One piece of advice she was given repeatedly she later ignored or forgot about and, to her detriment, nearly perished over Kakadu.

They had turned away a number of would-be managers and a business contact of her father recommended a professional public relations company that began to handle all of her affairs in the venture. Her support team extracted maximum sponsorships and product endorsements for her, and arrangements and payment for TV appearances. All of this money, after expenses, she presented as a donation to the local community in a series of grants.

But one charity close to her heart was the Rockhampton Hospital, which was the referring hospital for the region and whose medical and nursing staff had saved the lives of many very sick and injured locals, some relatives and one or two close friends. When that was revealed in one of her interviews, some locals got together and, with her permission, turned it into the catalyst for a fund raiser that eventually ended in the presentation of a magnificent sum to the hospital board.

Elise was a tremendous success, attracting huge crowds at all her way points and bringing priceless publicity for her sponsors. She was even offered a speaking part in a television drama series which was discussed and rejected without regret. Discussed and rejected, that is, by her agency, much to her disappointment and the relief of her parents.

The flight path had to pass some compulsory navigation points to be official and the longitude and latitudeof them were provided by the adjudicators. Officials at these points would log the time of her passing. The flight went well with one glaring exception.

The first leg of 780 kilometres from Longreach to Townsville was a bit of a shakeout cruise, enabling her to familiarise herself a little more with Tinker Bell. After refuelling and meeting the local press, she climbed out from her first stop over in Townsville. The predicted weather was clear with an easterly breeze blowing in off the Coral Sea; a lovely bank of altocumulus cloud appearing to starboard.

Her next stopover would be Burketown, 780 kilometres west, north west. After a four hour flight, bucking an unpredicted contrary wind, she was feted at the Burketown airfield as Tinker received another top up of fuel courtesy of her sponsors.

Elise was beginning to appreciate the vast emptiness of the country she was crossing, perhaps understanding for the first time that if anything went wrong out here, she would be very much on her own. The extra water and survival gear she carried would only go so far ifshe were forced to put down in the bush.

These things failed to trouble her thoughts too much and with a good meal in her tummy and a good night's sleep, she arrived back at the airfield to perform her pre-flight checks and submit her flight plan for the next leg of her journey, which would take her to Borroloola, 330 kilometres away for another refuelling before continuing on to Darwin. An hour after take-off she left Queensland for the first time and entered the Northern Territory.

Overflying Kakadu to Darwin would be the longest leg she had attempted so far. She would be in the air for a total of nine hours with a refuelling stop in the middle, but she felt she was more than capable. Once again, the weather forecast for the journey was mostly favourable with a slight chance of a thunderstorm in the Kakadu area.

Borroloola airfield was a little rough but she was used to landing on grass strips and the reception was very friendly and encouraging. An updated weather report suggested she might run into a little heavy rain towards Kakadu. She now faced approximately four hours in the air to Darwin, weather allowing. She gratefully scoffed down a hasty sandwich and tea provided by the local CWA ladies and was airborne again. With the added long range fuel tanks, she had sufficient fuel for the total 690 kilometre trip direct to Darwin, provided nothing went wrong on the way.

You can always depend on Murphy's Law to throw a spanner in the works. Some people say Murphy was an optimist and he was about to prove it again. After an uneventful three and a half hours, and just before Kakadu, the horizon to her right took on an ominous appearance with huge cumulonimbus clouds towering up into the stratosphere.

They were truly, awesomely beautiful but also deadly to aircraft of any size and would make short work of Tinker Bell with the extreme turbulence inside the clouds. However, Elise didn't think they would cut across her intended path so she maintained her current heading. She trimmed the little plane up so it would hold a straight and level course and consulted her charts for the nearest airfield should she need one. Finding none that was within a reasonable range, she was without a choice and pushed on determinedly.

When she next looked up from her charts, Elise found she was plunging into a heavy tropical shower that reduced visibility to mere metres. For 10 or 15 excruciating minutes Elise concentrated on her instruments to keep her straight and level and, as if tossed by the hand of a giant, she was almost thrown out of her harness as she had entered an area of massive turbulence. Then she realised, to her horror, that the storm clouds had moved with deceptive speed and she was flying through a thunderhead.

Visibility worsened, the cloud surrounding her grew darker and, like some malevolent monster, the thunderhead sent down an intense hailstorm which clattered with an incredible ear shattering roar, so loud and persistent that she could no longer hear her plane's engine. The little craft was thrown about in the turbulence like a leaf in a winter gale. One minute standing on a wing tip and the next climbing vertically. With a terrible shock, Elise realised she no longer had control of her aircraft and thought that this would be the end as she and her little aircraft would surely be torn to bits any minute now. But she hung on, grasping the control column with all her strength and working the throttle feverishly.

Lightning flashed constantly and the hail intensified. The temperature had dropped like a rock but Elise was sweating profusely as she bullied the controls through the turmoil.

Thunder crashed to add to the crescendo of noise so loud she thought she would lose her hearing if it continued much longer. She was tiring rapidly now with the tremendous effort and the adrenaline surge; her arms were aching as if she had just finished a heavy gym session. Sweat stung her eyes and she was holding back a scream of frustration and fear when, with a suddenness that took her breath away, it all ceased as Tinker Bell flew out of the cloud into clear air and sunshine.

As visibility cleared, she saw the danger was not yet over. The little plane was diving towards the ground which was now less than 300 feet below her. Elise closed the throttle and pulled back on the control yoke as hard as she could. When the gallant little aircraft levelled out, she applied full throttle to increase the space between her and the threatening ground, now very close below her wheels. The engine roared and her descent slowed completely and she eased the pressure on the control column while continuing to climb, keeping a wary eye open for any more of those blasted storm clouds. Eventually, she returned to a safe cruising height, badly shaken but still alive. The words of the old commercial pilot back in Longreach was echoing in her ears..

'Stay away from cu-nims.'

Now she had to focus on the remainder of the leg into Darwin.

The big question was, did she still have sufficient fuel to get there? Tinker Bell had burned up a lot in her brave fight against the thunderhead. A quick calculation gave her a rather comforting answer. She would or should arrive with plenty of fuel in reserve.

Her arrival at Darwin created a sensation and she was interviewed again and again. The press wanted to know more and more detail about her and her plans for the future. What did your parents think? Did she have a boyfriend? Was she planning on marriage? What were her thoughts on the current political situation in Canberra? What about the current beef prices and the drought in the southern states?

Her head began to throb and she was becoming very cross with some of the stupid questions that she felt were thrown in just for the sake of it. Just when she thought she would scream, the airport PR manager stepped in and turned off the microphones and ordered the journalists out. Five minutes later, a grateful Elise found herself in a cab on her way to a very nice hotel down on the waterfront where she dined and rested for two days before climbing back into Tinker Bell to continue the rest of her journey.

The lovely little plane looked a bit beaten up with a lot of her lovely white paint scoured off the leading edges of the flying surfaces by the hail. The mechanics had been all over it since she arrived and assured Elise her plane was very much airworthy and ready to go again. Her fuel tank was refilled to capacity. She may have miscalculated her fuel burn or was short served for fuel. They were aghast at how little remained in her tanks!

Oil was replaced, windscreen cleaned, all radio and electrical systems checked, flight controls double checked. Regardless, Elise walked around Tinker and checked everything herself as a wise pilot would. Elise left Darwin at first light the next morning and turned Tinker Bell's nose west by south aiming for Kununurra and East Kimberly Regional Airport, 860 kilometres away and the next leg of the huge journey that still lay ahead of her. She hoped those miles might be a little less eventful.

Flying over the Kimberly, she was reminded of the wonderful book she had recently read by Mary Durack called, *Kings in Grass Castles* relating the history of the family's massive cattle empire in the very early pioneering days. She had enjoyed the parallels between the Durack's and the Cuthbertson's regarding the role of women and families in the cattle industry and the collaboration with the Aborigines, to whom each family paid great respect, undoubtedly contributing to the enormous success of their individual ventures.

Then further south, she would be flying over the massive iron ore mines of Lang Hancock and the equally large shipping terminals created to carry the raw iron ore to the world. In the meantime, she would visit several key towns along the West Australian coast on her way south to Perth flying over or touching down at Broome, Port Hedland, Exmouth, Carnarvon and Geraldton, enjoying the magnificent scenery of the coastline and the hospitality of the citizenry on the way. Every time she had touched down, generous supporters pressed donations into her hand for the Rockhampton Hospital appeal she was collecting for.

It was a total travel time of fourteen days over more than 12,000 miles; her beautiful little Tinker Bell cruising along without a hitch before she arrived at Perth's International Airport. The major cities of Perth, Adelaide and Melbourne seemed to be trying to outdo each other in welcoming ceremonies and hosting. Elise was showered with television interviews and civic receptions in her honour, flattering speeches about her example to the youth of her country and invitations to come again.

At the completion of her great adventure, she was confirmed as not only the youngest female pilot, but the youngest pilot full stop, to have completed the circumnavigation of the country. Then the honours came flooding in. She was presented with the keys to the city of Longreach by the shire president in a long winded speech that took almost as long as her flight and almost forgot to mention her name. She was featured on a beautiful plaque commemorating her flight at the Qantas Founders' Museum in yet another long winded ceremony during which her father dug her in the ribs and whispered that he had warned her there was a price to be paid and they both laughed out loud which left those within earshot wondering what they had missed.

Without doubt the crowning glory for her was to be nominated and awarded "Young Queenslander of the Year" for her aviation achievement, highlighting awareness of the needs of the medical services in outback Australia and the huge funds she managed to raise for the Rockhampton Hospital. Her parents' hearts were bursting with pride for their daughter as she was presented with her award on Australia Day on the steps of the Sydney Opera House by the Governor General along with the recipients of each of the states. There were plenty of media providing national coverage of the event, pleasing Elise's sponsors and supporters, in particular, the Royal Flying Doctor Service, so vital to life in the vast outback. Elise spent a lot of time promoting and campaigning for them. The RFDS was one of the largest and most comprehensive aeromedical organisations in the world, providing extensive primary health care and 24-hour emergency service to people over an area of 7.3 million square kilometres. Without the RFDS, many thousands of people living in remote areas would have no contact with medical services. Although grateful for the exposure provided by Elise, their success was due largely to a number contributors large and small.

CHAPTER SIXTEEN

Instead of envy or resentment, Bill was supportive and excessively proud of his little 'sis.' He took a great interest in the entire adventure and whenever he could get away from his duties as property manager he read all the papers and hung out for the TV coverage which was getting a good airing on regional Television. But something was stirring inside him, a desire to emulate his little sister in some way. It came to him while he was thumbing through a photo album and came across some pictures of his grandfather, Big Bill, standing proudly with his navigator in front of his Bristol Beaufighter, before heading off to the war in New Guinea. This sparked an idea for a mission to pursue.

The 50th anniversary of his grandfather's disappearance somewhere in the Queensland outback, while on a mission from Port Moresby to Brisbane during World War Two, was coming up. What if he were to replicate that journey and do it in a Bristol Beaufighter just like Big Bill? It was a great idea, but where the hell would he get a Beau? There were nearly 6,000 built but very few remained and those were generally held in museums. Maybe he should consider an aircraft similar in profile and he thought he knew just the one.

He had seen an aircraft for sale in a flying magazine that would suit his purpose and had contacted the company that was the current owner. The plane was on the ground at Archerfield, Brisbane's secondary airport and Queensland's major centre for general aviation activities. The plane had done service as a commercial freight carrier around Australia for a company that was now feeling the pinch and had put it, their oldest aircraft, on the market to avoid increasing maintenance costs which ate into its profitability.

The plane had continued to meet its service schedule, a must as a commercial aircraft, so it should still have been in good condition. The reason it interested young Bill was that it was roughly similar to his grandfather's plane in its configuration. It was a Beechcraft Model 18, a twin radial engined, tail dragging plane, roughly resembling the profile of the Beaufighter. He would love to have found a Beau but they were very rare and very expensive and there was little chance he could even persuade a museum to let him have one on loan. He decided to fly down to Archerfield and take a look at the Beech before he exposed his plan to his father.

William Grant Cuthbertson had the plan, but it would take a lot of work to get his father's support, as it would take him away from his duties at Courtland Downs. The anniversary of Big Bill's disappearance provided an imperative that could not be ignored if the venture was to have a back story. It was a story that young Bill knew would create interest around the country.

Bill met with the selling agent at Archerfield who walked him over to the Beech. It was love at first sight. She was a gorgeous beast, glistening silver fuselage and wings, her Pratt & Whitney nine cylinder radial engines producing 450HP each, driving the Beech to a top speed of 195 knots or 360 kph. But the most striking thing about the Beech was its twin tail configuration. It looked very retro sitting there with the sun glinting off its silver fuselage.

She had a few dings here and there, but nothing to be worried about. He climbed aboard and found, as the agent said, she had been stripped of her passenger seats which didn't concern Bill too much; in fact it might have been a bonus. When asked, the agent said she had current airworthy certificates for airframe, engines and radios. When he was satisfied that Bill was a genuine buyer, he offered a trial flight and they returned to the office for keys.

Terry, the agent, had a sense of humour and when Bill pointed to the puddles of oil under each engine, he said the only time they didn't leak was when they were out of oil.

They completed a pre-flight check, part of which meant turning the big props by hand a few times to distribute the aforementioned oil. Climbing into their seats and securing seatbelts, Terry hit the switches and turned the radials over. They coughed and spluttered, belched big puffs of blue exhaust smoke and burst into life with a clattering roar typical of radial engines.

He signalled to an employee of Terry's to remove their wheel chocks and they taxied out to the holding point. Clearance for take-off was granted from the tower and Terry smoothly opened the throttles. Take-off went without a hitch and the lovely old plane was climbing away into the blue, the sun glinting from its twin tail fins as the undercarriage came up with a thump, flaps were raised and they gained airspeed quickly, climbing out effortlessly as Terry turned her away to the south.

Bill Jnr took the controls when they had gained altitude and was surprised at how light it was to handle. On first sight of the Beech, one tended to think of it as a bit of a truck and, while it was hardly a sports car, it was certainly very gentle on the pilot. Bill climbed and banked and went through a few manoeuvres to satisfy his curiosity. In the end he was reluctant to hand the controls back. Terry took over and brought the Beech in for an impressive smooth landing. After taxiing in and parking, Bill was still grinning like a fool in love. He was sold. Now, all he had to do was sell his parents on the idea.

Because of the success of his sister and the reflected glory it had brought to the family and the collateral benefits it brought to the community, he was confident they would go for it, especially because of the very personal nature of his project.

Bill decided to have a full family meeting to lay out his project and he gathered his parents and, in particular his grandmother, into the dining room of the homestead. His sister had got wind of his plan and sat there excited for him, hoping there might be a part in it for her. After everyone was settled he began.

His plan was simple really. He wanted to replicate the last flight of his deceased grandfather, Big Bill, from Port Moresby to Australia but finishing the flight safely at the intended destination. He would touch down at various way points on the return trip north for publicity and perhaps fund raising. He went on to tell them he had found a plane and planned to complete the journey on the 50th anniversary of Big Bill's disappearance as a tribute to the courageous grandfather he never knew.

Lydia sat quietly saying nothing, but young Bill noticed a single tear trickle down her cheek. They couldn't tell if she was overjoyed or caught up in grief again; they all agreed later, probably both, after she had retired to her room.

Bill's plan would have him celebrate the occasion at Jackson Field, Port Moresby and complete a flyover at Longreach before continuing on to Archerfield.

Bobby started asking questions about the plane Bill Jnr said he had located. Was it airworthy? How much was it and did he have the money to buy it or was the family expected to dig deep for it?

This was a good sign as far as Bill was concerned. Bobby's questions showed an interest in the project that might presage agreement. And then there were the 100 questions Elise was hurling at him like machine gun bullets. Each and every one answered convincingly.

Bill Jnr pulled out a sales leaflet that Terry the agent had printed off for him. Terry would also sit in the right hand seat while Bill was doing his rating on the plane, even though he had a twin engine rating already. Pilots needed to qualify on different types before they could take command of them.

His parents were not sold on the idea yet. This could be a dangerous journey, both getting the plane to New Guinea and then following the supposed route of his grandfather's last flight, which ended God alone knew where.

Bill Jnr tried to set their minds at rest but, taking a cue from his sister, he promised them he would not do anything without their express knowledge and permission. They ended the discussion on that note and Bill Jnr was left feeling a little flat. He went to the homestead's office to check on a couple of things that might help his cause and was surprised by a knock on the door. It was Elise who had come to give some encouragement, if he wouldn't be insulted by a little feminine support.

The asking price for his plane, he was already taking ownership mentally, was fairly modest given the circumstances of the sale. He had money in the bank and his share of the current wool clip, and other bonuses from their station, would easily cover it. His family accountant had put his affairs through a shelf company that provided records for his income from all sources and registering the aircraft in his company name would help offset some costs against income tax liability. He could see the day when it would be handy for transporting various items from and to the station.

Maintenance on those big radials was expensive, but he didn't plan on making it his regular commute when his commemorative flight was over. He would still have to do some restoration work on it; in all probability a fit out with some modern avionics providing up to date navigation and communication.

After some consideration and a little heartburn, Bobby and Jo decided that if their daughter was capable of navigating around the country, then there was no real argument against Bill Jnr doing much the same thing. Bill had time constraints and, if he were to do it, they would need to give him the go ahead immediately. Bill Jnr was delirious with joy when they gave him the word and he jumped on the phone to Terry at Archerfield and made his offer which was accepted on the spot. Bill Jnr had filled Terry in on his intentions and the salesman became very excited about Bill's mission. He could see a lot of value in supporting the young man.

Terry was positive that Bill Jnr, with the famous aviatrix sister, would achieve his mission and offered to assist him with some sponsorship from his company, for which Bill was very grateful.

Bill Jnr's intended flight had him entering and leaving Papua New Guinea which, as a foreign country, required a small snow storm of paperwork. Permits had to be sought and, with the assistance of his local Federal MP, who was an enthusiastic supporter of the mission and a Vietnam Veteran, permits were soon granted. The Port Moresby sub branch of the RSL had pledged support and looked forward to meeting young Bill, who would be honoured with a special dinner at the club when he arrived.

Australians hold their returned servicemen and women in very high regard and celebrate them at two important dates each year. Armistice Day, or Remembrance Day, falls on 11th November and commemorates the day on which the guns of World War One fell silent. ANZAC Day falls on 25th April and commemorates all service personnel from all conflicts and, in particular, the events that occurred at Gallipoli in the Great War.

Another issue was the passage there and back which involved a long flight over open water and, of course, special rules applied. Bill would be required to carry a life jacket and life raft that was accessible during flight and, if he was flying below 2000 feet, he had to wear his life jacket, which in a hot climate would be unbearable.

With the assistance this time of his club's senior pilot, and taking advice from manuals available to them, they worked out a reporting schedule for the "wet" passage of the journey. Reporting in to Air Traffic Control would give him peace of mind knowing his flight was being monitored.

Bill Cuthbertson Jnr faced some of the problems his sister had in terms of funding his flight, but there was some overflow from Elise's venture and his. Some of Elise's sponsors heard of Bill's plans and could see another round of valuable exposure for their products and services associated with this adventurous flying family. This adventure had the added attraction of being linked to a World War Two forgotten hero, who had never come home.

Sentiment for such stories had risen astronomically in recent years as the old warriors began to pass away and their grandchildren took a passionate interest in their forebears' sacrifices. Nothing but upside for the right product placement and didn't the advertising men know it. Elise's former agency was at Bill Jnr's elbow with an offer, due to a quick phone call from his now influential little sister. They decided on the right alignment of sponsors and conducted several local and national radio and television interviews. The local paper gave him headlines like, "The Flying Cuthbertsons". Bill Jnr took it all in his stride. Having shared some of Elise's limelight he was aware of how these things could easily go to his head and distract him from his mission.

After many hours of labour and testing, Bill Jnr and his technical supporters had finally got the Beech ready for the flight. Bill Jnr had named his plane with due ceremony, "Big Bill", with his service number underneath in honour of his grandfather.

The press had been notified and local television and press were elbowed out of the way by the big city guys who seemed to appear out of nowhere and were all over them. Bill's agency guys were almost overwhelmed, but managed to steer Bill out of trouble and make sure the right questions were asked and answered.

Lydia stood on a set of steps and poured champagne over the nose cone of the plane and another emotional speech was made by their Federal MP about sacrifice and honour and the usual earbashing about himself. The aircraft, "Big Bill", was bedecked with sponsor logos against the burnished aluminium fuselage and looked very smart. Young Bill's name was stencilled just below the pilot's cockpit window. The plane's name was painted stylishly on the nose in much larger type. The whole presentation was sign written very similar to professional racing cars with lots of bright colours and fancy logos with their current slogans.

All was in readiness. "Big Bill" was fully fuelled, totally restored and serviced to the hilt and loaded with every conceivable item that might be needed on the journey. Nothing was being left to chance.

The family gathered to wish him well and indulge in the traditional, magnificent roast lamb dinner re-created by Lydia as the last meal she prepared for her husband as he headed off to war. There was another speech from his dad and Lydia was once again overcome with emotion, telling young Bill how proud she was of him and that she was sure Big Bill would be as well. She hugged him in a warm embrace and pressed a small parcel into his hand and told him not to open it until he was airborne. He slipped it into his pocket and thanked her sincerely and swore that he would bring honour to his grandfather and return in one piece. Then Bill retired, as he planned to be up early to meet Rick at the Longreach Airfield where the Beech was now housed.

Elise was up early preparing breakfast for him and had already packed sandwiches for his trip and was busy brewing a thermos of coffee. He had fitted a small icebox within arm's reach in the cockpit and these supplies would fit nicely into the netting on the back of the right hand seat. He met with his club's chief pilot, Rick, who was still on the job after mentoring Elise a couple of years ago now.

They started with the latest weather reports, taking note of wind vectors at various altitudes that would work for or against him. Wind streams varied remarkably as an aircraft climbed to height. Balloons were launched regularly by the Bureau of Meteorology that sent back information on wind strength and direction, as well as air temperature to earthbound computers, as they climbed into the stratosphere. A pilot could gain a lot of advantage by reading these reports and factoring the information into his flight plan.

Having that information, they now worked on the actual flight plan that would be lodged with Air Traffic Control. They filled in a series of cards with relevant information, such as the call sign and frequencies for Port Moresby, as well as ILS and VOR. Instrument Landing System is a precision approach it provides direction and height information that will allow to follow a path down to the runway landing point.

Both were navigation aids to direct an aircraft to the duty runway of an intended landing field.

After lodging the flight plan and getting the okay from ATC that all was well and everything seemed to be in order, Rick and Bill strode towards the Beech for the pre-flight checks. The sun was beginning to have an influence on the eastern sky, heralding the beginning of a beautiful day for Bill's adventure. Elise was there, of course, and hugged her big brother.

A member of the local press insisted on taking a few photos of the three together, then Bill and Elise, and Bill climbing aboard the Beech looking into the rising sun, until Bill finally snapped and sent him on his way. He shook hands with Rick and kissed his sister farewell, then closed the door behind him. He made his way forward and settled into the left hand seat after securing his food and drink supplies.

Now it was time to start the engines and get serious young Bill, he said to himself and offered a prayer that his grandfather would be with him in the right hand seat.

Bill Jnr slid the cockpit window open and gave the thumbs up to Rick and Elise. The powerful 450 horse power Pratt and Whitney nine cylinder radial engines fired up in the usual clouds of blue smoke and roared into life, rocking the Beech on its main wheels. Rick pulled the chocks out of the way obligingly and Bill rolled out to commence his adventure right on time and slightly over budget.

After tuning his radio in for the local area information service that would tell him which runway was in service, wind direction and weather outlook, he called the tower and was met with good wishes for a safe flight. He then tuned to the ground control frequency and gained clearance to taxi to the holding point of the duty runway. On arrival there, he changed frequency again to ATC and asked for clearance for take-off. Granted, and he was again sent good wishes for a successful flight and without further ado, he rolled out and took off, climbing into the cloudless sky finally on his way.

The television guy was still hanging about and managed to video some good footage of Bill taking off and climbing out into the eastern sky, which was used extensively on the evening news services across Australia.

CHAPTER SEVENTEEN

The weather bureau had predicted a fairly typical Longreach day. The current temperature at 0630 hours was around 10 degrees and would probably rise to a warm 28 to 30 degrees later in the day when Bill Jnr and his plane would be well away.

The sky was clear and as the Local Area Information informed him, there was a light scattered scud under a layer of three eighths alto cumulus with a base of 6500 feet. Bill would have very pleasant flying conditions for his trip.

Bill recalled Lydia pressing the little parcel into his hand which now nestled in his breast pocket. The Beech was now trimmed and flying straight and level, so the time was right to see what she had presented to him last night. It was a small, grey felt bag with a draw string top. He undid the knot with a little difficulty and tipped it up into his left hand. Out slid a gold locket with a stylised letter L on the front. He opened it to find a photograph of his grandfather in a studio type pose, looking young, handsome and confident. He would have been the same age as young Bill was at that moment. He had to wipe away a small tear that had crept from the corner of his eye.

Bill quickly brought himself back to the job at hand. The slightly metallic and matter of fact voice of the tower requested he change frequency to ATC for Northern Australia which would oversee his flight into New Guinea air space. His heading was NNE and the distance 1580 kilometres, well within the range of his wonderful Beech 18 and the time was 0635. At a comfortable and economical cruising speed of just over 300 kilometres per hour, after five plus hours, he should be touching down around midday approximately, allowing for weather. He would recalculate these numbers as he flew several times over. Port Moresby in Papua New Guinea was in the same time zone, making things a bit easier for Bill.

The Beech had now levelled out at 6500 feet and performing immaculately. Bill was impressed with the solid old plane. The radials were throttled down slightly and the engine roar eased back to a moderate and more bearable rumble. Bill settled back in his seat and gazed out at the same scene his grandfather would have experienced.

From 6500 feet, the sea below looks relatively calm with the flecks of white wave crests providing definition for the deep cobalt sea. There were still some small patches of low lying cloud sliding under his aircraft, casting their shadows on the ocean. He had seen one or two fishing vessels closer inshore as they went about their business, dwarfed by a huge container ship forging a path inside the outer reef. No other sign of human activity was visible until he was within the coastal zone of New Guinea, where there were a lot of fishing and commercial vessels everywhere he looked.

The flight was otherwise uneventful and he farewelled ATC Northern Australia and changed frequency to Port Moresby ATC and reported 10 miles south in-bound. Bill had been advised that conditions over Jackson Field could be cloudy with moderate breezes and the usual high humidity.

He was welcomed and directed to the duty runway and made a slightly bumpy landing in the humid, turbulent air. From there he was directed to a parking spot in front of a hangar where, to his surprise, there was a gathering of people and press. He had a welcoming committee who had come together because his story had reached them and touched a lot of people interested in meeting the grandson of a World War Two pilot who perished in defence of his country and theirs. The greeting party was, of course, led by a politician, a member the local Returned Serviceman's Club and an historian.

Bill had been expecting the RSL man as they had corresponded during his planning and he knew the local sub branch had organised some special events for him and some old servicemen to meet.

Speeches were made for the sake of the television cameras and press and, after standing in the tropical midday sun for half an hour, Bill was asked to say a few words, which he managed and then thankfully was ushered into an air-conditioned office area at the front of the hangar.

By this time he was drenched in sweat and looking for a way out and, although his flight was uneventful, it was, nonetheless, draining. Bill's support team had booked him into a nice hotel 20 minutes from the airfield and the comfy bed in it was calling his name.

The RSL guys had outdone themselves and an escort had been appointed to look after him. Even though it hadn't formed part of his plans, he was delighted to be told a trip had been organised for him to Milne Bay by the Returned Serviceman's Club. It was in conjunction with the local aero club and sponsored by The Papua New Guinea Post-Courier, a News Corp paper following up on their Australian colleagues. They would fly down and land at Gurney Airport, where he would tour around the battle grounds where his grandfather flew and fought.

Bill was flown over the Milne Bay area and the key geographic spots of the battle zones were pointed out to him. He was surprised to see how much agricultural activity was evident from the sky. The less mountainous areas were being farmed for a wide variety of crops, which demonstrated a certain level of prosperity for the locals and in Bill's mind this was the payoff for the efforts and sacrifices of the allies.

He was genuinely touched by the kindness being shown to him and this tour put a lot of things into perspective for him. It was driven home to him what a desperate and hard fought battle it had been and how important it was in the overall outcome of the war against a fierce and merciless enemy right on Australia's doorstep. The courage and sacrifice of the allied forces, made up of men like Bill's grandfather. Men from Australia, the USA, Britain and an alliance of other nations and forces, bravely met and threw back the Japanese bent on domination of the Asia Pacific region who, suffered their first substantial defeat at Milne Bay.

Bill Jnr learned the airfield was named *Gurney Field* on 14 September 1942 in honour of RAAF Squadron Leader RC Gurney, who was killed in an air crash. The RSL guys had researched the records and established that Big Bill had been one of the three Beaus despatched to Fall River, but would certainly have been with 30 Squadron when it moved to Port Moresby under the control of the Fifth Air Force USAAF on 12 September, and established itself on Ward's Strip, eight kilometres north-east of town.

The Beaufighters of Big Bill's squadron were used to attack Japanese shipping in the Bismarck Strait and had earlier attacked Japanese shipping in the Coral Sea as they island hopped southwards. All of this was fascinating for Bill and he was feted by the press and his guides, who were all falling over themselves to be helpful.

Ward's Strip was closed at the end of the war and no longer existed, otherwise Bill may have chosen to replicate his return flight from there. But Jackson's Field was near enough; it was the gesture that was important. Bill laid out his plans to a group of his supporters at a farewell dinner at the RSL Club, on the eve of his departure. In a very touching surprise, Bill was presented with a plaque created from the tip of a Beaufighter propeller, commemorating his journey. This was overwhelming for Bill; he reckoned this would have taken a lot of planning and research and where the heck did they get hold of a Beau's propeller?

Meanwhile, his Beech had been serviced and refuelled and was waiting for him on the tarmac. The ground crew, who had performed this service, were standing about waiting to see Bill off and refused payment despite Bill's insistence.

He promised all of them would be welcome at Courtland Downs any time they wanted a holiday. After all, it was just across the water and down the road a bit, which brought a bit of a laugh but reinforced his gratitude for the friendship and generosity he had received when he had more or less just blown in.

His mission was simply picked up by the locals who saw an opportunity to demonstrate their gratitude and remembrance of a generation who selflessly put their lives on hold and took up arms to rid the islands of a savage invader. His plan was to depart at first light and keep the sun behind him as he followed his grandfather's flight plan.

He had given that flight plan a lot of thought at home when he was planning his journey. There was a big question mark over Big Bill's disappearance. The reports on the
incident revealed that weather conditions on the day were a little patchy with only a limited amount of cloud cover. There were no sign of sudden storms reported and certainly no enemy activity over the Australian mainland. So, if Squadron Leader William Cuthbertson DFC followed the heading from Townsville to Brisbane (160 degrees magnetic) and crashed enroute, why did the extensive air search not find any trace of him?

Bill Jnr concluded that while his ancestor was a talented pilot, he was in fact, a young man of 27 from the bush and the larrikin attitudes carried with him from home were deeply ingrained in his DNA. He would never have had a better chance to get brief contact with his beloved wife and family and mischievously may have chosen to fly off track by 10 degrees and overfly Courtland Downs before swinging east south east to Archerfield to complete his mission.

Young Bill decided to test his theory, by flying down that course to see what he could see. Obviously, he didn't expect to find the wreckage of his grandfather's plane after all this time, but it was simply part of the respectful commemorative flight he was undertaking in his memory.

Bill knew his ancestor was spotted by a naval vessel under tow off the Queensland coast and had plotted that position into his GPS. He would then turn inland and report his position to Townsville before going over the Great Divide to Charters Towers. Again, he would report to ATC his position and intention to turn onto a southerly course roughly approximating Big Bill's trip as reported by the Americans stationed there during the war, who had recorded his apparent heading. He knew this sighting was not fully appreciated when the search for Big Bill got underway, but it seemed logical to young Bill that he would have taken the opportunity to overfly his home on the way to Archerfield. He would have had plenty of fuel and who would know? Certainly not the brass who would have had the hide off his back if they knew he had deviated from his strict orders.

This theory would not leave young Bill alone; it was like a bush fly buzzing around his head. By trying to put himself in Big Bill's flying boots, his thoughts went this way. Big Bill had been away for a fair while and here he would be flying over his homeland, unexpectedly. If he took a heading from Charters Towers south and west, it would take him well west of White Mountains National Park and remain east of Bladensburg National Park. He would arrive over Longreach. He would then have a chance to buzz Courtland Downs, a little undisciplined perhaps, but Big Bill was not out of any ordinary mould. An incentive was, with the war still raging and knowing he would be back in the thick of it, this could be the last time he saw his home.

The temptation would have been mighty strong and it would have been well within the Beau's range. Young Bill decided to follow this hunch and buzz Courtland Downs as he believed Big Bill had intended. After which, Bill Jnr, as Big Bill, would continue south east to Archerfield. Bill Snr would still have plenty of fuel in reserve for this diversion, even allowing for adverse weather.

Young Bill would be flying over some rough country but he'd flown it before and was confident that he would have no navigation problems. The only concern was weather over the mountains which could change abruptly, so he would be seeking up to date information as he went. Satisfied with his planning, which had been well chewed over before he departed for Port Moresby, Bill made several phone calls to home, bringing people up to date with his progress. He had spent time on lengthy calls to his parents and his flying mates and supporters and had taken more calls from Australian press and radio, who were hanging out for his arrival home. He gave them a rough idea of his ETA at Archerfield and a few pieces of information that would give them a bit of colour, 'feeding the chooks' old Sir Jo Bjelke Peterson, controversial premier of Queensland, called it.

Bill set his alarm early to allow plenty of time to check-out and get to the airfield for a pre-flight check of his aircraft. He had collected plenty of admirers in his quest to celebrate his grandfather and many admirers of his beautiful Beech 18. It had been painted up to reflect his cause and provide some exposure of his sponsors' logos. All in all, it resembled a flying bulletin board or race car.

Bill had polo shirts and baseball style caps with the same adornments and a very nice rendition of the Beech on the front with the legend "Big Bill's Spirit". He gave these as

souvenirs to the people he met, including sponsors, supporters and kids that flocked around. The more exposure he gave his sponsors, the more he knew they would be susceptible to future projects, yet to be dreamed up, but he was sure there would be one.

The Beech had been made ready for him, thanks to the guys from the aero club who had given it a bit of a wash and spruce up for the television cameras. She absolutely sparkled in the tropical sun.

Bill threw his baggage in through the rear door and did a thorough walk around, checking control surfaces and connections, taking a fuel sample here and there, turning over the big radials by hand and checking oil levels. A couple of the lads did the walk around with him, keeping up a steady friendly chatter. Bill knew he had made some good friends here and that he would be back one day to another warm welcome.

Satisfied, he walked over and presented his flight plan to the local ATC representative who checked it over and gave it the all clear. His next call was to the weather bureau where he received a thorough rundown on what he could expect on the leg from Port Moresby to Queensland, where updates would be available from weathermen on route.

Take off was at 0800 precisely. Bill had had a great time and met some wonderful people he would always be grateful to and never forget. He was determined to come back on a more relaxed visit next time and maybe bring his sister and grandmother along with him. Somehow he knew Lydia would be very reluctant to visit the scene of her husband's conflict. He would make the offer and let her decide.

Clearance was given for take-off and the big Pratt and Whitney radials roared into life, hauling the Twin Beech down the runway and into the Papuan sky, which was populated by lazy little clouds as usual; some of which were still painted with a faint pink blush. He did a circuit around the city, taking in the view towards the Owen Stanley Ranges that had so much significance to Australians. Clothed in a deep green cloak of jungle growth, they looked benign, belying the horrors that were experienced there by allied soldiers fighting back the Japanese in dreadful conditions. This was a view his grandfather would have looked down on many times but with a vastly different mindset, seeking out targets for his deadly bombs and cannon fire.

Swinging back out over the ocean and continuing to climb, Bill carefully checked all his instruments and double checked his heading. Thanking Jackson's Field ATC, he switched frequencies to pick up Northern Australia ATC who would be his unseen companion for the next five or six hours.

The Coral Sea was an artist's palette of green and blue shades, commencing from the jade colour of the shallows just off the coast, into the deeper ocean waters. Looking down through the broken cloud layer, he wondered how many shades of blue there were. Bill was sure they were all represented here: azure; lapis lazuli; sky blue; cobalt and turquoise, all highlighted by startling white breaking wave tops over coral reefs. It was all very beautiful and he felt very small and very privileged to be where he was.

His call to the ATC had been acknowledged as he reached his cruising altitude of 6000 feet. Synchronising his engines, he set the throttles for cruise and the roar became a steady drumming through the aircraft. He reflected on what may have been going through Big Bill's mind at this stage. Perhaps he thought of completing his mission and, if he was lucky, getting some leave to visit his wife and new born son before going back to the awful conflict he had just left behind. He would know this was out of the question as his orders were very strict. Perhaps this was why he may have diverted to overfly Courtland Downs, as he would have no opportunity to see his wife and son while he was back on Australian soil, even it was for the briefest embrace.

CHAPTER EIGHTEEN

The Queensland coast was coming up quickly and although he had hardly been away for an extended time, like all Australians returning home, he felt that strange, pleasant homecoming warmth in his heart. He was now passing over Magnetic Island with the Great Dividing Range looming up in the far distance. Townsville was almost due south from Port Moresby and his navigation had, so far, been straightforward.

Bill decided to gain more altitude and opened the throttles, climbing to 8000 feet. He advised ATC he was abeam of Townsville and turned on 210 degrees for Charters Towers. His call was acknowledged and he gently banked away to his new course. The Beech was humming along; all systems were in the right zone and he felt a little more at ease now that he was over terra firma once again.

Twenty minutes later Charters Towers came up under the nose as Bill was advised of a change of weather conditions to the south over the ranges. Young Bill had assessed the weather with a cattleman's eye and decided it shouldn't be a hindrance. He calculated he should leave that front behind before it had any influence on his progress. Bill advised ATC that he was over Charters Towers at 1205 hours, 8000 feet turning 235 degrees and would report again over Longreach, ETA 1350 hours.

ATC heard nothing more from Bill for approximately 20 to 25 minutes when over the airwaves, they received a call that no one ever wanted to hear.

'Mayday, mayday, mayday.'

The call was heavy with static and the caller's voice high pitched with stress. Bill gave his call sign and repeated the mayday call. He reported both engines had cut out and he was descending rapidly in the area.

Like his sister before him, he had been caught out by tropical weather; the storm front he was advised of earlier, had hit him hard. While wise enough to avoid flying through the massive anvil-topped cumulonimbus that presented itself across his flight path, he thought it had sufficient clearance below its base for him to maintain his heading with relative safety. He had decided to drop down to 4000 feet where he fully expected some turbulence, but otherwise it should be okay. It only took a few seconds to realise he had made a huge mistake. His cattleman's weather eye should have been a little keener. He had no sooner committed his aircraft to his new course when he was hit with a torrential downpour of biblical proportions.

Blinding rain obscured his vision and the turbulence was indescribable, forcing Bill to tighten his harness to the point of nearly cutting off his circulation. The cockpit was in chaos with charts and manuals flying about. Bill was struck on the back of the head with something hard and heavy, giving him something else to think about. All sunlight was suddenly shut out and now an eerie grey darkness enveloped him.

The rain had become incredibly intense and now hail stones joined the fray. The noise level was horrific as the Beechcraft bucked and tossed about. Bill was no longer flying the plane; he was just hanging on hoping for survival. The control panel was a blur with the vibration and shuddering of the old plane, but his astonished eyes fell on his altimeter which was showing his height as 7000 feet and climbing at an incredible 1500 feet per minute. He had been caught in a powerful updraught drawing him into the very maw of a meteorological monster that had rocketed his aircraft up the best part of 4000 feet in the blink of an eye. He could only hang on and pray his tough Beech would live up to its looks as a truck and stay in one piece.

The noise, the darkness and the juddering and shaking had totally disoriented Bill.

His neck ached from the g-forces and his shoulders were screaming with pain as he was thrown against the limits of his harness. His windscreen was laminated glass with a tough polyurethane type material sandwiched in between three sheets of toughened glass. It had been shattered by the massive hail inside the furore of the destructive cloud and had his windscreen collapsed inwards he would most certainly be dead, either hammered by the hail or rendered unconscious to ride the plane into a high speed impact. Somehow, in answer to Bill's prayer, it had resisted any further pressure, but was still teetering on total collapse if the massive hail, or ice chunks, continued.

The starboard engine was the first to go. Its air intakes either drowned or were stuffed solid with hail. Another turbulent interlude threw the plane on its back, pushing it into a dive. Bill found it impossible to tell up from down, but one thing had improved. The noise had abated slightly but then he realised, ironically, that it was because he was down to one engine. Just as his thoughts go in that direction, the port engine gave up the struggle.

Checking his altitude again, he was now below 3000 feet. This rapid change of altitude might be an everyday event in a stunt plane, but not an old flying truck which was proving tough enough to hold together through the tremendous changes from positive to negative G-force. The one bright point was, judging by the sun shining in his eyes, she had been freed from the influence of the evil monster now sitting benignly above and behind him.

Bill was too busy to take in the view, however, because without its engines, the Beechcraft was now flying like a brick with wings and he needed to find somewhere to put it down in a *controlled* landing. No one liked the term *crash* landing anymore; it conjured up the wrong sort of image.

Bill desperately looked for a landing spot, while going through the drills to restart his engines, checking electrics, fuel pressure, fuel on and at the same time, putting out his mayday call.

There was not much promise in the terrain below, which was heavily timbered and undulating. An ironic thought pops into his head, that the Cuthbertson family were becoming experts in emergency landings. Perhaps, if he survived, he could write a book on the subject. He shook his head and concentrated, admonishing himself for his lack of professionalism.

He was losing height rapidly now and his earphones were filled with the insistent response from ATC, requesting further details. Radar coverage in the area was very patchy and so was radio communication; they had lost contact some time ago. Bill's hands were shaking so violently, he was thankful he was wearing headphones and a microphone which were forced down around his neck in the storm's rough and tumble. Holding a microphone and guiding his plane at the same time would be very difficult.

Bill was experiencing mild panic now. Instinctively, he knew he had to gain control of himself if he was to survive and the discipline of hours of training kicked in. He did his best to keep the plane straight and level while searching for a landing place within a small arc in his glide path. He called ATC again and gave his current position as 10 kilometres due West of Lake Buchanan. He was now down to 1000 feet hoping for a stretch of roadway or a cleared paddock but there was nothing but rugged looking bush as far as he could see.

Eight hundred feet and he still had the same set of problems. He lowered one stage of flap trying to stretch his glide. This was not good. Try as he might, the engines would not respond. Who knew why? Obviously, the water had done a lot of damage but he couldn't be bothered with that now as the ground was rushing up at him.

Bill thought he had prepared well for this journey, but some lessons were hard- learned and despite hearing of his sister's experience in the tropical storm with her own cumulonimbus, or thunder cloud, he allowed his concentration to lapse long enough to be destroyed by this malevolent monster so close to home. Lesson learned far too late. He was now down to 500 feet, still calling Mayday and not a roadway or clearing anywhere. Mercifully, he was over patchy bushland with stunted eucalypts, accompanied by an understory of scrubby bushes and native grasses. He lowered another stage of flap trying to reduce speed, his mind racing. Wheels down, wheels up? He elected to go in wheels up, as the undercarriage could snag in the canopy of a tree and put him in nose first... very hard.

The only thing he could do was guide the plane down and try to "kick a goal" between the trees. He would lose the wings but if he could preserve the integrity of the cabin and fuselage he may stand a chance of survival.

He had long since shut off the fuel to prevent fire and also shut down the ignition systems. He had two exits from the plane; the hatch by his left elbow, which he had cracked open in preparation for the possibility of it jamming, or by the rear entry door, if it did.

'Here we go,' he thought in dread.

A strange reflex action had him clenching his buttocks

Any further thought was drowned out by the incredible noise as the first and tallest trees made contact with the bottom of his plane and the big propellers, that were still spinning, had started to carve into the tree tops and then disintegrate.

He saw a gap between the trees and, while he still has some control by yawing the plane with the rudder, he steered for the centre of the space. And then everything happened very quickly. He couldn't believe the force of the initial impact which almost jolted him out of his harness; he was thrown back and then forward in his seat several times. His hands were jolted off the steering yoke. Through eyes blurring from the vibration, he locked onto the windshield, praying it would not cave in. He is aware, but not really registering, of the cacophony of noise as his Twin Beech broke up and was thrown sideways, colliding with another tree and throwing up impenetrable clouds of dust and clods of earth. And then utter blackness.

Search and Rescue, Townsville had notified Bill's parents, who received the shocking news, as any parent would, with tears at first and numb with dread for their son; they came together for mutual support. Bobby reacted first and started issuing orders. They should head into town to the airfield and see what could be done. Lydia and Jo decided to wait at home for any news that may be phoned through from Townsville; Elise had already decided she would join the air search for her big brother and headed for the car with her dad.

Before Bobby and Elise were halfway to the airfield, the home phone had been ringing off the hook with friends and neighbours all concerned for young Bill. Back in Townsville, search and rescue operations had already swung into action, since Bill's first mayday call.

A search plane was up and had been vectored to the position of Bill's last report. Ground parties would take a long time to get to the general area because there were no roads, so helicopters would be needed to get medics and rescuers in to the crash site when they located it. Longreach Police had been notified and a search party was being organised from there. Bill's aero club had received the dreadful news and the Cuthbertson family had been notified. They reacted with typical stoicism and resolve.

Several of Bill's aero club members had volunteered and were meeting at the club to discuss tactics if they were called on to assist. They were quickly joined by Elise and Bobby.

Then the media got wind of the story and the phone calls became continuous and repetitive. Jo hung up on the last persistent journalist and left the phone off the hook for the bit of temporary peace it brought them. A Brisbane television station had despatched its helicopter ostensibly to aid the search, but in fact to make sure they got some sensational footage for the evening news. Headlines were already out with all the hourly news breaks on radio and television. Headlines like, "Tribute Turns to Tragedy. Famous aviation family son crashes! Search begins!", were being splashed out to a voracious audience.

The survivor of any crash in a motor vehicle or airplane would experience a similar return to awareness. First, a blurred vision becomes clear, the realisation that they had come through and then the self-examination for injuries. Shock provided an initial buffer against the pain of shattered limbs and battered flesh. But for the injured, pain was inescapable.

Bill stirred slowly in the cockpit of his wrecked plane, awareness and memory came in flashes as he climbed out of the black abyss. He had a moment of panic, thinking he had been blinded, but his eyes were glued shut with oil or blood. He felt around and his hand fell on the cooler with his drinks and snacks. He located a bottle of water and doused his face, rubbing away whatever was causing the trouble.

Opening his eyes, he realised it was blood; his shirt front was saturated and when his hand contacted his nose, the shock of pain indicated it was possibly broken, to go with the large gash on his forehead. He quickly did an inventory and gave thanks to his God, as there didn't appear to be any major injuries.

He remained in his seat, getting his head together. He had no idea how long he had been unconscious. He recalled the first sign of engine trouble and the intensity of the turbulence and hail; the last thing he was thinking about was the time of day. His wristwatch was smashed and the hands were showing 1249. Dear God, he was over Charters Towers only 40 minutes ago, with everything going like clockwork and now he was sitting amongst the wreckage of his plane.

He suddenly jolted upright. Smoke! Was he on fire? All pain and discomfort was pushed aside by the old primeval terror. He could smell smoke but where was it coming from? Bill realised it was' a very familiar aroma to anyone who has lived in the bush and had to deal with bushfires.

The super-hot exhaust had burned the grass and shrubs gathered up as the engines ploughed through the bush with the momentum of the Beechcraft carrying the remains forward in a mad sleigh ride. He breathed a little easier and his heart resumed a near normal rate. He started to take in his surrounds; the starboard wing had snapped off at the root and was God knows where. The port wing tip outboard of the engine had gone as well. He knew he had to get out of the wreckage and dragged himself up screaming from a sharp stabbing pain in his left knee, but he was up and his will and sense of urgency denied him the luxury of returning to the familiarity and comfort of his pilot's seat.

His head was down as he ducked back through the fuselage to the cabin door and when he looked up, he was shocked to see the fuselage ended about five feet away. Through the gaping hole, where the lovely twin tails had been, he could now see where they were - upside down, resting against a coolabah tree. There were other bits and pieces mixed up in the brush and sand. This was one landing he wouldn't be bragging about.

He contemplated jumping to the ground but elected to ease himself down. Cursing his stupidity, he aborted his evacuation, climbed painfully to his feet and recovered the emergency pack hanging in its place beside the cabin door. It contained some rations and survival gear like a compass and a signalling mirror but also a package of flares. He added the first aid kit to his haul, as well as the cooler with his drinks and the remains of his food. He was almost out of the door when, once again, he recalled a very special item. Grandmother Lydia's locket was still in its felt bag swinging from the centre console. He swiftly retrieved it and secured it in the bottom of the survival bag.

Now he took in the whole big picture, he sent out a rough position report so authorities would have activated a search for him. There was still plenty of daylight so a fair chance he would be found quickly as he was fortunate enough to put the Beech down in an area where the bush was thin. To the east and west of him, the bush was quite dense. Had he gone down there, he may not have survived the impact and if he had, he may never have been seen again, anyway. His sense of humour came to the fore and he started laughing, maybe as a release from shock, with the way his plane was spread over the Queensland bush. He'd given them a big target to find. The laughter subsided pretty quickly; he was very lucky to be alive in a very sticky situation and he could save his hilarity for when he got out of it.

A thought flashed through his mind, linking up to an earlier idea he had about his grandfather's disappearance. Did Big Bill's choice of heading, as Bill Jnr earlier theorised, lead him to this part of the country? And could his grandfather have crashed, just as he had been thinking, in an inaccessible and dense patch of bush where his camouflaged aircraft would have been invisible to an airborne search? A search that would have focused further east toward the coast, along the course Big Bill would have been expected to traverse.

A shiver ran up young Bill's spine, which may have been from shock or maybe a kind of extrasensory perception. He sat on the damaged port wing and started to assemble the contents of the first aid kit that he'd need to doctor himself. He also made sure the flares were handy for the first rescue aircraft that would surely come along any minute now.

He had a few bruises and a deep cut on his knee that must have smashed into the control panel at some stage. He poured the little bottle of hydrogen peroxide over the wound which stung like hell, and then, as best as he could, he bandaged the wound which was bleeding steadily.

His nose and scalp had stopped bleeding, but the pain there had kicked in now and he searched for the Panadol. After a deep drink of water from the cooler he began to take a serious look around at the wreckage.

It had been a beautiful plane, and he would like to think it could be recovered and restored. He had seen worse wrecks of planes and cars restored to glory, but this would be a logistical nightmare.

He suddenly remembered he had an Emergency Location Transmitter. Damn fool! He struggled back into the wreckage to retrieve it and switch it on.

There was remarkably little fuel spilled which was a lucky break because a fire may have burnt him to death as he had lain unconscious in the cockpit. The only sign of fire was the bush scorched by the heat of the engines the ice and rain had failed to quell. While he was thinking about fire, he realised he should try and get a nice smoky one going to aid searchers as a back up to his Emergency Locater Transmitter. His bush craft was up to scratch and, despite his injuries, he soon had the start of a nice little signal fire crackling away. He would try to find some oil or trash from the wreck to give the smoke a bit of body. Having got his immediate environment in order, Bill settled down to wait for his saviours, who should be coming soon.

The signal from the Emergency Location Transmitter, when activated automatically or manually, would be picked up by a satellite which transferred the beacon's signal to the rescue coordination centre. The distress call would be escalated through a local user terminal, mission control centre and then the rescue coordination centre (RCC) responsible in that region for arranging search operations. The rescue authority uses its own receiving equipment afterwards to locate the beacon and commence its own rescue or recovery.

'But you have to switch the bloody thing on,' Bill scolded himself.

The system seemed a bit roundabout, but it was a system that had saved many lives and considering the vast area it covered, it had a remarkable success rate.

Trying to calculate his current position was complicated by the run in with the massive cloud which may have driven him many miles off course. At the 300 kilometres per hour the Beech was doing when Bill put in his first mayday call, and the final crash, the plane would have covered approximately five kilometres per minute and now possibly rested some 40 or 45 clicks away. But in which direction?

That meant there was a lot of bush to search and it had to be done methodically. At Townsville Search and Rescue, authorities had, with some difficulty, located detailed army survey maps of the area and were allocating a search grid to the assembled volunteer pilots, while further south at Longreach, a similar scene was being played out.

Radio frequencies were allotted and schedules devised. When everything was in reasonable shape, six planes and two helicopters transferred to Charters Towers, refuelled and became airborne again, heading along Bill's track as reported to ATC. They had now received the ELT (emergency locator transmitter) information but that was still only approximate. The fixed wing aircraft maintained an altitude of about 500 feet above the terrain. That will give them a chance to spot any wreckage and hopefully a survivor. They were in a broad line, stretching out with about 500 metres between each aircraft, covering a pretty good patch of bush as they went.

Thirty minutes later, the search planes were in the general area and each one broke off to their assigned patch of the grid and the bush was scoured for any trace of Bill and his plane. ATV news chopper followed up and had been requested to stay clear.

While they circled and waited for news, they began to film some of the thick scrub that lay to the east of Bill's crash site for use as 'colour' in any subsequent news story.

Bill had got his signal fire going and a rich plume of oily smoke was climbing into the sky above him, providing a clear target for the searchers and, as if by magic, a plane was circling overhead. An arm was waving out of the passenger window, indicating that he had been spotted. Within seconds, word had spread over the airwaves and a ground party was briefed on his position in case a helicopter rescue was not feasible.

The television mob heard the news and zeroed in to get their shots and were rewarded with a smiling, and bloodied young Bill Cuthbertson, standing beside his wrecked aircraft, waving cheerfully at them. Thankfully, the film didn't pick up the blood soaked shirt or the rapidly swelling knee or his black eye, an image guaranteed to horrify family and friends alike.

The good news reached Courtland Downs and Lydia and Jo were once again dancing about with relief as Elise and Bobby headed home. They had hardly got off the ground when the news broke, to their great joy. Bill had only been away a few days really, but the family's concern for his safety and the desire to see him home safe and well, made it seem much longer. Now, they waited anxiously to see their son and brother, the survivor of a plane crash.

'Stress and anxiety will play games with a person's thoughts,' said Elise in an attempt to ease the tension with the wisdom of a seasoned veteran.

Lydia sat on the couch in the living room, waiting on further news. She lapsed into and out of a restless "nanna nap" brought on by the immense relief that surged through her when news of young Bill's discovery was announced. In Lydia's mind, images of her deceased husband and her very much living grandson, flashed and merged and separated only to merge again.

The surreal semi-dreaming state only lasted a few seconds, but it stayed in her mind's eye for the remainder of the day only to be expunged by that night's peaceful sleep.

The family members, minus their much-loved son, joined hands in a prayer of thanks when they all came together to wait for further news of the distressed young aviator now in the hands of his rescuers.

CHAPTER NINETEEN

Young Bill was getting more than his 15 seconds of fame right then. Every newspaper had the story on its front page and the six o'clock television news carried the full story, including footage of the crash site and the rescue chopper winching Bill out on a stretcher. When Bill was eventually discharged from hospital, his parents and Elise were there to bring him home after fighting their way through a phalanx of press and television reporters. Bill didn't truly feel at home until they motored through the main gate at Courtland Downs, where he let out a huge sigh of relief and a yelp as the vehicle hit one or two potholes in the gravel drive.

His mother and Elise fussed about like a pair of mother hens bringing food and drinks, propping up his pillows and slapping a cool face cloth over his brow, despite protestations that he was just fine. The television remote was placed at his side; newspapers, flying magazines and books were heaped on the coffee table within arm's reach, along with a big tin of his favourite sweet biscuits.

He had been featured on the front page of most of the daily papers while he was in hospital and the family had kept the major ones for him to catch up on when he got home.

Television had provided a heap of coverage and his face was now up there with the Prime Minister in terms of recognisability.

The video shot by the television helicopter that was first on the scene, was pretty extensive and included the colour piece filmed over the denser bush before Bill was located. Of course, it was heavily edited and only about 20 seconds was ultimately used in the news story. Bill's publicist was still on the job and wouldn't miss this golden opportunity to pump the story for all it was worth. He had assembled the press into a conference room at the hospital and the family were ushered in there by their agent and positioned behind a battery of microphones, facing a room full of television and still cameras from the media.

Their publicist directed the flow and, after 15 minutes of intense grilling and a barrage of inane questions, he cut it short by declaring Bill exhausted and needing rest. In fact, the wily devil had already sold the exclusive interview rights to one of the biggest Sunday night current affairs programs and didn't want the lesser lights tiring out his client. He wanted him fresh and unrehearsed for the major program. He ushered them out and then turned to his clients and told them the story was now under a strict embargo. No one was to speak to the press unless it had been cleared by him.

The next morning, all the details were in print with Bill's poor old, battered visage on the front page of all the Queensland and some southern newspapers, with a photo insert of the wreckage of the Beech laying in pieces in the bush where it had come to rest.

The back story about Big Bill being lost during the war and Bill Jnr's quest to honour his memory with this flight was not forgotten and an interested journalist, Cliff Carter, was reviewing some of the rejected video when he noticed something peculiar. He called the production guy in and got him to run the video that was shot of the broader bush area by his team as background filler, until he was able to isolate the object he had seen. A technician was called in and they were able to clarify the image until they could clearly see itwas the remains of an old aircraft of World War Two vintage.

Could it be? No, impossible! And yet, there it was. Unmistakably World War Two vintage, and in an area that could just possibly be where Squadron Leader William Cuthbertson DFC came to grief. This was sensational and could be award- winning journalism if they could get in there and confirm it. Cliff swore his two colleagues to secrecy and promised they would both share in the credits if they could get this story up.

But first, they needed to get out there and confirm their discovery and hopefully tie it up in an exclusive. Cliff's heart was pounding with excitement. This was just what every young fledgling journo dreamed of. Not that he was a rookie by any means. Cliff had commenced his career in a small, regional television station in northern New South

Wales, Prime 7, where he learnt the basics of the job, but it was only when he gained an appointment to mainstream television that his eyes were opened to the cut and thrust of commercial television. This was where it was dog eat dog, as far as newsroom rank and minutes on air were concerned. He had his grass cut by one devious reporter when he naively asked for advice on a sporting scandal he had come across. Next thing he knew, the story was on air over the deceitful bastard's name as an exclusive. When he confronted the guy, all he got was a rueful smile and a wink which said it all. It would be a long time before he fell for that one again.

A true believer in karma Cliff was privately ecstatic when the traitor was discovered in a store room with the wife of an on air and very important colleague and was summarily sacked in disgrace.

Cliff was tempted to run to his boss with the story but decided to moderate his excitement and prepare the ground work soundly. He drew up a broadsheet of possible costs and weighed the benefits against it and also built his story around the legendary flying Cuthbertson's, Queensland's favourite family. The presentation of his discovery was so persuasive he had the go ahead immediately and a budget that included a helicopter and film crew. The now more experienced Cliff recognised the value of his discovery and hastily instructed his accountant to pull a shelf company and register it in his name. The story was hush-hush and those involved were asked to sign a confidentiality agreement that would have them consigned to the network bureau in the worst conflict between warring tribes on the African continent if they were stupid enough to leak the story.

Cliff was in a hurry, but he would not ruin the story with careless haste. He planned the flight with great care, telling the pilot exactly what he expected to find and how he wanted to film it. He delivered the same set of instructions and cautions to his film crew, telling them they were on the cusp of one of the nation's great news stories, literally creating history.

The helicopter took them back over the site and they confirmed with their eyes that what they saw on the video tape was in fact a World War Two aircraft. What they couldn't confirm from the air was the type. It certainly looked like their idea of a Beaufighter, but never having seen one in the flesh as it were, they couldn't be sure. Cliff had consulted *Jane's Fighting Aircraft of World War II* and thought he knew what he was looking for, but this pile of junk was not all there and more than half was buried by the bush. The bulk of the fuselage and the twin engine configuration was very positive, but they would need to go in on foot to absolutely confirm what Cliff prayed was the scoop of the year.

The group sought assistance from a well-known bushman to organise the expedition and, before anyone else could get a sniff of their mission, they were deep in the bush and closing on their target. They reached the wreckage after a couple of frustrating days, seemingly going around in circles, which is precisely what they were doing as their action man guide padded out his fee, negotiated on a daily rate. He had to deliver the goods eventually and so, they stumbled through the scrub, insect bitten and sunburnt, to the wreck site. But hey, what the hell? There was a silver lining, it gave the journos a real taste of the bush and some interest to their story.

A Bristol Beaufighter was a distinctive aircraft, with an unmistakeable appearance at ground level; the two mighty radial engines were easy to pick and jungle coloured camouflage and squadron markings were another clue. They had researched the details of Big Bill's aircraft and it wasn't long, all filmed in living colour, before it was a positive ID. They filmed the plane as it was, overgrown and settled in the undergrowth. Then Cliff decided he would check inside for remains.

This would need to be done carefully and respectfully, especially for the camera, as similar wreckage had been declared as war graves and were sacrosanct. The aircraft had broken in half a couple of metres behind the pilot's position. The tail plane, possibly including the navigator, had been thrown clear and lay in the scrub 30 metres away.

Cliff walked gingerly into the fuselage through the rear where the plane had snapped in half, all the time talking to the camera and secretly shaking in his boots, fearful of snakes and spiders.

There were tricks to using a microphone and Cliff knew most of them. By holding it close up to his mouth and breathing hoarsely into it as he spoke to the camera in extreme close up, he gave the impression he was in a dangerous environment, fearlessly risking life and limb to bring this incredible story to his loyal television audience at great personal risk Lathered in perspiration and a carefully dirtied face, he was seen on one knee inside the wreckage, apparently in prayer, getting emotional for the deceased flyers. No, this was not about ratings or sponsors' money; he was on a sacred mission to bring this story, concerning one of his country's great heroes, home to his viewing audience.

Filming continued, taking in the navigator/rear gunner's position in the tail section and moving about zeroing in on the cockpit with many of the instruments still intact. The pilot's single seat, perversely with the remains of what could possibly be a parachute on the back of it, looking as if the pilot had discarded it on his way out of the wreckage. The entry and exit to the cockpit was by way of a lift up hatch above the pilot's seat to the port side. If this was the plane in question, Cliff could well imagine it would have been difficult for a big bloke to open that hatch and bail out, with or without a parachute, and he could see the reason for ditching it quickly.

There was another object that looked like a small attaché case just at the back of the cockpit that caught Cliff's eye. It was, or had been, painted bright red, across which was printed in large black letters, "Most Secret". All now faded but still legible. Cliff managed to prise it from its rusted rack and hauled it to the hatch. All of this filmed as it happened, for the consumption of his avid viewers.

Cliff called for a "cut". He stood back and pondered the situation. What could be inside the despatch case? What secrets did it hold and could he build something out of this find? His camera man pointed out that he might be prosecuted for interfering with military intelligence, no matter how old.

Cliff's ambition and ego quickly shrugged that idea off as his imagination began to spin. Instead of a one off, he suddenly had an inspirational vision of building this into an audience grabber, stretching out the curiosity and intrigue for a couple of episodes building the tension levels until finally, the case would be opened and its contents revealed to a captivated audience.

Cliff ordered the camera to fire up again to continue shooting in and around the wreckage and the surrounding bush, taking in some of the landmarks visible from the site, until they had enough for half a dozen telemovies. The station's four wheel drive had finally beaten a path to them and it was time to go.

The camera guy was getting a little feisty. He had been bitten by ants and mosquitos and, what he swore was, a deadly spider and was mentally counting down the time until he expired. But he was reassured by the great white hunter that, of the many hundreds of species of spiders living in this patch of bush, none were possessed of the Sydney funnel web spider's virulence.

Cliff finally agreed to pull the pin and pack up, much to everyone's relief and after one more uncomfortable night in their camp, they set off at first light for the comforts of the city and a hot shower.

Led by the canny bush bashing expert, the retreat was no easier than the advance, although in covering the same distance, it appeared to be a lot shorter. A few suspicious looks were cast in the direction of "paid by the day Jungle Jim" which he artfully avoided.

A huge question had arisen over the wreckage. What had become of Big Bill and his crewman, Flight Sergeant Bluey Mansfield? Was there any trace of their remains? If they had been killed on impact, surely there would be some trace of their skeletal remains or uniforms in the wreckage. Did they survive and were maybe badly injured trying to walk out, only to perish in the inhospitable Queensland bush?

Certainly, the main fuselage was largely intact and it could be expected that any crewman in it, at impact, could possibly have survived, but could the same be said of the navigator in the torn off section so violently thrown aside?

There were many questions to be asked and answered yet. Such was the solemn first episode roundup of Cliff's television program airedin prime time to a huge audience, which included the Cuthbertson family.

The family looked on, to learn about Cliff Carter's expedition and they were rightly outraged and wanted to know who had authorised this team of newshounds to go trampling all over the last resting place of their ancestor, a war hero and WWII air ace? A king sized legal dust up followed with the press and lawyers having a field day.

Meanwhile, the despatch case had been transported to Cliff's television station and put under lock and key in Cliff's office, but for dramatic effect the viewers would believe it sat in a security lockup in the bowels of a well-known bank. They put an image to air of the box sitting on a cell floor behind bars like a high profile and dangerous felon.

The despatch case seemed to have a magnetism, an aura that radiated out from it, like something spiritually possessed. As it sat, its secrets unresolved, curiosity grew into intrigue and quickly became obsession. Cliff and the television station had to endure an avalanche of calls from the public demanding answers. Print media, from home and abroad, camped on the doorstep waylaying anyone who looked like they might give them a scintilla of information to feed the ravening hordes that read their papers or watched their news services.

The media, and therefore the public, could not have had any idea of the power and the shattering import of the items in that lockup but they soon would. What they would ultimately discover would be an explosive scandal with not only national significance, but the potential to bring down the serving government and shame a famous first family.

There is no hint of this diabolical outcome at this juncture. The **despatch case** was finally placed under 24 hour armed guard. All of this was sensationally reported on the national news, with the right amount of drama and speculation of course.

Unbeknownst to Cliff, he was about to receive a shock, because this exposure had been witnessed, reported and queried by more than one zealous public servant. Cliff would soon receive a visit from the Federal Police, acting on behalf of the military, to put a claim on the item and its contents as property of the Crown, at the insistence of Chief of Air force, Air Marshall Hector O'Brian AO DSO.

An expensive and intense court battle ensued over the ownership of the **despatch case** with Cliff's claim being recognised ultimately on the basis of precedence and the moot point of the millennium, 'the public's right to know.' Many aircraft around Australia and the world had been recovered by restorers without question. Why should this be different?

Plus, the crew apparently survived the impact and walked away, so it could not be classified as a war grave. Cliff would have access to the **despatch case** and its contents, but had agreed magnanimously to gift it to the Crown when he had completed his project. What possible harm could come from that?

But that was down the track and a deliriously excited, and blissfully unaware, Cliff was going to build this into an epic television event. Cliff was already scratching pointers in his note book, sketching in episode titles and promotional pointers, all featuring him, of course. His last great assignment had been looking into dodgy fish shops substituting imported catfish from Vietnam, labelling it "local" wild barramundi.

The way this sensation was rolling out, it would lift him above the pack of the ordinary try-hard reporters, into the stratospheric heights of elite television journalism. He was even practising his sign off in front of the bathroom mirror.

Late nights were spent in writing up a script and planning the sequence in which things would be revealed. It looked like they would get at least five to ten episodes out of this.

This was huge for Cliff. Previously, his biggest exposé after the blasted stinking imported fish scandal, was about a dodgy used car salesman he had to chase up an alley way in classic shock journo style. This would surely be the breakthrough he dreamed about; a wiser head would have advised Cliff to wind back his eagerness a little.

There was no holding him back now though; he had the scent of a tremendous victory in his nostrils and could already envisage the presentation of the Walkley Award.

Episode One 'The Hero' would give all the background on Big Bill and his war service.

Episode Two 'The last Tragic Flight of Lieutenant W L Cuthbertson DFC' would focus on Big Bill's last journey.

Episode Three 'An Ace Down' would be the futile search, including speculation on the reason for Big Bill leaving the war zone on a secret mission and why did he divert from his flight plan?

Episode Four 'Salute to a Hero' would be focused on young Bill and his mission to honour his grandfather and the young pilot's subsequent crash and rescue. There would be some copyright issues with this part of the story, he realised.

Episode Five 'Amazing Discovery' Cliff's discovery of the air ace's aircraft when the entire RAAF failed., How Cliff fought his way through the impenetrable jungle, clashing with spiders and venomous snakes, to the wreck site.

Episode Six 'The Secret Mission' The recovery of the Top Secret despatch case.

Episode Seven "'Expert Opinion Divided' Military experts to debate the possibilities.

Episode Eight 'Recovery' experts to reveal what may have gone wrong and can the Beaufighter actually be recovered?

Episode Nine 'The Story so Far' A summary and revisitation of the story to date.

Episode Ten 'The Reveal' The despatch case will be opened and the contents revealed 'LIVE!!'

There is no doubt Cliff's expectations are rising like a well prepared soufflé and like a soufflé too much haste may cause an embarrassing collapse. Cliff's rapidly formed television Production Company "Clifftop

Productions" was into full production. Background research had been undertaken, interviews sought from a variety of experts on military aircraft and shadowy security experts, eerily obscured for effect, who would give reluctant opinions but reveal nothing of substance.

War historians were grilled about the Battle of Milne Bay and the Kokoda Track. Survival experts were interrogated on surviving in the conditions they would expect to find in south west Queensland at the time that Cuthbertson's plane ditched.

Young Bill and his famous sister were filmed as they entered court seeking an injunction on Cliff's enterprise and were added to the growing list of interviewees reluctant, willing or otherwise. The injunction was granted, which put the brakes on Cliffs' ambitions for the moment. Cliff was made of the stuff of hard core journalism the world over and gave it scant regard.

The teaser campaign had sparked a lot of interest, not only with the general public, but withthe general media who could detect a faint smell of sensation.

There was another individual who should have shown intense interest in this affair, but was currently too involved in the federal political scene and internal party politics, jostling for position and power. A ripple of disquiet was soon to spread across the waters and was yet to reach him from the depths of modern tabloid journalism.

The full production was completely vetted by the station's legal department, polished and edited, over and over, until Cliff was totally satisfied. At this stage, no one knew what would be revealed from the top secret despatch case.

The television promos hit the airwaves soon after, which should have increased the stridency of the alarm bells from a certain character in Canberra but, so far, not a tremor of interest.

A high powered legal posse with a security detail was despatched by the government in an attempt to recover the item they still contended was, and always should, remain the property of the Commonwealth despite the earlier court ruling to the contrary. Secretly, they were alarmed at the revelation of secret military reports contained in the despatch case.

Why would a highly decorated air ace be taken out of a crucial conflict as a courier if the despatch case contained only routine reports on troop displacements? It had to be something of a very sensitive nature. They believed the Defence Department would be wearing this as another scandalous spot on its already heavily stained escutcheon.

Cliff's plans could crumble to dust if this second legal attack were successful and he had to watch the despatch case, with its intriguing secrets, loaded into a government vehicle to depart down the highway, along with his career, into obscurity. But all was not lost. Cliff called his legal department who immediately appealed against the injunction.

After a lot of back and forth which wound up being settled in the High Court, Cliff once again won the rights to the despatch case and its contents. This was through some obscure law relating to salvage. The decision led to celebrations with his team in his production company offices, which ended in tears, as usual.

Two of the team were discovered in the stationery cupboard, being anything but stationary. What was the attraction of stationery cupboards in television stations? Cliff couldn't figure. Thankfully, they were a hetero couple. Another did his licence on a breath test and a long standing feud between the sales rep and a production guy came to fisticuffs in the boardroom. Actually, it was a pretty standard performance in television land where, like oil and water, alcohol and egos did not mix.

CHAPTER TWENTY

1949

Lawrence Garret Parnham VC was elected to the House of Representatives on, what was then, the Country Party ticket, to great acclamation. After the results of the election were announced, his triumphant supporters celebrated long into the night. The Parnham couple of Lawrence and his adoring wife savour the victory at the Australia Hotel along with Lawrence's major supporters and chief political advisers.

Traditionally, representing graziers, farmers and rural voters generally, the Country Party began as the Progressive Party from the 1922 split until 1925. It then used the name the Country Party until 1977, when it became the National Country Party. The party commonly referred to as "The Nationals," or the "Nats", had generally been the minor party in a centre- right Coalition with the Liberal Party in government. In opposition it worked in formal coalition or separately, but generally in co-operation with the Liberal Party and its predecessor, the United Australia Party. During periods of conservative government, the leader also served as Deputy Prime Minister.

Against this background of change and challenge, Lawrence seemed to emerge unscathed, riding all the right waves and avoiding the deadly undertows that swept away lesser political hopefuls. He rose through the ranks effortlessly and was tagged as "leader in waiting". Lawrence was seen as a natural leader about whom his acolytes joked could heal the sick and raise the dead. A natural and eloquent orator drawing on a huge vocabulary, he easily bettered any interjector or rival in a debate or in the bar rooms of the rural hotels that were a mandatory stop when out on the rural hustings. The politician's best defence, when on the road, is a razor sharp wit and Lawrence's repartee was becoming legend. Between himself and party leader, Bob Menzies, they were formidable in town hall debates.

Due to war time shortages, housing had become a huge problem and at one meeting a heckler repeatedly demanded to know what Menzies would do about the housing problem.

'Whaddya gunnado about 'ousing.'

Menzies' response to great laughter and applause was classical. 'Put an aitch in front of it!'

The Honourable Lawrence Parnham VC MP was an enormously influential and popular politician who was admired by both sides of the House and in his private life as a farmer and grazier, whose family had been a huge positive influence on the quality and consistency of the wool industry. The examples they presented on land management and stock controls were a direct influence on the prosperity of their district.

Chatsworth Park had been expanded by the addition of entertaining areas and even a luxurious swimming pool, sporting a spa and a tasteful bar which supplied restorative drinks to guests. This was now the scene of many gatherings of the party faithful with Frances acting as a most gracious host.

Sometimes these affairs were staged as an example of Australian rural life for overseas visitors, who would be delighted to watch the sheep dogs work the flock, penning them up with a few whistles and calls from their handler. Once yarded, one of the prize sheep would be used in a demonstration of shearing and the fleece laid out for inspection. Then, depending on the status of the visitor, Frances would present the principal couple with a matching wrap for the ladies and a handsome scarf for the gents, made from their prize winning wool. The VIPs would then be served a delicious barbeque luncheon washed down with Hunter Valley wines on the terrace overlooking the pool, weather permitting, otherwise in the spacious dining room with a huge open fire adding warmth and ambience to the occasion.

Very often, guests were delighted to be invited to join in at the barbeque, wearing one of the souvenir aprons bearing the logo of Chatsworth Park, designed especially for the purpose, brandishing the cooking implements for the cameras. These happy snaps never failed to make the social pages. Important guests were sent away feeling they had experienced something very special and generally with a proposal or request for co-operation as the last word from their charming host.

Supporters and party contributors were also entertained at Hotel Australia following the family tradition. Before his passing, Alexander would be in attendance, bringing some of his heavy hitters in for support. Other soirees were to help raise funds for the Parnham Family Trust, a philanthropic instrument through which they distributed welcome funds to a range of charities.

Their political enemies grumbled that the lining of their own pockets was a collateral benefit of these fundraisers, but proof was hard to find. The cutting down of tall poppies was a national sport in Australia and the Parnham's were a particularly rich field of tall blooms for the chattering masses to disparage.

The net result was the making of what would appear to be the politician of the ages: war hero; leader; philanthropist; socialite and business entrepreneur. Frances, his glamorous partner, shone as his escort, always by his side when it counted and working harder than any other wife or partner on either side of the House. Their two beautiful children, when they eventually came along, Gordon Alexander and Estelle Charlotte, were favourites of the press cameras, being regulars in women's magazines. An over exuberant sub-editor had once dubbed the Parnham's as "Australia's answer to the Kennedys".

Lawrence and Frances were held in very high regard in high society but enjoyed the popular support of the admiring working class in the city and strong support from Lawrence's constituents in the rural communities. Powerful business people were ardent supporters, but not obviously so; many worthwhile crumbs fell or were tipped from the Parnham table and it paid well to stay close.

Now as they seemed to glide into their senior years, they could look back proudly on many years, in fact decades, of public service that had earned them both many accolades from grateful community groups and their government.

Together, they had travelled the world and met royalty and celebrities of all types. Sometimes this was done in the line of ministerial duty and sometimes it was private or business travel. Lawrence was scrupulous in keeping his official and private travel separate. He had seen one or two naïve or plain stupid and greedy MPs on both sides of the House, forced to fall on their swords having been caught rorting the system of paltry sums with their guilty-looking mugs spread over the front pages of the tabloids.

The thought of such shame was the stuff of nightmares for Lawrence and he could not imagine what his long passed father Sir Alexander would say should he be caught up in such cheap corruption. These petty breaches of trust by a serving MP or senior civil servant became a crack in the veneer of their reputations. It would then result in some aggressive journalist prising the crack wider to reveal darker secrets buried deep within.

Lawrence felt secure in his standing. Sure, there were a few shadowy deals made in the past, one or two matters overlooked that others might be held answerable to. His father's reputation had often been the subject of enquiry as rumours swirled around his involvement in some property deals that had a faint scent of corruption about them. But the old knight was a wily adversary and one or two complainants, who foolishly took him on without sound evidence to enforce their claims, wound up having their heads handed to them.

Lawrence enjoyed the lucrative perks of a senior politician, without needing to join the greedy self-serving lesser lights dipping their snouts in the public trough. He did very well on the quieter fringes, always at arm's length and with plausible deniability paramount.

That is not to say that Alexander, or his celebrated son had never used their knowledge or contacts to comfortably feather the family nest. This was looked upon as deserved and clever tactics that were earned by the sacrifice of providing public service and, after all, "*locum habet privilegium*" (rank hath privilege). Life was good and rewards, taken subtly and avoiding greed, were plenty for the hero of New Guinea.

It is a sad fact that no one passed through life without creating enemies whose enmity, or even deep hatred, was engendered, not by insult or injury, but by envy or feelings of inferiority from people that simply wanted the achievers to be cut down. Despite the broad adoration of the Parnham family, and all their good works, they had enemies aplenty. These enemies were united in their determination to find the fissure in the surface of the Parnham façade that could provide a lead into deeper, darker faults within.

There comes a time in the life of some men when things may change. Not cataclysmically, nor with some seismic shift of the tectonic plates of his being, but some small misalignment in the rhythms of his daily life. The warning comes as some involuntary half registered flicker of his subconscious thought. Some men try to fool themselves into believing there is nothing to it, just tiredness, jaded nerves, too much to drink the night before.

But some men had less to lose than Lawrence, who put himself above those lesser men. The portents were there, if only for a nanosecond, a momentary flash across the synapses. Then followed the first tremors of what may lay ahead; the tremors built to a noticeable and disturbing vibration and then came the tsunami. And nothing was ever the same again.

Lawrence's feelings of disquiet came about as Cliff Carter's pre-program promotional campaign reached saturation point and finally entered his cognisance. Increasingly frequent nightmares were troubling Lawrence in recent years and he had lapsed into heavy drinking again. Insomnia led to exhaustion and subsequent bad tempered outbursts at home and in his office. And to make matters worse, his son, his pride and joy and the next generation of the illustrious Parnhams seemed to be running off the rails. The last thing he needed right now was an intergenerational spat. But here it was in an era of social change which he'd heard referred to as a time of free love, drugs, sex and rock 'n' roll.

Gordon Alexander followed tradition in his education, being enrolled at Kings School and was welcomed as the fourth generation of Parnhams to throw a shadow across the school's threshold. Gordon's sister was a star pupil at SCEGGS Darlinghurst, her mother's old alma mater. Both seemed destined for the life and careers of their esteemed parents but with one exception; it was Estelle who studied law and was admitted to the bar, eventually joining her father and grandfather's law firm as a junior partner.

Much to the horror of Frances and Lawrence, Gordon had decided to quit university, where he had been showing promise in jurisprudence, to form a rock band and disappear on the road for months at a time, emerging now and again with his hair growing longer and sporting a straggly beard and enough hippy beads to purchase Manhattan from the Indians. He was also showing signs of substance abuse, although he denied it vehemently, declaring it a filthy bourgeois distraction. Apparently, so was soap, thought Lawrence.

The greatest shock came when he appeared with a waif-thin girl with a shock of hair, called an Afro, and declared her his wife. They had been joined in 'perpetual peace and unity' by their Zen master in a hippy commune in Byron Bay. Her name was Lesley Martine Robards, the daughter of a Sydney industrialist manufacturer of some sort, of nasty weapons for the American war effort in Vietnam. It was the age of flower power, she declared with the frequent use of words like groovy and baby. Make love not war. Oh Christ!

Against this unsettling melodrama, Lawrence's dreams tortured him nightly and were always the same; the screaming Japanese officer, the beating he suffered, the shaking hand writing and finally his men, the poor buggers executed by samurai sword, talking to him, their eerie voices coming from headless corpses standing at attention, saluting him. He would wake confused, tired and hung over. Typically, he would stagger into his bathroom to vomit and stand under a cold shower, letting the icy needles hammer down on his head driving away his hangover. If only it could drive away the nightmares.

To add to his agonies, some of his parliamentary colleagues had taken great interest in the Cliff Carter series promotional ads. There had been rumours for years, rumbling about in certain quarters, concerning a serious indiscretion by an officer in the frontline that may have been the cause of some Australian losses. Nothing solid was ever offered in support of these anecdotes, just 'some fella said to my old sergeant's second cousin twice removed that...'

Some of these old timers about the House, because of Lawrence's military background, would bail him up in the corridors for his opinions on the speculations that there could be a serious breach of military discipline involved in this television exposé of a wartime mystery. The same anecdotes were also hinted at in one or two biographies written by senior military officers on their retirement.

What did Lawrence know? Was there anything to these rumblings? These vague yet disquieting tales, which may or may not involve a current incumbent senior politician, had echoed around the close knit Lower House environment and military circles, coming initially from senior military and political types for years without anybody being able to flesh them out. No one wanted to take a risk on the legal backlash that would result by taking an educated guess, nor could anyone come up with any real and acceptable level of evidence. They just continued on as vague chatter when conversation had dried up over the last port of the night in the various club bars frequented by the political intelligentsia and gossip mongers.

CHAPTER TWENTY ONE

1993

By now, there was nation-wide public fascination with the contents of that damned despatchcase, frustrating and tantalising the audience during the 24 hour, seven day a week promotion.

Rival television networks employed experts who could throw some light on the matter, hoping to gain some spin off for the attention-starved programs that had missed out on this huge human interest story. Military historians had linked Cuthbertson's plane all the way back to the Battle of Milne Bay and speculated on why an important leader and experienced combat pilot would be pulled out of the conflict and sent south on this secret mission. The despatch case must contain some incredibly important and possibly explosive war time intelligence. The historians and conspiracy theorists were slavering over the possibilities.

Finally, Cliff brought his program to air, obviously in prime time, dominating the 7.30 Sunday evening timeslot. His network had never experienced ratings like this and advertising revenues reflected the success of the series. The massive ratings created equally massive sales records as well. The network shareholders were rubbing their hands together with glee as the revenue poured in at unprecedented volumes. Each week, as the story rolled out, the audience numbers grew and a variety of spin offs began to germinate.

Repeats were run in week day nine to five time slots. To say that management were deliriously happy with Cliff was to understate the situation, and if they were delirious, so too were the shareholders as they watched their share price soar.

Television was an industry that fed on itself, so it followed that there were teams commissioned by all the rival networks to come up with something, anything, that could perhaps rival, or at least take the heat out of, the sensational ratings winning series that was growing like topsy and now reaching stratospheric heights. It was already being spoken of as one of the greatest current affairs programs of all time. It would surely win a Walkley Award for Carter and sweep all before it, for every other media or entertainment award, both locally and nationally.

The Monday daily newspapers carried analysis and comment on the previous night's episodes and The Courier Mail had even run an editorial on it insisting the story must be run to its completion and its truths, however shocking, must be revealed to the public.

Each week following the schedule laid out by Cliff's team, the story continued on its enthralling way, dragging in more and more viewers. Not so subtle hints were fed into the weekly post episode wrap ups and previews of the following week's content, which seemed to indicate there was a massive political connection to the final reveal. But this was, of course, only speculation. The Pandora's Box, as some were calling it, was yet to be opened and its contents revealed.

The disconcertion and uncertainty created by all this promotion had created a ripple of concern with Cliff's legal team who were feeling a little nervous as to what might actually explode out of the wretched thing. A late night discussion with Cliff and his production crew came to the rational conclusion that it might be wise to secretly preview the contents of the top secret **despatch case**, ensuring they were protected against potential blowback.

The despatch case was brought into the boardroom and laid on the table with all due solemnity, and for the record, the lawyers insisted on the event being filmed. Bolt cutters were required to access the contents and, after a bit of a struggle, they managed to cut through the still intact padlock. They carefully filmed every step of the process which would be cut into the "live"presentation later.

Someone had produced some cotton gloves from the props department, which Cliff, as the centre of this investigation, donned and carefully opened the case slowly and dramatically, revealing several folders which he slid out onto the table. Each one was marked in very bold upper case type TOP SECRET and EYES ONLY FOR General Officer, Commanding Home Forces, Lieutenant-General Iven Mackay. The date was stamped 20th September 1942, marked with handwritten notes on the sender, bearing the 55th Battalion colour patch of brown and green.

Its original destination would have been the AMP Building in Queen Street, Brisbane which was the headquarters of the Allied Forces in the South West Pacific. Follow up research showed the date to be some two weeks after the battle of Milne Bay was concluded and the Japanese had departed.

The first folder contained a number of odd-looking hand drawn maps and another two page document that appeared to be of Japanese origin. It carried a long handwritten report signed and dated on the bottom. It had been counter signed by a Lieutenant Kerrison and dated some days earlier.

Cliff gingerly opened the second folder to reveal an action report, this time written by Lieutenant Kerrison. He scanned it quickly and reeled back, eyes wide with shock. The import of this report was not lost on him regardless of his relative youth and inexperience. He looked about at the group, shaking with excitement, totally unsure what he should do or say. After a few moments he gathered himself and shut the folder, before anyone else could glimpse the contents, and sat down heavily in one of the leather upholstered chairs. His team was staring at him, unaware of the gravity that had now descended on Cliff's narrow shoulders while the cameras continued rolling.

Cliff recovered his self-control and looked around the room at his people one at a time, making firm eye contact to ensure they heard what he said. He told them that this was a political bombshell, with the potential to bring down the government. He emphasised each point with an extended forefinger, stabbing into the boardroom table forcibly. In journalistic terms though its value was beyond any old gold mine. This was King bloody Solomon's Mines.

He did not wish to reveal it to them, even though he trusted them implicitly, as it may actually be dangerous to possess this knowledge. There was no telling what the subject of this report might do to prevent its publication.

His team shuffled their feet looking nervously at each other wondering what's to come. He made an executive decision to return the files to the despatch case and then into the safe hands of high security and brought in some expert legal and technical advice before proceeding. He reminded those in the room of their obligation to absolute secrecy and the ramifications should anyone be tempted to leak any information to a rival news group or even their mothers. He relaxed the threats by promising them he was now absolutely certain this event would be historic and earth shattering and they would all share in the spoils, but only if they all stayed tight.

A super confidential meeting was set up in the offices of Clifftop Productions Inc. Naturally, it was filmed in living colour and strictly limited to those deemed to be in the "need to know" category. That list had grown on the advice of his legal team and the portfolio of signed secrecy agreements was growing fat, too fat for a nervous Cliff Carter's liking.

A search was undertaken to find a military expert who was fluent in written Japanese. The candidate had to be savvy enough to understand military jargon, both Japanese and Australian, and project it against the wartime campaign that this package came from. One of the militarists who served as a consultant for the show suggested a senior intelligence officer, recently retired, who would fit the bill and volunteered to contact him and set up a confidential meeting. He also suggested that, given the age of the documents and the conditions in which they had been discovered, it may be wise to also employ the services of someone familiar with handling delicate documents. Again he knew someone and, with permission, would involve them as well. And so the confidentiality file grew again.

The despatch case was placed reverentially on the boardroom table once again and the antiquarian expert delicately removed the contents and laid them out, one at a time, on a section of cotton cloth covering the timber surface of the table.

The gathered participants were drawn in to get a first look at the frail documents. They were carefully photographed and catalogued. A notary public had also been employed to verify the veracity of proceedings and satisfied that such was the case, he signed a prepared form to that affect and was thanked for his services and escorted from the room. He was reminded to maintain strict confidence about what he had witnessed or face the legal consequences.

The military expert looked at the documents and declared they were of official AIF origin. He verified the signatures as those of Australia's top brass in the conflict of 1942-43, stationed in Port Moresby and the stationery was standard army issue for that period.

It would take time to read all the documents and translate the Japanese component, so after everything had been expertly curated and confirmed, the ex-intelligence officer was given the task of completing his translation in the shortest possible time against the ticking clock, that was Cliff's program schedule already rolling. Cliff told him he could not take more than a few days and a week was out of the question. Colonel Roger Hampstead DCM (Ret.) took a deep breath and seized the moment to ask for his fee. Cliff offered him a fee that had the old boy's eyes rolling. He told Cliff that, despite the generous emolument, it may not be possible to have a comprehensive report completed in such short time span. Cliff told him he had better work nights then and he would double the fee if he delivered the result on time.

Well, you didn't have to tell this old military hack twice; he was ready and rarin' to go. Hell, for that amount of money he was quite willing to assassinate a few people if Cliff so desired. A stack of writing paper, a supply of pens and a stenographer were laid on for his convenience and he wasted no time getting stuck in immediately. But not until after gaining permission to phone his wife and asking her to bring his toiletries and a change of clothing for a week. In response to her demands for an explanation, he told her he had been assigned an important and top secret task that would result in a success fee that would help their retirement fund in a most positive way. Being the wife of an army officer of his standing and experience she knew when to speak up and when to shut up and jumped to his request.

Colonel Roger Hampstead DCM (Ret.) plunged forth into the documents with a will. He examined the battle report of Lieutenant Kerrison first and was aghast at what he read. Lieutenant Lawrence Garret Parnham's name leapt off the page at him and as he read, he was beginning to wish he were somewhere else. His shaking hand reached out for the Japanese captain's written report. He produced his Japanese to English dictionary and started the onerous task of the translation, not made easy by the fact that the report was apparently written in the field and badly contaminated by water and mould in places. However, he completed the authentication of the document by identifying typical Imperial Japanese Army headers and battalion numbers and many tell tales in the presentation style. The paper and its header were the real thing and the salutation seemed correct for the time. The Japanese Captains name was reasonably clear in his signature and should be easy to identify and confirm if he had more time. This would really prove the authenticity of the document, by placing the Japanese officer in the Milne Bay campaign and at the right time.

He reached for a pen and began the literal translation, word by word. After three hours, he had a splitting headache and a raging thirst. The secretary assigned to him as a stenographer was summoned to bring him refreshments and fended off his cheeky flirtations. The old womaniser chuckled wickedly as she laid out a pot of tea and a plate of sandwiches.

Hampstead got back to work and started to reveal a story that he found hard to believe. Alongside the Japanese report was a pair of crude hand drawn maps which appeared to show allied defensive displacements around both Milne Bay and Port Moresby. The maps bore notations in Japanese on the margins, indicating weak points and defensive blind spots, underground bunkers and anti-aircraft weapons pits. Alarmingly, some of the notations were clearly written in English by a shaky, western hand.

Colonel Hampstead was becoming emotionally wrung out by what he was discovering. Quite clearly, the reports of Lieutenant Kerrison, having interviewed the Japanese interpreter, indicated that the subject of his report, fellow officer Lieutenant Parnham, had been guilty of revealing critical intelligence to an enemy in time of war. The conclusion was backed up by the Japanese version. A further element in the story was the question mark over the death of the translator, who would have been a key witness in the matter. It seemed there were as many questions as answers coming out of this explosive package.

Hampstead worked through the night, going over and over the translation and attached reports. After a brief catnap and another gallon of tea, he began working on his conclusions.

Being unable to stay away, Cliff called in to see how Hampstead was going. What the old told him was a massive shock and confirmed his own assessment from his brief reading of the Kerrison document. He was compelled to immediately call in his legal team.

His shock soon transitioned into excitement as he realised the immensity of the information he had in his hands. Hampstead was asked to accelerate his efforts and was left in the boardroom, his head spinning with fatigue and fear. He could understand why the senior field officers wanted to kick this mess down the road as careers would be on the line. He was sure those old boys were gone to their reward by now, which in a way left him holding the bag. Well, there was nothing for it but to do what his military predecessors had done; hand it off to someone else. He would take his well-earned fee and hit the road, grateful to leave this disgrace behind. He prayed his involvement wouldn't bring him into a legal stoush.

Cliff returned with the lawyers and asked Hampstead to sign a more binding confidentiality agreement, carrying crushing penalties should he let slip a single syllable and was handed an envelope containing a cheque for his services. A security guard escorted him to the front door, suitcase in hand. He stepped into a waiting cab, feeling soiled and looked forward to a cleansing shower which he knew would do little to wash away the foul stench he felt was hanging over him.

Back in the boardroom, a fierce debate raged about the Hampstead findings, with Cliff insisting the results should go to air and his lawyers arguing he may wind up facing a law suit that would bankrupt him and destroy the careers of everyone associated with the program. Voices were raised and tempers were hot. The normally placid lawyers Cliff had often declared an emotion free zone, were out of their chairs, screaming at Cliff's production team across the table. The board room became redolent with the stench of nervous sweat the air crackling with tension.

Cliff threatened to sack the whole blasted legal team until it was pointed out to him, they were employed by the network and not Clifftop Productions Inc. Cliff exploded. Pointing at the door, he told them he would find his own advisors and to get the hell out of his office. They left Cliff with fists clenched at the boardroom table grinding his teeth so hard he threatened several hundred dollars of dental work.

Cliff's new legal advisor, Calvin J Holden, was one of those lawyers depicted in a thousand derisory jokes. This guy would sue his own mother if the occasion arose and, after considering the evidence, gave his new client a go-ahead to broadcast in full and damn the consequences as if he would conclude otherwise. Confidentially, he could only see a long and lucrative string of lawsuits coming out of this, well into his future and he, Calvin J Holden, would be there, conducting Cliff's defence because he was gonna need plenty of defence! Hardly reassuring!

Q. What's the difference between a catfish and a lawyer. A. One's a bottom dwelling scum sucker, the other is a fish.

Cliff was in turmoil, especially when he was tipped off that his new legal advisor was a long-time member and contributor to the ALP cause and therefore an avowed enemy of the coalition and not one who could be counted on to help deliver this king hit with a relish.

Cliff decided discretion was the better part of valour and dismissed the snake in the grass and called in the company hacks again and scheduled a meeting. Eating humble pie was not usually on the diet list of your average egotistical television journalist, but he was made to devour a bigslab of it before they presented him with a way out. But if that slab of humble pie gave him heartburn, the next piece of advice could stop his heart. This is an area for a specialist and they had already been in touch with just the man. He was expected at the studio any minute. His assessment would be decisive and critical to their next step and the continuation of the series to its end. The legal eagle hired by the network's lawyers was a high profile international corporate lawyer, who had defended governments and tyrants, genocidal terrorists and Hollywood celebrities. J Whitfield Carbury, QC.

Carbury's decision was simple really, but it would be incredibly confrontational. Cliff would take the accusation to the subject of the reports; Lawrence Garret VC MP and Deputy Leader of the Country Party, and lay it on the table in front of him. He would film the whole affair and let the cards fall where they may. With luck, he may breakdown and confess, or pull a gun and shoot.

Lawrence was theoretically just two beating hearts from the Prime Minister's lodge and leadership of the nation. He must be given a chance to defend himself against the apparent accusations contained in these reports. Of course, he would be expected to mount a massive defence beginning with a suppression order. And then Cliff could expect all kinds of hell to rain down on him personally and through his employers whose moral courage in this matter would be sorely tested, setting the standard of their reporting for the future. Shareholders could also be expected to raise hell if it all went wrong. The other side of the coin was the reasonable chance that Cliff's case would succeed. Then the tremendous upside was an unshakable right to pursue the truth of the matter and present the series' finale, unfettered.

Having come this far, and having invested so much, Cliff was really backed up against the wall and accepted the legal guru's advice and handed J Whitfield Carbury QC his cheque. His payment was relative to his status as a guru rather than the quality of his advice which was delivered at the end of a five minute consultation.

Cliff swallowed deeply. He was not sure his shaking hand around the glass of water in front of him would carry the liquid to his mouth without losing the lot. He was still a relatively untried TV journalist with little experience of interviewing people in powerful positions. So far his portfolio of material would include such interviewing highlights as the series he did the previous year at the Royal Easter Show.

He had interviewed winners of all sorts of Blue Ribbands from Best Fleece, Champion Bull, that stood on his foot nearly crippling him, Best Sponge Cake, which carried the bonus of a slice of the winning entry, to Champion Rooster. A fierce little shit of a thing that pecked a hole in the back of his hand. After that, he declared himself free of agricultural shows for life.

But this would really be a test of his resolve and if he could steel himself to conduct a civil interview with one Australia's most senior politicians and get it on film, it would be a brilliant addition to his series. He knew it was an explosive accusation and he could expect hell and damnation from an aggressive and hardened pollie who had fought off many bloody challenges in his career. Parnham was a man born to lead if not rule, from a long line of similar men, stretching back to early settlement. Here was a man many felt was above reproach, who would have many equally powerful and influential supporters.

Cliff was beginning to crack. He was panicked by the prospect and said so. He started looking for a way out. His production chief and the company chairman both sat him down and delivered a strong affirming lecture to him, emphasising the importance of this opportunity to further his career and the responsibility he had to deliver the goods for his colleagues and his company. He must also look at the bigger picture, his responsibility to the nation in providing the truth about a significant historical event and the men at the centre of it who, like Big Bill Cuthbertson, willingly put their lives on the line for King and country.

By the end of the chairman's oration, Cliff almost felt obliged to stand and sing the national anthem, but he got the message and with the assistance of the company psychologist, was able to develop a technique to take on the task.

CHAPTER TWENTY TWO

1993

The reception at Government House was a glittering celebration of the life, times and community contributions of Lawrence Garret Parnham VC MP, hosted by the governor- general. To Lawrence, the night swept by so swiftly that he barely had time to draw breath, much less enjoy the fine champagne, delicate canapés and the delectable feast that was waiting on the gorgeously laid tables. It seemed every significant celebrity he had ever met or did business with, over his long and illustrious career, demanded his attention, smiling and applauding him as he moved about.

Highlights of his stellar career were being shown on television screens set around the perimeter of the ballroom: his medal presentation; his passionate speeches in defence of his constituents; a meeting with the Queen; surrounded by cheering supporters as he won his first election.

The music from the orchestra filled the air, compelling couples to fill the dance floor swirling and dipping to the demanding rhythms of the band. Coloured lights flashed on and off and a huge shower of balloons fell from the roof to reveal a massive television screen with the grim face of a Japanese officer, pointing a pistol directly at the camera, screaming in Japanese, 'Anata ga shindeshimau.' (You will die!)

The image faded and was replaced by a distorted grinning image of Cliff Carter holding up a noose and a placard with the word 'GOTCHA' written in blood, still running in rivulets dripping to the floor. Cliff's image was yelling at the screen in the high pitched excessive hard sell style of top television presenters the world over. His words coming up on a banner across the bottom of the screen.

'Tune in at 7.30 for full details of the biggest political scandal in Australia's history!'

Lawrence screamed and woke in a lather of perspiration from the nightmare to a reality even more horrible, which flooded his fevered mind. He collapsed back onto his sweat-soaked pillow, shaking uncontrollably and finally vomited a vile substance onto his chest.

Fortunately, Frances was sleeping at the other end of the house and didn't witness his terror attack. With his one remaining hand shaking and mind still churning from the impact of the dreadful nightmare, Lawrence took a cold shower and regained self-control. He had never allowed Frances to witness his night terrors and swore she never would. He donned fresh nightclothes and made his way to the kitchen for a coffee and brandy.

Lawrence couldn't be sure why he was so unsettled; he was just overwhelmed with a deep, dark feeling of foreboding. Was this a symptom of growing old; work related stress, or something more sinister, like some creeping illness overtaking him? For many years he had been a successful and popular citizen and he was unable to highlight any threats, real or imagined.

He had the strongest surge of panic following the news each night and yet, he still couldn't put his finger on it. It was as if some sixth sense was trying to warn him of an approaching threat. Was it something involved in this damned current affairs program that was being tirelessly flogged in the broadcast media? There was definitely something about it, some thread that begged to be pulled, to unravel the hidden meaning within it. But what was it that bedevilled him?

The program had been lately banging on about a lost RAAF pilot flying a Beaufighter back to Brisbane from Port Moresby. Lawrence recalled the excellent work those aircraft did when they establishing the defences around Port Moresby and Jackson Field. But why were they targeting this chap's mission which came to a sad end apparently? But many did during the war, why select this particular bloke? Alright, he was a decorated air ace but so was Bluey Truscott and Lawrence couldn't recall this sort of fuss about his demise.

It was the Battle of Milne Bay in particular, which came up

repeatedly that raised the hairs on the back of his neck, along with many mentions of the brave lads of 55th Battalion at Port Moresby and the Kokoda Track. Perhaps, it was just the flashback to the horrors he endured in losing so many men in close combat and the hideous wound he suffered and the...

Here his memory shut off from what was really at the core of his unrest. What was it that troubled him so much? He was decorated with the Victoria Cross for Christ's sake? He didn't ask for it; he was judged a fitting recipient by his comrades and superiors. Was it survivor's guilt? And what was this hullabaloo about an old RAAF crash site and its contents? What the hell had that got to do with anything? There were lots of old wreck sites around the country.

And yet, there was this stirring inside him. It was the dreams, the flashbacks that had been troubling him, generated from his time as a captive of that damned Japanese captain that tortured him so thoroughly and comprehensively. There were a lot of memory blanks over that time; he knew there was much he didn't know and couldn't possibly recall.

It was very hard to escape the circus of speculation generated, as the morning newspapers were feeding off the television reports and interviews with key political pundits and party power brokers who were sought to pad out information released the night before. High ranking veterans from the New Guinea conflict were button holed and pestered for anything they might know about rumours of a military scandal. The newshounds were being driven nuts by short-tempered editors desperate to extract something from this continuously building, totally dominating sensational story.

The whole of Australia was enthralled by the unfolding drama that had rolled out from Cliff Carter's incredible program. The instigator of all this appalling mish-mash of speculation and innuendo, Cliff Carter, was now himself being interviewed by international news syndicates like CNN and BBC. He had become an instant celebrity and an expert on everything from World War Two aircraft, military tactics, the Geneva Convention and the law relating to treason. And if asked, his ego would drive him to speculate on the best method for sexing a chicken!

Before the sun coloured the eastern sky with its hopeful shades of pink and red, Lawrence was fully dressed, shaved and primed for the day ahead. He managed to eat some breakfast of eggs and toast prepared for him by the cook and washed down with scalding tea. The radio in the kitchen was broadcasting the morning news from the ABC. Much of it concerned rural matters, weather conditions and rehashed stories from the previous day. No mention was made of the television production and its fallout. Lawrence sucked it all up and headed for his electorate office. Perhaps the familiar surrounds and routine would help to settle him. His office manager, Marjorie, was pleased to see him and, after handing him the recent mail, she left him to open and read it before she headed off to make a pot of his favourite Bushell's tea.

Lawrence laid back in the wonderfully comfortable old swivel chair that had received his weary backside for over 30 years. The padding of the old chesterfield was as good as new and seemed to fold around him like the arms of a long-time lover. He rested his head on his remaining left hand and drew in a deep breath. Marjorie returned with his tea and they exchanged a few pleasantries about family, friends and farming. They were more than employer and employee. They had been lifelong friends and confidantes from school days.Marjorie poured his tea and proffered a plate of fruit cake to him, then took her leave.

She had waited years for Lawrence to make advances towards her, from the first moments of her feminine awareness until middle age, by which time, such a union was totally out of the question. Without question, she would throw herself in front of the assassin's bullet to save him but, sadly for her, they remained in a purely platonic relationship.

Lawrence began to attend to his mail which had been sorted, by the ever efficient Marjorie, into the order of importance she gave to each envelope, judged by the sender's return address details on the top left hand of each item. She had become very skilled at this over the years and she could even include in her assessments, the plain envelopes, based on some female instinct that a mere male would fail to understand or appreciate. Each envelope had been neatly slit open along the top without revealing the contents, to enable Lawrence to easily access them one handed.

It was the third letter in the pile that, for perhaps a similar instinct, caught Lawrence's eye. It was a standard DL landscape business envelope with the exception of being Priority Paid and felt as if it would contain only a single sheet. The sender's details were, as usual, in the top left-hand reading, *Mallard Partners, Attorneys at Law,* with the address in the Brisbane CBD. He removed the single sheet he predicted it would contain and scanned it quickly.

What the hell? These lawyers represented the television channel and the presenter that was running that blasted program everyone is on about. And for some damned reason they were demanding an immediate meeting with Lawrence and advised him to make sure his legal representatives were in attendance. Lawrence snatched up the phone and called his lawyer and was put straight through.

After reading the faxed copy of the letter, Lawrence's lawyer, Gordon Reynolds, called his Brisbane colleague for further information and got it. He was quickly on the return call to Lawrence and advised him that a meeting was an absolute must. After hanging up, he sent a message to his wife to have an overnight bag packed and ordered his secretary to book two first class seats on the earliest Qantas flight to Brisbane. Within three hours of receiving the letter, Lawrence and Gordon were 35,000 feet in the air, half way to the Queensland capital.

On the way, Gordon started to prepare for what he knew would be a torrid ordeal for his client. He explained to Lawrence that they were to meet with the producers of *that* program to discuss the contents of the top secret satchel they had recovered from an RAAF aircraft that went missing in 1942, on its way back to Brisbane, carrying some highly sensitive reports concerning the Battle of Milne Bay.

What could Lawrence recall of his time there that could have something to do with all of this? Lawrence's brain was spinning like a top. He felt like he might make use of the sick bag in the sleeve on the back of the seat in front of him. Now a sickening certainty crept over him, making him cower involuntarily down in his first class seat. He was almost certain he was being pulled inexorably into this televised scandal monger's programme and that it had something to do with his capture and torture at the hands of that infernal Japanese captain and what transpired during his brutal interrogation at his hands. But full recall seemed to be just as far from his grasp as ever. The complimentary cocktail that was served to him on take-off sat untouched before him on his food tray, the ice cubes long since melted. Gordon summoned the steward to bring him a fresh drink and Lawrence interrupted to demand a double scotch, no ice and when it arrived he threw it down his gullet as if it was the panacea for all his woes.

Gordon, on his right, was totally absorbed in reading some heavy legal literature and was oblivious to Lawrence's discomfort, intent on having some sort of legal rejoinder to the accusations he was anticipating would be thrown at his illustrious client, having read and reread the legal letter from the Queensland firm against what he had gleaned from the program that had aired so far.

Lawrence and Gordon emerged from the Brisbane Airport passenger terminal into the humid sub-tropical air, shirts immediately damp with perspiration. As they slipped their jackets off they were met by a driver, provided by the legal firm Mallard Partners, responsible for their presence in Brisbane. It was early evening, with the mercury still hovering around 30 degrees and the vehicle's air conditioning was appreciated. It was only a short run into the city and their meeting at the television station overlooking the Brisbane CBD.

The journey was unremarkable, Lawrence lost in his own thoughts and Gordon still perusing some documents of some sort and saying nothing. Twenty minutes later, they found themselves in an undercover car park beneath the television station from which they take the lift to the 10th floor. They were met in the foyer by a well-groomed, very attractive young lady who led them into the corporate area of the station and handed them off to an immaculately suited man who introduced himself as the station CEO. He led the way into the boardroom and conducted the introductions to the people gathered there. They met the station's legal representative and Lloyd Mallard, the signatory of the letter that Lawrence received, along with the programme producer and finally, Cliff Carter. There was a secretary there to record the minutes and, after a few awkward moments, Cliff's CEO sorted everyone out.

When they say, 'if looks could kill', Cliff Carter would be a lifeless corpse on the boardroom floor right then and there, as he and Lawrence locked eyes. Cliff proffered his right hand and then awkwardly withdrew it with a stuttering apology for his gaff, but Lawrence, used to this situation, had ignored it anyway. The station CEO read the body language and deftly stepped in between them, before arranging everyone into non-combative positions around the large, polished blackwood table that had seen plenty of heated debate on the subject of that evening's very tense meeting.

The CEO called the meeting to order and they got under way. Lawrence could feel the sweat running down his spine and was feeling light-headed and almost faint. Gordon leaned in to him and patted his thigh, looked him in the eye and nodded reassuringly.

CHAPTER TWENTY THREE

Bill Jnr had recovered from his ordeal and, while recuperating at home on the couch, he had been caught up in the television series that had enthralled the rest of the country. He felt a deep sense of loss, or more like an invasion of the family privacy. This was his pop's plane and he was on a memorial flight to honour his grandfather and all of this nonsense came as a result of his failure to complete that journey. Only as a result of his mishap did they find Big Bill's plane. That should have led to an immediate attempt to locate and, if possible, recover any remains of the unfortunate air crew and treat the wreckage as a war grave. Instead, this little upstart journalist had come along and was making money out of the family's misfortune. Something should be done about it, but what?

Their attempt to block the program in the courts failed and they were required to pay the defendant's costs, which came as a double whack in the eye. And now it seemed the sole focus had been on producing this blasted current affair program while their courageous ancestor had simply been forgotten. Bobby and his son had talked of little else but staging a search for their ancestor's final resting place.

Elise had listened to the men talking about a lack of initiative by the government or other authorities, to follow up on the discovery of the wreckage of the Beaufighter. She decided to intercede and became involved in the discussion, taking a firm hand on things and was all positive action. She suggested they petition the Queensland government for funds to commence a search and undertake the project themselves. After all, they had all the resources themselves to conduct a preliminary aerial search and plenty of experienced stockmen to provide support on the ground.

The hard part has been done with the discovery of the plane. That gave them a positive starting point from which to commence the ground search.

This was just the spark they needed. Bobby and Bill were all for it and started to formulate an action plan. They would need financial backing to cover the cost of fuel, food, aircraft etc, plus the hire of a helicopter which would be an essential part of the expedition. Elise's point about the state government putting funds into the scheme made sense and so did Bill's proposal to immediately start calling their sponsor for backup. But the clincher came from Bobby when he accused them, good-naturedly, of overlooking the obvious. Why not get television to work for them and shoot their own reality program?

Sometimes things could be right under your nose and go unnoticed. What a great idea, by God, and why didn't they think of it before? It might give them a chance of funding the whole thing, with luck.

Their campaign began with their local MP and their media contacts. Elise and Bill both had an impressive black book of media friends as a result of their individual exploits. Every one of them, press, radio and especially Cliff's rival television networks were starved for an involvement somehow or other and were eager to get on board. The rival television network of Nine Entertainment QTQ would film the whole search as a documentary series and were paying a fat fee for the exclusive rights.

Applying for government funding, given the background turmoil of Queensland politics, was like shooting fish in a barrel, as the ruling party were desperate to hang on to precious votes and the story behind the Cuthbertsons' request was too compelling to be ignored. Brother and sister aviation heroes searching for the remains of the war hero grandfather! Who would be stupid enough to ignore this? It was vote catching gold.

Before you could say popularity poll, the grant was approved to underwrite the expedition to search for, and recover, the remains of the two airmen who had lost their lives in the aircraft, currently being shamelessly exploited by commercial television. The government spin masters were sure they could tie that bit of shame back on to the opposition. This was a win-win for the incumbents. The Cuthbertsons had little interest in the snake pit of Queensland politics, but were still grateful for the support of their local member.

The Cuthbertson clan naturally expected to be at the centre of the search and the media insisted that they were accepted, already seeing the headlines, or composing their "to camera audio". They would pump this up to the point of saturation in an effort to drown out and shame Cliff's exploitative programme. The television promos were already being produced with an impassioned announcer ever so subtly pouring scorn on the opposition networks disregard for the nation's war dead and how his programme would take up the solemn responsibility to "bring the heroes home" which became their tag line, repeated ad-nauseam.

The Cuthbertsons' expedition got underway with its own film crew. A land-based assault was the obvious first step, following the track already beaten into the bush by Bill Jnr's rescuers earlier. The bush-bashing was still hard work. The plan was to take a convoy of vehicles and equipment into the crash site of Big Bill's plane, where they would set up a base camp and begin the search for Squadron Leader, William Luther Cuthbertson DFC and his crewman, Flight Sergeant Robert Arthur (Bluey) Mansfield.

The Cuthbertsons' expedition was soon organised with much fanfare from all concerned. The politician wanted to get recognition for his part in this government part-funded adventure and also make sure his big boof head was on telly alongside the famous flying siblings. Sponsors were falling over each other to get exposure and there was also a pretty big fan base that had begun to build and they wanted autographs, photos and whatever fans wanted. Too slow, the publicity guy suggested they should have produced some memorabilia for sale. It was not too late, Bobby suggested and set off to get t-shirts and caps printed by the guy that supplied Bill Jnr's needs on his trip to New Guinea.

The family had agreed, whether or not the expedition was successful, they would try to earn as much from it as they could for the charities they had supported and who had been the beneficiaries from all of their adventures so far.

The political power brokers took note of this and the public reaction to it and already had Bill in their sights. They were almost smacking their lips in anticipation of the thought of him as a potential young preselect for an election not too far distant.

The organisation was a lot like gearing up for mustering, which they conducted with practiced ease. The expedition set off in high spirits with hope in their hearts that a mystery, that had bedevilled the Cuthbertson family for five decades, may finally be resolved.

They left Longreach along traveling east along the A4 then they turned north onto the Aramac-Torrens Creek Road to take them deep into the bush to the crash site. The vehicles used were all rugged off-road military style four-wheel drives that didn't need much in the way of roadway surfaces and could smash their way through all but mature trees.

Bill had plotted the turn-off point that would take them directly through the bush to the site of his own downed aircraft. Equipped with the accurate latitude and longitude, they pushed through quickly once they left the highway heading out east towards the Lake Buchanan crash site of Bill Jnr's Beech 18 and further east to where Big Bill's plane laid waiting for them.

The going was pretty rough and almost monotonous in its similarity – mature coolabah woodlands, sand plains and vast dune fields – all adapted to a climate of infrequent rain that fell in short, but massive deluges, quick to evaporate in the harsh outback sun. Underfoot they stumbled over the densely tufted kangaroo grass, native legumes, windmill grass and common wheat grass.

The distance they would need to cover was about 70 kilometres. At the rate they were forced to travel, it would take them six to eight hours to reach Bill's Beechcraft wreckage, given several stops to check navigation, deal with punctured tyre changes and refreshment breaks. The occasional razor sharp rocks and jagged stumps of small broken trees were unavoidable and hard on the toughest tyres.

Finally, they came onto the crash site. Without the latitude and longitude it would have been very difficult to locate, as it was lying on its belly amongst stunted shrubs and immature trees with one or two larger trees filling in the sky line.

The wreck was scattered about, just as they had seen it on the aerial shots on television. The camera crew began filming as Bill and Elise walked around, inspecting the shattered Beech. Elise was amazed that her brother survived this mess, but it appeared he had been both lucky and skilful in putting it down in an area fairly clear of large trees, anthills and boulders. Bill speculated on the possibility of recovering the plane but, before he got too worked up about it, Elise urged him to continue on with their main mission and think about this later while stifling tears as she couldn't avoid the thought of how close her brother had come to death in this shattered aircraft.

They pushed on. Bill was a little reluctant to leave the plane he had grown to love, feeling like a grieving lover walking away from a loved one's grave. They had good fix on the wreckage of the Beaufighter, again courtesy of the television coverage and began to make good progress.

After a few false starts, they found the wreckage of the Beaufighter and didn't wonder that it was difficult to find back in the day. Like an apparition, it seemed to materialise out of the bush it had been lying in for decades. The jungle camouflage on the fuselage and the blue and white RAAF roundel on the starboard side, ahead of a large upper case 'F' was now faded, but still clearly visible. All sorts of bush had added to the cover up by growing up, over, through and around it, almost burying it in foliage. The team started clearing a site quickly to set up camp for cooking and a sleeping tent.

Obviously, there was a tremendous amount of curiosity in the old Beaufighter and everyone wandered over to take a first-hand look. They were all a little edgy in the thick grass and low scrub surrounding the wreck. This was a good spot to find a taipan snake if you wanted one. Time and weather had taken a toll on what remained of the aircraft. Bill was strangely proud that his revered grandfather, like him, had elected to perform a "wheels up" emergency landing with a very similar outcome.

Oddly, the cockpit was well preserved considering, although the perspex windows had become opaque and denied the curious a view of the interior. Bill Jnr took a particular interest in the cockpit area and, was filmed climbing in through the still functioning hinged cockpit hatch, which opened from the port side with a creaking resistance. Checking carefully for unfriendly occupants, he slid down into the pilot's seat, his feet finding the rudder pedals as if the layout had been tailored for him. The camera man moved in behind him, shooting over his shoulder, recording the moment he took the control column in his hands. He reverently placed both hands on the butterfly control yoke and sat there staring through the cracked and discoloured windscreen toward the horizon partly obscured by the heavily overgrown bush. A flood of emotion ran through him as he imagined what it must have been like for his grandfather to sit here in combat.

How privileged was he to be sitting here in the pilot's seat that was occupied by his ancestor in the biggest conflict of the 20th century. The camera guy climbed out to complete some all-round shots and left Bill Jnr sitting there in wonderment.

Big Bill had sat here in this very cockpit and would have looked at the enemy through that three piece windscreen as he lined up his targets. Bill Jnr's right hand found the firing button on the control column and he absent-mindedly pushed it down.

Bill Jnr would never know the shuddering roar of the armaments under the nose of the deadly aircraft or the shattering damage inflicted on the enemy and his aircraft and shipping. He could only imagine the shocking noises of war, the fear and excitement, mixed with the smell of cordite, aviation fuel and his own sweat.

Then he experienced something that would stay with him for life. A peculiar warmth suddenly flooded through his chest and he felt his face flush. He would later swear that he felt a hand resting on his shoulder, so intense was it that he jumped with fright and spun around to see who was there.

Elise was standing on the wing now looking in at him. She later denied the suggestion that it was her hand that laid gently on his shoulder to comfort him, but commented on her brother's shocked expression and pallor as he turned wide- eyed to return her gaze. She was stunned to see tears flowing down his ashen cheeks. She also felt the presence of their grandfather, but not at the same emotional level as her brother. She offered her hand as he climbed out of the plane and stood on the port wing with his head in his hands momentarily.

Finally, he shook his head like a swimmer coming up for air and dismounted to help his team with the clearing. Big Bill would stay with him for a long time after that ethereal experience.

One task tackled immediately was to hack out a helicopter landing pad from the raw scrub. This was an arduous job and a little dangerous, due to a number of disgruntled snakes, bull- ants and the odd scorpion. The chore took the best part of the day and, in the current climate, the team finished pretty much wrung out. They were re-energised with the arrival of the chopper, carrying plenty of cold drinks and refrigerators powered by portable generators that would also provide lighting.

Tents were set up on the bit of rough ground previously cleared for the purpose, providing valuable protection from the sun. One of the team, who had been nominated as chef, got on with cooking up some hot food in the tent commandeered as the kitchen.

Sitting around the campfire after their evening meal, a discussion began, trying to ascertain what might have happened here after the crash. Did both men survive unscathed? The one thing they had all agreed on was one or both men may have been injured in the crash, otherwise with Bill's bush craft, they would more than likely have walked out. Big Bill would have realised that search planes were looking well to the east of their position on the most likely direct route he should have followed to Archerfield, as per his original flight plan. In this, Big Bill had become his own worst enemy by deliberately taking a course further west, in order to do a flyover of his home. In the end he had suffered a double jeopardy.

Someone suggested they scout around in the morning to look for any sign of an old signal fire, for surely they would have had one going nonstop. It would be possible even after all this time, to find traces of scorched rocks or charcoal. With the certainty the site could have been drenched in fuel, that fire may have been built well away from the actual wreck.

Bill occupied a folding table inside one of the tents with a cup of tea and a bulky sandwich of egg, sausage and lettuce, spreading out his maps and photos. Elise joined him and they discussed what they knew about their granddad. They had heard all the stories from their grandmother, Lydia, about her husband's exploits, which were repeated or backed up by their mother Joanne. They knew he was an excellent horseman and had spent many hours and days on the track with the Aboriginal stockman from whom he learned many survival tips. That had given him the knowledge and ability to live off the land for weeks at a time. So Big Bill could be expected to almost make light of a situation like this, unless he was disabled by injury in the crash or, alternatively, supporting his injured crewman, Bluey Mansfield. And the reverse was highly probable as well.

An examination of the Beau's wreckage seemed to indicate a "controlled crash landing", if there was such a thing. As many an old pilot has said, 'It was a good landing if you could walk away from it'. The cockpit was comparatively intact, as was the main section of the fuselage. Both wings had been ripped off and parts scattered; the tail section, still emblazoned with the squadron's blue and white vertical stripes, lay some 75 metres away. Both engines were visible, one still attached to a wing stub and the other lying in the bush, back along the impact path. Despite this, Bill and Elise believed Big Bill and Bluey would be lucky to have walked away unscathed.

The search party had already undertaken a lot of research and planning. Aerial photographs of the area had been studied and a search pattern devised, but on the ground in the actual search area, Bill was hesitant. He believed he could "feel" his grandfather's presence and he sat among the remains of Big Bill's plane and began to try and think like Big Bill, as the bushman he was.

Given that one, or both of them, were injured, then Bill's instincts may have been to seek a source of water and perhaps bush tucker within a pretty short hike. Young Bill examined the maps and photos again and saw there were several directions he could have gone and found water. But Big Bill didn't have maps and photos to guide him. He would have gone on instinct. Perhaps he would have headed for high ground first, to get the lay of the land.

Looking around, he and Elise decide a prominent hill to the north east of them was a likely starting point. After discussion with the rest of the team, Bill and Elise headed in that direction as the rest of the search party began a grid search in the immediate area.

Day two saw the camp well established and everyone exhausted after another hard day's work. The crew enjoyed a barbeque dinner and a couple of cold beers before settling down for the night again.

The film crew had been busy recording every move and every discussion, as well as a lot of background shots of spiders and snakes and weird clouds and anything they thought would add colour to their video. They collapsed, absolutely drained, into their camp cots. Young Bill reminded them of the importance of keeping up their intake of water and easing up on the beer.

The camp to a hot and dusty dawn, bird calls echoed among the trees. Cooky got a great breakfast going. The standard bacon and eggs, plus some lamb chops, steak, onions, baked beans and toast. If that was not enough, they had lashings of jam and honey to go with the toast and a huge pot of tea. Vegetarians if there were any looked on and wept.

Bill gave a briefing and established the communication frequency they would use on their walkie-talkies. They were required to keep to a strict radio schedule for safety reasons and report anything they found and if they did find anything, it must not be disturbed. They were provided with a number of stakes with high visibility ribbons on the ends. If something significant was found, they must mark it, photograph it and report it, and please limit radio chatter.

They all set out through the bush to their allotted search areas, full of hope. Bill and Elise headed for the hill they had discussed the night before, with the television crew following dutifully along behind them. Perhaps their journalistic instincts told them where the story would be and they were not going to miss it.

While the tree canopy was not all that thick, the undergrowth of scrubby plants, rough saw grass and Mitchell grass growing under the trees, made a straight line passage very difficult. They pushed on and after several stops for rest and a drink from their canteens, they agreed that if the men were carrying injuries this would have been a tough journey. There was no telling if they would have had food or water with them from the wreckage. It was hard to imagine doing this while injured and without food and water, but with your life depending on it, little more incentive is needed and anything becomes possible.

The two siblings began the climb up the side of the hill, slipping and sliding on the unforgiving surface which consisted of broken shale rock, hard loose clay and sand. It was two steps forward and one back, causing a little doubt to creep into Bill's mind. It had taken them two and a half hours to get to the base of the hill and they finally crested the top of it a further hour later.

They found that the very summit consisted of several huge boulders in an untidy heap that appeared to be the core remains of the ancient peak which should provide a good viewing platform if they could find a way to the top of the pile. After circling it, they found some footholds that would give them access to the top, where they discovered a broad view of the wooded plain on which the Beaufighter wreckage sat.

Bill took out the maps and survey photos and laid them out on a flat area of the rock and aligned his hand held compass. Elise produced her binoculars and scanned the horizon for any clues.

Bill's gaze fell to the rock they were standing on and noticed some discolouration, as if a fire had been burning here at one time. The both of them take a more thorough look around and Elise let out a shout. Wedged deep down between the rocks was a small food tin. It was old and rusted but had the shape of the emergency ration tin of military issue that would have been part of the supplies carried by Big Bill. Bill Jnr called the camera guys to come and record the find. He brought a stick with him and, as there was limited space, Elise had to move away to make room for him and nearly toppled off the rock.

They managed, after a lot of mucking about, to lever the tin out of its resting place and were surprised to find that almost all of its printed labelling was intact.

It read in upper case across the front: *A.M.F. OPERATION RATION*, and below that, in smaller print, D2, and it appeared to have instructions across the top. It had been opened and discarded. This, plus the sign of a fire, was proof that someone from the military had been here.

Could Bill have built a signal fire and eaten the rations while they waited for rescue? They believed their assumptions have proved correct. If it wasn't Big Bill here, then who else could it have been in such a remote place? What would be the odds? The camera guys got all the shots of the can with Bill speaking to camera on the find and his theory.

They re-enacted the discovery and recovery several times, including the landscape spread out before them. They carefully scanned the area again for any more clues but come up empty-handed. Meanwhile, Elise had been scoping the area systematically with her binoculars and believed she could see a patch of green dense scrub several miles away to the south west, that might indicate the presence of water. Perhaps Big Bill had the same thought and made his way there.

Bill and Elise set themselves to hike to that spot and see if they could pick up any more clues. They all climbed down carefully and Bill put in a radio report on their findings. Now they needed to get back to the base camp as quickly as they could to beat nightfall as they were not equipped to camp out overnight.

The radio contact with the other three groups revealed nothing and everyone was heading back to camp, hoping to get there before dark. No one expected the going to be quite so tough and everyone had underestimated travelling times. No one had experienced tougher going than the siblings who, despite being buoyed up by optimism, were struggling. The heat sapped their strength, beating down through the broken forest canopy. Even as the sun slipped below the tree line, there was no respite from the heat. The television crew was doubly under pressure, lugging heavy camera and sound equipment through the scrub, but they were also excited with the film they had in the can.

The discovery of the ration tin, which was returning with them, was a real highlight. Although not absolute proof that the survivors included Lt Cuthbertson, it was very promising. The video they had shot would be flown out on the chopper as soon as they got back and hopefully would be cut and edited in time to pre-promote their series on the six o'clock news service and have it to air in time for the seven thirty programme.

When dinner had been prepared, served and eaten, they downed a few ice cold beers, courtesy of their recently arrived refrigerator, and reviewed the day. Bill summarized and filled everyone in on their findings and the theory they intended to follow up on the next day. Everyone contributed to the conversation, adding some theories and hunches. Meanwhile, Bill thought they should still cover all bases and continue the grid search because, if his theory didn't pay off, they'd have wasted time and resources. Better to continue with his "belt and braces" approach, leaving nothing to chance. He wished everyone a goodnight and retired to his tent.

The sun jumped up out of the east and it suddenly sounded like every bird in Queensland had gathered to celebrate the occasion and joined in the joyful cacophony. Kookaburras cackled away, rainbow lorikeets flashed noisily by in large colourful numbers and small flocks of ravens tumbled about haphazardly across the sky Was it a murder of ravens or did that remain the domain of crows with their distinctive harsh cry? While budgerigars, in countless numbers, almost blotted out the sun. The stridency of their calls were deafening as they headed out for food or water.

And overall, at a greater altitude, looking for the main chance were the carrion birds and birds of prey. Wedge-tailed eagles, kestrels and goshawks.

On the ground, the humanity was up and about, charged with the optimism the discovery by Bill and Elise yesterday had given them. Most of the crew slept like lords after their exhausting day and were now aware of aches, painful cuts and insect bites, all requiring some medical attention at one level or another.

Breakfast was bolted down and each group carefully checked their gear, making sure radio batteries were charged, water bottles were filled and first aid kits were packed and that they had sufficient food rations for a day in the field.

Bill called in the group leaders and reminded them to be careful, pointing out a track across the recently exposed sand in the middle of their campsite. It was the unmistakable serpentine track of a snake that had meandered through during the night.

'Be bloody careful if you need to take a pee during the night,' he admonished them.

They had been lucky and there had been only one minor injury the preceding day and, considering the rough terrain, it could have been a lot worse. Bill would hate to lose anyone to snake bite at this juncture. Finally, he thanked them again for their devotion and enthusiasm and broke off to go back to his tent to pick up his gear.

The television guys were sticking with him and Elise, as they could smell blood and would bet their last dollar that something amazing was about to happen. It was an infectious feeling and Bill thought he could feel his grandfather calling to him. He spoke quietly to his brave young sister, who had proved her courage on more than one occasion, and gave her a reassuring hug and a peck on the cheek. It was time to go, and after double checking his map and compass bearing, they set off toward the waterhole inside that green oasis they had seen from the hilltop.

The going was just as tough as the day before and, after about two or three miles, they came across a gully that was fairly wide and deep. The gully ran north-east to south-west right across their intended path.

'You could easily throw a stone across it,' thought Bill, 'but how the hell do we get down without breaking a leg and then scale the opposite side?'

The sides of the gully were vertical and about five metres deep; too deep to take any risks and the bottom was littered with large boulders exposed by flood waters that had long since dried up.

Bill studied his map closely again, looking for contours that might indicate a safe crossing point. The best bet for what he wanted was off to their right. So after a brief rest, they bashed their way along in that direction parallel to the washed out creek bed.

Elise was ever the competitive country girl and had moved on ahead like a scout. They heard her shout and picked up the pace to catch up with her. After a couple of hundred yards, Bill was starting to get worried as she hasn't responded to any of his calls. The bush was thick but not that thick that they could have by-passed her.

Bill and the camera crew, who were getting some drama out of the day, decided to back track. It didn't take long, now that Bill was actually looking for a sign to find where she had turned left in the direction of the creek again, which was only 50 metres away.

Bill kicked himself when he found Elise had left a distinctive mark, indicating her path and he had walked right past it. He followed her tracks through the scrub until he got to the edge of the drop into the creek bed. He was surprised to find his sister standing on the opposite bank waving at him, with a big grin on her face. She pointed out where the bank had caved in on both sides, giving a steep, but manageable crossing point.

'Step carefully,' she advised the team as she had seen a couple of snakes in the creek bottom and was not sure what variety they were.

They could be just browns and not the deadly taipan species that inhabited the area.

Bill spotted a bit of a shake in the camera man's hands all of a sudden, and he thought the next film shot would more than likely be a little blurred. Country boys and girls loved pulling a city slicker's leg!

There were many different species of snakes, venomous and non-venomous, in southern Queensland, which no one minded but when one came into your tent like the carpet python that had invaded the girls' tent the previous night, it could cause an issue. There wasn't a creature alive that could match the scream that had rent the air at two in the morning. After the reptile was identified and assurances given, everyone settled down again except for the outbursts of laughter coming from the guys' tent for the next 30 or 40 minutes.

The girls were now questioning if it had been an accidental visitation or an introduction to, as one larrikin dubbed it, a new team member, Mr Joe Blake. There was far too much male hilarity about the constrictor and this was a typical practical joke in the bush. Bill had laid the law down, forbidding a repeat of the trick if that's what it was.

They negotiated the obstacle and stopped to confer. They reviewed what they knew. First, the weather in July and August, when Big Bill went missing, was cool during the day and chilly at night. Rainfall was moderate as a rule, so the creek may not have been flowing, so there would have been little reason to bivouac here. And if they were confronted by the washout, if it existed then, would they have been determined as Young Bill's team to cross it?

Thirst and desperation to survive would have provided the necessary incentive. They were now about a mile from their target and decided to push on as quickly as possible. Bill checked his compass again and away they went pushing through the spikey, unpleasant scrub, throwing up some quail startled into flight with that peculiar whirring, whistling sound from their wings when alarmed. While it was an awful place for a human, it seemed a paradise for birds that made themselves known by an incredible variety of calls.

After another half hour they had reached their target; a large, lush, green oasis stood in stark comparison with the withered surrounds that stretched out around them to the horizon. Scrub thick and tough enough to stop a tank.

Bill asked Elise to complete their radio schedule. The other parties, once more, had nothing to report which was disappointing, but at least they were covering a wide area, which would leave no lingering doubts later. They were confronted by a dense wall of exotic, green foliage consisting of an incredible range of plants and palms. Tropical ginger, cabbage palms, foxtail palms, cycads and ferns.

The bird song was deafening and they were on alert in case they ran into a cassowary, which sometimes inhabited places like this and could be a bit feisty. They were startled by a brush turkey which squawked a protest and disappeared in a clatter of wings and flying feathers into the deep underbrush. A Sacred Kingfisher flashed past like an iridescent firework; Grey Fantails, Rufus Whistlers and the iconic kookaburra chuckling away somewhere in the bush while overhead. They caught an occasional glimpse of a circling kestrel through the thick canopy as it worked its way out to more open ground in search of prey.

But they were not here to bird watch and ignoring the plethora of native feathered creatures, which would have had your average ornithologist foaming at the mouth, they pushed into the close, jungle-like growth. It closed over them like a cloak and forced them to adopt a zigzag path to make any progress.

They broke through to an exquisite, tropical oasis, a deep clear waterhole surrounded by lush flora, alive with fauna. The ambient temperature had dropped by about 10 degrees and when they felt the water temperature of the pond, Elise said it felt like the run off from a mountain stream. This billabong was obviously fed from the Great Artesian Basin deep underground and would most likely be permanent. But again, Bill reminded them that, while this was all very nice, they needed to be looking for signs of his grandfather. The chance of that was slim, because if they made it to here, and that was a big if, and made camp within this mini jungle, any sign of that occupation would have been grown over long ago. But they decided to give it a go anyway.

On a suggestion coming from their camera man, they scouted the outer edge of the jungle growth. Big Bill would still be hoping for rescue coming from the sky and if they plunged too deeply into the bush, they would have been invisible. That made a lot of sense. They would have set up somewhere with an easy access to the water hole but still in the open, so they could keep a signal fire going and be visible.

Instead of a camp site, what they found instead, shocked them to the core. On rounding a clump of growth, they came across, what was clearly a crude grave site. It was marked by a mound of rocks with a vertical pile about half a metre high, assembled to represent a crude headstone and it gave some dignity to the bush burial site. The surrounding grass lands were not exactly covered with the rocks that were needed for this interment, if that's what it was. Alot of work had to be done to have completed the grave.

They gathered reverently around the site. The camera crew was going nuts shooting film from every angle and from all over the place. First, the bare grave itself, then with Bill and Elise standing behind it, gazing down mournfully, arm in arm, then an artful shot, crouching beside the headstone arrangement, tidying some of the stones. But wait, how did they know who was buried here?

On instinct, Elise scratched away at the base of the monument and made a startling discovery. Beneath a flat stone placed right at the front and centre of the rock pile, she uncovered a small tobacco tin with its imprinted label still readable. "Wills Vice Regal Mixture". It appeared to be of the correct vintage. She had to wait for the camera crew to catch up, recreating the discovery before they allowed her to open it. Her shaking hands worked at the lid and failed to open it. Bill stepped in and applied a bit of muscle. It finally gave up its secrets as the lid surrendered to her brother's stronger grip.

Inside the tin were two ID discs, a round one and an octagonal one. These discs were issued by the air force and carried name rank and serial number of the service men and women. In the unfortunate event of the bearer's death, the round disc was taken to record the loss of the service person. The second one was octagonal with the same details On the front side was a service number, surname and the initials RAAF and an abbreviation CC, possibly the owner's religion. The initials were JT and the surname was Mansfield. This was the final resting place of Big Bill's navigator and rear gunner, Bluey Mansfield. Inside the underside of the lid, they discovered a message scratched into the surface. Simple initials again. W L C and a date. Elises hand shook as the importance of what she was holding sunk in.

There was nothing else. They were right. This was where Big Bill hiked to from the hilltop lookout; a permanent water supply, plenty of game and protection from the elements, provided by the dense foliage. It made sense on all levels.

Bill reported their find to the rest of the team still searching their grids and received a jubilant response. Bill reminded them that what they have discovered is the grave of a brave Australian airman and, while it was a significant find, it was something to celebrate with all due solemnity and asked them to remember that in their prayers.

All groups reported their progress and Bill received three negatives. He told them their efforts were appreciated but they must complete their search because at this stage they were yet to discover the fate of Big Bill.

The camera crew wanted the chopper to pick up their latest video and Bill put in the call. It was getting late in the day and they needed to complete the search of this little patch of paradise. Bill requested sleeping gear and supplies for the night ahead.

They would need a landing pad for the chopper and they only had one machete with them, but by carefully selecting a lightly wooded area to the west about 200 metres away, they managed to clear a suitable site, taking it in turns with the big blade. Bill lit a small, smoky fire to give the chopper pilot some assistance finding them and indicating wind direction as a bonus, not that a helicopter needed to land into the wind.

When Dusty Springfield the pilot arrived, he landed his craft without any fuss but raised a massive cloud of choking dust. Hence his nickname, further reinforced by the British female pop star of the same surname. For him, this was a very familiar exercise being an ex-military pilot with two tours of Vietnam behind him. They off loaded their gear and the excited television guys handed over their precious video tape and received replacements. Dusty was curious about their find and wanted to chat. He was a very intelligent guy with a lot of bush flying behind him and he was always worth talking to. His experience had told him the search party would need leg protection in the coarse scrub they were battling. Not only to prevent scratches and cuts from the stubborn flora that could quickly become dangerously infected, but also from the myriad snakes that inhabited that part of the country. He handed Bill Jnr a carton of stiff leggings or chaps that covered the lower legs.

Bill theorised that if Big Bill had been still fit, he could have set out to the east from here to walk to the Gregory Developmental Road which was about sixty kilometres away and would take him back to Charters Towers. The road would have been carrying a fair bit of military traffic in those days. If he was lucky, he could have flagged down a passing vehicle fairly promptly. They tossed this idea around for a bit and decided to sleep on it. Dusty clattered off on his mission to get the precious video back to the Brisbane television station. Bill asked him to contact his parents and let them know everyone was okay, and to bring them up to date.

They ate a cold meal and sat around discussing the situation. Their medical adviser, a full time paramedic, naturally referred to as Doc, delivered a hypothetical on the probable cause of Bluey's demise. He surmised that Bluey Mansfield had been badly injured in the crash and Big Bill brought him to this spot hoping to keep his mate alive until they were rescued. This waterhole would certainly have given them the best chance of that. Why Bluey died is anybody's guess, but Doc believed infection was the likely cause. Any open wounds would quickly succumb to the persistent attack of the virulent bush flies. Once infection set in, it would not take long to poison the whole system. Sepsis was when the infection reached the bloodstream and caused inflammation in the body. When the infection was severe enough to affect the function of organs, such as the heart, brain, and kidneys, septic shock and a significant drop in blood pressure followed, leading to respiratory or heart failure, stroke, failure of other organs, and death. He used this as an opportunity to remind everyone to be careful of any cuts and abrasions and take proper precautions to avoid infection.

As Doc finished his discourse on Bluey's likely demise, a sombre mood settled over the camp until Bill produced his mouth organ and played a favourite country and western ballad. Elise joined in with her lovely, lilting voice and the mood soon picked up. They enjoyed a few familiar songs together with one of the film crew revealing himself, to everyone's surprise, as a pretty fair tenor. He was of Italian heritage and had a love for opera. His name, appropriately, was Giacomo, after the great Italian composer, Puccini.

The sound man, who you might expect to have an interest in music, let everyone down by professing to be a fan of "heavy metal" and was hooted at roundly with a lot of loud laughter. But he did know a lot of smutty jokes which kept them laughing and made up for his poor taste in music.

In the morning, Bill pored over his maps and aerial photographs and decided that Dusty's theory could be correct. Taking a compass reading from the grave site in the direction of the nearest stretch of the Gordon Development Road Bill noticed on the map, a steep escarpment about 25 kilometres to the east. The ridge stretched away almost north to south across the intended path, which would provide a bit of a challenge to any hiker, even one as experienced and determined as Big Bill. It would be tempting to follow along this line by air with Dusty's assistance, but they would be bound to miss something from that high. There was nothing for it but to hike out the same way as Big Bill must have done. Young Bill concluded that they needed to re-equip and employ some expert bush men and he knew where to get them.

The recovery team at the oasis was recalled to the base camp where Bill informed them of his decision to suspend the search until they re-organised and recruited some specialist assistance. Bill thanked everyone for their diligence and loyalty and invited anyone who wanted to join him and Elise in the next phase of the operation, to let him know. Anyone who would like to stay and help, would be most welcome to be a part of this concluding chapter in the search. With luck, the break should only be a couple of days so they could continue to camp out, enjoy the outdoors and maintain the base until he returned.

A question arose about the grave. He told them protocol required that he should contact the Commonwealth War Graves Commission and give them the details of Bluey Mansfield's resting place and it would be up to them if his remains were to be removed. Certainly his descendants would be pleased to hear that their father, grandfather or uncle had been found. It would be a difficult trek for any of them to come to pay their respects and should they so desire, perhaps the Cuthbertsons could assist them reach there by helicopter. It would be the very least they could do for the man who perished in the presence of their grandfather.

The team was under instructions to clean up the site if they intended to leave. Bill wanted the camp site as it was when they arrived, if not better. Bill was a fanatical conservationist and made sure that what was carried in would be carried out, so all their trash was bagged and put on the trucks to be disposed of correctly in the city.

A couple of the younger volunteers had decided to stay, as the experience would give them credit in their studies and they would spend the time collecting and cataloguing insects and plants, hoping to find previously undiscovered species. Their chances were pretty good, thought Elise, judging by the number of creepy crawlies trying to share her tent. The bonus would be that they would maintain the site until the core team returned.

CHAPTER TWENTY FOUR

The scene was the boardroom at the television station, peopled by lawyers and, of course, Cliff Carter and the station CEO, Warwick Hargreaves. Lawrence sat in this extremely alien environment, wondering just what the hell was about to break. Why had his legal advisor been so insistent that he put himself out to be here when there was so much turmoil in the party currently and he needed to be there, lending his support to his leader.

The group around the board room table had been sitting quietly looking down at their hands folded in front of them, giving Lawrence the impression that he was in the presence of some very pious group attending to their prayers. There was a subdued atmosphere in the room and an almost palpable tension directed at him, or due to him. One thing he had learned over the years, was to always be on the front foot, especially when you were under attack and he demanded someone to speak up and explain to him what the bloody hell was going on. His anger was rising and he felt he was being treated with great disrespect. His lawyer laid a gentle, placating hand on Lawrence's shoulder and, by raising his eyebrows and nodding towards the network's lawyer, without a word, indicated said lawyer should put their cards on the table.

A flat type of file box was placed on the table and the lawyer removed the lid and took out a small stack of documents which proved to be photocopies of the original older and more delicate documents that were now under lock and key in a hermetically sealed safe. Every precaution had been taken as the network company had been sworn to protect the top secret file for the government, for the duration of the court hearing, to decide their right to publish. This was a most unusual situation and was certainly unprecedented in Commonwealth law.

In a flat monotone, common to legal types everywhere, the lawyer listed the documents, one by one, and then continuing in a suddenly more ponderous voice that came from somewhere deep in his chest, he gave a summary of the contents and the dreadful charges they contained levelled against Lieutenant Lawrence Garret Parnham VC.

Lawrence was on his feet screaming at these upstarts. Who the bloody hell were they and who did they think would believe this communist conspiracy? This was a typical tactic of the foul left of politics that now permeated Australian politics; is there nothing they wouldn't stoop to in order to defame him and demoralise his party? He continued to rant in this fashion until he ran out of steam.

Lawrence locked his eyes on Cliff Carter, who appeared to be shrinking into his shell under the old politician's death stare. The boardroom was so quiet, you could almost hear the cockroaches attacking the biscuits in the staff room. The air crackled audibly with the static electricity generated by the tension. No one said a word, as they were waiting for the expected outburst to subside.

Lawrence's blood pressure was at record heights and the veins were standing out like vines across his forehead; his heart was thumping in his chest so loudly it was almost audible. He turned to his lawyer for support and got none. He slumped into his chair like an electronic robot that had had its plug pulled and stared at the profile of his lawyer, willing him to say something.

He didn't let Lawrence down; he was on his feet and in his most impressive court room voice, trained to impress unmoving juries, he protested loudly that they would deny all of this inflammatory propaganda-driven nonsense and sue everyone in the room if one word was revealed to the public.

The station CEO was a master salesman and negotiator and raised his hands in a placatory gesture, asking for calm. His velvety voice, that he used to great effect in his day to day activities, had the desired effect and everyone drew a deep breath. He explained there was no pre knowledge of these documents; they were discovered in the course of filming the production that journalist Cliff Carter was working on. The materials, including the satchel they came in, had been authenticated by military experts and its ownership contested by the military in the courts with federal government support.

Lawrence surged angrily forward as if to leap to his feet again and was restrained firmly by his lawyer, Gordon, who was feeling his client's rising anger to the point when he thought he was about to explode. Around the table the participants all seemed to suffer a simultaneous raging thirst as they grabbed for the water filled glasses in front of them. All eyes were on the CEO as he continued.

Warwick explained in his honeyed tones, that the television network had won the temporary rights to the possession of the material and here he emphasised the next words. *Out of respect for Lawrence Parnham and his status* they had asked them to be here to be informed about the material and, in fairness, take whatever action they felt was warranted. There would certainly be a demand from the public for a full and frank enquiry and he should be in readiness for the coming public outcry.

Lawrence was stunned. How could this be happening? He had never been able to recall any accurate details of the actual events except in abstract nightmares. This information being revealed, supposedly written by the long dead Japanese captain, in this report and the supporting material was manifestly damning, if true. But how could he defend himself if all memory was lost?

Lieutenant Kerrison's report asserting an interview with the Japanese translator could likewise be devastating. The Japanese attested that everything in his superior's report was accurate. The translator claimed the Australian officer, Lawrence, broke under interrogation and, in return for his life, co-operated to reveal the defenders' dispositions in Milne Bay and Port Moresby. Kerrison's report also went on to speculate on the cause of death of the translator. Obviously a bullet through the head, but there was speculation that under cover of the Japanese counter attack, it may have been possible for "someone" to make sure the translator wasn't around to provide testimony in support of these incredible allegations.

At this point, Lawrence was almost leaping across the table, incandescent with rage and demanded that this vile, thinly veiled accusation of murder be withdrawn immediately. He looked down at his ashen-faced lawyer and lifelong friend for support again.

It was Gordon's turn to be outraged and he joined Lawrence on his feet again, waving an admonishing finger at the CEO and warning him that he was skating on very thin ice. He appealed to the network's legal team to withdraw these preposterous claims.

Warwick seemed to be losing his cool a little with this very serious additional allegation and was darting looks at his lawyers who requested a short break for everyone to calm down and regain their composure. They ushered Warwick into a side room and advised him to back off on the charge of murder in relation to the Japanese interpreter, which could only be supported by the hearsay evidence of a long dead Australian officer.

In short, these war time documents recovered from the downed Beaufighter seemed to carry enough weight to have The Honourable Minister Lawrence Parnham VC charged with cowardice, treason and possibly causing the improper death of a prisoner of war. Was there a statute of limitations for these serious war crimes and even if there were, the mere hint of this scandal against the family's shady past would destroy his reputation and career, stone cold dead.

Lawrence's head was swimming and his heart pounding. He felt on the point of collapse. This couldn't be true; his entire world, his entire belief system was based on courage and honour. He had a Victoria Cross and multiple awards to testify to his courage, strength of purpose and devotion as a public servant and soldier.

This, if true, could cause the collapse, not only of his family's reputation and business interests, but also his political party to which he had devoted much of his adult life serving since the war. The Country Party was currently entangled in an internecine war which was threat enough, but this? If convicted of the charges, could he spend the rest of his life in jail? Maybe not, but certainly he would be living with irredeemable shame.

Now that the bomb had exploded in the room, it was time to calculate the direct and collateral damage. What did they want from him? There was no suggestion they wouldn't continue with the broadcast.

The media always fell back on the line that it was in the public interest and the public's right to know, that dictated the release of this information, regardless of the damage to the subject or the pain and suffering of his family and friends. The damage in this case though, would be very far reaching and a very heavy responsibility rested on the shoulders of the television executives.

Warwick Hargreaves showed no sign of giving up on the most

explosive story that any of them could have ever imagined. This could match, or even be bigger than the Whitlam dismissal.

Lawrence was aware of scandals in the army and public life that had been made to go away in the public interest. Perhaps they could negotiate with these avaricious and soulless parasites. He turned to his lawyer again and saw Gordon's pallor. They looked at each other in disbelief.

Gordon Reynolds asked for a minute or two of privacy with his client. The executives departed the boardroom, leaving them sitting there like mutes. As the door closed, leaving them in silence, Gordon pointed to the roof and then his ears, indicating that the room could have listening devices and to be careful of what was said.

Lawrence immediately instructed Gordon to obtain a suppression order, but Gordon told him that may be more difficult than it appeared. Attack or defend? That was the question. How could you mount a defence against this? Attack was the only way forward. Gordon suggested that it was all down to the strength of the evidence against him, which in his vast legal experience fell into the area of *potior est conditio defendetis* or 'The condition of the defendant (Lawrence) is the better' i.e. 'the onus of proof is on the plaintiff'.

Lawrence looked askance at his lawyer who was looking rather smug, having pulled that one out of his hat. But would that Latin crap keep this out of the press? Lawrence demanded. The two angry men could see no point in discussing the matter further.

Without another word, Lawrence and Gordon stormed out of the television station's offices brushing aside attempts to stall them and engage them in pointless chatter. It was quite clear where the network wanted to go and Lawrence must make damn sure that they were met with maximum resistance. No, not just resistance; they must somehow bury these vile slurs, bury them deep and under six feet of concrete. Gordon disagreed and gave his opinion that the only way to handle this would be to confront the allegations and disprove them. Because, no matter how deep you buried this sort of thing, one day it would rise up like the living dead and come for you. Better he went down in flames now than to have this hanging over Lawrence forever.

Gordon Reynold's ever efficient secretary had booked the two men into separate rooms in a five star hotel with wonderful views over the Brisbane River. Neither one was interested in the view, so the curtains remained closed. Gordon Reynolds requested a private corporate room from reception and was ushered to an unoccupied room, equipped with several phones and a facsimile. He hit the phone, confident it was not tapped or the room bugged and within minutes he had stirred up some trusted legal experts in a number of pertinent areas of law.

The concierge tapped quietly on the door and delivered a bottle of scotch, two crystal tumblers and a bucket of ice. Gordon poured two very large drinks and they got stuck into business.

Phones started to ring all over Sydney, Canberra and Melbourne. Faxes were fired out at an astonishing rate. The book of torts was being thumbed by a small, tight group of loyal interns determined to work around the clock, looking for loopholes and precedence's that would stop or stall proceedings. They were turning over everything they could find in regard to defamation, nuisance, trespass, unlawful harassment, deceit, conspiracy, slander and malicious falsehood. All without really knowing what was behind all of the fuss. Within three days, they had a small truck load of writs to be served on the network which would tie them up for years.

A petition had been put before the High Court to slap a suppression order on the release, publication or broadcast of any information relating to, or emanating from, the documents currently held by QLD TV Network, Clifftop Productions or any and all of their associates, partners or affiliates and materials, either completed, in production or planned.

Any party breeching this suppression order would be subjected to the full weight of the law being the High Court of Australia, Canberra ACT and may result in fines of up to $1,000,000 and/or incarceration for up to five years. This was a very heavy duty attack carrying all the weight of over four decades in the rough, cut and thrust of Australian politics and three generations of Parnham's legal professional expertise. They were circling the wagons because it was not just Lawrence under attack; it was his life, his civilisation, culture and the honour of the Parnham dynasty.

But far from congratulating themselves, or sitting back on their haunches, or shouting their successes from the roof tops, they knew that when the lion made a kill and announced it with his ear shattering roar, he attracted every opportunistic scavenger for miles. He knew he would have a new battle on his hands with many new enemies.

And so it would be if he were to allow one syllable of this to fall into the hands of his enemies. Walking through a minefield was a walk in the park by comparison with the journey Lawrence was embarking upon. His reputation, his career, his family, his fortune, his awards and all his good works would all be for naught.

Having lit the fire under Gordon's contemporaries, they caught the early flight back to Sydney to regroup and reassess. Lawrence firstly went from the airport to his city apartment and freshened up before meeting with Gordon again. He and Gordon Reynolds were then in lock down in Lawrence's Sydney office for days without a break, trying to pull his defence together.

Gordon had raised a curious feature of this entire event. Harking back to the time in question, why didn't the senior officers bring these charges against Lawrence in the field? The charges were of sufficient seriousness that if found guilty of treason or cowardice in the face of the enemy, a soldier could expect to be summarily executed. Although the Australian military had never held an execution for any reason, it did not detract from the seriousness of the charges.

Aside, that is, for the British execution of Harry "Breaker" Morant and Peter Handcock in 1902 at the end of the Boer War. Gordon found the appropriate ruling in a dusty old military tome and read the relative passage to his client.

According to Section 98 of the Commonwealth Defence Act 1903, no member of the Defence Force shall be sentenced to death by any court martial except for four offences: mutiny, desertion to the enemy, or traitorously delivering up to the enemy any garrison, fortress, post, guard or ship, vessel, boat, aircraft or having traitorous correspondence with the enemy. Significantly, this sentence cannot be carried out until it was confirmed by the Governor General.

So then why, given the gravity of the situation, had no action been taken immediately? Obviously, the hesitation had been due to the fact he was the son and heir to a very senior Australian politician.

The resulting scandal would have been very damaging to war time morale. The senior ranks had dithered for weeks and finally decided to kick it down the road on the pretext that they were too busy fighting a war to deal with it. And so a pilot had been despatched to carry the report back to Australia to be dealt with by senior command at Headquarters, letting the officers in the field off the hook.

Then, by some incredible stroke of luck for both the officers in the field and Lawrence, the plane carrying the inflammatory documents, crashed in the Australian outback, never to be seen again. That is, until another aircraft crashed in the same area and, stretching the laws of probability to their extreme, the war plane with its toxic documents intact was discovered by the second aircraft's search and rescue party.

Back in the war zone, Lawrence had recovered from the rough treatment he received at the hands of the Japanese and, with the defence of Milne Bay at a critical stage, he was then ordered to lead a patrol against the enemy again. Secretly, HQ had hoped he may have met his fate, thus clearing up a murky event. In another deadly fire fight, when in defence of the wounded in his charge, and while seriously wounded himself, Lawrence proved his incredible courage in the battle repelling the enemy's attack and driving them off with heavy losses, earning the very highest gallantry award!

This report had been signed, sealed and delivered, arriving promptly and safely back in Australia and was acted upon immediately. The announcement of a heroic act such as this was an important boost for military and civilian morale. But whether this speculation proved accurate or not, the fact was the incriminatory material had now surfaced.

How and why the documents came to the surface, is of little concern to Lawrence. The fact was, they had been discovered and were now being used to attack everything he believed in and held dear. His lawyer had performed magnificently and his application to the high court for an injunction on Lawrence's behalf was powerfully argued and word perfect. But if Gordon were being perfectly candid, he knew his client had as much chance of survival as a chocolate teapot.

Tired and disillusioned, Lawrence retired to Chatsworth Park and dived deeply into the golden depths of several bottles of Dalwhinnie whiskey, his preferred brand, and failed to surface for three days. He refused food, phone calls, imprecations from his wife and closest friends, his priest, and even his much respected party leader, who all recognised the symptoms of acute anxiety and depression.

The only person he admitted to his study was his legal representative, Gordon Reynolds. Gordon confronted Lawrence who looked like a wrung out human wreck, dressed in clothes he must have dredged from the bottom of the laundry basket. His eyes, in contrast with his pallid countenance, were so red they seemed to be bleeding; his thinning hair was a tangled mess and his breath was foul. A powerful smell of alcohol oozed from every pore, uniting with the general fug of the study. The whole disgusting aspect was so bad that Gordon ignored etiquette and threw open the windows to allow some fresh air into the room, despite the outside temperature. His suggestion that Lawrence took a shower and freshened up was ignored as Lawrence's shaking hand reached out for the bottle again.

Gordon moved like a striking taipan, scooped it up and hurled it straight out of the open window. He heard a satisfying smash of glass against the garden wall. His client was stunned but Gordon was unflinching and adamant. Lawrence must straighten up right now and make himself presentable to stand before his party leader and reveal the whole sordid story and how he planned to defend himself and prevent the scandal from damaging the party.

Lawrence knew he must bring his party leader into it eventually and he didn't have to be Nostradamus to predict the outcome of that particular meeting. There was a chance they may be able to gain the support of Lawrence's leader, who was Deputy PM to make this go away in the national interest. But again, that was a very slim hope. God, what would he do? This was a perfect situation for the opposition, who would give neither Lawrence, nor his leader, any leeway. This would be a knife at the throat of the Country Party that he loved and Labor would be feeling out their carotid artery. On advice from Gordon, he decided to "grasp the nettle" as his lawyer put it, though that hardly fit the fate that he anticipated.

With much trepidation, Lawrence called his leader and requested an immediate audience. Lawrence gave him the address of a secure private venue, well away from the prying eyes of Canberra. He informed him that Gordon would be in attendance and perhaps they should involve the attorney general. His leader was no fool and, suspecting this was an extremely serious matter, let forth a torrent of questions which Lawrence was forced to fend off with the rather lame explanation that all would be explained at the meeting and he would prefer not to say a word before then.

Gordon's proposal was to have the meeting in the vacant apartment of a friend and colleague who was away overseas. It was in an area of Sydney well away from the mainstream and would provide the security they required with its protected entry and off street parking. It was doubtful that any of the press would accidentally stumble across three of the most senior politicians in the land conducting a clandestine meeting in a part of town seldom frequented by press, pollies, or their acolytes and start a round of rumour and speculation.

When the four men, Lawrence and Gordon, the party leader and the attorney general were settled and everyone had a drink in front of them, Lawrence nervously commenced the conversation by apologising for the cloak and dagger situation he had subjected them to. Lawrence was confronted by some very grim visaged faces that mumbled, in less than friendly tones, acceptance of the circumstances. Their political radar had alerted them to some impending bad news that was coming their way from Lawrence, who then asked permission if he may defer to his legal representative to open the meeting with an explanation as to why they were there.

The party leader and deputy prime minister nodded his assent and asked Gordon to get on with it. Lawrence coughed nervously and turned to Gordon and indicated he should now open the conversation as they had planned earlier.

Gordon drew breath and began a long and detailed summary of the whole messy media affair.

There were signs of impatience brewing around the table as everyone present was very familiar with the story so far. The television promotions, which had run ad-nausea, had seen to that. It had been almost impossible to avoid the blasted things. They were banged out in the middle of the news and plastered in print in all the major dailies. Gordon moved on to the crux of the matter and despite having repeated and rehearsed this address in preparation for the meeting, he was still struggling, under the steely gaze of the two politicians, to adequately explain in a favourable light the ugliness of the allegations being levelled at Lawrence.

Before he revealed the awful mess, he assured them that what they were about to hear had been heavily protected by the unbreakable suppression orders he had instigated. Furthermore, at this stage, very few people were aware of the full story, which was limited by partitioning and sectioning it in such a way that no one person could now have access to the full story. Outside of the key executives of the programme and television station, no more than six people, plus Gordon and Lawrence, knew the full alleged story.

At the impatient urging of the party leader, supported by the attorney general, Gordon finally revealed the staggering story.

'Here seated before you,' he said, 'is one of the great heroes of the war in New Guinea, who is now accused of cowardice and treason.

'The documents contained within the top secret satchel that was scheduled to be opened live on television, until the producers, realising the enormity of the allegations, had the wit to bring it to the attention of Lawrence, fearing a legal backlash.

'Although costing them dearly, they had enough empathy to give Lawrence a briefing on the matter.'

Gordon's nervousness had him tripping over his words in his anxiety to get them out.

He was urged to give more detail of the allegations and when he related the shocking contents the documents contained, the listeners were gobsmacked. The Deputy PM felt the breath sucked out of his chest and slumped backward in his chair with a curse. This was worse than anything they had imagined or expected. These days it was an MP's admission of adultery or with increasing frequency, MP's admitting to being gay and, in one or two sad cases, suffering from what was wrongly referred to as the gay disease, AIDS.

The two men opposite were unable to utter a word. It was, to say the least, astounding, well beyond the bounds of any sort of run-of-the-mill human folly. This was catastrophic. Cowardice and treason?! Dear God! If this did get out, it would not only ruin Lawrence but it had the potential to bring about the destruction of the Country Party and, by association, the ruin of the entire coalition government. Lawrence was separated from the Prime Ministership by a mere two heartbeats, and whether these allegations could be proved or not, the ghastly stain that would spread across the entire governing body would be indelible and taint Australian politics for years to come.

The room had fallen in to what could only be described as a heavily pregnant silence as each took on the weight of this bombshell. No one was brave enough to make eye contact with another as they all sought to find words to express their feelings and keep their anger under control. Were they angry at Lawrence, assuming him guilty? Or were they inwardly seething at the blasted media who were using this information to build ratings and drive up their revenues, or both? There was almost a hint of treason right there. The leader left his chair and paced the room seeking answers that would not come and were not there anyway.

A miserable television programme holding the fate of the entire nation, and its standing in world affairs, in their grubby hands for the sake of winning a damned ratings survey and a pissy profit. A survey result would be forgotten within a couple of weeks and the profit would soon be dissipated on some worthless twat of an overpaid announcer, or the latest young blonde bimbo with a big chest and a tiny intellect.

The attorney general broke the silence by declaring that the key to the whole scandal was the veracity, or otherwise, of the documents and also whether a statute of limitations could be brought to bear to shut the matter down. They must immediately gain access to the documents at all costs. A court order was to be issued for the immediate surrender of all documents recovered from the wreckage of the RAAF aircraft and any and all copies that they held.

The court order extended to the suppression of any scripts written or produced and further, any programming and promotional material that was already in the can and had been scheduled to be released for publicity. The order was hand delivered by a security officer also charged with the responsibility of taking possession of the seized documents and delivering them directly into the hands of the attorney general.

The network executives were advised that when the papers had been seen, read and evaluated, a meeting would be called and the attorney general would deliver his decision on how, or if, they would relinquish the explosive material.

As always, the attorney general knew the network would be pushing the usual publics need to know line, hoping it would be an influential factor in his decision making. On the other side of the debate, information had been supressed during the war years in the interest of public morale; it would be argued by Parnham's legal team that such was the case now.

Cliff Top Productions' lawyers duly received a summons from the office of the attorney general. They were to present themselves to his office at a scheduled time. A refusal would be considered as contempt of the federal court from which the summons had been issued.

While not exactly shivering in their hand-made Italian leather boots and Versace suits, the networks lawyers had very little experience of the high court, outside one or two infamous cases of slander, and approached this like an interview with the devil knowing full well that should they slip up, somehow the network could be crushed as the government moved to protect itself and the sanctity of the Australian political system. In any event, the television station knew there was no such thing as a hurried decision by a government department. They would delay, delay, delay until the point of exhaustion.

True to form, the attorney general seemed to spend an inordinate amount of time examining the evidence and measuring the value of the information for public consumption against the television network's need to return revenue for their shareholders.

The opposing legal teams assembled in their home bases, before setting off for Canberra and their meeting with the attorney general. Cliff Carter argued vehemently with the station's lawyers and management to be included in their journey south. They finally got sick of his moaning and acquiesced. But Cliff's triumph was short-lived as, on arrival at parliament house, he ran into the stiff arm of the parliamentary security officers, who pointed out that his name was not included on their security list of participants and directed him to the public canteen.

The lawyers and their briefcases and the attendant files and reference books were scanned by security as they passed into the imposing offices of the attorney general. They were met by a senior member of his staff who escorted them to the centre of the great man's dominion. Cliff cools his heels in the nearby staff canteen with a dreadful cup of tepid coffee.

The attorney general was sitting behind his imposing desk with a grim-looking entourage on either side. This was, to the astonishment of the network guys, the core of the Australian National Security Committee (NSC) which focused on major international security issues of strategic importance to Australia. Border protection policy, national responses to developing situations, either domestic or international, and classified matters relating to aspects of the operation and activities of the Australian Intelligence Community. The NSC was chaired by the prime minister with the deputy prime minister as deputy chair and included the attorney general, the minister for foreign affairs, the minister for defence, the treasurer, the minister for immigration and border protection, and the cabinet secretary.

Arranged before the network team was a cut down version without the PM, treasurer, cabinet secretary and minister for immigration, but never-the-less a very powerful unit. The attorney general took the lead in the meeting and didn't waste time getting down to tin tacks. He immediately informed the network group that despite their earlier court success in claiming ownership of the documents he, on the advice of the Australian government solicitor, had been advised, the documents forming a report on a military action, and subject to strict top secret classification, had been ruled to be the property of the Australian government and would be placed under indefinite embargo pending further investigation and deliberation by the attorney general's office.

The network guys began to stammer out their protests and were brought to order by the raised hand of the attorney general, in the classic stop sign of a traffic policeman. He then went on, reading from a prepared statement which agreed the network had rights to the rest of the top secret despatch case's contents which outlined details of intended actions by the allies, battle orders and action reports.

Then there were the Japanese documents which were found to be fascinating from a historical vantage point. The documents seemed to hint that planned attacks on Port Moresby would be aided by the acquisition of some key intelligence. The report did not indicate where the intelligence had come from, but it was a very strong indication of the Japanese army's confidence in overthrowing the allies, and gaining a valuable springboard for its attack on the Australian mainland. This was, in itself, an alarmingly explosive fact, previously unreported which, had they been successful, would almost certainly have led to the ultimate invasion of Australia.

The network executive interrupted forcefully, declaring that was an interesting historical fact, but not the juicy exposé they had led their viewers to expect. They would be howled down by the audience, critics and their sponsors, if that was all they had for them.

'Bad luck,' stressed the attorney general, 'at stake here is the future stability of the Australian government and this matter will be dealt with as though it was a foreign incursion. The government respects that the network has invested a lot into the series they have been running and understand that, having this very inflammatory rug pulled out from under you, is a bit debilitating but nothing like the cataclysmic result, if you are stupid enough to ignore my order and go ahead to reveal all the details in your television program.'

The attorney general pointed out they were the masters of inventive and addictive drama and they had a great story to tell here about the gallant allied forces that protected us from the scourge of a foreign invader.

'Go away and do your thing, and note that this meeting has never taken place and these documents do not exist. Be very sure of that.'

The look on the lawyers' faces as they exited the building were all Cliff needed to understand that the network had been royally screwed and him along with it. The sad little television posse head back to the airport in stunned silence.

They had pulled a miracle out of the fire before today, but how on earth would they turn this around? With visions of plunging ratings in their heads and, in Cliff's case, bankruptcy as a result of share prices spiralling down, pulled sponsorships and a lame programme following the sensationalism of the promotions, they did make a tragic group. Cliff's thoughts of repaying the loans he had acquired, based on the revenue projections, made his stomach churn.

Once the room was cleared of visitors, the attorney general turned to the deputy PM and told him, in no uncertain terms, that Parnham was gone, dead, wiped from history. He must never show his traitorous head in the house again. However they choose to do it, was entirely up to the deputy PM, but it would be done and it would be done immediately. This toxic stain on the face of Australian politics would be wiped clean.

The deputy PM asked for a moment or two. He told those remaining in the room, to cool their jets, as it were. It was very easy to get steamed up over this matter but before acting rashly, take a long look at the Parnham legacy. Let's start with old Jefferson G Parnham who served in the early government of New South Wales and spent many years in the service of the public helping to establish many of the institutions that benefited the community then and were still enjoyed by the people to this day.

Then Lawrence's father, Sir Alexander Parnham, a great legal advocate and member of the NSW legislature, who spent many years fighting for the rights of working people and the rural community, in particular. A great man who introduced legislation, altering the very fabric of the Australian society he served with great distinction for many years. He was also a very important foundation member of the Country Party that had now become an integral part of Australia's political system.

Lawrence Parnham, whether guilty of the charges put before them or not was, by the same token, a proven and attested war hero who at great personal risk saved the lives of the men under his command. That was an indisputable fact which earned him the highest gallantry award his grateful country could bestow. Since that time he had shrugged off the injuries he suffered due to his war service, where lesser men may have used this as an excuse to sit back on their laurels and wait for the world to support them. He had been an energetic and productive politician who, like his forebears, had on a private basis been a generous philanthropist who was adored by the rich and poor alike. He had been responsible for many significant rural developments, particularly in educational opportunities and medical services. All of this on top of his untiring service to his military comrades, ensuring they received every advantage they deserved. He had provided as many pro-bono hours as any lawyer in the land and many more than some, defending people who otherwise stood unrepresented before the courts.

In short, he had been an outstanding citizen who should be looking forward to a much deserved retirement and maybe writing his memoirs now that he had reached his declining years. To treat him this way was to the detriment of, not only the party, but to the society they served. Another thing to consider was how this would be explained to the public? And how in God's name could they prevent the media dogs from sniffing out this mess? Why give them an invitation by virtually putting Lawrence Parnham in stocks to receive the derision and mockery of the public. No, this would not reflect well on any of them.

The latest Morgan Gallup poll had revealed that the party was losing support across the board and this scandal would drive them down even further. While agreeing in principal with the attorney general, he proposed another tactic to take Parnham away from the public eye.

He suggested the idea that Parnham was literally put away anonymously in a secure place like a rehabilitation centre where he would receive counselling and care. A press release would be created and presented at a suitable time, sadly announcing the awful fate that had befallen one of the country's great heroes. It was well known that he had a problem with alcohol, which had finally reached out its evil hand and delivered a massive stroke, leaving him paralysed and incoherent. This would account for his sudden departure from public life and the lack of coherence would provide a rational screen for a no interviews embargo.

In the words of several banana republic dictatorships, Lawrence Garret Parnham VC MP was to be disappeared. And his narcissistic colleagues acting only to protect their careers and entitlements were thinking, *and long may he stay disappeared.*

CHAPTER TWENTY FIVE

Bill and Elise arrived back home, tired, dusty and dirty from their exertions. They had been flown out, courtesy of Dusty Springfield and his helicopter that conveniently put them down 50 metres from the homestead.

They had left the base camp of the search expedition in the care of a group of young and very enthusiastic student volunteers, who were happy to use the opportunity to flesh out their research into the entomology of south western Queensland. The expedition's vehicles had all been left in the care of the volunteers, as it didn't make much sense to bash their way out overland, only to have to repeat the exercise in a couple of days and besides, the crew could use them if they wished.

Over dinner at Courtland Downs, Bill and Elise brought Bobby, Joanne and Lydia up to date with their findings. Lydia became emotional as she listened to the confirmation that her greatly loved husband had been trying to reach her when he came to grief. Elise's photos and description of Big Bill's efforts to provide a decent burial for his mate, broke her heart.

Bobby patted her hand and assured her she mustn't feel any blame for their misfortune. To Lydia, it was as though it happened only yesterday and yet, here was her middle-aged son, Bobby, and mature grandchildren now dedicated to finding him. Bobby and Joanne, more or less, chaired the discussion and pledged support until Bill and Elise reached a resolution. Lydia believed her husband, Big Bill, was capable of anything and if Bluey Mansfield was still alive he would have carried him on his back.

They shared their suspicion that Big Bill may have tried to walk out after caring for and finally burying his mate Bluey. There was no doubt, knowing Big Bill's character, that he had the bush skills to survive a 60 odd kilometre hike, possibly injured and with limited supplies.

They decided to consult with the oldest indigenous worker they had on the station, Jimmy Magpie, and see if he or his son, Junior Magpie, could help them look for sign of Big Bill's tracks even after fifty years. Father and son Magpie weren't too sure, but Junior willing to give it a go. In fact, Junior Magpie was deliriously happy to be a part of this thing. He dashed about getting his gear ready which, as it turned out, was a curious bundle containing some of his black man's magic and his new bush hat.

The brother and sister team sat at the big table in the dining room with maps spread out before them, explaining to their father what they had done and where they had been. He agreed that their conclusions about Big Bill's movements had proved sound so far and it seemed logical that he would try to walk out if he were capable. Since Big Bill had flown over this territory many times, he would have had a pretty good idea of what it held for him and could be counted on to be aware of the Gregory Developmental Road and the salvation it offered. Bobby believed they were on the right track and should follow their instincts.

A phone call summoned Dusty and the next morning his helicopter was sitting out in the house paddock, fuelled up and ready for them at first light. The trio of Lydia, Bobby and Joanne were there to watch them climb aboard and clatter away to the north-west, back to their last camp at the billabong. Poor old Junior Magpie was hanging on for dear life on his first chopper flight, his eyeballs popping out of his head and his mouth almost a blur as he muttered non- stop in his own tribal language, perhaps calling on the spirits of his ancestors for protection as the machine lifted off into the air.

The line from Bluey Mansfield's resting place to the Gregory Developmental Road was the area along which the search for any sign of Big Bill would be conducted. And while the distance to be covered, as the crow flies, was not great, only about 60 to 70 kilometres, it was very harsh terrain that they would be searching. Everyone would be thankful for Dusty Springfield's gift of leggings by the time they had travelled too far through the coarse scrub.

This promised to be a gruelling venture as it would be ground based and would need a lot of support and, given they would be conducting a search for some fifty year old sign of their grandfather, it would done slowly and thoroughly.

After all this time, they didn't really expect to discover footprints or bent grass, or whatever the skilled trackers looked for when tracking game in the bush, but more of a spiritual instinctive kind of tracking where they would scan the landscape for the most likely route that Bill would take. Junior Magpie, thinking as a skilled bushman would hopefully mirror Big Bill's inclinations, by choosing a similar track towards the ridge in the distance.

Jimmy Magpie had spent a lot of time in the scrub passing on his incredible knowledge to Bill senior and would expect him to react in a particular way to landscape features, to find food and water. Junior Magpie, at an age that would qualify for retirement, had spent much of those years living off the land as his father and their ancestors had done for thousands of years and despite his age, was as agile as a man half his age.

Having inherited his father's skills, he was quite a bit younger and fitter than his now quite ancient patriarch and would be a great asset in the search for Big Bill's remains. He would look for marks cut into tree trunks as they always did when they went into new country. A slash or deep scarring of the tree would indicate the passage taken and would also provide a guide back to the way they had come. Perhaps old habits died hard and Big Bill had left marks that might still be visible as scars on the trees to Junior Magpie's eyes.

When a tree was injured, it reacted in a way similar to a human that has an injury or laceration, in that the tree would attempt to heal itself by growing over the injury. This repair could take many years to heal, leaving an anomaly in the trunk that an educated eye could discern, long after the wound had been inflicted. Exposed sapwood would be surrounded by regrowth and, in some circumstances, the axe or knife used to inflict the damage may have left cuts partly covered by regrowth.

All the planning and preparation went on under the scrutiny of the television camera crew who, it seemed, were almost grafted onto young Bill and Elise. The resulting video would be picked up and sped off to the station for the broadcast in their rival program which was definitely beginning to put a dent in Cliff Carter's current affairs show, which had stalled due to the legal battle between the network, the attorney general and Lawrence Parnham's lawyers.

As Bobby waved off the helicopter heading back out into the scrub to resume the search for his father, he couldn't help but feel a little left out. He was still a very fit man in his mid-life and would have loved to go with his children on the search. However, there were many matters on the station that needed his undivided attention and reluctantly he left it in the hands of the younger generation. Joanne, sensing his fretfulness, told him to let them finish what they started. It was their mission and they were best suited to the task as he was to his. Okay, point taken. He shook his head and got on with the day's chores.

The trip felt more like a joy flight to the passengers as they traversed the vast patchwork of cultivated and wild country below. The helicopter was piloted by the legendary Dusty Springfield, who guided his flying machine to the landing pad that was prepared only a few days ago at the billabong site from where they would recommence their search. First out of the chopper was Junior Magpie, who walked about sniffing the air and feeling the soil with his bare toes like a man landing on an alien landscape.

Magpie rejected the leggings, preferring to have direct contact with the earth he was so familiar with. Having returned to the billabong campsite, they set about establishing it as a more serious and semi-permanent new forward base camp. The chopper departed in the usual cloud of dust and clatter, leaving them to an eerie silence which was soon broken by the orchestra of bird calls once the helicopter was out of range.

At this stage, everyone knew what they were required to do and the first chore was to rebuild the fire pit and get some combustion going. The team had no trouble finding fuel and the fire was burning down to a magnificent hot coal base, ideal for cooking. The night was a bit chilly and one or two wandered over to enjoy their beers by the cooking fire. Before too long, a bit of a sing song got up and going and the laughs began. These were the times they would remember later, the camaraderie, the fun that got them through the tough days ahead.

The helicopter had returned a bit later in the day, transporting the support crew who, up until now, had been camped at the original base camp, supporting the volunteers. Now they were here to handle things like cooking, handling supplies, maintaining a radio contact and shifting camp etc. They melded into the new base camp seamlessly.

In truth, Bill confided in Elise, they were well and truly over staffed, but he hadn't the heart to tell anyone to go home. To hell with it, they were such a great bunch, Bill wouldn't care if they all stayed out here together for a year, except for the fact they had a solemn duty. If they failed, it would not be due to lack of effort by Big Bill's grandchildren. They would literally turn over every rock and stone to ensure the discovery and repatriation of their grandfather's remains to his home, to join his ancestors in the family plot at Courtland Downs.

Young Bill had his reliable maps and aerial photos spread out on the table again for further closer examination. Bill called the whole team together and proceeded to give them a briefing, telling them what they could expect. Warnings were issued regarding safety, in particular venomous snakes and proper hydration. Bill confirmed everyone had access to a First Aid kit and there were people with the training and experience to use them.

Radio schedules were organised from Bill and Elise to base camp and people were appointed as radio operators. They were charged with the responsibility to receive and record the time and subject of incoming calls and to minimise radio usage. It was possible the rival network could have someone monitoring their frequency.

They spent the day getting their gear in shape and then settled down to spend the night on this hallowed ground. The team ate an excellent barbequed meal of steak and salad, washed down with a very nice Hunter River red. After all, no one said they had to suffer cold baked beans and stale bread just because they were on an expedition. They had wonderful support from Dusty in his reliable chopper, bringing in fresh supplies daily, so why not bring in the good stuff? This daily delivery of meals to the camp reminded Dusty of a related story of his time in Vietnam when he said the US troops out in jungle on patrol often had hot meals choppered in and then wondered how the enemy knew where they were.

In the morning, the sun came up as usual to see the team already stirring. Elise had picked some wild flowers and she placed them reverently on Bluey Mansfield's grave with a silent prayer, asking his guidance in finding his loyal comrade, Big Bill. A large billy of tea was keeping hot on the camp stove as they enjoyed some bacon and eggs, sausages and toast.

The camera crew was already shooting mood pieces and there were some in-jokes flying about, causing a bit of laughter and mock punches. Junior Magpie was shaking his head thinking,

'White fella's pretty bloody strange,' but enjoying himself on this new adventure all the same.

Junior enjoyed the music provided by Bill and Elise and sang along with many songs he knew. Like a lot of his kin, Junior had a natural flair for theatre and music and loved to join in enthusiastically clapping and jigging about.

It was a happy camp and, as he looked about, Bill reflected on how fortunate they were to have such friends, and how proud his grandfather would have been of them. He shook his head and tried to think happy thoughts to avoid the maudlin mood he could feel creeping up on him.

Bill was itching to get going and rounded up the search team. Junior Magpie led off in a crouch, eyes moving left and right across the immediate ground and along the horizon. He looked for signs that only he understood, ripples in the broadcloth of the land that would lead to water, or to food or shelter or just leading to the next camp ground.

Where were the kangaroos going for fresh feed? Where were magpie geese landing? What put those parakeets in flight? All of these signs, ignored by the white fellas, told a story to Junior Magpie. He looked for what the white fellas would call "the path of least resistance" through the mulga scrub and tough Mitchell grass. This would be the direction an experienced bushman would go in order to save energy.

They started moving at a steady, controlled pace, pushing through the scrub directly east on Bill's compass, which was the direction confirmed by Junior Magpie. Most of the area was semi desert scrubland consisting of mulga, saltbush, gidyea and brigalow, spinifex and different species of grasses, depending on the soil type they travelled over. It was a diverse but hungry patch of ground. Occasionally, they met small sand hills with shifting sand under their feet, clothed sparsely in Mitchell grass. Dry creek beds, that would run full in the rainy season, threw up stands of red river gums and coolabah. It was harsh but starkly beautiful.

Junior Magpie had names of his own for all of these species. Some of them would provide edible berries; bark and leaves from some were used as spices or antiseptics. Other food came from the plant's root systems themselves or the creatures living within them. But he wasn't looking for food right now, his eyes were scouring the tree trunks for old scars at chest height where a man passing by would blaze a mark to follow back home on his return or allow someone to follow him.

They had been hiking for several hours now, Junior Magpie covering more ground than anyone else zigzagging back and forth. Bill called a halt for a rest break and to take on some food. Elise called for the chopper and Dusty arrived overhead with a crewman lowering a basket down with their lunches of sandwiches, cold drinks, fruit and some high energy bars. That's the way to bush bash, lunches "par avion". The television guys dropped some video into the basket and Dusty's crew hauled it up and they swung away noisily back to the base camp.

The heat was building now and they suffered through minor dust storms kicked up by sudden mischievous gusts that come out of nowhere to form into little willy-willies that created temporary havoc and then disappeared into nothing. After lunch they pressed on, following Bill who had been checking his headings against his map and believed they were still on the right track.

He was looking at the map, explaining his theory to Elise for the hundredth time when they heard Junior shout. He was gesturing excitedly to them, a slash of white teeth highlighting his cheerful grin, to come and see as he pointed at a large gum. Sure enough, there was a definite old scar, partly overgrown by bark but still quite clear. This was cause for a celebration. They posed for the camera, acting out the discovery for the sake of the documentary. They looked carefully at the mark to confirm their conviction. Junior pointed to the cuts, partly covered now by the slow growing bark, as proof.

This was just the sort of thing they had been looking for, but it was far from conclusive. There had been cattlemen and indigenous people through here for generations; the mark could have been made by any one of them. But they were convinced that it was the right vintage and asked Junior Magpie for the direction from here. Junior was in a state of high excitement, now following his discovery and was keen to build on that success. Pointing to the east, he headed off again.

Bill took a compass reading from the mark, back to the camp and made notes in his diary and on the map. Looking in the direction to the east, there was nothing to indicate why or where his grandfather might have gone from here, except due east, of course. He took a sight on a small hillock a couple of miles away, which proved to be roughly on the line they needed to take. Using this as a guide, they set off again.

An experienced bush walker would pick out a landmark, like the hilltop ahead of them, to keep on a straight line and maintain the desired compass heading. From there, a new landmark could be spotted and the hiker's course would once again go in a positive direction, instead of wandering off in circles.

Elise had been on the radio, giving the news back to base camp. She had given them a brief description of their progress before confirming that they would call again with their position when they were making the night's bivouac at approximately 1900 hours.

Things seemed to be going great but "Murphy's Law" kicked in with a vengeance. The sound guy, who entertained them with his wonderful tenor voice, gave his vocal chords another airing, but this time with a high C scream. He had made the city boy blunder of stepping over a log without checking the other side. The other side of this particular log was providing a sheltered sunny spot for a large death adder that was warming itself sleepily after consuming a nice big fat bush rat. That was, until his peace was shattered by a large boot coming from nowhere and landing squarely on his back.

The snake's peace was shattered and so was his spine by the great hiking boot of Giacomo the sound guy, who looked down for the source of the searing pain in his right calf. To his horror, he saw the snake had somehow buried its fangs deeply into his flesh. Giacomo had been in a rush to gather up his gear and join the hiking party and foolishly decided the leggings were surplus.

Chaos reigned for the next few minutes as Giacomo danced about screaming – in perfect pitch – until he was tackled to the ground. Magpie Junior made quick work of the death adder while Bill screamed at Giacomo to keep still. He dived into his backpack for the first aid kit and came out with a long gauze bandage that he wrapped tightly from just below the wound, all the way up to the top of Giacomo's thigh.

Elise was on the radio calling for urgent assistance. It was essential to get the poor man to hospital where shots of antivenene would save his life. He was in for an interesting couple of weeks in recovery but first they had to get him to a clearing so they could load him into the chopper. Junior Magpie pointed out a suitable clearing on top of a small, sandy ridge a couple of hundred metres away. There was one saving grace for Giacomo. His assailant may have just used a fair amount of its venom on the bush rat, so sparing his human victim from a full dose.

Getting Giacomo to the pick-up point was no mean feat and they had no sooner started a smoke signal when Elise had talked Dusty into the landing zone. Giacomo was practically thrown aboard and away the chopper roared, heading south to Longreach Hospital and he was seen no more.

Now the television network had a problem. How and where to get another sound man at short notice to pick up where the Italian tenor had left off? Apparently, sound men were in plentiful supply and the replacement arrived on the return flight with Dusty, wide-eyed and just a little bit nervous. His name was nowhere near as romantic as his predecessor.

Barry jumped down from the helicopter and was instantly put to work. Dusty reported that he had stayed at the hospital until he could get a report from the medics, who assured him Giacomo was in safe hands and should make a full recovery.

In his absence, the team had continued on, determined to find the next sign from Big Bill. It didn't take long. Junior discovered a line of rocks on a flat ledge of stone pointing in the easterly direction. It was a deliberate construction obviously left to provide a searcher with further direction. It had half an arrow head, but clearly the other half had been dislodged at some point as there were several similar rocks in size and shape within a couple of feet. Bill noted the formation and its compass heading and marked the position on his map. By now they had enough way points to draw a line through them from the camp to where they stood now. The whole thing was filmed, as usual, with the team posing around the prominent rock formation, carrying its message from the past.

It wasn't exact, nor did they expect it to be, but it was steady in its purpose heading east towards the escarpment that had now come clearly into view. There was a notch in the ridge at which the recently discovered arrow pointed directly. It was clear that was the route Big Bill intended to follow, hoping the notch would be a pass through the escarpment, allowing him an easier passage to the Gregory Developmental Road and salvation.

They decided to continue with the tracking exercise and ignored short cuts which could lure them into taking an assumed and incorrect path. Junior Magpie led them away again and the mission continued with renewed energy. The television guys were getting what they wanted, with the new sound guy Barry struggling with his phobias:

Arachnophobia (spiders), Ophidiophobia (snakes) and Agoraphobia (fear of open spaces).

'What? No way princess. How could anyone have that many phobias?' muttered one of the team.

Bazza laughed at their disbelief. He said he also suffered from coulrophobia, which was a morbid fear of clowns; a pretty common phobia apparently and he was starting to develop a rash when he looked at certain team members.

They had uncovered his not so subtle sense of humour. Around the fire, Bazza, as he preferred to be called, kept up a steady patter of jokes that had them rocking back with laughter. He confessed to having an ambition to be a successful stand-up comedian and cracked the old line that when he told his family he wanted to be a comedian, they all laughed at him, but when he got his first paid gig they weren't laughing anymore!

News comes back with their resupply that poor Giacomo had taken a turn for the worse and was in critical care but still expected to make a full recovery. He was making news himself as an integral part of the documentary he had been involved in. But the upside was a bit of collateral in the form of fresh promotion at his expense. They would have preferred to earn it by other means, than having their sound man chewed by a death adder.

Another interesting piece of news from a different quarter came back to them with their resupply and that was the results of the latest television survey. There was clear evidence that public interest was growing in their documentary and their ratings were climbing wonderfully. Curiously, "The Cliff Carter Exposé" had, for some reason, been taken off air. They were not to know what had transpired behind the scenes at Cliff Top Productions.

All this time, young Bill had been mulling over the possible recovery and restoration of his Twin Beech and would there be a possibility of rescuing the remains of Big Bill's Beaufighter?

The Twin Beech might be achievable, but would it be financially viable, even allowing for insurance? There were plenty of airworthy models available and probably at a tenth of the cost of recovery and restoration. On the other hand, his grandfather's plane would be impossible to restore to flying condition, but the Beaus were exceedingly rare and this one had special significance, not only to the descendants of the man who flew it, but as a memorial to all the gallant airmen who lost their lives, many of whom came from Queensland and more than one from Longreach. A plan began to hatch in Bill's fertile mind forming a fitting memorial for his grandfather. But the priority now was to press on and find Big Bill, who seemed to be calling him onward.

During his upbringing, young Bill had had enough contact with the Aborigines to be well educated with their beliefs and the spirits of the dead who looked over them and guided them when they needed help, or punished them if they broke any tribal traditions.

The natives working on Courtland Downs were from the Iningai tribe and had their own distinct dialect and system of understanding of the world around them. Bill had seen enough in his time to convince him that they did have some form of spiritual connection with the plants and animals, as well as their ancestors. How else could they have survived out here for as long as they had and how else did they gain the knowledge that they passed on from generation to generation over eons?

Junior Magpie was at that very minute, putting some of his powers to work for them in their search and was already scouting ahead over the sand hills and through thick scrub, looking for further confirmation of Big Bill's passing. He was feeling pretty pleased with himself so far and the boss, young Bill, was also pleased with him as well and enjoyed Junior Magpie's insights into the bush they were passing through. He had already learned how to find and identify some edible berries and the most likely spot to find a goanna.

CHAPTER TWENTY SIX

While the legal war was raging, Cliff found himself at a loose end. He was advised not to do anything further until he heard from the legal team. He was very concerned at the tapering off of audience numbers before they went into a forced break. He needed to find another angle that could inject further life into the current version, or work as a spin off. He needed to do some research.

A meeting was called at Cliff Top Productions and all his troops wandered in disconsolately, expecting the worst of news. Cliff looked worried, but not that worried as he stood to address them. He brought them up to date with the limited knowledge he had. Glumly, he told them that they, that is, Cliff Top Productions and the network were still in a fierce battle with the lawyers opposing them. They couldn't afford to stand still, so he proposed that if it all fell over, they should see if there was another angle of attack on this bloke, this super hero who they now knew had very dark secrets.

That's all the crew knew; the real story was still a heavily guarded secret. Did he have any more secrets? That would be the subject of their research, starting right now. He ordered them to get hold of everything they could on Lawrence Parnham, in particular his family trust and his political history. Look for anything that could connect their major allegation of treason with any dealings he may have had inside the House or in his commercial activities as a private citizen.

The team was eager to get to work, disappearing into their cubicles and punching phone numbers. A couple headed for the public library to access microfiche and copies of the Hansard. The Hansard was the report of the proceedings of the Australian parliament and its committees. This included the Senate, House of Representatives, the Federation Chamber and all parliamentary committees.

So there would be plenty for them to plough through. Clever researchers knew some short cuts and ignored the Senate and reserved the parliamentary committees, if they needed to access them later. By searching for keywords on microfiche they could narrow the search even further. Soon they were in an efficient rhythm and coming up with lots of material but nothing jumped out at them. There were a couple of matters raised in question time that seemed to be either ignored or sidelined with unseemly haste. But there was something there, like a shadow that moved at the corner of the eye; illusory, ephemeral but, nonetheless, there. The team continued to dig.

Back at the office, Cliff was studying the survey details and was displeased to see a programme he believed was bordering on plagiarism. The programme was produced very professionally and had a magnetic appeal to it, similar in suspense to his own programme that drew the audience in, teasing them with more intriguing yet to be revealed in next week's episode stuff.

Personally, he didn't give a damn if they ever found dear old Cuthbertson's bones or whatever; he, Cliff Carter had the real story, the explosive exposé that would rock Australian society and politics to their very foundations. He ploughed on through his latest revenue reports.

The advertising reps were becoming very nervous and beginning to soften their rates to keep clients on board. He had already knocked back a couple of silly deals that would have cost money to schedule and it was past time to straighten the buggers out. He called his secretary and told her to notify all reps of a meeting in the boardroom at 4p.m. that afternoon. No one was to miss it or arrive late on pain of instant dismissal.

The reps slouched in, all Hugo Boss suits, hand-made Italian leather shoes and Izzy Miyake aftershave lotion and truck loads of arrogance which would not last as long as Cliff's come to Jesus talk hit home and a few self-inflated reputations received a big pin.

Fifteen seconds into his rev session, a few heads have dropped and a few faces reddened with embarrassment as he told them the facts of life and accused one or two, without being specific, that they were soft pedalling, coasting along on reputation and wouldn't get a sales job in a toy store at Christmas. He delivered a new set of rules, governing the protection of their advertising rates and their precious inventory, time, which could not be put on the shelf. Neither could it be replaced, if frittered away on freebies. Then he announced a new special award for the rep, male or female, who maintained an average unit rate higher than the stations for three months in a row. The winner would receive an extra week's annual leave with pay plus average commission.

That put a brighter light on things and the team all bounced out of the room full of determination again. Nothing spoke louder to a sales team than money.

Cliff understood why the public had turned on them. It came down to respect for the nation's fallen servicemen and women. Here was a decorated airman and his equally gallant crewman, who have come to grief while flying a top secret mission back to Australia from a war zone.

In retrospect, he realised his mistake and started to write a script which was basically a big suck up, but in his eyes was a salute to the gallant men who gave their lives and to whom this programme was solemnly dedicated blah, blah. A meeting with production reminded him that they were miles behind in payments to contractors and, for that matter, all production staff, so where the hell was the money going to come from for this brain fart?

As if on cue, his secretary put her finely coiffed head in the door and reminded him he had a meeting in five minutes. Oh crap! It was the bankers! He dismissed the production guys with an instruction to do what they could as he saw it as vital to preserving their integrity. The guys chuckled under their breath and jokes about integrity and Cliff Top Productions started flying about. CTP's integrity was on a par with the average schoolyard crack dealer.

Cliff bounded into the meeting with the two bankers, all piss and wind, trying hard to look the confident executive in charge of a sure fire money-making organisation and was met with blank poker faces showing little of Cliff's confidence in his situation. Oops, this was not good. He sat down and the meeting commenced with a thick sheaf of spreadsheets that hit the table with a thump. These were his current income and expenditure reports, very heavily weighted to the expenditure side of the ledger, unfortunately.

The bankers bore expressions you would expect from your GP when he announced you have six months to live, as a result of diagnosing a vile disease, but in this case life expectancy was way shorter. In fact, if he could not bring his accounts into some sort of reasonable viability by the end of the month, which was two weeks away, then they would have no choice but to close him down and bring in the liquidators.

Incidentally, they had been intrigued by his programme and couldn't wait to see it conclude. Could he give them a hint of what was contained in the top secret box? No he could not he responded emphatically! Jesus, what bloody front, they'd just delivered the death sentence and still expected to be treated like friendly insiders. Anyway, the bankers were sure he understood, it was not personal, it was just business.

Now where had he heard that line before? The meeting wrapped up on that note and the two immaculately clad bankers gathered their brief cases and, careful not to crease their Armani suits, slid out of their chairs like a pair of synchronised performers, and through the door in one smooth motion.

The liquor cabinet in the boardroom was heavily patronised that night. Cliff subsided into another alcoholic coma where he was found by his loyal and long suffering secretary next morning on the floor in a foetal position.

She had requested some time off that afternoon to attend a medical appointment. What she didn't say was, it was really to attend an interview for a secretarial role in a radio station not that far distant. Muriel may have been loyal but only up to a point, and one thing she excelled at was reading the winds of change and she was not going to be left wondering or, worse still, left in the lurch. She'd be there if he survived but, would he survive? If he didn't, she had to take care of number one.

When Cliff finally surfaced from his alcoholic binge, he sat up with difficulty, his head spinning and threatening to explode, leaving a puddle of drool staining the carpet where he had lain. His hair was matted and he had a pronounced two day growth. He tried to lick his lips with a raspy tongue that was stuck to the roof of his mouth. Gagging, he staggered to his feet into the adjoining washroom, shoved his head under the tap and had a little heave.

His expensive jacket was a rough ball on the floor where it had served as a pillow for the last 12 hours. He shook it out trying to iron out some of the major creases but gave up in disgust and hurled it into the corner.

A sharp rap on the door revealed an excited and nervous little researcher, with the rest of the research team waiting on tenterhooks for him. Their noses crinkled at the powerful alcoholic fumes being exuded by their leader. Their non-stop digging at the library into the Hansard reports had shown signs of colour, as they would say in gold-mining terms.

It seemed, on the surface there appeared to be a number of critical foreign investments in property and mining development, plus one or two lucrative beef growing concerns, that may have received preferential support for two Japanese companies. The interesting thing was that one of the directors, who served on both company boards, bore the same surname as the long dead Japanese captain, who was the catalyst in the allegations brought against Lawrence Parnham VC MP. But the very red hot connection which you would only notice if you were pre-disposed to finding it, was the fact that Parnham had power of veto in favour of more than one of the applications. Suddenly, Cliff was sparking on all cylinders, wide-eyed and bushy-tailed, his adrenaline surging. Someone shoved a strong coffee at him and from somewhere hot sugary donuts were on offer. He gulped these offerings down hungrily and, with sugar levels restored, he was energised and all action.

'Right, let's get on with it,' he declared.

Great work so far team, but he needed solid proof. They needed a bullet proof case to be successful. He emphasised solid, unshakeable proof because he refused to go through the torment of another round of lawsuits. Don't even bother coming back with rumour, innuendo or supposition.

Whatever it takes, dig and dig. Get this rock solid and we'll have this crook on toast. See what else can be found from company annual reports. Look at the social pages and see if the Honourable Minister was careless enough to be seen socialising with the Japanese. Is it possible to find any evidence of bribery or extortion? Were there any scratchy donations to the Parnham Foundation or Electoral Fund?

Cliff had been temporarily diverted from his company's financial issues in his excitement, but was quickly brought back to earth when his secretary pointed out that he had only a few days to meet the bank's demands. She had returned from her interview with the rival company and was confident she had the job offered and, in cold hard terms, couldn't care less about this over rated blow hard. Her feelings toward Cliff weren't hatred exactly. He hadn't been a bad boss, apart from groping her a couple of times, but she despised the way he spoke to his staff while bragging about his accomplishments and he clearly deceived his sponsors with bloated stats. He was going to get his though and she didn't want to be around when the bomb went off. She was going to time her resignation to create the most impact.

Cliff called all his major sponsors and investors, setting up a series of meetings designed to elicit more investment funds that would deflect any moves from the bank to petition him for bankruptcy. He prepared a proposal for each one of them which delicately hinted at the dark side of a very senior politician. The sponsors were united in their morbid desire to see a senior politician in the incumbent party get a well-deserved smack. They were not dissimilar in this attitude to the famous 'Tricoteuses,' a group of morbid women who sat knitting beside the scaffold between beheadings. As to who it might be, they had no idea. All they did know was Cliff had a very senior politician in his sights with a promise of an earth-shattering exposé and they would savour every moment of it.

They had invested a lot of money based only on their ill-placed faith in Cliff.

Cliff understood that most politicians had shadowy areas in their past, but most politicians didn't come to power on the back of a war service record the way this one did. In any event, there were always at least two sides in Australian politics and one of them would be very keen to hear some of these salacious accusations. The major charge of treason and cowardice in the face of the enemy would be enough to destroy the subject and his party. Cliff could think of more than one cold-hearted reptilian on both sides of the house. Even within Parnham's own party, there were the over ambitious and greedy types whose lust for power exceeded any sense of duty to their constituents or the good of the nation. To paraphrase JFK, 'Ask not what you had to do to repay your lucrative lifestyle but what more can the taxpayer fund for you.'

Now he had a clear priority order on which to pedal the results of his muck raking to the most loyal supporter, or highest bidder, and pull in some badly needed funding to get rid of those banking parasites. The banks, who were his best mates and partners, in the original enterprise had now become parasites, a derogative term he didn't recognise as having any currency in his "profession". Really?

Cliff's researchers came back with the sort of material he could build another series on and maybe he would have to if the banks got their way and shut down Cliff Top Productions. They hadn't been able to uncover any more suspicious foreign investments bearing Parnham's finger prints but they had dug into the Parnham Foundation and discovered a series of regular small donations over a long period, almost like an automatic deduction, on an account connected to the Japanese investors by a number of links through a network of shelf companies. The deposits were small enough to avoid mandatory reporting and go unremarked by authorities, but adding up to a very sizable amount over time. So what was going on?

Did Parnham award these contracts and investments as some sort of reparation to the dead captain's family in an attempt at hushing them up? And how would they know enough about the affair to be able to convincingly bring Parnham to heel? If they did know and were blackmailing Parnham, why would they then reward him through his foundation? Besides, the foundation's coffers were locked up like Fort Knox and administered by a committee made up of a number of impeccably qualified and unimpeachable individuals.

None of this made sense, or at least none of it could be linked into a coherent form. What the hell, where there's smoke there's fire, right? So he'd sell the smoke and let the buyer find the fire for themselves.

Cliff interviewed a series of sponsors and political power brokers. The sponsors could appreciate the exposure they would benefit from, but were a little queasy about getting on the wrong side of either colour of politics, on the very sensible reasoning that whatever your political leanings, they'd always be a potential customer. This could be great for the audience or it could just grate on the audience.

Cliff assured them, with some research from out of the archives, the more salacious the scandal, the higher the ratings. Everyone struck the "holier than thou" pose until the show rolled out and then they were glued to their screens. Don't worry they will lap this up and look for more.

The power brokers went away, one after the other, to assess what they had heard and feed it into their systems. These guys didn't make rash decisions and the supporters and friends of this high level politician would surely have long memories and many ways to make a man regret his unfortunate alignments, never mind what Cliff Carter said.

Cliff had been here before. Maybe not at this level, but a sale was a sale and the techniques, the body language, the cut and thrust as two minds seek advantage over another, was a familiar dance. He learned early about the law of scarcity in a market place. If something became scarce, naturally the price goes up with demand and so it became a matter of creating an air of scarcity or, in his case, a lack of availability, and then watch them come running. Then he spiced it up with a bit of urgency; be quick or miss out.

Cliff came up with a cunning tactic that would serve the purpose and called in an old mate in print media, who wrote a financial gossip column called "The Inside Trader" and asked him out for a drink. Cliff knew he could rely on this bloke to be unreliable! Over a few beers in "The Drip Tray", one of the many bars Cliff called home, he hooked up with his mate. They settled down with their drinks and, after a bit of the usual back and forth, Cliff feigned nervousness as he finally got around to the real reason for the convivial drinks.

Cliff swore his mate, Clancy Doherty, to secrecy and told him he had a huge ethical problem. (As if he even knew the meaning of the word.) He told him he had proof positive of corruption at the very highest level and at the centre of it was a man admired and loved by the whole country. If he put the story to air, he knew the man would be vilified, but so would Cliff and his network. But he had a duty as a journalist to allow the public to know the truth, however, he was a little nervous and thinking of holding it back. What did Clancy think he should do? The old Clancy, pillar of morality and ethical journalism (industry nickname, 'Clancy of the Overheard') muttered some garbage in sympathy and suggested he should be very careful, to seek legal advice, maybe dig up a few similar cases from his archives and see what the public reaction was.

Perhaps he could invite a small select audience from his demographic into a neutral venue and subtly feed the story to them over cheap wine and cheese and then ask them to complete a brief questionnaire which could be used to gauge their acceptance, or otherwise, of the theme. Cunning Clancy then made a suggestion; a tactic designed to give him, not Cliff an advantage.

'Aside from that, take your time,' he said soothingly. 'Don't rush into it, and hasten slowly.'

Then he suddenly remembered a previous engagement, wished Cliff good fortune, thanked him for the drink and scuttled off as fast as his bandy little legs could carry him, and his head full of treachery, back to his typewriter.

The story would be in the morning edition of his column, subtly referred to, shrouded in double entendres and shadowy phrases that only financial and political aficionados would claim to have unravelled, and the less well informed would be convinced they knew who and what he was writing about. But the desired result for Cliff would be the reaction of his potential sponsors. He was hoping that coming from a second source, in this case the well-established columnist Clancy Doherty, would create more than a little interest.

Cliff watched as Clancy's stubby form, in its ill-fitting grubby suit, threaded a hasty path through the lunch crowd and smiled beatifically with the self-satisfaction of knowing the seed was well sown. Before 9 a.m. the following day, his phone had started ringing off the hook and his potential sponsors were on a different kind of hook.

CHAPTER TWENTY SEVEN

In the same state, northwest from Cliff's Brisbane office, another exciting rival documentary, with a common medium, was taking shape with far less controversy.

Bill and Elise had arrived at the base of the escarpment that had been their destination for two days. Junior Magpie had conducted a master class in bush-craft, brilliantly identifying a whole series of blazes cut into the more mature trees that would have been ignored by less talented eyes. Some of them were almost completely healed or overgrown, but close examination proved them for what they were; scars cut into the tree trunks as a sign many years before by another skilled bushman.

The team halted to brew a billy of tea and had something to eat before going on. Bill had his map and survey photos laid out on a convenient flat rock again and, adding some further notes, located their exact position on the map. He was examining the ridge above them for a gully or break in the rock wall that confronted them. He and Junior Magpie headed off to do a little scouting while the rest of the team, minus the camera crew who followed along, a little unhappily, leaving their half-finished mugs of tea behind, stayed behind.

Bill was assuming his grandfather would have been weakened by his ordeal and possibly hungry and dehydrated and certainly less fit than he himself was right now. There was no way of knowing if, in fact, he was carrying an injury from the forced landing. Common sense dictated he would have looked for a passage over or through the escarpment that would require a minimum of effort.

They discovered a likely entry point screened by a large bush. It was a narrow gap, forming a steep lead between two enormous boulders standing on their ends like gigantic dominos.

They followed the lead into deep shadow that dropped the temperature pleasantly, making the job a little easier. Almost immediately, Junior found a series of marks on the right hand side of the passage. They seemed to form the initials WLC, but weather, probably rain cascading down these rocks, had almost erased them. The rock face was very hard and it would have taken quite a bit of time and effort to score it like that. Was this wishful thinking? Upon reflection, and taking a pragmatic view of the situation, they agreed there is no doubt now that this was the way Big Bill would have come. The two men and the camera crew, who had captured the dramatic moment on film, headed back to the rest stop and enjoyed a refreshing cuppa and some fruit cake, thoughtfully included in their supplies. Everyone was very excited by their news and eager to get going again, except for the camera crew who were just starting to relax.

Bazza, the would-be comedian sound man, seemed to have lost a bit of spark but was still cracking jokes, comparing his situation to being a porter on a safari. Will the sahib and memsahib be having a hot bath this evening? And were they aware they may have to call in emergency assistance as they had run out of fresh mint for their gin and tonic?

Junior Magpie was given the honour of leading the team to the lead that he and Bill found earlier. It needed to be tackled single file and the camera man jumped ahead to get his shots, while Elise and Bill paused by the rock wall, etched by their grandfather years ago as he had struggled to survive. Bill poured some water from his bottle over the carvings that highlighted the faint letters on the rock face.

What had been going through his mind at that time? Had he been totally focused on the journey ahead, or did he stop and think about his wife and young son Robert? Had he been confident of his skills? Would he be anticipating a joyful reunion with his family when he was finally recovered from his predicament?

The lead wound up and around several more boulders and then out across a flat small ledge-like area that gave a view back towards their base camp in the west, some 35 or 40 kilometres away. Elise chose that moment to update the base camp guys about their progress and findings.

Junior Magpie was scouting a number of different leads that could have been the way forward, putting himself in Big Bill's shoes, using his knowledge and instincts to assess the best alternative. He settled on a lead slightly left again, between some dominating boulders and breaking to the right. It reminded Junior of a snake's track in the desert sand, the way it seemed to wriggle back and forth.

Bill estimated they were about three quarters of the way to the top of the ridge, when he heard Junior calling him forward. Junior Magpie pointed to a gap off to their right which took a turn before breaking into a number steps, formed by a series of smaller, flat rocks that looked like they had been laid there by a landscaper. Bill felt himself being compelled to climb the steps to see where they ended.

On impulse, he called his sister to come up and join him, which she did. They climbed the steps which took them up and through a series of gaps and ledges, until they were confronted by a strange aggregation of boulders, some small, some large, that begged to be climbed in the promise of a view of the opposite side of the escarpment.

Bill lead the way, with Elise holding his hand. It was not a difficult climb but there were many loose rocks and slippery gravel in places that could cause grief to the unwary. At the top, the promise was fulfilled by a glorious outlook to the east. The horizon must have been 100 miles away but Bill's sharp eyes focused on a number of flashes of light he could see in the mid distance, which must have been the sun reflecting off a car's windscreen travelling north on the Gregory Development Highway.

Away to their left, they could see an opening in the cliff face that provided a relatively gentle descent onto the plain below. Big Bill had found the way to his own salvation with unerring bush-craft, endurance and courage. Surely it would have been a relatively easy stroll down the eastern side of this escarpment and a day or two hike to the highway. So what had happened to him? Why didn't he make it after coming this far and getting this close? Would they find the answer somewhere along the line from the bottom of the descending track to the Gregory Developmental Road in the east? Young Bill was pondering this enigma wondering if they would ever find the answer.

Bill borrowed Elise's binoculars for a closer look. Sure enough, it was the highway and he turned to tell Elise about his thoughts and observations when he saw her peering down past her feet into the deep crevasse below. The sun had just reached a point where it was almost vertically above them, penetrating the deep shadows at the bottom of the void below her feet. Five minutes earlier, or perhaps five minutes later, and the bottom of the crevasse would have remained invisible and the material laying there would never have been seen. But what was that material? It appeared to be a cloth of some indiscernible type, possibly cotton or linen, but definitely human in origin.

Bill handed Elise her binoculars for a closer look. It took a moment or two to focus and she dropped down in a crouch, holding the glasses aside with her head in her one free hand. Bill retrieved them from her shaking hand and took a look. What he saw was unmistakable. There, among a pile of rags and leaf litter was a glint of white bone. Was it human or animal? Oh dear God, could it be the remains of their ancestor? Elise obviously thought they had found him and was sitting on a rock ledge with her head still in her hands, sobbing quietly.

The only way they would know was to somehow get down there and recover whatever it was. This would be a very hazardous undertaking, requiring infinite care and more equipment than they had with them.

Bill patted his sister's back sympathetically, muttering some comforting words to her. Then reminded her, that if it was Big Bill down there, then they had succeeded in their mission and now they needed to toughen up and work out how to retrieve his remains. Magpie Junior had disappeared already, possibly because of his people's religious attitudes to the dead.

Elise pulled herself together and they decided to follow Magpie Junior and go back down the way they came and call base camp for support. This recovery would require some specialist expertise which none of their team had, nor do they know anyone vaguely qualified for this type of recovery operation.

Back at their camp, they were resolved to stay overnight and get a fire going. The smoke would guide Dusty in to their position in the morning. There shouldn't be a problem landing the helicopter as there was a wide sandy area about 100 metres away from the base of the cliff, a rare relief in the middle of the tough chest-high scrub in the area.

Bill and Elise sat on opposite rocks holding each other's shocked gaze across the gap between them. Elise, with tears in her eyes, asked the question hanging in the air. Was that the remains of their grandfather lying at the bottom of the crevasse up there? Could he have done as they had done and climbed up on the rocks to look for a way across the terrain in the valley below?

If they were his remains, then it was highly probable that was what he had done. Possibly weakened by hunger and thirst, the effort of gaining the apex of the escarpment may have left him light-headed or he may have slipped on the loose footing and fallen to his death at the bottom of the crevasse.

How tragic to think that his well-documented bush skills had brought him this far, to have endured so much and, when he could almost touch salvation, he should slip and fall like some stumble-footed city boy who had never ventured off the bitumen. It was at least a 15 metre drop into the gap between the massive boulders up there that had held their secret captive for all these years. A fall from that height would surely have been instantly fatal and if there was any comfort to be had from this, his remains would have been protected from the scavenging dingoes and crows that in other circumstances would have scattered them far and wide, never to be discovered.

A recovery operation got under way immediately. A firm embargo was placed on the news. Only those that needed to know, heard about the discovery. At that point they could not say for certain that the remains were those of the big man and if word got to Lydia, and it was proved incorrect, it would be tragic.

A radio conference advised base camp of their needs. The helicopter was being loaded with all the rope they could find but it was probably not enough and with personal safety a priority, they would be well advised to obtain some expert assistance.

Dusty headed for the coast for some climbing gear and to see if he could recruit a volunteer from the state rescue team to actually conduct the recovery. Bill agreed with the idea. They certainly didn't want any more casualties now if they could possibly avoid it.

What they needed right now was something to break the sombre mood that had enveloped the camp and, right on cue, Junior Magpie provided a bit of indigenous relief.

He got a fire going and afterwards disappeared for a half hour coming back into camp with a great big happy grin on his face with some bush tucker, a bloody great big goanna which he threw straight into the hot coals and looked about for approval, licking his lips. This set Bazza off on another string of jokes about nouveau cuisine and protocols for eating goanna straight from the fire. Did one take a bite and pass to the left or right? If Magpie Junior had intended to raise a few laughs, as well as supper, he had succeeded mightily.

After a few pointed dares, they all had a crack at the huge, charcoaled lizard with varying reactions. Junior couldn't understand these white fellas. This was top tucker. His chin was glistening and greasy with the rich, yellow fat that was a delicacy for him and his kin. It reflected in the light of the campfire, giving him the appearance of a wild man with his perfect, white teeth gleaming in his dark face. All of this was captured by the skilful cameraman as colour for the doco they were developing. Everyone had a taste of Junior's reptile roast now and they all offered flattering comment as Junior stood back proudly, flashing his big, wide smile.

Cookie still put together a more European style meal which did not contain a single native animal, not counting Australian beef, much to everyone's relief.

Despite the awful reality that awaited them on the summit of the escarpment, there was a sense of relief and a burgeoning happiness that they may have achieved what the public and experts of all stripes chorused as mission impossible. The general opinion was that no human remains could possibly last in the harsh climate of south west Queensland's outback for 50 years. No doubt, there was a deep and abiding sorrow attached to their find and a wretched function to be carried out when they confronted their still grieving grandmother with this news.

The individual members of the party were, in fact ecstatic, to have been a part of this amazing mission and before too long, Bazza cracked some more of his oddball humour and the laughs produced a general feeling of wellbeing. From somewhere in his subconscious, Bill summoned up one the family's favourite old songs and was supported by Elise's lovely voice. One or two more songs and Bazza was inspired to add his musical talents to the evening, bursting out with a bawdy ditty about two sailors and a pregnant barmaid which had them all joining in on the hilarious chorus. The whole fireside concert faithfully recorded for posterity, if not for prime-time viewing, by the television guys.

Bill and Elise spent a very sleepless night sitting around Junior Magpie's fire discussing possibilities, while the camera crew had been busy filming Junior's bush cuisine. The dawn sun rose like an explosion of light and heat bathing the eastern face of the escarpment in a golden hue, while a sound track, provided by the birdlife, rose up from the surrounding bush as usual. To quote Rudyard Kipling from the poem Mandalay:

'an the dawn comes up like thunder outer China crost the bay.'

There was not a drop of water anywhere near here, let alone a bay, but the sentiment remained the same. They were still a long way from the bay or any sea, for that matter.

Nor did they see the sun until it was well up in the western shadow of the escarpment, but they felt its power. The thunder was provided by Dusty, returning in his reliable helicopter. Bill had been on the radio directing him to the landing site to the west of their camp and they jogged across to assist in the unloading of the gear. They were introduced to the climbing specialist Dusty had dug up through his Search and Rescue mates. Andrew 'Spiderman' Bates had a long history of difficult rescues from cliff falls, sinking yachts and stranded bush walkers. He knew his ropes.

While they were all in a hurry to discover the truth about the bundle of rags and bone at the bottom of the crevasse, they still took time to breakfast and down a hot cup of tea, while they got to know Spiderman and briefed him on his mission, emphasising the sacred nature of the remains that may or may not belong to their grandfather.

Spiderman Bates accepted their sentiments without comment. He had recovered many human remains and been confronted by grieving relatives on many occasions. He always had empathy for them. His job was to recover the remains as professionally as he could.

They geared up again with full water bottles and then headed off straight away to the top of the escarpment to get on with the recovery. With familiarity's it didn't take long to reach their objective.

The trek up the escarpment was only a couple of hundred feet but still a bit of a challenge carrying the climbing equipment, sound and camera gear, as well as some food and water. This would be a forensic recovery and Spiderman would need to be very careful of the material if it proved to be Big Bill's uniform, which would bear his squadron insignia, providing undeniable evidence of who the wearer was. Then there were his remains, which must be little more than bleached bones now, and must be gathered with all possible care and reverence.

Would his ID tags be there? It went without saying that Spiderman was well versed in these matters. Every stage of the recovery would be photographed and an audio description made by Spiderman before he moved anything. The television guys had persuaded him to take their delicate camera below to shoot a few precious, but very telling, seconds of the remains. That footage would be a real sentimental highlight and guaranteed to bring a few tears to the viewers' eyes. It was paramount they paid all due respect to the remains of the revered ancestor whose widow waited, and to the two young people, who had put their heart and soul into the search.

Spiderman was familiar with a variety of cameras and he had the hang of this one in a few minutes. He had had the sad duty of recovering all manner of human remains in his career, including the tiny bodies of toddlers and older children who came back to visit him in his dreams. He got it!

Bill led the way back through the crevasse, assisting Spiderman with all his climbing gear which, thankfully, was packed into two hold-all bags of the type that sportsmen used. The gear was heavy and the bags awkward, making the climb a little tricky but they soon broke out to where they had left off the night before. They set up on the small space in front of the rocks that led down into the crevasse.

Spiderman set about organising his gear, anchoring pitons into cracks in the rocks, checking and double checking everything. Bill was impressed with his thoroughness and obvious capability.

Spiderman hooked up and began to abseil carefully down to his target. Three feet from touch down he paused and called for the television camera to be lowered down to take the shots the crew had asked him to secure. With that done and the camera out of the way, he got on with the main objective. Bill lowered a small basket down to him. He would load the remains into it to be slowly raised to the surface. But first, Spiderman took his photographs of the scene and laid a right angle measuring device down to provide some measure of scale. When he was finished he very carefully parted some of the material to expose the secrets beneath. Almost the first thing he saw was a set of ID tags. They were still around the neck of the skeletal remains that were of a much loved and admired war hero, grandfather to the two young people who waited anxiously above him and husband to his widow who was waiting at home for word about the husband for whom she mourned.

The uniform still retained the insignia of the 30th Squadron and Bill's wings on the chest. Spiderman uncovered a water bottle and a few items like a knife and his watch. This was a sad tragedy that told its own story. This brave man had overcome every obstacle in trying vainly to save his mate and then struggling across this inhospitable terrain to fight his way home, only to meet his end in this way.

Spiderman believed he would have died instantly as the fall was over fifteen metres and, as his photographs would verify, his neck was broken on impact. Presumably, the spinal cord would have severed between a fractured C2 and C3. This would be some comfort to his family, at least. The thought of him being trapped at the bottom of this natural rock shaft waiting to die of thirst was intolerably cruel.

Spiderman got on with the grim task and reverently loaded the basket with its fragile cargo. When the basket was ready and secure, he gave the line a couple of tugs and a whistle and carefully guided it to the top with an attached guide line from below. He scoured the tiny area scrupulously once more to be certain he had missed nothing, then he ascended.

The void was what climber's call a chimney with vertical sides, mostly parallel and not much larger than the climber's body. To climb this structure he would use his whole body to apply pressure to the opposite vertical wall. He judged it to be impossible for a man in a debilitated state to climb. Spiderman found it a tough climb, even aided by a line attached to his harness, and depended on the team at the top to provide lift. When he reached the top, he was helped over the edge by Bill and Junior Magpie drenched with the sweat of his exertions. Magpie Junior was looking askance at the collection of bones. Bill realizing their effect on Junior, gave him an out by suggesting he head down to attend to the camp fire and get the kettle on for tea. Junior wasted no time clearing the area and when they caught up to him, he was just taking a magnificent damper out of the camp oven.

At the top of the escarpment, Bill and Elise stood together looking down at the sad bundle of rags and bone. Bill reached down and gently touched the skull as if stroking the head of an infant. Carefully, lovingly and quietly, he told his grandfather he was finally going home. Elise was blinded by tears and even the cynical TV guys were moved by the occasion, still capturing every emotion-filled second of the moment. The siblings, relying on their strong religious beliefs for emotional strength, knelt and offered a prayer for their ancestor and thanks for the guidance to this spot.

An hour later, they walked out of the shadow of the boulders that marked the entry to Big Bill's last walk, into the bright sunshine, carrying the revered bundle with them. Junior had done his duty and stoked up a good fire and the support crew had been preparing a hot meal. The television crew was anxious to get their film away and Dusty was only too happy to oblige. But first they had to make arrangements to decamp, both here and back at their billabong base camp. Both bush sites would be left in pristine condition, all trace of their temporary occupation gone.

First things first, though. The recovery team grabbed a big mug of Junior's tea and a slab of his damper, lathered with butter and strawberry jam. Nothing better in the bush. Another night in the scrub after a barbequed meal and a couple of frosty beers and everyone was sparking on all cylinders when the sun came up.

Bill was unsure of the legalities surrounding the recovery of his grandfather's remains and Spiderman suggested, based on his previous experience in such matters, that the state coroner would provide the answers. Meanwhile, he advised to keep everything secure and be assured Big Bill would be turned over to the family when officialdom had had its say.

Elise was on the radio advising base camp back at the waterhole of their success and that they would re-join them soon for the trip back to civilisation and to start getting organised.

It took two days to clear both sites. They gathered all the gear up and spent a considerable amount of time restoring the site to leave the bush the way they found it. The Cuthbertson's were well schooled in conservation and this site would always be, in their minds, as sacred ground. To have left it in an untidy state would be unconscionable.

Special attention was given to the gravesite of Flight Sergeant Bluey Mansfield with more stones collected and added to the monument and fresh wild flowers gathered by Elise.

Big Bill's remains were turned over to the coroner at the Brisbane Magistrate's Court, who officiated on the matter and ruled the cause of death was accidental. The court appointed an undertaker with the family's permission and Bill's remains were transferred to a beautiful casket for the trip home to Courtland Downs and his family's burial ground. The coffin was draped with an Australian flag and sent on its way with a brief ceremony performed by the RAAF for one of its own at Archerfield airport, Bill's original destination, supported by veterans from the Brisbane Returned Serviceman's League.

The still air was shattered by the firing of a salute from half a dozen airmen in impeccable full-dress uniform. The Last Post concluded the service and, as always, drew tears from the assembly gathered together to pay their respects and send Squadron Leader William L Cuthbertson DFC home.

CHAPTER TWENTY EIGHT

Have you ever been at sea on a small boat and watched in dread as a massive storm front approaches from over the horizon? Drawing inexorably closer, as it grows darker and more threatening, lightning flashing, clouds looking like they have been carved from granite with a black impenetrable gloom below them. The whole roiling violent threat gaining speed as it closes in on your fragile craft, and the only possible outcome would be a fight to the end that you know in your heart you cannot win. Then you would know what Lawrence Parnham was experiencing.

While the dark secrets to be released in a massively popular television live documentary, had been suppressed, quite literally by a ton of writs, the insatiable political animal that was the federal government had somehow picked up on a faint, but unmistakable, stench of death surrounding Lawrence. His health was rumoured to be deteriorating rapidly and his once robust and energetic demeanour was descending into inertia. Those closest to him bore the brunt of his frequent ferocious rages where items were thrown about as he screamed and raged at some inner demons or imagined slight.

As the perceived noose tightened around his neck, Lawrence became more and more irrational and his rages more intense. Frances had long since left Chatsworth Park and taken refuge with a friend in the city. If Lawrence thought the going was tough, he would find out soon enough just how tough life could get when his leader returned from Canberra.

His subsequent meeting with his party leader was cold blooded and brutal to the point of inhumanity. Lawrence had caused the greatest threat to national security in Australia's history and was virtually given the bad news in such a way as to conjure up the image of a loaded revolver in an empty library of British melodramas. The leader told him that he wouldn't be getting off quite that easy.

The decision of the attorney general was that he would be going into isolation at a private location in the Blue Mountains. His presence there would be a closely guarded secret, but he would be within daily visiting range of his wife. He was to receive no other visitors, nor was he to have any contact with the media in any form, nor to discuss his situation with anyone, not even his priest. The media would be told he had had a critical stroke, which had left him immobile and incoherent and therefore of no interest to anyone in the media for interviews.

In time, the leader told him, he may be reinstated to the world by a medical miracle. This would not be for some time and, for the moment, highly unlikely. The party leader and the attorney general were the only government members to have this knowledge and their wrath over the potentially party destroying scandal was white hot. If this should somehow be leaked by hospital staff, or some member of Lawrence's family or coterie, thinking they were helping him out of the mire, the party would be devastated by the revelation and the damage would be catastrophic.

Shortly, some paramedics summoned by the attorney general, would come by and take him out of the building that housed his office, to a waiting ambulance and deliver him to his destination, which would help fuel the rumour of a stroke cutting him down. He was well known in the building and, before the ambulance doors closed, someone would be on the phone to the press. The paramedics, by the way, were from ASIO and wouldn't hesitate to administer a powerful sedative if he chose not to co-operate. His resignation from the party was effective immediately, with his personal belongings to be forwarded to him later. There would be no further contact or correspondence and, should he be so stupid as to initiate any legal action to counteract this decision, then be advised the attorney General's department would institute a very unpalatable response. In the meantime, he would receive full benefits due to him from his generous superannuation fund and disability insurance.

While all of this sounded draconian, the AG reminded the party leader, to bear in mind the extreme gravity of the charges against their former, and he emphasized *former*, colleague and party member. Treason, cowardice in the face of the enemy and, if that was not enough, he was suspected of the murder of a captured Japanese interpreter. This entire dreadful state of affairs he had shamefully kept to himself by the grace of God and the death of two gallant airmen.

In due course, a small team of paramedics arrived to administer strong debilitating sedatives to the stricken MP, who sat in his office chair, that had been his solace for the beginning of many busy mornings. He was in a state of shock, his face grey and his mouth hung open. It would not be hard to believe he had indeed suffered a cerebral haemorrhage. The medics had been briefed to expect trouble, given the number and size of the guys bringing in the stretcher. Lawrence was inconsolable and, in the opinion of the paramedics, capable of self-harm, so a powerful sedative was administered. Lawrence was strapped down firmly on the stretcher and, without further ceremony, taken down to the waiting ambulance. It transported the now shattered and semi-conscious Lawrence Parnham from his illustrious position as one of the most respected and universally admired MPs in the land from his electoral office.

Simultaneously, he was removed from the political party he and his father, Sir Alexander Parnham, had helped to found and, with great irony, to the rehabilitation hospital built in his fathers' name where he was treated with the respect due to his standing in the community from which he was now effectively excised like a cancerous tumour. The staff was aware of who he might be, but could not be sure as only the admitting staff had seen his face. All attending nursing staff had been required to sign a confidentiality agreement.

He was said to have suffered a stroke, rendering him mute and was to be shown respect but kept in strict isolation from other patients. They were sworn to utmost secrecy with the, by now familiar threats of prison terms and massive fines, should they breach these rules.

This was a crushing blow to Lawrence and his self-esteem. His sense of who he was and his place in his proud family, his place in his political party and his once assured place in the history of the country he loved. This once proud and industrious representative of his rural community, who was now in utter disgrace, was now in black despair and heading for banishment in a place he had never had cause to be admitted and from which he may never return.

Lawrence Parnham had built up an extensive business empire beyond Chatsworth Park. He had been a very shrewd trader and developer, investing in a number of burgeoning enterprises that had given him a steady cash flow which he parlayed against property development. The holdings of Chatsworth Future Build Pty Ltd were complex and their success depended on increasing demand and capital growth driving sales and providing a cash flow that would cover the heavy interest incurred by the massive loans that CFB Pty Ltd had sourced from various banks and venture capitalists always impatient for their returns.

Now with Lawrence taken away from the helm of his ship, the state of his business dealings, according to Murphy's Law, started to deteriorate. A severe local drought caused a massive loss of pasture at Chatsworth Park at the same time as a glut of superfine wool drove prices down 40%. The partner in one of Lawrence's key enterprises was found to have been embezzling a non-related charitable fund, which cast a pall over Lawrence's business which, as a consequence, suffered a forensic audit and the cancellation of a number of contracts. The revenue from this business had been channelled into the merchant bank holding the note on a property development on the city's fringe.

After the second default, the merchant bank became nervous and sent out a credit control adviser who had previously been a union thug and a suspected member of a criminal bikie organisation. He had built a reputation as a hard man and traded on it, but it failed to serve him here as he was chasing a phantom. Parnham had been thoroughly "disappeared" and there was no one who could enlighten the frustrated thug. His barely disguised intimidation of Parnham's former employees and political supporters failed to shake any information from them or, in fact, put much fear into them with his overly dramatic growling and dark scowls.

So the first domino in the long line had fallen. The bank swiftly placed a caveat on the development; the contractors realised they weren't going to get paid and quickly pulled out of the job. After a very short while, the once vibrant building site became a small ghost town with newspapers and food wrappers blowing around behind the high cyclone wire security fencing, decorated with warning notices advising trespassers they would be prosecuted.

Lawrence may have found a way around these gathering problems had he been there, but he was not, nor was he in a position to be. Trusted employees were letting him down and the one he counted on most of all, was one of the first to jump ship and nor did he go empty-handed. Parnham's trusted business manager smelt a rat and, in the spirit of *carpe diem,* he seized, not only the day, but as much cash as he felt was due to him after 20 years of faithful service, and a good bit more. He also took with him a couple of key account books that traced the names and percentage share in a number of "fortunate arrangements" that had paid extraordinary dividends to the participants. They might just prove to be very valuable some time down the line.

Things moved rather rapidly after that and, before too long, the creditors were at the door of Chatsworth Park waving court orders and seizing computer hard drives, artworks and basically any asset that could be offset against the enormous debt that was now laying on Lawrence's figurative doorstep. The hard drives revealed the full extent of the Parnham estate and made search and seizure easy. The luxury apartment at one of the best addresses in Sydney's CBD, which had been passed down from Sir Alexander to his son, was impounded by order of the sheriff and the locks changed. A notice posted on the door and in the commercial pages of the daily papers, advised the public and creditors of a forthcoming auction.

Lawrence's law office was also raided and several classic artworks removed, along with the hard drive from Lawrence's PC. The office floor space was also part of the Chatsworth Holdings assets and, as such, was impounded. Law partners and staff were generously granted 24 hours to find alternative accommodation and remove their files and personal property. A small private airplane parked at Bankstown airfield was placed under a notice of seizure by the sheriff's office and clamped, as were a small fleet of luxury and collectible cars. Snug in a berth at Sydney's Cruising Yacht Club was a beautifully maintained 45 foot Halverson motor yacht, MV Frances, also now impounded.

Parnham had accounts in Swiss banks and the Cayman Islands that were being pursued by the liquidators, now picking over his bones. It became like peeling an onion, one layer of Blue Riband holdings from another. The appearance of solid financial stability and respectability built up over generations was stripped away as the Parnham corporate structure was revealed as fragile under the withering attack of the creditors. The whole structure was balanced on the narrow platform of generous low interest rates and the capacity to feed the machine from funds borrowed against developments that existed only on paper. At one time, the wool clip provided that stability, but no more. Just one default saw the whole organisation begin to tumble like a child's game of Jenga, where the player removes the wrong piece and brings the whole tower of wooden blocks crashing down.

None of these failures on their own would rate a mention in the financial pages, except for the association with the Parnham name. The government authorities could impose penalties for wrongful behaviour and, in some cases in the past, had imposed jail terms through the courts on miscreants for blatant disregard for the law and the failure to meet their civic responsibilities. Lawrence's corporate crimes would carry no more than a good behaviour bond and some heavy fines taken on their own, but it was the sheer numbers of these misdemeanours that weighed heavily against Lawrence in the finish who, as a Member of Parliament, was expected to hold unimpeachable standards.

Then the real threat moved in like the Grim Reaper. The Australian Tax Office began to notice the goings on and orders were struck to have a closer look at Lawrence Parnham's taxation returns! There would be no denying the ATO their pound of flesh.

CHAPTER TWENTY NINE

The aircraft bearing Bill and Elise, and their sad cargo, touched down on the Longreach runway where they were met by the family. Another contingent of local veterans provided a solemn welcome ceremony at the airfield as the coffin was transferred to a hearse waiting to transport it to Courtland Downs, where a service would be held and Big Bill would join his ancestors in the station's cemetery.

More than two weeks had passed since Big Bill's remains had been handed to the coroner in Brisbane and his family had waited patiently to hear the coroner's report and have them delivered into their care. The coroner confirmed a verdict of accidental death due to a fall, resulting in several fractured vertebrae (C2 & C3) and instant death.

The television documentary that had been filmed during their expedition was screened to great acclaim and destined to be an award winner. The television crew who had made up the party that followed in the footsteps of Bill and Elise, were to be honoured guests at the memorial service and were given exclusive permission to record the entire service that would be a follow up to the main program and aired in peak time.

Junior Magpie had not been forgotten either once he had gotten over his superstitious fears of the dead. His efforts had been central to the success of the mission. Giacomo, the original sound man, was out of hospital and limping noticeably. The death adder's venom had caused some permanent damage to his calf muscle, which he would carry for the rest of his life. A man like Giacomo, with that golden voice and appreciation for music, fun and dance, had more than earned his place as a friend of the family.

The Cuthbertsons had posted a notice in the local paper, *The Longreach Leader*, inviting friends of the family, and especially old friends of Big Bill, to attend the service and wake afterwards at Courtland Downs. There had been a number of Bill's old squadron members who had survived the war and now made their way to Longreach.

One group flew a chartered plane to arrive there in style. The shire had put a number of its school buses on duty to ferry mourners out to Courtland Downs from Longreach airfield and the old chaps took advantage of that facility. Some of the guests piloting smaller aircraft were invited to use the Courtland Downs runway and were guided to an area cleared of long grass to park their planes. Several decided to camp under the wings of their planes.

The news services were there in force: television; radio and press. CNN and BBC had a presence, sending their local agency guys out to report on this story which had made its way around the world. This was a lot more than the usual run of the mill human interest stuff they were used to seeing from outback Australia, such as crocodile attacks or backpackers going missing.

The same notice was placed in the newsletter of the family church. A large crowd was expected to attend and the family was not disappointed. Such was the popularity of the family due to the recent saga that had been playing out on television. But also, their long record of community service over many years and several generations. Some deeds were well-known and a lot more were done quietly, just simply to help out a friend or neighbour, but always appreciated and never forgotten.

Young Bill's quest to honour his grandfather, and then the expedition of both Bill and Elise to recover Big Bill's remains, were obviously a gripping local adventure that had enthralled the entire community.

William Cuthbertson was only the third generation of his family on the land and was being honoured by the fifth generation.

In the history of this vast ancient land this was less than the blink of an eye. But the Cuthbertson dynasty had managed to set a standard for future generations that would ensure their prosperity and place in the tapestry of Australia's development as a great and generous nation.

But it wasn't just that, it was the family's contribution as generous and hard-working citizens who could always be counted on to be the first to arrive at a fire front during bushfire season or filling and loading sandbags when floods ravaged the town. They were always among the first to open their doors wide to strangers in need and neighbours who had suffered a loss.

The station lacked a building that would provide enough room for the expected crowd and a large marquee had been set up on the grounds. Another one provided cover for tables laden with food and a bar for the drinkers as there would be very few non-drinkers in attendance. Some of the mourners were also world class elbow benders with insatiable thirsts that would keep the barman busy well into the small hours as they downed gallons of the golden ale and swapped yarns, exchanged news, stock prices and ideas and gave their best guess at predicted rainfall in the coming season. And being true Queenslanders, a gallon or two of Bundaberg rum made its way down some rough old gullets.

Bill's casket was set up on a stand at the front of the marquee, draped with the Australian flag. On an easel was a blown-up photo of Bill standing proudly in front of his Beaufighter. His medals were arrayed on a small table in front of the photo along with his wings, which were recovered with his remains.

The service got under way with young Bill reading the eulogy to his grandfather, which brought forth a torrent of tears.

Elise played the piano and was accompanied by Lydia as they sang Bill's favourite hymn. One of Big Bill's squadron members stood and spoke the words of Winston Churchill. 'Courage is rightly esteemed the first of human qualities, because it is the quality that guarantees all others. The same must be said of Squadron Leader William L Cuthbertson,' said the old flyer, 'who gave all for his country and for whom we are gathered here today to honour his sacrifice and lay him to rest in the soil, for which he gave his life.'

More tears flowed and a light applause rippled through the gathered mourners. Then the veterans were invited to come forth by the President of the RSL after reciting the traditional famous poem by Laurence Binyon, *For the Fallen*.

They shall grow not old, as we that are left grow old, age shall not weary them nor the years condemn, at the going down of the sun and in the morning we shall remember them. Lest we forget.

The old warriors solemnly placed a poppy on Bill's casket and, standing at attention, touched their right hand to their heart. A recorded version of the last post concluded the serious part of the service.

The casket was taken with great care to Bill's burial plot to lay in eternal rest beside his parents, Hugh and Lilly. The reverend recited a prayer as the casket was lowered and those that wished, passed by and spilt a handful of soil into the grave.

RIP Big Bill, you're home now. God Bless you and take you into His arms.

'This was not a time for tears or sadness,' said the reverend, 'but a time for celebration. A favourite son had returned home. Kill the fatted calf, pour the wine and raise your voices in song.'

Well you didn't need to hold a gun to the collective heads of country people when it came to celebrating. Everyone returned to the second marquee where the bar awaited the thirsty and a band struck up with a medley of Big Bill's song list.

The band was Lydia on piano with tears in her eyes and a sad smile on her lips, Elise playing violin and young Bill and his dad, Bobby, on guitar. Horry Oates, a neighbour, provided percussion on his well-worn drums. Horry was an old rocker who rejoiced in the moniker, Horrible Horry, who had toured with his band Road Kill for years on and off. (Mainly off.) But the result was an emotional explosion of country music that had everyone up and crushing the temporary dance floor.

Even Bobby's wife, Joanne, defied arthritis and her years and grabbed one of the young neighbours and was out there giving it a crack with the energy of a teenager. Giacomo, the recovering snake bite victim and sound man, was called on by Elise, recalling his wonderful voice from their expedition to give a recital and stunned the crowd with an aria from his namesake Giacomo Puccini's famous opera Turandot, 'Nessun Dorma', translated as, 'none shall sleep' which was particularly relevant to the night's proceedings. No one understood the lyrics sung in Italian, but his beautiful lilting voice enunciated the glorious composition so emotionally that as one tough old hand remarked, 'He would bring a tear to a glass eye.'

The stand-in sound guy, Bazza, had pushed back against all his phobias, including necrophobia, (fear of death or dead things), to be there. He claimed a comfortable spot against the bar from which point he enjoyed a view of the band and dance floor through the bottom of his glass, which was being emptied with monotonous regularity.

They partied on in Bill's honour into the wee small hours, providing lots of colourful infill for the camera crew whose focus was beginning to deteriorate somewhat as they freely sampled the Cuthbertson hospitality. All journalistic discipline gone with the sunset.

Magpie Junior was an enthusiastic participant, displaying his unique dancing skills and, after a couple of furtive beers, was charged with "enthusiasm" to celebrate his part in proceedings. Under Queensland law, the sale or supply of alcohol was restricted to indigenous people to reduce misuse and abuse, but no one seemed to mind that Magpie was having a couple after the wonderful effort he had contributed to the success of the expedition. His joie de vivre was shared by everyone on this momentous occasion.

A cavalier approach was taken by some of the departing operators of the vehicles that would hopefully carry them home, but most wisely elected to sleep off their alcohol consumption and depart the following day. That meant the fires were stoked up and a massive breakfast of bacon, eggs, chops and steaks were offered to the hungry and hungover. The survivors of the big bash crawled out of tents and from the backs of pick-ups and station wagons and from under the wings of their planes, drawn to the irresistible aromas of the barbeque. The mood was still festive as the previous evening's doings were revisited and rehashed, providing plenty of laughs and teasing.

It took a while, but the mourners all finally departed down the track in various stages of sobriety and an interesting variety of vehicles from tractors to limos, aircraft, both fixed wing and rotary helicopters, leaving behind what was celebrated as a fitting tribute to the great man.

Civil Aviation Crash Investigation Report.
(Extract)

Bill was convinced the cause of the simultaneous failure of his engines was due solely to the overwhelming force of the storm cell he had inadvertently entered. Ice in the form of hail and rain, with the force of a fire hose could most certainly do the trick. Civil Aviation authorities investigating the cause were not ones to take short cuts and examined the aircraft with the thoroughness of forensic scientists. Yes, their report found that weather was a contributing factor but not the only cause of the failure of the usually robust engines.

A report reached them from the management of Jackson Field

refuelling facility in Port Moresby that they had been supplied with a batch of contaminated fuel and this had been pumped into Bill's Beech, which in all likelihood led to the failure of young Bill's engines. Subsequently, officials took samples from the fuel tanks still accessible in the wreckage and discovered a high level of chemical contamination. Examination of the fuel lines showed they had gummed up with a tacky substance that ultimately shut off the fuel supply to both engines simultaneously, leading to loss of power and a controlled emergency landing. Young Bill was praised in the official report for his skill in putting the aircraft down where he did and his actions afterward to assist searchers.

But what of Big Bill's experience? Could anybody possible tell after all these years what had gone wrong with his aircraft and why he had failed to send a mayday call?

Examination of the wreckage was undertaken by the experts that checked out his grandson's plane, but in very different circumstances. There had been a lot of deterioration in most of the vital systems in the big Beaufighter but one thing was clear, the communications system was pretty much destroyed in the crash, preventing any attempt at a distress call.

But why wasn't a call put out when the pilot realised he was in trouble? All their training and instincts would be expected to kick in. A well-practiced forced landing procedure should have taken over which would include a mayday call, giving the aircraft's position. So why didn't an experienced pilot, a man who had fought in the Battle of Britain, an air ace who was in transit from a war zone, put out a call? It was highly unlikely that he would have been panicked and it must be assumed that his radio was operational so what went wrong?

Research of the time period, when he went missing, revealed the answer.

During World War Two, the United States Army Air Force established a series of airfields in Australia in preparation for a possible Japanese invasion. Some of these establishments were so top secret that even people living in the areas surrounding them were unaware of their presence. The crash site was literally surrounded by them at all points of the compass.

One of the Civil Aviation investigators was a very keen young amateur historian who started digging into World War Two records, which revealed very little that could offer an explanation for Big Bill's plight.

But digging into the archives of local newspapers of the time, revealed a startling article he found deep in the pages of a local newspaper.

A vast area surrounding the crash site, including some substantial rural towns, experienced an inexplicable radio blackout. Complaints flooded in to local radio stations that had no explanation for it. Suspicion fell on US 5th Air Force activity at one, or perhaps several, of their air bases dotted around Queensland. Could Big Bill's distress call have been blanketed by this communication blackout at the critical time? It seemed a reasonable hypothesis, but the conclusive evidence was buried or obscured by official censorship or simply lost over the years since when no one would have realised the significance of such a minor matter against the background of a world war.

After all the years they could only take an educated guess at why his plane came down. War time records revealed the Bristol Beaufighter to be a tough resilient aircraft that, even after sustaining significant damage in combat, it would get its crew home. One of Big Bill's squadron came back to base at Milne Bay with six feet of starboard wing shot off by anti-aircraft fire. But all mechanical devices have weaknesses and peculiar quirks and Big Bill's plane would be no different.

Although the Australian ground crews were as good as they came in the New Guinea climate, they were working under extreme pressure and extreme climatic conditions. Humidity was the great enemy of aircraft maintenance, providing an ideal environment for all manner of mould and rot, that would attack electrical wiring and instruments.

The aviation investigators had taken up this enigma as a challenge but, without hard evidence, they were groping in the dark. One suggestion came from an experienced technician who had spent a few years in the tropics and thought the problem may have been condensation in the instruments as a result of the high humidity giving false readings. Bill could well have been convinced that the engines were overheating or he was about to run out of gas. Perhaps the condensation had gathered in the fuel tanks and caused the engines to run fitfully, further convincing Bill he was running on vapour and needed to put the aircraft down while he still had control.

But truthfully, they could not report a definitive answer to his family and at the days end, what purpose would it serve now? It would always remain a sad and unsolved mystery.

CHAPTER THIRTY

Poor old Cliff Carter had been caught up in a punishing game of musical chairs. The original programme, which had promised an incredible climax to its fans, had fizzled out with a whimper, rather than a bang. The legal restraints put on his production meant he was confined to beating up the Japanese intelligence contained in the strong box and trying to make a sensation out of it. Sadly, only a handful of war historians took more than a cursory interest in it. Consequently, he had failed to hold the sponsors who had underwritten the show and he finished with his financial trousers down.

But Cliff was anything but a quitter. Having anticipated this turn of events, he had set his research team to work on a forensic analysis of the affairs of Lawrence Parnham VC MP and they had been rewarded with a rich compost that would prove so fertile as to justify another program debunking this straw hero who, as far as he could see, had been dipping his hands into public and private purses with a will, apparently believing he was above the law due to his status.

Cliff had once had a mate who played amateur football like a gladiator and consequently accumulated so many suspensions that his association finally banned him for life. But this individual was not to be denied and he had a plan. He re-registered himself under an assumed name, in another neighbouring competition, as a reverend and continued to play, believing that no one would ever question a man of the cloth. They did and he received another life suspension. Lawrence Parnham, thought Cliff, was a bit like that, believing he was above the law and no one would question the Parnham name, but guess again Big Boy, because here comes Cliff.

Cliff called in his team and they began work on the Lawrence Parnham story. Cliff was well aware he dared not mention the other matter as he suspected he would invite destruction, but they had played into his hands by creating this bullshit story of the old guy's ill health when, in fact, they had simply disappeared him. Well, Cliff was going to bring him out of the dark and put the spotlight right back on him and make him accountable to the rest of the world, like anybody else.

If Parnham had been disappeared, he would need to leave the planet or be killed and dissolved in a bath full of acid if he was to remain hidden from the investigative skills of Cliff's team. A brainstorm session got to work to whiteboard ideas. The first job was to eliminate as many alternatives as possible. Sleuths sniffing about Chatsworth Park had greased the palms of several key employees, some of whom owed no loyalty and were, in fact, owed wages that they were unlikely to ever see. The word coming out of the Parnham compound was there had been no sign of Lawrence for some time. His wife, Frances, well that was another story?

Frances had filed for divorce and reverted back to her maiden name Kingston. She had gathered what she could from the wreckage, mainly jewellery and cash from a safe in the homestead, before the sheriff arrived and was quick enough to beat them to the city apartment before it too was seized. She also managed to secure several bank accounts that were in joint fictitious names in the Cayman Islands, unknown to the financial bloodhounds. The accounts were rapidly closed and the cash balance, with the assistance of her agents in London, spirited away beyond the reach of all and any creditors, including Lawrence should he try get his one remaining hand on it. Once satisfied that every possible loose end had been gathered and bundled up in her favour, she fled back to Mother England and her family.

This was mostly supposition by the staff of Chatsworth Park, but enquiries in other areas confirmed a sighting of Frances Parnham, nee Kingston, at Sydney's International Airport departures lounge with a stack of suitcases and a pair of huge sunglasses which, instead of hiding her face, drew attention to her with their ostentatiousness. Frances held dual citizenship and chose to travel on her British passport. Photos and confirmation were supplied by an AFP officer on secondment to the network and Cliff and his border control cronies. At this point, no warrant had been issued for Frances and her passport was current so there was no reason to prevent her departure.

She was wearing a stunning amount of bling and an expensive fur. The outside temperature was sitting at about 28 degrees centigrade so if she was trying to avoid notice she was going about it all wrong.

But what of Lawrence? The whiteboard in Cliff's boardroom was disappearing under post-it notes and coloured marker jottings, with a column on the side, of ideas yet to be explored. They were beginning to come to an interesting conclusion. If Lawrence had left the country, he would have left evidentiary trail. Cliff had recruited an investigator to his team who was part of the network's contracted staff undertaking projects for their current affairs programmes. He had a background in policing, namely Australian Federal Police, and had kept an impressive and very handy list of contacts. The contacts Cliff wanted him to chat to were in Border Control. Despite a fairly diligent, yet unofficial, search of recent departures that failed to turn up any traveller that could be Lawrence, or Lawrence incognito, on false travel papers, the inescapable conclusion was their quarry was still in the country somewhere. The suspicion fell on a certain high security institution on the outer fringes of Sydney. Cliff despatched his most reliable and determined sleuth, Peeping Pete, to check it out. Peeping Pete spent a bit of time checking out a number of possible sites.

In frustration, he slapped himself on the forehead. Of course, there was only one institution that fit the bill and that was one that carries the name of Lawrence Parnham's father. Without further hesitation or enquiry, he pointed his car in that direction.

As he approached the entrance to the premises, he was forced to give way to a convoy of police and paramedics, all lit up, as the cops say with lights and brights. The noisy bustling convoy swept into the grounds of the hospital with no regard for the sign in the driveway demanding Quiet Please in bold letters. Pete tagged onto the back of the emergency vehicles, as though he was part of the convoy, although his hideous lime green Datsun 120Y was not fooling anyone.

The one thing Pete did really well was connect with people. He had a guileless look about him and a boyish smile that earned instant trust. That, and a few well- greased palms. He did his thing and took no time to discover a hysterical housemaid in the process of being interrogated by police. He sidled up as close as he dared, with a borrowed stethoscope around his neck, which allowed him entry without question. What he heard was stunning and soon confirmed by the appearance of a gurney bearing a covered body, being wheeled toward the waiting ambulance.

Peeping Pete was now at his best as he adopted what he hoped was the bearing and persona of a medical man. He strode purposefully to intercept the gurney as it arrived at the ambulance. He was now also armed with a clipboard which he used to wave down the paramedics. He boldly lifted the sheet and pretended to examine the wrists and nails on the remaining arm of the lifeless figure but, at the same time, managing to get a glimpse of the face and, despite his thick skin and cold heart, he was shocked to see it was of the man they had been searching for. The search was now over and the vicious red welts around the neck of the deceased told the story of his demise as clearly as any coroner's report.

Pete couldn't get to a phone quickly enough and was running back to the foyer in the belief there would be a public phone there, when he was intercepted by a keen eyed cop and asked for ID. Pete didn't miss a beat and told the plod his ID was with his jacket in the mortuary and he was running late for a post mortem examination of a man suspected to have died of aids. Would he, the policeman, like to come along and he'd happily show his ID? The cop suddenly discovered he was urgently needed elsewhere and Peeping Pete wasted no time disappearing in the opposite direction looking for a phone. His shaking hand misdialled three times before he took a deep breath and tried again.

When Cliff heard the news, he was jubilant, fist pumping and dancing around his office until he realised, to his shame, he was celebrating the death of a once honourable man. Anyway, he had the series end he needed desperately and the now contemptible Lawrence Garret Parnham VC MP was no more. There was only the disposal of his remains that was still of interest. Peeping Pete was sure the cause of death was suicide by hanging, so it would be interesting to see what the powerbrokers of the left put out, and would he be given a state funeral by party officials who couldn't wait to forget him or would he be quietly interred by family, sans Frances of course who sent a cheap wreath.

Sure enough, the family decided on a discreet, by invitation only, service at the family's church, despite the sin of suicide. Here was another example of the Parnhams' influence. The service was attended by Lawrence's aging twin sisters, Laura and Lilly, clad in impressive mourning wear of veils and long black gowns and gloves. They were attended by their loyal manservant, also in mourning wear, and their identical Pekinese dogs each with a black silk ribbon around their pudgy necks. Cliff's camera guy captured it all for the public. And not surprisingly, few public tears were shed.

Gordon and Estelle, the loving progeny of Lawrence and Frances, and their partners in a rare drug and alcohol-free state arrived in a noisy Kombi van. If they thought they were in for a big, fat juicy inheritance they were in for the shock of their soon to be hard-working, penniless lives. There would be very little left of the Parnham Estates when the banks were through. The trustees would auction Chatsworth Downs, its buildings, furnishings, and farming equipment. Finally, the land under the homestead itself would be sold to the highest bidder. The bargain hunting buzzards were circling and they would not leave a thing behind.

Many old veterans who had served alongside Lawrence, with long memories, posted heartfelt messages to him in the daily newspapers. After all, he had worked hard for them over the years and that part of his public service would be remembered long after his misdeeds were forgotten. But no state funeral was even discussed. The whole nasty business was being buried with him and the quicker the better.

A pompous, wholly insincere, eulogy had been delivered in the House by the party leader and endorsed with the equally insincere here's, here's of his once admiring colleagues, who mostly found themselves unprepared to deliver such speeches themselves.

The truth behind Parnham's demise was now universally known, if only by strong rumour and innuendo, and former faithful comrades were now walking around it like a puddle of vomit on a bar room floor.

CHAPTER THIRTY ONE

At the Sir Alexander Parnham Blue Mountains Special Resort, Lawrence Parnham sat on the edge of his bed, staring at the floor in the semi-darkness of the pre-dawn. Despite powerful sedatives, he had not slept in three days and looked it. Unshaven, drawn and haggard, he was in the depths of despair, trying to understand what had happened to the life of privilege and entitlement that had been laid out for him.

How quickly had it all departed? He would have done anything for his party, but when he desperately needed their support, they deserted him like the rats of a sinking ship. Not only had they deserted him, but they had cast him out of the party and out of society. He had been buried alive in this sanitised nuthouse. No access to family or friends, if he still had any, and certainly no contact with his former staff or press. A senior politician like he was, from a distinguished pioneering family, should be offered the staff and resources to write his memoirs.

He compared himself to The Prisoner of Zenda and was daydreaming of a miracle restoration of his fortune as in another classic novel, The Count of Monte Cristo, where the hero of the Alexandre Dumas novel escaped his wrongful incarceration, acquired a fortune and wreaked revenge on the enemies responsible for his misery. But tragic reality had come around and there would be no fairy tale ending for Lawrence Garret Parnham.

Was dishonour shared by a family like an inherited faulty gene? Certainly, the Parnham's, generation to generation, shared the same faulty gene that caused them to be blind to the sins they had committed and repeated over time. They truly believed that because they enriched themselves with their semi-legitimate enterprises, they were in the common interest. They were convinced the advantages they enjoyed, that were denied the common folk, could not in any way be considered immoral, let alone criminal.

They had bent the rules of governance and used influence and power to pass the demolition of an historic building or to block legislation that could have benefited the poor so instead a grant would fall to a select few. That grant would evolve into another development that ultimately created jobs and opportunities for the working class, wouldn't it? And if the Parnham's found a little extra in their bank accounts at the end of the day, then who was hurt?

And if it was found that his Victoria Cross could generate opportunity, then where was the harm? No disgrace in that. He had laid his life on the line, for God's sake and the sake of his nation. Why had they come now trying to tear him down? Why had this thing happened? Accusations from people long dead came to destroy him and his integrity. Frances has turned away from him, his beloved political party had disowned him and the slavering hounds of the press had been tearing at the fabric of his soul.

He was experiencing a pain like no other, a pain that wouldn't be assuaged by alcohol or drugs. A coward and a traitor, how could anyone, especially a Parnham, be guilty of such immorality? At 6.30 on a cold and depressing morning, Lawrence's attendant carried his breakfast tray with hot coffee and morning paper into his room. She had taken care to ensure his papers were smoothed out; she, in fact, ran a warm iron over them. When she threw back the heavy curtains to admit the morning light, something at the corner of her eye caught her attention. When she turned, she threw her hands up in horror and screamed as only a hysterical woman can.

Lawrence Garret Parnham, disgraced MP and VC hero, had hung himself from the bathroom shower rail and was no more. A sadly dishonourable man had died a dishonourable death.

EPILOGUE

That day at Chatsworth Park, a sign swung from the front gate post in the wind and chilling rain, with the details of the liquidator's auction that had been held the month before to clear the remaining machinery and household goods of the Parnham dynasty. It bore the contact details for anyone believing they had a claim on the Parnham estate to contact the company of Goodwin Smythe: Auctioneers and Liquidation Specialists.

The Parnham name was erased with the death of Gordon Parnham from a hotshot of heroin while backpacking in Amsterdam. His wife, Leslie, had returned home childless to her father, having anticipated the life of wealth and luxury with Gordon Parnham and been disappointed. Instead, after he overdosed, she married a stockbroker and moved into his family home at Point Piper and subsequently gave birth to four sons. She never mentioned her father or Gordon again.

Estelle and her new husband, Thomas Newstead, moved to Tasmania and developed a rundown hobby farm into an organic goat's milk farm and added vegetables and honey to the organic products they sold their products out of a converted, barely roadworthy, Toyota HiAce van at Hobart's regular markets. They had five children that Estelle home-schooled.

Lawrence Garret Parnham VC, former state MP, lay in an overgrown grave amongst less distinguished and anonymous graves and was seldom visited.

At Courtland Downs, 1250 kilometres to the north west, in Queensland's south west, a sign swung in the wind from the gate post at the entry to the property, inviting friends and admirers of a great

Australian war hero, to come and join the celebrated Cuthbertson family, to rejoice in his life at a funeral service and wake held in remembrance of an honourable man by his loving widow and proud descendants.

Young Bill eventually recovered a major component of his grandfather's Beaufighter. It consisted of the cockpit and wing stubs, including one engine which, after extensive preservation treatment, formed the centre piece of a permanent stunning abstract memorial on a lovely piece of treed public ground on the road into Longreach, gifted to the cause by the shire.

It became something of a local shrine for RAAF pilots who would drive many thousands of miles to pay homage to the memory of Squadron Leader William Luther Cuthbertson DFC, who earned the title of air ace in this very aircraft. 'A brave and honourable man.'

A plaque on the memorial plinth read:

A grateful nation gives thanks to the men and women of the 30th Squadron RAAF who gave their lives during World War Two.

Lest we forget.

For the Cuthbertson family, life continued as it had for 120 years on the land. Weddings, births, deaths. Bumper beef and sheep meat prices came along and fell away in a familiar rhythm. Droughts and floods were met with equal stoicism. Young Bill was wooed by the conservative government, winning preselection and eventually contesting the state seat of Gregory, carrying it with a comfortable margin. As the Member for Gregory, he served his constituents with energy and purpose, using his new Cessna to cover his electorate, introducing many legislative changes that brought much needed infrastructure and investment into his rural neighbourhood.

Elise continued her flying career becoming one of Australia's first female airline captains, bringing further distinction to a great family with an enviable history.

All the great things are simple and can be expressed in a single word: Freedom, justice, honour, duty, mercy, hope.

Winston Churchill

TIMELINE

1805. Chatsworth Park established Parramatta district by Jonas Oliver Parnham.

1807-1808. Merino sheep delivered to Chatsworth Park.

1864-66 and 1868. Serious drought across Queensland and the East coast.

1865. Death of Jonas Oliver Parnham.

1866. Death of Almira Genevieve Parnham (nee Hartwell)

1876. Courtland Downs established by Harold Eldon Cuthbertson.

1881. Plymouth 3rd March. Henrietta Constance Croft departs Plymouth aboard 'Scottish Knight.'

1881. 15th June. Arrives in Townsville after a voyage of 104 days. P17.

1892. Rail arrives in Longreach.

1895-1903. Australia wide drought.

1910. Alexander Parham appointed Kings Counsel and takes silk.

1914. World War One commences.

1916. December 27th Major flood Clermont Qld.

1918. 11th November Armistice Day. The Great War ends.

1918-1920. Queensland and NSW drought.

1927. Death of Harold Clement Cuthbertson.

1927. Death of Henrietta Constance Cuthbertson (nee Croft)

1930. Alexander Parnham became Knight Bachelor Sir Alexander Parnham MP KC.

1939-1945. World War Two.

1940. 10th July-31st October.

1942. 23rd January-August 1945 War in New Guinea.

1942. May. Battle of the Coral Sea.

1942. May. 55th Battalion arrives in Port Moresby

1942. July F Company to Milne Bay.

1942. August 25th Japanese landing at Milne Bay.

1942. August 30th Lt. Lawrence Parnham captured and tortured by Japanese.

1942. September 6th Battle of Milne Bay is over, Japanese pull out.

1942. October 8th. Lt. Lawrence Parnham act of supreme courage.

1942. October 10th. Squadron Leader W Cuthbertson departs Port Moresby for Archerfield.

1942. October 15th Search for Squadron Leader W Cuthbertson's aircraft abandoned.

1942. 21st July-November 16th Kokoda Campaign.

1945. July 5th John Curtin PM died at the lodge aged 60.

1945. Joseph Benedict Chifley becomes 16th PM and Labour Party leader.

1946. Sir Alexander Morris Parnham MP KC knighted by King George V.

1949. Australian Coal Strike.

1949. Lawrence Parnham wins a seat in the House of Reps for the Country Liberal Party.

1949. Robert Menzies becomes PM for the second time.

1963. August. Death of Sir Alexander Parnham.

1966. Robert Cuthbertson meets Joanne Wheatley.

1968. Birth of William Cuthbertson Junior.

1970. Birth of Elise Cuthbertson.

1973. Death of Francis Lilly Cuthbertson (nee McLeod).

1975. Death of Hugh Clement Cuthbertson.

1987. Elise Joy Cuthbertson solo circumnavigation of Australia.

1992. William Grant Cuthbertson memorial flight.

1992. October. Young Bill crashes.

1993. Release of the war time documents.

1994. Death of Lawrence Garret Parnham. Aged 74.

THE FAMILIES

The Parnham Family

Chatsworth Park established 1805. 500 Acres. 45 kilometres southwest of Sydney. Nearest settlement Campbelltown, Liverpool. Parramatta to the west of Sydney where John Macarthur established his merino flock.

Jonas Oliver Parnham b 1780 d 1865 M Almira Genevieve Hartwell b1786 d 1866

Julian Wesley Parnham b 1815 d 1876 M Victoria Elvira Westchester b 1817 d 1882

Jefferson Gideon Parnham b 1841 d 1913 M Charlotte Hope McWilliams b 1846 d 1917

Mary Frances Parnham b 1842 d 1917

Alexander Morris Parnham MP KC b 1875 d 1963 M Winifred Jane Stevenson b 1877 d 1970

Lawrence Garret Parnham VC b 1918 d 1993 M Frances Esther Kingston b 1920 d 1990

Laura Grace and Lilly Madeline (twins) Parnham b 1917

Gordon Alexander Parnham b 1947 m Leslie Martine Robards b 1953

Estelle Charlotte Parnham b 1951 m Thomas Maxwell Newstead b 1948

The Cuthbertson Family

Courtland Downs established 1876 Longreach Queensland. Approximately 30,000 hectares. Cattle and some sheep.

Harold Clement b 1854 d 1927 M Henrietta Constance Croft b 1864 d

Hugh Clement b 1890 d 1975 M Francis Lilly McLeod b 1895 d 1973

William Luther (Big Bill) b 1916 d 1942 M Lydia Collette Grantham b 1920 d 2002

George Clement (Books) b 1920

Elsie Henrietta b 1926

Edwina Joy b 1928 d 1930

Robert Arthur Cuthbertson b 1943 M Joanne Rose Wheatley b 1945 d

William Grant Cuthbertson b 1968

Elise Joy Cuthbertson b 1970

Flight Sergeant Bluey Mansfield KIA

Lloyd Mansfield – older brother to Bluey

Charlie Mansfield – Bluey's grandson

Magpie Junior – Aboriginal tracker

Horry Oates – neighbour and crazy drummer

Cliff Carter – TV journalist

ACKNOWLEDGEMENTS

The RAAF's Forgotten Finest Hour
http://www.3squadron.org.au/subpages/MilneBayBattle.htm
RAAF 75th Squadron. History.
Armidale New South Wales. Wikipedia Year Book Australia 1988
History of Australia since 1945 Wikipedia Beechcraft Model 18 Pilot
Friend.com
Beech Model 18 history, performance and specifications. Pilot Friend.
com Bristol Beaufighter History and Performance. Wikipedia
List of Birds of Queensland. Wikipedia
The end of transportation by Lucy Hughes Turnbull, 2008
Australian farming and agriculture – grazing and cropping. Australia.
com.au

Shawline Publishing Group Pty Ltd
www.shawlinepublishing.com.au

SHAWLINE
PUBLISHING
GROUP

9 781923 171145